Passion's Coaxing

Sabrina gazed up into Clay's intent blue eyes, aware that she wanted to hold this moment forever. She wanted again to feel his arms about her and the touch of his lips on hers. She could have wept with the intense need that inflamed and consumed her.

Clay took her hand and rose to his feet drawing her with him. He was aware of everything about her.

He put his arms around her waist and drew her against him. Their bodies touched and the flame of mutual need leapt between them. He bent his head to touch the sweet parted lips that lifted to meet his.

He took her mouth lightly, savoring the seeking of hers, tasting, touching, blending until both were lost in the magic of it. His lips traced a flaming path from her mouth to touch her cheeks, her eyes, then roamed in passionate discovery down her slender throat to the pulse that beat wildly. . . .

Tame
My Wild
Heart

SYLVIE F. SOMMERFIELD

ZEBRA BOOKS
KENSINGTON PUBLISHING CORP.

ZEBRA BOOKS

are published by

KENSINGTON PUBLISHING CORP.
475 PARK AVENUE SOUTH
NEW YORK, NY 10016

First printing: April, 1984

Printed in the United States of America

This book is dedicated to Zayna Notar — with sincere thanks for her kindness, her generosity, and above all for her friendship.

Prologue

The sun, at its zenith, beat down on the lone figure who worked with slow rhythmic movements. He shoveled the dry earth, and sorrow emanated from him. It could be seen in the drawn lines of his face and the tears that lingered in the red-rimmed eyes.

He lay the shovel down, then turned away from the dark hole he had dug and bent to lift the blanket-covered body which lay beside him. He lifted its slim lightness with an attitude of care and reverence. He held it close to him for a moment, then laid it in the ground. He stood as if exhaustion almost overwhelmed him, then he again turned and lifted the shovel and began to fill the earth back in.

When the mound of earth was finished he knelt beside it. His hand lay against the earth as if there were still some contact between him and the one who lay within.

He sighed raggedly and rose again to his feet. His mind was lost to the past for a moment and only drawn back to the present when a whimpering cry came from another small bundle that lay near him. He went to lift it into his arms, then he bent again and lifted the long rifle that lay beside it.

He had been in a small clearing and he slowly left the freshly mounded earth and walked toward the trees that bordered it. He had almost reached them when he stopped suddenly.

A shadowed form moved from the cover of the trees. The two stood looking at each other for several moments.

"You have buried her?" the shadowed form said softly. "It is not our way."

"It is my way, Hawk. She was my wife."

"You never should have taken her from her people. She was not meant to live your way. You have taken her life, now you must repay your debt to her people."

"Hawk, I don't want any trouble with you or your people. Get off my land and leave me alone. No one is responsible for her death. Don't you think I would have done anything to keep her with me? I loved her, don't you understand? She came to me of her own will."

"She would be alive today if you had not come. Go from here . . . Go . . . but leave the child here."

"Hawk," the man's face hardened; and he held the child so close it whimpered. The rifle tipped upward until it was aligned with the Indian's broad chest. "I'm here to stay. This is my land, this is my child. We were friends, Hawk. I would hate to see it end this way."

They were still for a moment, then the Indian smiled.

"One day, you will balance the debt. We were friends, but you took something from me."

"No! I took nothing, and I valued our friendship. Let the past be buried, Hawk, and leave me in peace if we cannot mend our friendship, because I intend to stay here. The child could be the link between us."

"One day it will come to us . . . one day I will take something from you, something you value. Then the debt will be paid, then we will both have peace."

He turned and walked away and the lone figure stood watching until he disappeared. Then he sighed deeply and his blue eyes clouded with renewed pain.

He looked down on the child and silently prayed that his words would come true, that the child he carried could mend a tragedy and bridge the gap death had made.

At this moment he felt lonelier and more miserable than he had ever felt before. Almost angrily he braced the rifle against his shoulder and walked in the opposite direction from the one the tall Indian had taken. He had walked for less than half an hour when he came to another clearing.

In it stood a rather large cabin. He opened the door and went inside, closing and bolting the door behind him. Standing the rifle in the corner he took the child to a small hand-carved cradle that sat in front of the fireplace and laid it inside.

Fear that had not shown in his face before became apparent as he whispered softly.

"I'll never give her up, Singing Bells. You can rest in peace. Someday I will again make peace with Hawk. Someday I will find a way to take the bitterness from his heart and make us friends again."

One

England, 1760

Sabrina McNeil hummed lightly as she walked along the gravelled path that wove through the well-laid gardens of Waverly Hall. Occasionally, she stopped by a blooming bush and with a pair of scissors clipped a long-stemmed rose and laid it in the basket she carried.

When the basket held a satisfactory number of beautiful blooms, she walked across an expanse of green lawn and entered the back door that led first to a pantry, then into a large kitchen.

"Good morning, Ellen," she said to the cook who was rolling out fresh biscuits for the family's breakfast. Ellen was round and rosy and her eyes sparkled in pleasure at the girl's arrival.

"Good mornin', Miss. You do look pretty this mornin'. I see you been cuttin' flowers again."

"Uncle Eustice likes flowers in his room. It brightens his day and makes him feel better."

"You're the one makes him feel better," the cook laughed.

11

"Tis the only time he isn't cranky is when you're about. You could be his own daughter and he wouldn't love you more."

Sabrina took a vase from beneath the sink and began to arrange the flowers in it.

"He's been good to me, Ellen; taking me in when my parents died and caring for me, educating me and filling my life with good things. I love him very much and a few flowers is a small thing. I wish I could make him well again."

"Yes," Ellen replied, "maybe we could get rid of the leeches if he could get well. I can't abide their standing about waiting for him to die so they can grab the money. By rights it should be yours."

"Oh, Ellen, I don't want the money. Uncle Eustice has equipped me to carry on somehow. I'll be all right."

"You're the only one what cares for him," she replied stubbornly. "And no matter what you say, it should be yours."

"Ummm, those biscuits do smell good. Are any ready? I can take some up with the flowers. With a little butter and jam maybe I can convince him to eat a little."

"I'll help you fix a tray," Ellen replied.

Together they prepared a small breakfast; then Sabrina placed the vase of flowers on it and lifted the tray. When she left the kitchen she had to pass down a long hall, cross the immense dining room and foyer to the bottom of the stairs. She thought of what Ellen had said. Sabrina had been ten when her parents had been killed in an accident. Eustice Waverly had been her oldest living relative, the brother of her mother. He was the oldest of the Waverly family, and had been several years older than Sabrina's mother. Sabrina had been a frightened and lonely child when Eustice had taken her in, but she was soon to realize that Eustice had been lonely also since he had never married. His heart opened to her and hers to him from the moment they met. He had filled the next few years with understanding and love. She was eighteen now, and because of Eustice, was a bright, intelligent young woman.

She thought also of the 'they' to whom Ellen had referred. She would never tell either Eustice or Ellen of the shattering fear she carried within her.

Eustice had another sister who had lived a wayward life. She had run off at fifteen and married a man who was at the least an opportunist and at most things that would have made Sabrina more frightened if she had known. There was a son of this union, not too much older than Sabrina. It was him she feared most for she could read well the hungry look of lust in his eyes, both for her and for her uncle's money.

She crossed the foyer and started up the stairs. Less than half way up she looked up to see her Uncle Clyde on the way down. A tremor of fear ran through her, yet her pride would not allow her to show it. Clyde stopped, and she continued her climb, hoping he would let her pass without trying to stop her. She was mistaken. His eyes glowed with pleasure as he watched her walk toward him.

"Good morning, Uncle Clyde," she smiled, and tried to continue on. His hand reached out to stop her. He took hold of her arm. Outside of dropping the tray and running, there was nothing she could do but stop.

"Good morning, Sabrina," his voice caressed her name.

"Taking Eustice his breakfast again, I see. You must brighten his hours considerably. The old man is not a fool, is he?" Clyde chuckled suggestively. "You look very pretty this morning."

With both of her hands occupied, she could do nothing to stop him as he reached out and brushed his fingers lightly across her cheek and caught a tendril of her long hair between his fingers.

"Like spun gold," he murmured softly and his eyes warmed as he looked at her. Panic nearly choked her as she searched for a way to escape him. Then a voice from the bottom of the stairs sent a flood of relief through her. Clyde jumped at the sound of it, and he turned a dark scowling face toward Ellen who stood at the bottom of the stairs, her face beaming with an innocent smile.

"Sabrina, you had better get that breakfast to him while it is still warm."

Sabrina flashed Ellen a quick warm smile of gratitude as Clyde dropped her hair and she fled as quickly as she could.

Clyde continued on down the stairs toward Ellen. If he meant to intimidate her by his dark frown it was useless, for Ellen was not afraid of him at all. She knew him for what he was, just as she knew the intentions he had for Sabrina. Her eyes held his defiantly.

"You had best see to your business in the kitchen, Ellen," he said in a deceptively soft voice. "If you neglect your duties you might find yourself unemployed one day soon."

"Oh no, sir," Ellen smiled sweetly. "I've no intention of neglecting my duties. I make a point of doin' everything Sir

Eustice tells me to do . . . everything," she added softly, watching his cheeks flush with anger as he understood her words. Even from a sick bed Eustice Waverly was watching over the welfare of Sabrina.

Angrily, Clyde walked away and Ellen watched after him.

"Nasty old lecher," she muttered. "Ye'll never get her or the money. Not while there's still a breath in my body." She went back to her labors in the kitchen.

Sabrina continued down the long hall to her uncle's room. There she braced the edge of the tray against her hip while she reached out and opened the door.

The room was dim because of the heavy drapes that were drawn over the huge windows. She sat the tray down and went to the windows. She drew the drapes open, letting in the bright morning sun. Then she opened the window so the summer air could clear the room. Before she turned about, a warm chuckle sounded from the bed.

"You always bring sunshine, child."

She turned around, a smile on her face. "Good morning, Uncle. Do you feel well enough to eat a little? I've brought you some of Ellen's fresh biscuits and some jam and tea."

"Come and sit with me and I'll eat a little."

"Good," she said, as she lifted the tray and carried it to the bed. Then she sat on a chair beside the bed and poured his tea. He watched her closely as she did.

"Sabrina?"

"Yes, Uncle?"

"Are you happy here?"

"I've been happy with you from the moment I came,

15

Uncle. You have been everything to me."

"With me . . . but not necessarily Waverly Hall?"

"Waverly Hall is beautiful, but it is you who have given me everything."

"Would you be happy here when I am gone?"

"I don't want to talk about your being gone. I intend for you to get out of this bed and on your feet. You have many good years yet."

She bent forward and took his hand in hers. "I love you, Uncle, and I need you. Please, try and get well . . . for me."

"You are frightened, child," he said softly. "You cannot keep things from me. I've seen it for some time. I know just what it is that you are frightened of. Tell me . . . is it Clyde, or is it Thomas?"

She said nothing, but her head dropped so he could not see her eyes. Gently he put a finger under her chin and lifted her face. He loved this girl more dearly than he had ever loved anyone before. For the past eight years she had been his life. Now, whether she would admit it or not, he knew his time was slowly running out. She was so pretty, a prettiness that would soon turn into a very rare beauty. Her wide eyes were the color of new spring violets. Her skin was dewy soft, and blooming with radiant life. Her mouth wide and ready to smile. Her hair filled with vibrant life was a vision of pale gold that hung in a mass of wayward curls to her hips. Now she had tied it back hastily with a scrap of ribbon. Her eyes were filled with pain.

"Do you think I don't know them? Do you think I don't know how their twisted minds think? Do you also think I

16

don't know they are sitting about waiting for me to die so they can collect all my money? And," he added with a soft chuckle, "do you think I do not love you enough to have prepared for the time I am gone? Do not let them worry you Sabrina, my child. You will be beyond their reach when I am no longer here."

"I know you love me, Uncle, and I'm sorry to be so frightened. It's just . . . when they look at me as if . . . as if. . ."

"As if you were a possession. You are not, and you never will be. Clyde and Thomas will have to find another place, for I plan on leaving Waverly Hall to you, and explicit orders they are to be evicted the day I am no longer here."

"I don't care about Waverly Hall, Uncle, or the money. I just want you to get well so we can share our time together again. I won't be afraid then, not if you are here."

"Child, you cannot spend your time in chains to an old man. You are young and full of life. You have a great future and a great deal of love to share with the right man, and I intend to see you get the chance to enjoy everything."

"Oh, Uncle, please," she begged. "I only want you to get well, please, that's enough to make me happy."

"It really is, isn't it?" he smiled. "Well, to humor you I shall eat my breakfast. Then you and I shall go and see the rest of those beautiful roses in the garden. I can have Joseph take me down. The fresh air will make this weak old heart feel better."

"Wonderful! It won't be too much?" she said worriedly.

"No, I shall enjoy it. Then this afternoon I have an appointment to speak with my lawyer. I intend to take care of your future."

"Take care of the present," she commanded with a smile. "Eat."

"Yes, you slave driver, I shall eat. Come, share my tea with me."

For the next hour they sipped tea and talked together. Then Joseph, Eustice's valet, with the aid of a young gardener, took Eustice down to the garden and made him comfortable in a chair beneath the shade of a tree. There Sabrina read to him for a while, then they discussed changes that could be made in the garden, what could be added or changed to improve it.

Before lunch, Eustice's eyes closed and Sabrina sat quietly by while he took a nap. She sat watching the garden daydreaming, without knowing that interested eyes were watching her. At the second floor window, Thomas Waverly held the curtain aside so he could get a better view of Sabrina. He watched her intently, his eyes filled with desire and a need to possess her. She had eluded him so often, a thing that rarely happened to Thomas. He licked his lips, then smiled as he bent forward to watch even more closely as Sabrina turned and looked toward the house as if she sensed someone was watching her.

Thomas was startled when he heard the door to his room close sharply. He turned to see his father standing by the door smiling at him.

"I don't need to ask whom you were watching. Lush little piece, isn't she? I expect it shall be a pleasure to live in this house once old Eustice is gone."

"I agree, but you had best be careful."

"Careful? Of what?"

"Eustice's lawyer is on his way over here this afternoon. If I'm not mistaken the old man intends to change his will. If he does, we'll be in the street and Sabrina will be out of our reach."

"Thomas, Thomas," Clyde said softly. "Do you continue to underestimate me? Do you really think I did not take everything into consideration? Did you really think I would let a loose thread take Sabrina and all that wealth out of my hands?"

"What are you going to do?"

"I suggest you keep your eyes and ears open. I shall show you how an expert takes care of loose ends."

Thomas turned back to the window and Clyde walked up beside him. They watched as Eustice woke from his sleep, and he said something to Sabrina as she laughed.

"She's a lovely creature," Clyde said in a quiet intense voice. "I shall enjoy her most thoroughly."

"We," Thomas added, "We shall enjoy her most thoroughly."

"Yes . . . yes of course. Shall we go down and have lunch with them and await the arrival of the legal brains?"

He chuckled as he walked to the door and Thomas followed after him. He had seen the maneuverings of his father before and an excitement tingled within him. He knew his father had devised a means to throw the Waverly wealth into their hands . . . and Sabrina. Even if he had to share her, he didn't care, all he knew was that he wanted her and soon . . . he would have her.

Eustice noticed Sabrina's withdrawal when Clyde and

Thomas joined them for lunch. Now he was sure he was right in what he planned to do. When lunch was over, Clyde rose to his feet.

"If you will excuse me, please, I have some urgent business to attend to."

"Of course, Clyde," Eustice said. "Go along. I shall be in conference with Mr. Chapin most of the afternoon."

"I shall see you at dinner," Clyde replied as he bowed slightly to Sabrina. He turned to Thomas. "Thomas, would you mind driving me into town? I should like to discuss a few things with you."

Just as Thomas rose, the butler appeared. He spoke to Eustice in a low voice.

"Mr. Waverly, Mr. Poltice is here, sir."

"Mr. Poltice? Chapin's assistant? Please show him in."

The butler left, and in a few minutes returned with a small bespectacled man who seemed somewhat in awe of the Waverlys.

"Mr. Poltice, I was expecting Mr. Chapin."

"I'm sorry sir, there has been somewhat of a difficulty. Mr. Chapin has told me to come and make what changes you wanted and bring them to him."

"Well, come into my study."

"Yes, sir."

Eustice rose and stood watching both Clyde and Thomas who took his look for exactly what it was and left.

Eustice and Mr. Poltice enclosed themselves in the study for well over three hours. When they came out, Mr. Poltice seemed to be anxious to be on his way and Eustice, though very tired, seemed to be satisfied with the afternoon's accomplishments.

He might not have felt so secure or so pleased had he followed Mr. Poltice when he left Waverly Hall. His carriage had gone only three or four miles down the road when it stopped beside another that had been waiting for him. He disembarked, then dismissed his carriage, watching it roll out of sight. Then he walked to the other carriage, opened the door and climbed inside. He sat down and looked into the satisfied smiling faces of Clyde and Thomas.

"My dear, Jacob," Clyde said. "I believe you have something for me?"

"Mr. Mellon . . . please . . . this is wrong."

Clyde chuckled. "Jacob," he said softly. "Do not antagonize me. I might become unhappy with you. In that case, I may have to make a visit to Mr. Chapin. We wouldn't want that, now would we?"

Jacob's face paled, but he reached inside his briefcase and withdrew the papers he had so recently completed in Eustice's study. He quite reluctantly handed them to Clyde. Clyde took them and read them very carefully.

"We were quite right, Thomas. He has bequeathed Waverly Hall, all his money . . . everything he possesses to that child."

"I knew he had that in mind," Thomas replied. "What are we going to do?"

"Do? Why Thomas," Clyde replied. "We shall simply correct the so obvious mistake our dear Eustice has committed."

Clyde slowly tore the papers in several pieces.

"My God!" Jacob said. "You cannot do that. I have to

have those papers to put away."

Clyde drew a matching set of papers from his breast pocket. "These are the papers you shall file. These are the papers that will dispense the Waverly wealth at the death of Eustice Waverly."

"But . . ."

"Do not say a word Jacob. File this will. When Eustice is dead, you, Thomas and I will be a great deal wealthier, and no one will ever know any other will ever existed."

"I hope you are right," Jacob said.

"I know I am right. There is no one else who knows of this second will but us. You were the one who witnessed it, who were the other witnesses?"

"Joseph, his valet and Stewart his secretary."

"Did they read it?"

"No."

"Then we need only have a copy of their signatures on our will and there is no one who can contradict it."

"But how . . .?"

"How will we get their signatures? Again you underestimate me. Within a week both names will be affixed to the bottom of that document. Now," Clyde smiled again, his particularly cold smile. "Can we drop you at your office? We wouldn't want Mr. Chapin to wonder where you are. He might even think you were at Waverly Hall and begin to ask questions. We don't want that to happen now, do we?"

"No . . . no," Jacob stammered.

"Then let us get you back to the office. I don't want any stir about this until I'm ready."

Clyde ordered his carriage on and in less than an hour

deposited Jacob in front of the Chapin law office.

The days drifted along in a warm lethargy. Both Thomas and Clyde kept their distance from Sabrina until she relaxed and let them slip from her mind. She spent her days making Eustice as comfortable and happy as possible, and was rewarded when her attentions seemed to renew his strength. He was able to spend much more time out of bed, and his heart seemed to gather strength and energy from her youth and faith.

They spent hours together in the garden, digging in the earth and planting flowers while they talked of the future.

It was over three weeks later that Eustice decided to celebrate Sabrina's forthcoming nineteenth birthday with a small gathering of their friends.

"But uncle, it will be too much for you."

"Nonsense child, I have not felt as well in a long time. It is time you had some friends about of your own age." He smiled at her. "It is time you met a nice young man and enjoyed your life."

"I do enjoy my life, and I love being here with you."

"Sabrina, you are a sweet child. I want you to have a good life — a family, someone to love you and to share the balance of your days with. I . . . I never had a wife or children of my own. I missed that, but I should like to think of your children as my grandchildren. I should like to see them bring Waverly to life again. Can you humor an old man who loves you?"

She smiled, and reached out and took his hand in both of hers. "All right, Uncle. We will have your party. One day I hope to make Waverly all you want it to be."

"Thank you my pet. Now, suppose you go into town today and buy yourself the prettiest dress you can find. I want everyone to see the prettiest bloom the Waverly garden has to offer."

She nodded her agreement. Ellen accompanied her to town and they enjoyed the afternoon shopping. Ellen agreed that the gown they chose was extraordinarily beautiful.

She found, when she returned, that her uncle had already retired to his room for a late afternoon nap before dinner. She took the time to practice a few styles in which to wear her hair, and to sort through the jewelry her mother had left her and her uncle had given her to find what would match the gown.

It was nearly seven o'clock in the evening when a light rap sounded on her door.

"Yes?"

"Dinner is ready, miss," came the young maid's voice.

"I'll be right down."

She hung the gown in the closet, and put the jewelry back in the jewelbox. Then she gave herself one last hasty look the in mirror and left the room. She rushed quickly down the stairs, for she knew her uncle frowned on tardiness of any sort.

When she entered the dining room she was surprised to find only Clyde and Thomas there.

"Eustice has not come down yet, my dear," Clyde said. "Shall we wait a few more minutes or start dinner without him?"

"Let's wait," she replied.

Clyde nodded and pulled out her chair so she could sit down. She shivered with the knowledge of what it would be like in this huge house if she did not have the warmth of her uncle's love as a shield.

They waited what seemed to her to be hours, then she heard the huge grandfather clock in the front hall strike seven-thirty. Somewhere deep inside she sensed something was drastically wrong.

"Uncle Clyde, I think I will go up and see what is wrong. It is not like Uncle Eustice to keep dinner waiting."

"Never mind, my dear," Clyde said as he rose. "I shall go."

Before she could say anything else he was already walking across the room. Again time ticked slowly by. Then she heard the slow heavy steps return. She knew something was wrong and she began to rise as Clyde reentered the room. His eyes held hers as he slowly walked to her side. She trembled in fear at the next words he said.

"Sabrina, my child . . . my poor child."

"Uncle Eustice," she whispered.

"In his sleep, my dear . . . peacefully. He is dead."

A deep buzzing began in her ears and suddenly everything turned black. She did not see the exchanged look of satisfaction between father and son as slowly she collapsed into Clyde's arms.

Two

When Sabrina awoke Ellen was bending over her, and past her shoulder she could see Clyde and Thomas. Ellen had seen them carry her upstairs and she had followed immediately, unwilling to let them be alone with her even for a few minutes.

Sabrina's eyes filled with tears as Ellen took her hand with sympathy in her eyes.

"Ellen," Sabrina whispered. "Tell me it isn't so. Not Uncle Eustice."

"I'm afraid so, child. He must have died in his sleep. 'Tis a peaceful way to go."

"Oh, God," Sabrina sobbed. She threw herself into Ellen's arms. Ellen held her and tried to comfort her with soothing words.

Clyde and Thomas quietly left the room. After some time, Sabrina regained control and lay back against the pillows. They talked for some time, then Ellen said, "You had best get some sleep, child. In the next few days, there will be much to do and it will be a terrible strain on you."

"Yes," Sabrina replied. Ellen helped her undress and get into bed. "Oh, Ellen. What shall I do without him?"

"It will be hard, but I have a feeling he has done something to care for you. If he has, you must carry out his wishes and care for Waverly Hall as he would have. You have an obligation to him even though he is gone."

"You're right, Ellen. I'm sorry. I . . . I'll do the very best I can."

"Of course you will," Ellen smiled. "Now get yourself some sleep. I'll bring you a tray in the morning, then we will handle things one at a time as they come."

Ellen walked to the door.

"Ellen?"

"Yes?"

"Thank you."

"For what?"

"For the 'we'," Sabrina smiled.

When Ellen was gone Sabrina lay in the large quiet room. Hot tears slid down her cheeks as painfully memories overcame her. It was some time before she was able to control them and begin to search for sleep. As she drifted off into troubled sleep she wondered why she had the strange feeling her life had suddenly taken a strange new course. A course she could not control.

The next three days were dark shadowed days for Sabrina. People came to call and extend their condolences. Then came the funeral, which took every ounce of strength Sabrina had. She had never felt more lonely and frightened in her life.

For the next week, the house seemed to be an empty cavern where her thoughts and memories echoed from room to empty room.

Clyde had already warned Thomas to keep his distance from Sabrina. He did not want her to alarm outsiders and make them curious about her fear until he had her completely entrapped and he knew that was only a few days away. The will was to be read at Waverly Hall. Everyone gathered in the study, including all the servants, because

Eustice had bequeathed each of them something.

Mr. Chapin sat behind the large oak desk and facing him sat Clyde, Thomas, and Sabrina. Behind them, and scattered about the room stood Ellen and the rest of the servants who had served Eustice for many years.

Mr. Chapin began to read in a deep resonant voice.

"I, Eustice Waverly, being of sound mind . . ."

His voice went on and on, to Sabrina it seemed like an interminable time. One bequest followed another, each servant getting a small amount of money. The last person to receive a bequest was Ellen, and it was the first surprise.

". . . to Ellen Doyle I leave the sum of three hundred pounds per month, and the small house near the bend of the river. Her employment at Waverly Hall is to cease from the moment this will is read, and she is to enjoy her retirement with my best wishes."

There was a startled gasp both from Ellen and Sabrina. This would successfully separate Sabrina and Ellen, and it brought a suspicious narrowing of Ellen's eyes as she gazed at a very innocent looking Thomas and Clyde. It also brought the first warning chill to Ellen that this will was not going to be what she and all the others expected it to be. The next words proved her right.

"To my brother in law, Clyde Mellon and his son, Thomas I leave the balance of my estate, Waverly Hall and all the properties. I also leave my niece, Sabrina in his care as his legal ward. He is to be her guardian until she reaches the age of twenty-one, then she is to receive one third of the estate he holds. If she marries after the age of twenty-one all of my estate shall remain in the custody of Clyde Mellon."

There was a complete and absolute silence as everyone slowly digested the words. Sabrina was stunned. She had no one and no place to go except Clyde Mellon and Waverly Hall.

Clyde rose, then Thomas followed. The words they spoke to the lawyer were barely heard by the frozen Sabrina. Then Clyde came to her side and took her elbow.

"Come Sabrina. We have many guests coming to Waverly Hall. We must be here to greet them."

Sabrina trembled with a fear she could not name. There was nothing she could do at the moment but go with him. No one noticed Ellen who had slipped from the room several minutes before. They stood together at the bottom of the stairs. "Would you like to go upstairs and change before our guests arrive?" Clyde said. "I want my hostess to be at her beautiful best. I hope to entertain a lot and I expect you to add charm to all my engagements."

"Uncle Clyde," Sabrina said softly, "I cannot. I . . . I would like to lie down."

Clyde took her wrist in an iron grip. His smile was cold and self-satisfied. "You must understand your position my dear. You are under age. I am your legal guardian, you will do exactly as I say."

"Please, Uncle."

"Sabrina," he said, his cold eyes holding hers, "there are institutions in which one can incarcerate obstinate children. I would not like to see you locked away in Breed Institution for years."

She sucked in her breath and her face turned white in terror. Breed was a mental institution of which she had heard many stories, and she knew that legally her uncle could sign papers to lock her away in it for at least three years until she was twenty-one. By then, she knew, she would be insane.

"Now go up and change your clothes," he said in a firm voice.

She walked slowly up the steps, and Clyde and Thomas stood below watching.

"You've frightened her," Thomas smiled.

"Yes, but she is a willful girl. I shall have to discipline her well, until all she knows is my will. Come let's get ready for our guests. Soon we will begin to enjoy all . . . everything Waverly Hall has to offer."

They laughed as they climbed the stairs together.

The guests were several men who had been in business with Eustice and wanted to know what Clyde's plans were concerning them.

When Sabrina came down she was shaken and pale. She had changed into a deep green dress that was plain and unadorned. She had bound her hair in a chignon at the nape of her neck, yet no matter what she had done to make herself look plain and unobtrusive her pale gold beauty among the drab men sparkled like a rare diamond against black velvet.

Clyde watched her effect on them and smiled to himself. He intended to use that beauty combined with Eustice's wealth to make him one of the most influential men in all of England.

After tonight, he thought, she will do whatever I choose her to do. His body trembled in suppressed excitement at the prospect of what he planned for later.

When the last guest had gone, Sabrina was almost overcome by mental and physical exhaustion. She started slowly up the stairs.

"Good night Sabrina," Clyde said. She turned to look down at him. The look in his eyes was unfathomable, but his smile sent a shiver of fear through her.

"Good night, Uncle Clyde," she whispered, then she fled swiftly to her room. Inside she turned to lock the door, resting her entire body against it for a moment. When she reached down for the key, she found it wasn't there. She looked about but there was no sign of it. Too exhausted to think clearly she supposed one of the maids had taken it out and misplaced it. She would have to find it in the morning.

She took off her clothes and slipped into her nightgown, then she brushed out her hair and prepared for bed. She sat for a moment at her dressing table and looked at a small portrait of her Uncle Eustice that sat on it. She still could not believe what had happened. Had her uncle really believed that leaving her in Clyde's care would make her life safer and better? Lost in her reverie she did not hear the door slowly open, nor did she see her uncle step inside and close it behind him. He stood watching her, enjoying her rare and gentle beauty, an innocent beauty he intended to taste to the fullest.

The thin nightgown and her unawareness did nothing to hide her charms from his seated gaze. Golden hair tumbled over creamy shoulders and the outline of her slim ripe curves could be clearly seen through the transparent material. He felt the blood rush through his body at the mere thought of possessing them.

He was only a step or two away from her when she became aware of his presence. She spun about, her wide violet eyes growing wider with fear. Paralyzed with fright, she could not move as he came close to her. He reached out and gently caressed her hair.

"Like silk," he said softly. "I knew it would be. I imagined you just as you are. So very beautiful."

His eyes raked over her with such a look of heated lust that she uttered a soft cry and crossed her arms before her as if to protect herself from their attack.

"Uncle Clyde!"

"You needn't be afraid of me," he said in a velvet smooth voice. "I promise you I shall teach you to enjoy your lessons. Soon you will look forward to having me come to you."

He reached out again to grasp her arm, but now she came to sudden frightened life. She dodged his hand and tried to run past him only to feel his hard arm about her waist. She was caught against him and she struggled furiously as his other hand closed over her mouth.

"You will listen," he said in an amused voice. "There is no one in the house except you, Thomas and I. He is making sure of that. You can scream and fight all you want and it will be useless. I should hate to have to punish you for I would hate to see that beautiful body bruised, especially since I plan to enjoy you most thoroughly. Are you going to be sensible and remain quiet, or must I prove to you escape is impossible?"

Panic overwhelmed her as she realized Thomas would soon be here too and she would have no time to escape. She fought with all her strength, but his laughter taunted her as easily he turned her in his arms and struck her brutally across the face, knocking her to the floor in a trembling heap. She sobbed as she felt him twine his hands in her hair and she cried out as he drew her to her feet. Wildly she fought, but he gripped the front of the thin gown and tore it from her. Then another blow brought bright sparkling lights before her eyes and she would have sagged to the floor except that he held her bound to him.

He looked down into her frightened eyes and laughed softly. Then slowly, deliberately he captured her mouth with his. Brutally, forceably he ground his mouth against hers until she could taste the salty taste of blood. Desperately her mind groped for control. If Thomas came there would be no way for her to escape. Slowly she began to force control over her mind and her body. It took every bit of effort she could muster but she relaxed in his arms.

He lifted his head in surprise, and he watched her suspiciously as she gave him a weak tentative smile.

"Please," she whispered softly, "don't hurt me. I . . . I'll do whatever you want. I know I cannot get away."

For a moment his eyes narrowed, and she gave him what

he searched for. She let fear wash over her face and fill her eyes with tears. Her naked body trembled against his.

Slowly he relaxed his arms and smiled at her again. "Very wise my dear, you will find it much easier to surrender and enjoy it than to fight me."

"What . . . what do you intend for me?"

"I intend, my sweet," he said gently, "for you to be my mistress, my hostess and the most beautiful decoration I own."

"And Thomas?" she replied.

"That depends on how well you obey me. I can contol Thomas, I always have. You will be obedient to me and," he chuckled, "stop fighting me. Then we shall share an enjoyable time here at Waverly. If you refuse," he shrugged. "I shall have to have Thomas aid me in teaching you that all resistance is useless." He took hold of her shoulders and moved her a few inches away from him. He let his eyes roam over her slim curves. She held herself in control, but she wanted to lash out at him, to rip the smirking gleam from his eyes, to tear at him until he lay bloody at her feet. It was the first time in her life she had ever felt hatred and the desire to kill another human being.

He gently slid his hand from her shoulder to cup one breast and he moved his fingers gently savoring the soft firm skin, then he let his hand slide down the curve of her waist and rest on her hip.

"Such a joy you will be," he said huskily. "I cannot wait to taste the pleasure of possessing you." His voice lowered to a whisper. "Let me see your obedience Sabrina . . . go to the bed."

She shivered with distaste, but kept her face as impassive as she could. Knowing his eyes were upon her, she turned and walked slowly toward the bed. She cast her eyes in every direction to see if she could find a weapon to defend herself, for she knew she would rather die than to submit to either Clyde or Thomas.

Beside the bed, on a small table, sat a cut glass decanter of water. It was heavy, and she realized it was the only thing resembling a weapon that was in sight. She stopped by the table.

"Do you mind if I have a drink?" she said softly as she again turned to face him.

His eyes glowed with passion, for she was a vision he would never forget. The light behind her touched her skin with a pale golden light and gleamed through the mass of her pale gold hair that hung to her slim hips. "Drink," he said hoarsely as he slowly began to move toward her. She turned back to the table and poured the water into a glass, then she grasped the neck of the container firmly. She would only have one chance and she had to make it good. One hand held the container, with the other she lifted the glass and sipped the water, then she sat the glass back down. He came up behind her and put his hands on her hips. Grimly, she clenched the container, and as he slowly turned her about she suddenly swung it up and brought it crashing down on his head. She saw the blood and the startled look in his eyes as they glazed and he slowly slumped to the floor at her feet.

Her body shook as if she were caught in a cold wind, and her teeth chattered in fear. Gripping her shattered nerves, she stepped past him and ran to the closet where she grasped the first dress she could find and slipped it over her trembling body. Then, watching Clyde's motionless form as if at any moment he would leap up and catch her, she backed toward the door.

All her strength left her and a cry of defeat and misery choked her as a hand touched her shoulder. "Thomas!" she thought in desperation, and knew now there was no final escape. She knew she would fight him to the last of her strength, she spun about and came face to face with Ellen.

She almost collapsed with relief.

"Oh, Ellen," she cried as the older woman took her in her arms and held her for a moment. Then she looked at Ellen, renewed panic in her eyes. "Thomas, where's Thomas?"

Ellen smiled. "He's sleepin' like this one, and I imagine for enough time for us to get out of here. I tapped him none too gently when I realized what these two were about."

"What will I do, Ellen?"

"Come with me. I have a brother in the city, he will keep you safe until we decide what can be done about all this. There's something very wrong and we've got to find out what before we let them get their hands on you again."

Sabrina gasped. "Oh, Ellen, I could not bear it. I must get away from here, as far away as I can."

"Come along darlin', my brother will care for us until we find out just what can be done about this terrible thing."

Sabrina left the house with Ellen, who had made a carriage ready before she had come to find Sabrina.

When they arrived at Ellen's brother's home they were made welcome, Sabrina was forced to drink some tea into which Lester, Ellen's brother, had slipped something to make her sleep. An hour later, Ellen helped her into bed and she drifted off into relaxed peaceful sleep.

She stirred awake and realized, from the sounds about her, that it must be late in the morning. When she opened the door and went to the top of the stairs she heard the murmuring sound of voices, and they sounded upset and strained.

She walked toward the room from which the voices came. The voices became recognizable as Ellen and her brother.

She could not understand why they seemed so full of alarm.

"I'm telling you, Ellen, there's no place about here to hide, not from that sort of thing. It puts a whole new light on it."

"Are you telling me you want us to go?"

"My God, Ellen, haven't you heard a word I've been saying? You're my sister and you know I would do anything for you, but in this case I'm helpless. They'll find out . . . sure as there's a God they'll find out."

Sabrina pushed the door open and both people turned to face her. Ellen rose from the table.

"Good morning, Sabrina. Do you feel a little better? Did you sleep well?"

Her voice was strained and her face was pale. Sabrina could see in a moment something drastic had happened, for Ellen seemed to be frightened and that was a rare thing for Ellen.

"I think I feel much better than you seem to, Ellen. I've known you too long to be fooled. What has happened?"

"Sabrina . . ."

"Ellen, please. I'm not a child. Please tell me what has happened. Have they found us . . . have they come for me?"

Ellen cast a quick look at her brother, then turned back to Sabrina.

"Sabrina, we have to get you away from here."

"Away from here . . . why? I thought I would be safe here."

"No . . . no, we're not safe here. In fact we are not safe anywhere."

Sabrina went to Ellen and took both her hands in hers. Then she kissed Ellen's cheek.

"Tell me what is wrong Ellen."

"Sabrina, child. I know what you did, you did in self defense, but with the will being the way it was nobody will believe you didn't do it on purpose."

"Do it? Do what, Ellen, what?"

"Sit down Sabrina," Lester said. "We have something to tell you that will be quite a shock. We have to find a way to get you out of England and to safety. The authorities have begun a search for you, a most thorough search, and it will not take long for them to trace you to Ellen, and then to me."

"Surely," Sabrina laughed, "they have not gone to the authorities. What would they tell them, that they tried to rape me and I fled. If anyone comes I shall just refuse to go back with them."

"No, Sabrina," Ellen said, "if they come for you it will mean you death, you see . . . Clyde Mellon is dead. It seems when you struck him last night . . . you killed him. Now they are looking for you. You do not stand a chance against Thomas' rage. We have to get you away from this town, away from this country. That man deserved to die and I will not let you pay for it."

Sabrina gazed at her, absorbing the shock of what she had just said. In a matter of days, she had gone from a wealthy loved girl, to a penniless frightened woman who had no recourse but to run.

Three

Two days later Lester set a folded piece of paper on the table in front of Ellen.

"I'm telling you it's the only way out of this. Who will look for you in the wilds of America? You can stay there until this is forgotten. At least you will be safe from that treacherous man's grasp."

"But to take that poor child . . ." Ellen began.

"Ellen," Lester said gently. "Would you rather see her tried and hung for the murder of that animal? You have read the papers these past few days, you know Thomas is crying for her head, claiming she killed his father in cold blood because he inherited Waverly Hall and the fortune that goes with it."

"How can they believe such a thing?" she demanded. "That poor child could not commit a murder. I told you how I found her. They must listen to me."

"Ellen," he replied in an exasperated voice. "You are a friend, you are also just the cook who could come into some money if old Clyde died."

Ellen gasped, and her face became pink from anger.

"I'm just telling you what they could say. You have got to get her away until we can find some proof of your suspicions. Are you frightened?"

"For myself, no, I've worked all my life, and who knows better than you that it has not been easy. But that child—to take her to such a wild place, to make her a servant, I don't know if she could stand it."

"I think she is stronger than you know."

Ellen sighed. "I shall go and tell her. When does the ship sail?"

"The day after tomorrow. I only hope they do not find you before that. I certainly do not want either of you to be seen by anyone who might run to the authorities."

"We'll be careful."

Ellen reluctantly rose to her feet. Slowly she walked up the stairs and knocked lightly on Sabrina's door.

"Come in," Sabrina called.

Ellen went in to find Sabrina just rising from bed.

"Good morning, Ellen. Is there any more news?"

"Everything's the same," Ellen said quietly as she sat on the bed. "Thomas is harassing the authorities for your capture. He wants to see you punished for the . . . 'tragic death of his beloved father' so he says."

Sabrina's face was pale and her wide eyes were filled with fear. "Oh Ellen, what shall I do? We both know it's only a matter of time until they trace me to you and your brother. I cannot stay here and make more problems for the two people who have been so kind to me."

"You don't need to, my dear child. Lester and I . . . well, we've come up with this idea. It might be a little hard on you for a while, but it's the only way we can see out of this."

"Idea, what kind of idea?"

"Well, Lester works for the courts," Ellen began and Sabrina could see she was nervous. "He's in charge of the indentured servants who leave here to go to the colonies."

"I don't understand Ellen. What does that have to do with our situation?"

"Well, you know how it works?"

"Not exactly."

"If someone here wants to go to the colonies and doesn't have the fare, then someone there pays for their fare. Once you get to the colonies you must work off the price of the passage."

"But . . . why couldn't we just pay our own fare?"

"Because the first time you go near a ship to book passage you would be arrested. Don't you think they're watching for just that sort of thing?"

"But aren't they watching these ships too?"

"Yes, but Lester is sure he can get us aboard without being spotted."

"What . . . what will we have to do when we get there?"

"Well, it seems like Lester got this letter from a man who is a friend of his. This man lives in the colonies. He wrote to Lester telling him that a friend of his was looking for someone to help take care of his house and a small child. It would be a contract for two years. I could go as the housekeeper, and you could be my daughter. I'm sure he would be quite pleased to get two for the price of one and in two years most of this problem might be forgotten, especially if they can't find us."

"Ellen," Sabrina smiled, "what would I ever do without you. I would be quite lost."

"Then you agree?" Ellen asked, relief in her voice.

"How can I not? You and Lester have jeopardized your lives for me. If you were caught both of you would be punished because of me. Two years is not so very long."

"Lester is searching out every way he can to help you. In the meantime we must keep you safe until he finds the way out of this."

"I'm grateful Ellen, I'm truly grateful both to you and your brother. I'll do whatever you think necessary."

Ellen put her arms about Sabrina and smiled. She was aware that Sabrina was not as confident and secure as she sounded by the way she clung to Ellen.

"We cannot carry much along with us, and we will have to slip out of here and onto the ship at night. We must be very careful."

"When do we leave?" Sabrina whispered, and Ellen could hear the fear in her voice.

"Midnight . . . tomorrow night."

They looked into each other's eyes with understanding for a few moments then Sabrina smiled hesitantly and Ellen nodded. They would do what was necessary.

When Ellen left her Sabrina lay back on the bed. Tears she refused to let Ellen see touched her cheeks. She thought of her uncle, sure now that his death was not what she had first thought. She thought of what Clyde had tried to do to her, and no matter what happened she could not find regret in her heart for what she had done. She was frightened of this unknowable future. In servitude for two years to a man she did not know, and in a strange land. Yet she knew there was no other way, for if she were caught, Lester and Ellen would be caught too and might be imprisoned for their love and charity to her. She closed her eyes, wondering what her new life would be like and what kind of man would send for someone to care for his child. Where was his wife, and why did he not just get someone from the area in which he lived to do the job? It would have been much easier, and certainly less expensive for him.

She was frightened in way she had never been before. Frightened of a dark uncertain future, frightened of the insecurity of not knowing if they would truly escape or if at the last moment the hand of fate would swoop her up and deliver her into the clutches of a man like Thomas who would delight in seeing her pay.

Finally she rose and went downstairs. Lester had already left for his office, so she and Ellen shared a quiet breakfast together. "You must have some clothes to take along with you," Ellen asserted. "Clothes that will make you look more like a servant than the lady you are. It is certain you cannot go out on the street where you might be seen and recognized. I shall have to go out today. I will go to a friend who can do the shopping. Will you be all right here for a while?"

"Yes, I'll be fine. Don't worry about me."

"Good, it's best I go now while it is early and not too many people are about. Keep the door locked and do not open it for anyone."

"I'll be careful," Sabrina replied.

Ellen rose and began to gather the breakfast dishes.

"You go on, Ellen, I shall do this. It's about time I learned to work for myself. I do not expect the man who is paying for our services will expect me to lounge about like a lady of leisure while you do all the work. He might become suspicious."

Ellen nodded. She went to a hook behind the door and took down a well worn cloak and flung it about her shoulders. She smiled at Sabrina as she opened the door.

"Now remember, don't open this door for anyone."

"Don't worry, Ellen," Sabrina laughed. "I'll be very careful."

Ellen closed the door behind her and soon the sound of her footsteps receded into silence. Sabrina stood in the quiet room. She had never felt so alone in her life.

Resolutely she pushed aside her fears and loneliness. She began to gather the dishes and wash them. When the kitchen was again neat and clean she took some polish and cloth and went about polishing the furniture in the other downstairs room.

Once the bottom floor of the house satisfied her, she ran

lightly up the steps into her small bedroom. Quickly she made the bed and tidied the room, then she smiled in satisfaction. She was pleased that she had handled her job well.

"I should make a very good maid," she laughed miserably to herself. She could see the bright morning sun as it filtered through the lace of the curtains. How she longed to be out in the sunlight, walking through the gardens of Waverly, digging in the fresh moist earth. She choked back the feeling of pain the vision of Waverly and her uncle brought.

At least I can have some fresh air, she thought; she went to her window and pushed it open, letting in the breeze and the sound of the birds.

Across the street from Lester's home was a small park where a relaxed afternoon could be spent. She gazed at it longingly, but she knew she could do nothing to jeopardize Lester and Ellen.

As she turned away her attention was drawn to a tall shady tree that stood near the entrance to the park. Her heart caught in her throat as she realized someone stood in the shadows of the tree watching the house.

She stepped back away from the window quickly, but knew it was too late. Whoever stood there had had a good view of her as she pushed open the window.

Again the feeling of deep relentless black fear gripped her. She stood out of sight now, but she kept the tree in her sight. At first she thought it might have been someone who was just engaging in an early morning stroll and had stopped by the tree to rest. But a cry of shock came unbidden and she shivered with a cold touch of terror as the man stepped away from the tree and stood in the open gazing up at the very window where she stood. There was no denying his identity or the cold malicious smile that touched his lips . . . Thomas!

"My God," she moaned softly. "He knows I'm here."

Thomas stood for a moment watching the window, then, to Sabrina's surprise he began to whistle lightly as he turned and strolled back through the park and out of her sight.

She stood shaking with fear. There was no place for her to run. She knew it would only be a matter of minutes before the authorities came for her. She was lost.

Grimly, she gathered her courage together. She left the room and ran down the stairs. But before she could reach the door, it opened and Ellen came in. In a moment Sabrina was in her arms and trying shakily to tell her what she had seen.

"Sabrina you must have been mistaken, there is a policeman on the corner and at least two in the park. He need only have called to them and you would have been taken already. It must have been a man who looked like Thomas. You are very frightened and your mind could play tricks on you in that state. Now come and sit down. Lester will be home for lunch soon, we'll tell him. He'll know what to do."

Sabrina was still shaking as she let Ellen lead her to a chair. She waited for Lester's return fearing at any moment to hear a pounding on the door and a cry for her capture.

More than an hour passed before Sabrina realized that the authorities could have been there long before. Yet she knew she had not been mistaken. It had been Thomas. She had felt the cold chill of his smile from across the street. He knew where she was, and she wondered if he was playing with her like a cat with a mouse. Would he wait until she had reached the ship then snatch her from safety at the last moment? It was like him to do such a thing. She felt trapped. Lester returned and Ellen quickly explained.

"That is impossible."

"Why?" Sabrina exclaimed. "It was Thomas! I know it was!"

44

"Sabrina, as I left my office a few minutes ago, Thomas Mellon was sitting outside in his carriage. He smiled and spoke to me and went on. Now if he knew you were in my home do you think he would have done that?"

"Yes! Yes! He is a monster. He would love nothing better than to capture me at the last moment. He is vicious and cruel and he would enjoy it!"

"Sabrina, calm yourself. I have some news that will make you feel better."

"What?"

"There is an earlier ship I can get you on. If he did know he would have no way of knowing if we change plans. This ship leaves tomorrow at dawn. We will slip out the back way just before dawn and you will be gone. Now try and calm yourself. It is best if the two of you get your things ready. I shall be home by seven and we will complete preparations."

Sabrina tried to draw her strength and courage together, but her face remained pale and her lips bloodless in fear. Her hands trembled as she helped Ellen fold the clothes she had just purchased and put them in a small satchel.

Lester returned promptly at seven that night, reassuring her with his calm attitude and patient understanding.

"If it had been Thomas you would be in prison by now. Your nerves have been stretched to the breaking point, and that's understandable, but you must not allow yourself to see shadows that are not there."

"I'm sorry," Sabrina said softly, "it's just that . . ."

"That the man has frightened you to death," Lester said gently, "but it will soon be over. Soon an ocean will separate you, and he has no way of knowing when, where or how you are going. The next two years may be difficult enough for you, don't carry your fears along with you. Tomorrow is always new, and you can start a whole new life. Put these bad memories behind you. Everything will work out, maybe better than you think."

He bent and brushed a gentle kiss on her cheek and patted her hand reassuringly.

"Now," he smiled. "Suppose we have some dinner. Then, I expect, it would be best if you two could get some rest. I will be waking you about three o'clock in the morning. By the time the sun rises you will be safely out of the harbor and on your way."

Sabrina tried her best to eat, but the food choked her and refused to go down. She talked with Ellen and Lester in a nervous jerky way and they silently realized that the only time Sabrina would feel safe would be when the ship was underway.

After dinner Ellen and Sabrina went to their rooms to do as Lester suggested and try to get some sleep. It was an impossibility for Sabrina, and when it came time to rise and Lester rapped gently on her door, she was still awake.

She rose and went downstairs. They ate some hastily prepared food in a dimly lit kitchen. Then Lester carried their cases down.

"I've forgotten my cloak," Sabrina said. She ran back up to her room and took a cloak from the closet. Then she stood for a moment and looked at the still open window. Reluctantly, as if drawn against her will, she walked to the window and looked out. There was a full moon and it lit the tree shrouded park in tiny clusters of light that left the shadows even darker. Quickly her eyes searched out the tree and she gasped softly. To her it still looked as if someone stood in the darkness below it.

Firmly she held herself in check and she pressed her lips together in determination. She would have succeeded, except at that moment she could hear the soft sound of someone whistling. Then a dark shadow pushed itself away from the tree and walked off into the night. "Thomas," she whispered. Did he know she was leaving now? Would he be at the dock waiting for her? Why! Why was he playing this game with her? Why did he not just call in the law and have her taken? She knew it would be useless to tell Ellen and Lester. They would think she was imagining things again. She left the room, closing the door firmly behind her. She would just have to take the chance that he did not know she was leaving now and if he returned tomorrow it would be too late to stop her.

She went downstairs again and they left the house as quietly as possible.

Lester drove the carriage himself for he felt the fewer people who knew of their nocturnal journey the better. They were quiet all the way to the dock and Sabrina had her hands clenched beneath the folds of her cloak, for her vivid imagination could hear the sounds of another carriage that followed them down the dark streets. She was sure that Thomas was ready to pounce on her at any moment.

Despite her fear the trip was uneventful, and they arrived safely at the dock. She looked up at the tall ship that would be carrying her toward an uncertain future. She had to smile at the name she saw in swirling letters on her bow *Good Fortune* they said. "Oh, I hope, I pray," she whispered.

Lester carried their few pieces of luggage up the gangplank and set them on the deck. Sabrina and Ellen followed, standing uncertainly beside him. It was only a few seconds before the sharp sounds of heavy footsteps sounded on the deck and a large figure walked toward them out of the dark.

"Captain Breed?" Lester questioned.

"Yes, I'm Captain Breed," the man answered, his voice sounded gruff. Sabrina could barely make out his features in the dark. "These are the two passengers I've been expecting, I take it. It's good you have finally arrived. We will be sailing very shortly. I'm afraid your quarters will be very cramped."

"It's all right, Captain," Sabrina said. "I'm grateful to be able to sail with you."

"Grateful," the captain questioned, "to sail on a cramped ship toward indentured service. I would hardly say that was something to be grateful for."

"But it is Captain . . . it is," she replied.

"Well, you may take your things below. The others will tell you where you can sleep. I hope you can find some comfort."

"Thank you," Ellen replied.

The ship was many miles at sea when the sun rose. Neither Sabrina or Ellen were to see Thomas arrive at Lester's home. They would not know of Lester's innocent protestation, or hear Thomas's rage. And neither of them would know of the hatred and evil desires that would follow them.

Four

Sabrina laughed gaily and everyone about her felt enclosed in her youthful enthusiasm. Ellen too was pleased. She had watched Sabrina relax as soon as the ship was safely away from danger.

Ellen sat close to her on the hatch of the deck and enjoyed the girl's relaxed pleasure as they listened to some tall tales being told by one of the sailors. But she knew that deep within Sabrina was as worried and frightened of her unsure future as Ellen was. If she had been alone, Ellen would not have worried, but Sabrina was so beautiful, so young and so very vulnerable that she worried about whether she was going from a teapot to a tempest. What kind of man mastered the home into which they would have to serve for two years as housekeeper and nursemaid for a child. It was something she could not get off her mind and she knew for Sabrina it was worse. Sabrina turned to Ellen.

"Shall we take a walk about the deck before we must go and eat more of that atrocious food?" she laughed.

"Yes," Ellen agreed. Together they rose and began to walk slowly around the deck. Sabrina watched the clear cloudless sky and Ellen watched her face.

"You needn't worry so, child. We'll be together, and I hardly think a man who wants someone to care for his child so badly he pays so much for her would be the kind to do us any harm. Don't let's jump to conclusions until we know what we have to face."

"I know you are right Ellen," Sabrina replied, "and I imagine he is some wealthy man who has such a magnificent home that he'll hardly know we're in it."

"That's the attitude," Ellen laughed. "We'll serve our two years and be gone before he even knows we were there."

"I wonder . . . " Sabrina mused.

"What?"

"How old the child is . . . what the child is like . . . what the father is like . . . oh all kinds of questions."

"Well, we'll have our answers soon enough. We'll be docking sometime tomorrow. Then we'll have the answers to all our questions and our future for the next two years."

"I wonder what America is like?"

"Somewhat like England I should say. I suppose the harbor we reach will be like London harbor. If we keep our senses about us, girl, maybe we can even enjoy our time here. I like the hustle and bustle of London. Yes . . . maybe we can even enjoy our stay a little."

They laughed together, and went below to eat some of the food Sabrina had coined some new words for. They slept a restless sleep that night and both of them were already at the rail when the first sign of land was on the distant horizon.

Sabrina felt a sudden chill, as if the hand of fate had reached out to touch her with the warning of something to come. She watched wordlessly as the ship neared the dock.

A crowd jammed the dock, for each coming ship brought news, friends and supplies. She watched the people as the ship tied to the dock and wondered if the man who had bought her services was among them. Her eyes moved from man to man . . . and then she saw him. He stood leaning against a crate. To her he looked like the Indians she had been told about so often. He seemed amused by all the activity about him, and she could sense the amusement from where she stood. She could also sense a tremendous aura of strength and power, as if he were condensing some deep fury within and restrained it only by sheer will. He was tall, and she could see the breadth of shoulder was his own for the cream colored fringed buckskin clung to his lean form like a second skin. He sent a shiver of latent fear down her spine, for it was as if he were a strong contained force about to explode. He was dark, his skin tanned from days in the sun, and his hair was thick and black. She watched as he spoke to a man near him and his teeth flashed white against his dark skin. He was wild, like an untamed whirlwind, and she was fascinated by his air of overwhelming strength and self assurance.

Her attention was drawn from him when Ellen came to her side. "Have you been trying to pick out who we will be working for?" Ellen smiled.

"Truthfully, Ellen, I was watching that man over there. What strange clothes he is wearing. I've never seen anything like them before."

Ellen's eyes followed Sabrina's until they rested on the one being spoken of.

"My goodness, he's a handsome bugger, isn't he?" Ellen said softly. "But he looks . . . dangerous."

"Dangerous?" Sabrina replied.

"Yes," Ellen said. "Dangerous in a way you don't know, child. He's the kind of man who gets what he wants, when he wants it . . . no matter what it is. I've a feeling he would never take no as the answer to anything."

"Welll he certainly doesn't look wealthy, so I doubt very much if he is the one."

Ellen pointed to a man who stood a little further away, a large ruddy faced man with a huge belly. He wore very rich clothes, and acted as if he were quite a bit better than the others about him.

"I wouldn't be surprised if he were the one. He looks as if he owns most of the town."

"Yes, but," Sabrina laughed softly, "I wonder what his wife looks like and," she giggled, "I can't imagine him siring children."

Ellen chuckled. "You'd be surprised child. That's one thing all men have in common."

Ellen turned to Sabrina. "You stay aboard until I find out where I'm to be working and how I can go about explaining that I brought my daughter along with me."

Sabrina nodded and watched Ellen join the group of newly indentured servants who were being taken ashore. Each would present their papers to a man who waited on the dock and he in turn would find the one to whom the servant belonged; then he would validate the transaction. Ellen waited with the group until it was her turn to present her papers. She handed them to a tall cadaverous man who scanned them quickly. Then he gave Ellen a half angry look.

"The papers say you and your daughter."

"Yes, she's still aboard."

"But 'twas only one sent for."

"I can't leave my child alone in England, now can I? He's getting a cheap price. She will work as hard as I."

"I don't know. Maybe he won't want two of ye. Then ye'll have to be separated."

"No! I will not be separated from my child," Ellen exclaimed.

"Ye will if he don't want the two of ye. She'll be sold to another to work out her time. What's the difference? Ye'll both be workin for two years."

"I won't be separated! At least let me talk to him. Surely he's not a heartless man to separate mother and child?"

Ellen's voice cracked in near panic and she was about to burst into tears when a deep masculine voice spoke from behind her.

"What seems to be the matter, Perkins, aren't all my papers in order?"

Ellen spun about and looked up at the same man she and Sabrina had admired from the ship. He smiled pleasantly at her and she smiled in return, for she did not seem to be able to help it.

"This is the one you sent for, Mr. Storm, but there seems to be a little problem."

"What's the problem?"

"She's had the nerve to bring her child along. I told her you only sent for one, and you only paid for one."

"Please," Ellen pleaded, "Don't take my child from me. She'll be no bother and she'll be frightened alone. Please let her stay with me. She'll be no bother—I swear—and she'll do her share of the work."

A strange dark look came over Storm's face as Perkins grabbed Ellen's wrist and gave her a shake.

"Shut up woman! Mr. Storm will tell you what will be done."

Ellen turned pleading eyes to Storm.

"Children should never be separated from their parents, Perkins. I see no harm in her bringing the child along. She can be a playmate for mine."

Ellen wisely kept silent about the fact that Sabrina could hardly be a playmate for a child when she was nineteen.

"Thank you, sir, you'll never regret it. How old is your child?" Ellen asked.

"Five."

"A boy?"

"No, a girl."

His face seemed to darken as if it hurt him to speak of the

child.

"I'll take your papers, and I'll go and get my wagon. We have a long trip ahead of us. You and your daughter be here when I return. What's your name?"

"Ellen."

"All right, Ellen. I've bought your papers for two years. You do your job well and I'll see you and your child are cared for."

"Thank you, sir."

"Good, I'll be back in about half an hour."

She watched him stride away from her, his lean body pushing his way through the crowd with ease. She wondered just how he was going to feel when he saw Sabrina. Then another idea came into her head and quickly she returned to the ship and went to Sabrina.

"Sabrina we have a problem and there is only one way out of it, now listen closely."

Sabrina's eyes widened as she listened to what Ellen said. At first resistance was in her eyes, then Ellen finally convinced her that what she wanted her to do was necessary for their safety.

A half hour later they stood together on the docks and watched Clayton Storm approach them.

Sabrina had put on a long cloak and covered her head with the hood until her face was shadowed. She stood with her head down like a shy child. She was small and slim so to all outward appearances she looked like a girl of no more than eleven or twelve.

She felt his presence beside her like a vibrant force and she wanted to look up into his face but Ellen's warning words came back to her.

"He'll separate us if he finds out your age, child. Keep yourself hidden until we're well on our way. Then it will be too late for him to send you back."

She clenched her hands beneath her cloak and allowed her eyes to rise only to the strong body that stood before her.

"This is your little girl?" She heard him say, his voice tinged with amusement. "How old is she?"

"She's twelve sir, but she's tall for her age," Ellen said worriedly.

"Well she'll be of use to you in caring for mine. Come along, we have to get going, it's a long way home."

"You mean we won't be in the city?" Ellen said unhappily.

He laughed a deep rumbling laugh that made Sabrina smile. She liked the deep resonant sound of his voice and the pleasant sound of his laughter. For the first time in a long time she felt strangely safe and at peace.

"We're about as far from the city as you can get," he replied. "You're not afraid, are you?"

The teasing laughter in his voice brought a protest to Ellen's lips and a smile to Sabrina's. The smile was quickly gone when two hard strong hands gripped her waist and lifted her onto the wagon.

"I'm not afraid of anything," Ellen stated firmly.

"Not even Indians?" he questioned.

"Indians?" Ellen questioned in a trembling voice. "Are there Indians where you live?"

"Not far, but they're peaceable," he replied as he slapped the reins to urge the horses into motion. "We go a good way by wagon, then by horseback the balance. We'll pick up my little girl at the first stop and take her home with us."

"She's being cared for now?"

"Yes, but I want her home with me and there's no one else about here that will . . . can come to do it. I need someone permanent. Maybe if you like it here you will consider working for me permanently."

Ellen and Sabrina had both caught his slip. That no one about the area would come to his place and stay. Both wondered about the reasons as they traveled along slowly and he tried to answer all of Ellen's questions about their destination, yet it annoyed him that he was strangely aware of the slim quiet hooded form that sat near him.

"Your child doesn't talk much?" he said.

"She's very timid and frightened. She'll be all right once we're there."

He could see Sabrina's small hands clasped in her lap and thought they looked so delicate and fine that he began to wonder just how much work they could do. They were restless, and twisted gently. He fought the urge to reach out and take them in his to reassure her of her safety.

To Ellen and Sabrina it seemed as if they travelled for hours. The city was left far behind and slowly the road began to appear less and less travelled upon. Eventually it turned into a narrow path through the wilderness. Both of them were surprised to see a cabin suddenly appear just ahead.

"We'll pick up Summer here," he said quietly.

"Summer?"

"My little girl," he replied.

"What a strange and beautiful name."

"Her name is Summer Moon," he said in a firm challenging voice. "She is half Indian. Does that make a difference?"

Ellen and Sabrina could hear the depth of resisting anger within him.

"A child is a child in the eyes of God, Mr. Storm. Their color or blood makes no difference to him, nor does it to us. I'm sure she is a beautiful child and you love her very much."

"Yes, she is beautiful," he said softly, then again they heard the hard steel in his voice beneath gentle words. "I love her . . . she's mine . . . mine."

It was as if he challenged someone to deny this. They remained silent, not sure of what answer they could make, yet for some unknown reason Sabrina felt a gentle sympathy. She wanted to assure him somehow of something that seemed to frighten him.

He pulled the wagon to a halt in front of the door, but almost before he could get down, the door opened and a child, clad in buckskin, ran out.

"Papa! Papa!" she cried excitedly as Clay leapt down and caught her up in his arms. He hugged her to him fiercely and her small arms entwined around his neck.

Behind them, in the doorway stood a rather buxom woman with a broad smile on her face. Clay smiled at her over the child's shoulder.

"She's been good for you, Mrs. Daugherty?"

"That child's a lamb, Clay. A real pleasure to have about. Me and Hank enjoy havin' her here. You could leave her as long as you wanted."

"Thanks," he grinned, "but I want her home with me where she belongs. I want you to meet Ellen and her little girl. They'll be staying with me and taking care of Summer and the house whenever I'm away."

"Hello Ellen, welcome to the territory."

"Hello," Ellen replied.

Mrs. Daugherty tried to see beneath Sabrina's cloak, but could not. "Do you want to rest a spell before you go on?"

"No, I want to get as close to the river as I can before I camp. I'd like to cross the river in the morning."

The woman's smile faded. "Do you think he's still watchin', Clay?"

"He's watching, I can feel him. I don't want to give him any opportunity to do anything that might cause an open break between me and her people. We have gotten along, I don't want to destroy that. One day I want Summer to know. One day when she's old enough to understand."

The woman nodded and Clay set the child in the wagon

and threw the bundle Mrs. Daugherty handed him in beside her.

"Goodbye for now," Clay said. "We'll come and visit one day soon."

"Don't you forget to do that," she called after them.

Again they rode for what seemed to be hours. Ellen and Sabrina listened to the bright happy laughter and the ceaseless chatter of the child as she talked to her father. They also enjoyed the amused and affectionate answers the man gave the child's multitude of questions.

Both Ellen and Sabrina were near exhaustion when another cabin came into view. Again Clay drew the horses to a halt and climbed down.

"We leave the wagon here," he said. "The rest of the way is on horseback. I forgot to ask either of you, can you ride?"

"Sabrina can," Ellen said. "I have always kept as much distance between me and a horse as I possibly could."

Clay laughed. "We'll only be traveling in short jumps. It won't be too bad."

He helped a stiffened Ellen down, then reached up for Sabrina. He lifted her from the wagon and set her gently on the ground. Then he turned to his daughter who leapt from the wagon into his arms. Their laughter blended.

"One of these days I'm not going to catch you, little one. Then what are you going to do when you find yourself flat on your nose in the dirt?"

"You'll catch me, Papa," she giggled. "You always do." The self assurance in her voice brought a smile to all their faces.

Sabrina watched her from beneath the hood. What a lovely creature she was. She was small and straight as an arrow. Her oval face was fine boned and two wide eyes as black as night looked at her father with intense love. Her hair was parted in the middle and two long black braids

58

hung well below her waist. Her skin spoke of her Indian blood. One look at her face as she watched her tall handsome father spoke eloquently of her near worship of him. Sabrina could see her love was returned twofold.

Again a cabin door was opened, but this time a tall man stood in the doorway.

"Afternoon, Clay."

"Caleb," Clay answered.

"You can leave the wagon by the barn."

"I'll see to the horses," Clay answered. "Are mine ready to go?"

"Yep."

"Afternoon, Uncle Caleb," Summer called.

"Afternoon, Summer," the man smiled. "Been a good girl while your papa was gone?"

"Yes, Uncle Caleb," she replied seriously. He nodded.

"Want to come in and sit a spell Clay?" Caleb said while his eyes lingered on Ellen and the slim form in the hooded cloak.

"I'd like to, Caleb, but I want to reach the river before I camp."

"That'll take some doin'. Your in a powerful hurry," the man said quietly. "Anything wrong?"

Sabrina watched Clay seem to grow still. It was a moment or two before he replied. "No, nothing's wrong, I just want to get Summer home and see to my place before too long."

Again the man nodded, but Sabrina was not sure it was in agreement with what Clay had just said.

"Caleb, this is Ellen, she'll be staying with Summer the times I'm gone. Sort of a general housekeeper. This is her little girl, Sabrina."

"Afternoon," Caleb said, his gaze intent on Sabrina's covered form.

"Afternoon," Ellen murmured, and Sabrina nodded her

head.

His curiosity almost got the best of him, but his knowledge of the frontier kept the questions in him silent.

Summer rode the wagon with Clay toward the barn while Ellen and Sabrina stood under Caleb's intent gaze in silence.

Soon Clay returned. He rode one horse with Summer perched before him, and he led two others. Sabrina needed no help to mount, but Ellen required Clay's help into an unsteady seat.

"I'll see you in a few weeks, Caleb. Thanks."

"Goodbye," Caleb said to them all, but Sabrina still felt uncomfortable as if he could see through the cloak. She was relieved when Clay led the way and they started off.

Clay kept a slow steady pace and they could hear his laugh often as Summer continued to chatter away.

When the sun was near the horizon and deep shadows stretched across the wooded path they could hear the murmuring flow of a river nearby. When they finally reached the banks Clay drew his horse to a stop.

"We'll camp here tonight," he said as he deposited Summer on the ground. He made camp quickly and expertly. First tethering the horses so they would not stray, he then built a fire and gave them food from the pack he had carried along.

"By this time tomorrow night we'll be home," he said to Ellen. Then he turned to Summer.

"Wrap yourself in a blanket Summer, near the fire and get some sleep. We'll be starting early."

Summer did as she was told and it was not long before she slept. Sabrina too rose, took a blanket and went to the edge of the fire where the shadows could hide her. There she wrapped the blanket around her and lay down. From where she was she could see Clay's face clearly in the pale light of the fire as he talked to Ellen. She had thought he was the handsomest man she had ever seen when he had stood a distance from her on the dock, now she was closer and she could breathlessly feel the warm touch of his startling blue eyes. Like the sky on a sunny day, she thought. They had been so startling in his dark face that she had not been able to keep her gaze from lingering on them.

He bent a little forward as he said something to Ellen, and Sabrina could almost feel the magnetism that wanted to draw her to his side and sit close to feel the sense of strength and protection he exuded. After a few more minutes Ellen too went to sleep, and again she watched as he sat gazing into the fire. Suddenly his face seemed so young . . . so hurt. She wondered what had crossed his mind that had been so painful.

Then she suddenly became more aware of him as he turned slightly and looked in her direction. Panic struck her as he rose and walked toward her.

When he reached her side he squatted on his haunches and spoke softly.

"Sabrina?"

"Yes," she whispered.

She trembled with a sudden electrical feeling of warmth as he reached out and took one of her hands in his. Then he spoke in a gentle voice as if he wanted to soothe her fears of the unknown.

"I know it's frightening for a little girl your age to be transplanted like this. Try not to be afraid. I'm sure you and Summer will get along well and there won't be so much work that you won't have time to play. I'd like you to be happy here, so if you have any worries, or you become afraid you will talk to me, won't you?"

She was trying her best to control the trembling as his large hard hand gently caressed hers. She fought the shocking urge to move into his arms and beg him to hold her and make her secure. Why did she feel there was safety within those arms?

"Yes," she whispered.

"Good girl. Now get some sleep. Don't worry about strange noises. I'll be on guard. There is nothing out here to harm you. From now on try to see the beauty of this place and you will enjoy it as I do; good night, child, sleep easy."

"Good night," she replied. For a moment he remained beside her holding her hand in his. Then gently he laid her hand down, rose and walked back to the fire. It was just before dawn broke that Sabrina awoke. She lay still for a moment listening to the early morning sounds. Then she thought it would be best to rise and wash and prepare for travel before the others. That way she could retain her cloak and her secret until they were at his home. Then it would be too late to send her back.

Quietly she rose and walked away from the camp. She lay aside the heavy inhibiting cloak and knelt by the water. She scooped up the water in her hands and bathed her face. Then she loosened her hair from the confining braids and ran her fingers through it. She unbuttoned her dress and pressed her cool hands against her skin. Then she rose, lifted her skirts and removed her shoes and stockings. Gathering her skirts high above her slim hips she waded into the cool water. She was humming lightly to herself when a snapping of the underbrush alarmed her. She spun about and gazed up into shocked blue eyes. Clay stood a few inches from the bank gazing in surprise at the beauty who stood before him.

Five

Clay Storm slept lightly. He was aware of every sound and movement around his camp. It surprised him when, in the dim light of early dawn, he saw Sabrina rise and walk quietly away.

He knew she knew nothing about the area she was in and was afraid if she wandered too far from camp she would become lost. She was an unsure frightened child, and he did not want her fears made any greater by stumbling across a wild animal or getting herself hurt. Aware that she might have just been going into the nearby brush to relieve herself he gave her a few minutes to accomplish this, then he rose and followed her tracks easily up the banks of the river. Through the brush he could see her as she began to wade into the water. He pushed the brush aside and walked out on the bank, she spun about in surprise when she heard him approach.

It was hard to tell who was more shocked—Clay or Sabrina. Unaware of her beauty she stood with the water swirling about her slender legs, the dress bundled in her arms, her hair tumbled in golden profusion about her, and her wide purple eyes filled with defiant fear as they met his.

"Good God," he muttered softly, then he smiled, "my my, you've aged overnight."

"Please," she stammered, "let me explain."

"I should like nothing better than to hear both you and your—mother's explanations. Come out of that water before you catch cold."

She waded to the bank and walked up beside him. Fear held her and she refused to look up into those all-knowing blue eyes again. She kept her eyes leveled at his chest. Doing so she missed the look in his eyes when she stood beside him. It was concern and compassion that filled them, not the laughter she had expected.

"How old are you?" he questioned gently.

"Nineteen."

"Is Ellen your mother?"

Sabrina gulped, but did not answer. A gentle finger lifted her chin and his eyes held hers. They seemed to be able to read every thought in her mind.

"I'm going to take you back to camp, then we are going to talk. This time I want the truth."

She could not answer, for she could not control the wild unfamiliar emotion that coursed through her at his touch. She watched his smile fade and a new look replace it.

"Be damned," he muttered as he stepped back from her. He was angry at his own reaction. No matter her beauty, she still looked like an innocent half child.

"Come on," he said more harshly than he intended.

"I . . . I have to put my shoes on," she mumbled helplessly.

He stood watching her as she sat on the ground and put on her stockings and shoes. He was alarmed at the urge to join her there and tumble her into the soft grass and taste that soft pouting mouth. Angrily he looked away, and waited until she again stood beside him. Then he motioned her ahead and followed her as she walked back toward the camp. Absently he appreciated the sway of her slim hips, and the glimmer of early morning sun on the soft gold strands of her hair. Firmly he controlled the desire to reach out and touch it. When they walked back into camp they found a very worried and frightened Ellen. She had wakened to find both Clay and Sabrina gone and she was afraid of what might have happened. When Sabrina came in sight with a cold faced Clay behind her she knew with a sinking heart their secret was out.

She rose and went to Sabrina quickly.

"My lamb, my sweet," she soothed as she put her arm about Sabrina and a glared defiantly at Clay, who returned her glare with a look of tolerant amusement.

"Has he hurt you, child?"

"Good heavens, Ellen," he snapped. "I have no intention of molesting children."

Sabrina's head snapped up at this and anger glittered in her eyes.

"I'm not a child," she said in a chilled voice, then she looked at Ellen.

"I'm sorry Ellen. I'm fine, but my stupidity has caused us a problem. I know he will surely take me back now. But I'll be all right. I'll find another position and we will be safe until word comes from Lester."

Ellen turned her eyes to Clay, who had stood regarding them as they spoke with an unreadable look in his eyes.

"I know you feel we have lied to you and in truth it is so," Ellen said, "but will you let me explain the reason why. Then, if we place ourselves on your mercy, you may be just and let us stay. You see, " she paused, then she added in a soft whisper, "it means her life if she is returned to England."

"Sit down," he said in a firm quiet voice, "and tell me what this is all about. This masquerade could not have gone on much longer anyway."

65

"We thought," Sabrina began, "that if we were already in your home it would be too late to send us back."

"I see," he watched them walk to the remains of the fire and sit down together. They lent each other strength. He rebuilt the fire to give them a chance to gather themselves together. When he finished he sat across from them and held their eyes with his.

"Now suppose you tell me what this is all about?"

Ellen squeezed Sabrina's hand encouragingly, then she began to talk. She told him the whole story. When she reached the part about Clyde's attempted rape of Sabrina the blue eyes switched to Sabrina and within them Ellen could see a deep cold rage. It was at that moment she became aware that Clay Storm was more aware of Sabrina as a woman than as a child in danger.

"What were your plans?"

"To stay in your home until we received word from my brother. Then we would decide what was best for the future."

There was a deep and penetrating silence as Clay continued to watch Sabrina. Her nerves were stretched to the breaking point, and she could take no more.

"Do not play with me!" she said. "Tell me if I must go or stay, but don't make this a game for your amusement."

"I hardly think the loss of your life would stir my amusement. I see no other way than to let you stay. In a few weeks I will be going back to the city. I shall check for any word from Ellen's brother. In the meantime, how am I supposed to look upon you?" he chuckled lightly. "I have bought your services for two years. That is no small sum of money. I expect," he added softly, "some form of return on my investment."

Somehow she sensed a double meaning to his words, but she could not read the eyes that suddenly became emotion-

66

less.

"I . . . I shall do my best to keep my side of the bargain," she said and again she watched humor touch his eyes.

"I think it would be best if Ellen were my housekeeper, and you were to care for Summer. She is a little wild at the moment. That comes from being alone with only me for all her young life."

His voice became gentle and touched with the warmth of love as he spoke of the child. "I would have her taught the ways of a lady and you would be good at that." He bent forward, his eyes intent. "Teach her to read and write, to be a woman of character. I would be more than grateful, and I would compensate you with whatever funds you might need when this is over. Is that agreed?"

Sabrina was aware only of an intent warm blue sea that held her mesmerized but Ellen was aware of something else. Clay Storm was no backwoodsman. He spoke too well, had too much money, and despite the way he tried to hide it he had all the bearing of gentry.

"Is that a bargain?" he repeated.

"Yes," Sabrina answered. "Yes, I will do what you want in return for your silence and my safety."

"Good," he murmured. "Very good."

He rose to his feet and went to Summer. Gently he shook her awake. "Come on sleepy head," he smiled as he bent to kiss her. "We want to get home tonight."

Summer rose eagerly and in less than an hour they had eaten and were again on their way.

Each kept their own thoughts, but each would have been surprised at the thoughts of the others.

They stopped only to rest the horses occasionally and to eat a very light lunch. When the sun began its descent it was Summer more than Clay who urged them along.

Sabrina, riding directly behind Clay and Summer could

hear their words drifting back to her.

"Papa?"

"What, Summer?"

"Why do we need anyone else to live at our house?"

"Don't you want them to?"

"No."

"Why?"

"I just don't. I want to stay with you."

"Summer, you know I have to go away sometimes a day or two at a time. There is no way I can always take you along."

"You did before."

"Yes, but you're growing up now and it's time you began to learn some things I can't teach you."

Summer looked up at her father and it was clear in her eyes that this was a statement she could not believe. In her mind there was nothing her father did not know.

"What?" she questioned.

Sabrina laughed for the imperturbable Clay Storm seemed to be momentarily without words. Then he spoke firmly.

"Just things, Summer. Why don't you give them a chance, see if you like them, see if there aren't some things you'll enjoy learning?"

"Okay . . . but."

"But what?"

"You still promised to take me on one of your trips for beaver again. If you take me, I'll be good, I promise."

"It seems," Clay muttered, "I'm making a hell of a lot of bargains lately. Going out to check beaver traps is not for little girls."

"I went before," she protested, "please, Papa, just one more time. Then I'll listen to the lady and learn what you want me to."

"All right, all right," he agreed. "One more time."

Sabrina could hear Summer's pleased laugh and Clay's even more pleased response as she put her arms about his waist and hugged him tightly. There was no doubt in Sabrina's mind that he loved this tiny child with his whole heart.

They crested a hill and Clay stopped the horses. Sabrina and Ellen came up beside him. Below them spread a lush green valley, and in it sat a house. It was much larger than Sabrina had expected and certainly much larger than Clay's two friends had owned. Behind it sat a small barn.

"Well, we're home," Clay said and Sabrina could hear the note of satisfaction in his voice. He nudged his horses forward and they followed. When they dismounted Clay took the reins of their horses.

"Summer, show Ellen and Sabrina about while I care for the horses."

He walked away leading the horses while Sabrina and Ellen picked up the packs he had left on the porch and followed Summer inside. The house was much larger than Sabrina had thought. It showed all the signs that the ones who lived there cared for their possessions. It was spotlessly clean. They walked into a large square room that had a fireplace on one wall and a doorway beside it that led to the kitchen. Two doors on another wall led to two bedrooms, and a door opposite led to another. All the rooms were large and made quite comfortable with large hand-made furniture.

Summer led them to the kitchen which also had a large fireplace. The huge wooden table had been polished to a smooth finish, and kitchen utensils hung on the stone wall. She then led them to each bedroom. The beds were also extremely large and solid looking. The covers looked to be hand woven of some Indian designs. Hanging on the wall of the largest bedroom was another intricately and brightly woven cover. Sabrina touched it lightly.

"How very beautiful."

"My mother made it," Summer said.

"It's really very beautiful."

Sabrina turned to see a dark thoughtful look in the child's eyes as she gazed at the hanging. It was a look of hunger and loneliness, a look of longing that fled the moment she saw Sabrina's eyes on her.

As they again reentered the main room, they could hear Clay's footsteps cross the wide front porch and come to the door.

Sabrina again felt the same sense of security as he entered the room with a load of wood under one arm.

"I'll light the fires and we'll have some supper. There's candles in the kitchen Summer, run and get them."

Summer returned with the candles and Clay laid them on the huge mantle for the time when they would have to light their way to bed. Ellen, when Clay had built the kitchen fire, set about making supper while Sabrina and Summer sat before the fire on a huge black bearskin rug.

Clay sat in a chair and watched them. Sabrina's gold head bent near Summer's dark one. He heard their light laughter and was pleased at the sound. It was the first moment of real peace he could remember in a long time, and he savored it completely.

Summer was explaining how Clay had killed the huge bear himself, skinned and cured it as a rug for the house.

"Papa wasn't even afraid," she said proudly.

"Well you're wrong there, little one. Papa was scared to death. I only killed him because I knew I couldn't outrun him. I had no choice, it was either kill him or let him eat me for supper."

This did not set well with Summer who looked for words to repudiate this statement.

"Well anyway," she said belligerently, "anyone else would have got eaten."

Clay threw back his head and laughed.

Ellen called them to supper. A supper Clay complimented over and over. "I've been eating my cooking for so long I'm deathly sick of it. You'll never know how I longed for a good meal."

Sabrina watched as Ellen melted under his charm and extended herself even more to please him. It occurred to her as it had to Ellen, that Clay was more than what he appeared to be. His manners and charm were too well refined to belong to a backwoodsman.

After dinner Clay sat with Summer on his lap until she went to sleep. Clay had told them that each of the two bedrooms belonged to Sabrina and Ellen.

"Does Summer sleep in my room?" Sabrina asked.

"No!" he said firmly. "There's a small bed in my room. She sleeps there,"

"But if I am to care for her and she needs me in the night . . ."

She stopped talking as a frigid gaze turned on her. The voice was just as chilled.

"If she needs anyone in the night I am here to protect her. Your job is to teach her during the day. Is that understood?"

"Yes," she replied softly. She watched his broad back as he carried Summer into his bedroom and put her to bed.

Ellen was exhausted and her head kept nodding, yet she was reluctant to go to bed before Sabrina. But under Sabrina's insistence she finally agreed that she was too stiff and tired to argue.

"I hate to leave you alone out here," she said.

"Oh, Ellen, the door is bolted, there's a bright fire. There's a rifle over the mantle and Mr. Storm is in the next room. There's nothing to be afraid of. Please, you're exhausted. Go to bed."

Ellen rose, took a candle from the mantle, lit it from the fireplace then she kissed Sabrina's cheek and said quietly, "You're safe child. Don't worry, and don't think back on the past. One day this will all be over and we can go home."

"Yes, Ellen, of course. Don't worry about me. I'm fine. Goodnight."

"Goodnight."

She watched Ellen's door close, then she sat on the rug and contemplated both her past and her future. She thought of Waverly Hall and all its splendor and realized she was more comfortable here in this small cabin than she had been there. She wondered if these thoughts were disloyal to her uncle whom she had loved so dearly.

She was so caught up in her reverie she did not hear Clay's door open. She did not hear as he entered the room and closed the door softly behind him.

She sat gazing into the fire and from the darkened corner of the room he stood and watched her. He admitted readily to himself that he had not seen another woman as beautiful as she. He remembered, with bitter pain, another, a dark eyed girl, little more than Sabrina's age. Firmly he put the memory from his mind. He was almost twelve years older than the girl who knelt by the fire, twelve years of painful experience that left him with a hunger he refused to recognize. Sternly controlling his emotions he took several steps toward her before she sensed he was there and turned to look at him. Her wide violet eyes all but shattered his reserve and the tremulous smile touched a place within him that no one had touched for a long time. He sat down in a chair a little away from her. He was determined to keep his distance.

"Aren't you tired? It's been a very long journey for you."

"I'm tired, but I cannot sleep. I was hoping you would return."

"Why?"

"To apologize."

"For what?" he replied, a touch of surprise in his voice.

"I am only hired help. It's not up to me to make decisions or question yours. I know you must want Summer near you for protection, since you have been her only protection all this time. I imagine it has been quite difficult trying to raise a little girl by yourself."

"It's not difficult to care for someone you love," he said softly.

She lifted her eyes to his and again she was held by the mystery that seemed to lurk in the depths of his eyes. She sat motionless, but she felt the urgent need to go to him, to reach out and touch him gently and to feel him reach for her and hold her close to him.

For her it was a new and a very frightening thing, but he recognized the dawn of desire for he had tasted it before.

"Go to bed, Sabrina," he said gently. The quiet words broke the spell she had been bound in. Turning her gaze away from him she slowly rose and walked into her room.

She sighed deeply as she closed the door, feeling a sense of loss she could not understand. She had taken a lighted candle with her and it cast the room into flickering shadows. She put it in a holder on the table and began to prepare for bed.

Each window in the house had wooden shutters that could be drawn in and bolted from the inside. Hers were bolted tightly now, and again it occurred to her that Clayton Storm's home seemed to be a well protected fortress.

Sabrina did not like the feeling of being shut in, so she went to the shutters, unbolted them and pushed them open letting in the cool night air.

She slipped into her nightgown and braided her long hair. Then she went to the window and leaned her elbows against

73

the frame. How beautiful it is here, she thought. The stars seemed so much closer and the wind whispered through the trees like a quiet song. She closed her eyes for a moment to enjoy the soft breeze that lightly touched her warm skin.

Then the sudden feeling came over her that she was being watched. For a startling moment she was afraid to open her eyes.

Determinedly she opened them and gazed about. No one was in sight. There was wide clearing between the house and the dark wooded area. She watched the edge of the woods. Was someone there? Standing in the shadows of the trees. She laughed at her own fear. How could someone be there? The people in the house were the only ones about for miles. Yet her skin prickled as if she could actually feel someone's presence. She was about to close the window and go to bed, when a strange eerie call came from the edge of the wilderness. It was a gentle mournful call, very quiet, very gentle, yet it made her shiver with a feeling she could not describe. Again she started to close the window. It was some kind of night animal she thought. Then her attention was drawn to the corner of the porch that she could see from where she was. She had heard no noise in the house, no opening or closing of the door and no footsteps on the porch, yet Clay stood there, a rifle tucked under his arm and his eyes intent on the edge of the woods.

How long they stood as they were she did not know. Clay's gaze never left the woods, and the rifle was pointed in that direction. Clouds skittered across the moon and a low rumbling of thunder in the distance caused Clay to lift his head and gaze at the sky. His attention was drawn again to the edge of the woods by a repetition of the soft mournful cry. This time he stepped down from the porch and out into the clearing.

Sabrina stepped back into the darkness of her room. She

didn't know why, but she had the feeling Clay would be angry if he saw her there. From the shadows she watched him as again he stood motionless, then the sound of his voice in a quiet whisper came to her. "Hawk," he said softly, "Damn you, Hawk."

Minutes ticked by and the thunder increased. Soon it was accompanied by flashes of lightning and an increase in the intensity of the breeze. It was only when the first drops of rain sounded against the ground that Clay turned and walked back to the porch, this time she heard his footsteps on the porch and the closing of the door. Again the house was silent. But now the feeling of another presence was also gone. Sabrina reached out and drew the shutters closed just as the storm broke about them. She returned to the bed and lay down. Soon the patter of rain on the roof made her drowsy and she began to slip into sleep. But with sleep came dreams, vague dreams of someone's touch, blue eyes, and a strange wide winged bird. Then she drifted into deeper sleep.

She awakened to bright sunlight and the call of early morning birds. She pushed the shadows of night away. There was nothing for her to be afraid of. She knew that Clay was watchful and he would let no harm come to them. She rose, dressed and went to the kitchen to help Ellen with breakfast, and to begin her duties with Summer.

Six

There were only three of them for breakfast, Ellen — Summer and Sabrina.

"Has your father slept late?" Sabrina asked Summer.

To this Summer looked completely taken aback. "Papa has been gone long before you got up."

"Gone? Where?"

"Maybe to his traps, maybe hunting, maybe," she shrugged, "somewhere. Sometimes he goes away for a while."

Sabrina and Ellen exhanged glances. "He certainly doesn't leave you alone?" Sabrina said cautiously.

"Of course not," Summer said. Now she was offended that any negative thoughts could be attached to her father. Again Sabrina and Ellen were amazed at the almost adult actions and reactions of this child.

"Well," Ellen said in a somewhat disconcerted voice. "Who comes to care for you?"

"Swift Doe."

"And who is Swift Doe?"

"She's my friend . . . she's Papa's friend too. He said . . . he said she used to be my mother's friend."

Sabrina felt a tug of another emotion she could not identify. Swift Doe as Papa's friend. She wondered just what kind of a friend Swift Doe was.

"Summer," Sabrina said, "we must get together and make up some kind of a schedule."

"A sch . . . sch . . ."

"Schedule."

"What's that?"

"A sort of a plan for how we will arrange our days. Your lessons, and the clothes we'll make for you and all sorts of things." Sabrina smiled encouragingly.

"Can't we wait for a while. I want to go to the village with Swift Doe again before we have to do all that stuff."

"I see," Sabrina said quietly. "Do . . . do you think I could go with you. I'd like to meet Swift Doe."

"We have to go before Papa gets back."

"Why?"

"He doesn't like my going over there so Swift Doe lets me visit when Papa is away."

"Do you think that's right, Summer?"

"What?"

"To lie to your father."

Summer's eyes grew wide. "I would never lie to Papa," she said, aghast that she had been accused of such a thing.

"But you said . . ."

"He doesn't like me to go, but he never said I couldn't."

"Maybe he thought he didn't have to. Maybe he thought you just wouldn't go if he didn't approve."

Summer thought about this and the bright light in her eyes faded. She looked unsure as she watched Sabrina closely.

"I suppose I should ask Papa," she said, but her voice gave away the knowledge that she was sure her father would not let her go. She slid down from her chair and walked to the door. With a last uncertain look at Sabrina she ran from the room and they could hear the front door slam behind her.

Sabrina ran to the front door and looked out; she saw Summer cross the clearing and enter the woods. Afraid that she would get hurt or lost, Sabrina ran after her. It was easy to follow her small soft prints in the earth that was moist after the rain. For a long time she followed the prints and her fears grew. Where was the child going? Was she trying to find Swift Doe? Sabrina began to worry as the time dragged along and still the prints led her deeper and deeper into the forest.

Suddenly she came to a small clearing. There, on her knees, was Summer. It took only a moment for Sabrina to realize why she had run here, for it was an obviously well cared for grave by which she knelt.

She was not sure of what she could say to comfort her, but the dejected little girl drew her sympathy.

She looked at the grass covered mound of earth and saw the flowers that surrounded it.

"Your mother?" she said softly.

A small sound accompanied by sniffles was her only answer.

"I'm sorry, Summer. I know how you feel. You see I lost both my parents when I was very young. My uncle took care of me. You are very lucky to have a father who loves you."

"I know," came the whispered reply, "but you don't understand." The black eyes filled with tears. "You see Papa doesn't allow me to come here either. He doesn't even know that I followed him here one day."

Sabrina was stunned, not only at the words but at the pain and uncertainty she found in the dark eyes. She wanted to hold the child close and comfort her, but she was not sure why Clay had done this and she did not want him angry.

"Summer, I want us to be friends. Suppose we keep all this a secret for a while? At least until we can decide what to do.

Maybe if we become good friends one day I can talk to your papa and tell him how much you want to know about your mother."

"Would you?" The eyes brightened with hope. Sabrina realized her father was the sun in her world.

"Yes, I would. Now why don't you go back to the house. I'll come in a few minutes. We can start your lessons."

"All right," she rose, "you won't forget . . . you promise?"

"I won't forget," Sabrina smiled, and enjoyed the hesitant smile in return. She watched as Summer retraced her path toward the house.

She looked back at the grave and a million questions filled her mind. Why would a father keep this place a secret from his own child? Why would he refuse her permission to come here?

She looked about her. It was a very beautiful place. Wild flowers spilled across the open field and tall trees shaded the circular area.

She sighed and was about to rise when again the same strange sensation struck her as it had the night before. Someone was watching her.

Quickly her eyes surveyed all the surrounding area, but there was no sign of anyone. Still the sensation caused her to tremble. Fear held her paralyzed for a moment as she realized just how far she was from the house. Slowly she rose to her feet and began to trace the footprints praying she would not get lost.

The trees seemed to close about her and she began to move faster and faster sensing without looking back that something or someone was behind her.

Now she broke into a run and for the first time looked back over her shoulder as she did.

A shrill scream escaped her as she ran into a tall solid

form that closed its arms about her. She was wild with fright and began automatically to fight.

"Sabrina!" It was Clay's voice. "What's the matter?"

She sobbed as she relaxed for a moment against him. He held her close feeling the pounding of her heart and the violent trembling.

"Summer told me you were in the woods," he said. "It isn't safe here unless you know what you're doing . . . what frightened you?"

"There's . . . there's someone out there. They were watching me, following me."

He gripped her shoulders and held her a little away from him.

"Did you see anyone?" he demanded.

She looked up into his eyes. The feeling burst within her that he expected her to see someone.

"No . . . but I felt . . ."

He chuckled. "The forest can be a very frightening place for a city child," he said. "Your imagination got the best of you."

Her violet eyes grew deeper with the combination of fear and anger as she looked up at him.

"I'm not a child! I don't get frightened of shadows!"

The smile faded from his lips as he looked down into her defiant eyes. Her hair fell about her in a tangled mass from her bout with the brush. Her cheeks were pink from exertion and anger. The wildness of her beauty matched the place in which they stood.

"No," he said softly, "you are not a child." He reached out and brushed his hand against her hair, then he touched the soft skin on her cheek and let his fingers caress for a moment. Again she was caught in the web of his intoxicating gaze as his blue eyes deepened. She was aware of a magnetic thing that drew her to him.

He watched the frantic beating of the pulse at her throat and knew he was awakening an emotion in her he was not prepared to handle. He did not want to recognize what he felt for this slim wisp of golden beauty. He refused determinedly to sink into that violet pool as he wanted to.

"But," he said allowing his voice to be firm and cold enough to startle her, "it is a childish thing to go off into the woods in a place you know nothing about. At least you could have been lost, at worst you could have been discovered by bears, snakes, or other deadly things. I'll take you back. Sabrina, don't wander away without me again."

She opened her mouth to tell him she had not just wandered carelessly away, then closed it immediately as she realized she would betray Summer's trust if she did.

"I won't," she said meekly.

"Good girl," he laughed. "Now come on. I'll take you home."

She walked toward the house and had gone several steps before she realized he was not with her. She turned to see him looking in the direction from which she had run. There was a dark thoughtful look on his face and again she felt the same sensation . . . he expected to see someone.

When he realized she had stopped, his attention came back to her. Quickly he walked in her direction and they both moved toward the house.

Questions tumbled in her mind. Were these people superstitious, did they believe ghosts walked about here? Who was Clay expecting to see? Questions about his secrets from Summer joined them. There was so much about this strong silent man she did not know.

Summer sat on the porch watching them walk toward her. There was a smile on her face for her father and this time it included Sabrina, for it took her only moments to understand that Sabrina had kept her promise and not said anything to Clay about where she had found Summer.

"I've brought a deer home, Summer," Clay said. "Suppose we show Sabrina how we tan the hide. Maybe, since it's so pretty, she could make a dress out of it."

"I'd like one like yours, Summer. I'd like to learn," Sabrina smiled at Summer.

Summer smiled back in her first real reaching for Sabrina's friendship. Sabrina was well aware that Clay's eyes were on her and that he seemed somewhat surprised.

"Run and ask Ellen if she would like a piece of venison to cook for supper," Clay said to Summer. "Then I'll take the rest to Swift Doe and her family."

Summer went through the house to the back to find Ellen.

"Who is Swift Doe?" Sabrina questioned.

"Friend of mine. She stays with Summer occasionally when I have to be away. Now you're here I won't have to have her come anymore."

She could see it was all the information that he intended to offer and that he had no intention that there would be a meeting anytime soon between her and Swift Doe.

She found she enjoyed her first lessons in tanning a hide. It was done Indian style. It was pegged to the ground and thoroughly and painstakingly scraped clean. Then a mixture of something she didn't know was spread over it and it was folded to absorb the mixture and to soften it.

She listened to Summer's ceaseless chatter and Clay's sometimes amused answers.

That afternoon Clay disappeared again. She surmised he had gone to see his mysterious friends. She and Summer began the first lessons in reading. Clay had surprisingly supplied her with pencils and paper.

They fell into some kind of regularity. Ellen seemed to be content and she and Summer were also becoming friends for Ellen, to Summer's wide-eyed wonder, supplied her with treats from a kitchen that had never been so prolific before.

Clay was often gone for a day or two at a time. Each time he took the time to again warn Sabrina to stay close to the cabin when he was gone.

Slowly, day after day, Sabrina and Summer began to become friends. They shared a secret and this was the strongest bond that drew them together. Sabrina could see after a while that Summer's young mind could not really understand why her mother and the Indian village were things of which Clay would not speak. She loved her father, yet she wanted to know her mother and longed for the comforts and feminine affection only a woman could give. Clay also could not see that Summer was mature beyond her years, and that her heart was full of questions only he could answer. They had been there several weeks, and days began to fall into a kind of order. Sabrina had forgotten the incident that had happened the first night she had been there and the strange night call that had seemed to upset Clay. Nothing like that had happened again.

Clay had not come home for supper and after a good meal and some lessons for Summer, Sabrina had tucked her into bed. It was a pleasure for Sabrina both for the fact that she was beginning to feel a deep affection for the child, and that she liked being in the room Summer shared with her father. It was large and very masculine. The furniture was immense and well made. More Indian hangings covered three walls. One wall, to Sabrina's pleasure, was lined with shelves that were filled with books. Again she was aware that there was much more to Clay Storm than they knew.

Seven

Pale beams of early morning sunlight found the cracks in the window shutters and cast Sabrina's room in soft light. She had been awake for some time. A dream she could not remember had wakened her and she could not sleep again.

She rose and gathered some clothes, then she donned her robe. While everyone else slept she decided to go to the small stream that ran near the cabin and take a bath.

She took some soap and towels from the kitchen then slipped out the back door. A warm morning breeze touched her skin and she listened as it joined the song of the birds for an early morning concert.

Walking across the clearing she found the stream. She walked its edge for a while until she found a wide place that was sheltered by trees.

There she deposited her clean clothes and slipped out of her robe and nightgown. She twisted her hair atop her head and caught it with a comb. Then she took the soap and stepped into the water. It felt cool to her body as she knelt and felt it swirl about her. She lathered herself with the soap then scooped up water with her hands and rinsed her body clean. She hummed lightly to herself as she leisurely continued to enjoy her bath.

Satisfied, she stood up and took the towel to pat herself

dry. Then she stood on the bank and slowly dressed. She loosened her hair and ran her fingers through it to rid it of some of the tangles, then she drew it over her shoulder and braided it in one long heavy braid.

She felt good as she bent to gather up her things. Then it was there again—the strange sensation that someone was near. She stood erect, and when she did she looked across the stream to the huge tree, by which stood the largest, handsomest man she had ever seen. His skin was deep bronze and his dark hair was braided on each side of his dark chiseled face.

His clothes were only fringed buckskin pants and moccasins. About his neck hung a necklace of strange silver figures. In his hand he carried a bow that stood taller than Sabrina. On his back hung a quiver of arrows held by a leather strap that crossed his broad chest.

White teeth glimmered in his bronze skin as he smiled at her, ignoring her wide-eyed fear and trembling amazement.

He stood, his broad shoulder braced against the tree and his dark eyes thoroughly examining her from head to foot. She had the sensation he might have been watching her long enough to know every inch of her. She was terrified—too terrified to move or even to breathe.

"You are very beautiful," he said, his voice a deep throbbing from his massive chest. "Storm has chosen his new woman well."

He must be a friend of Clay's, she thought, relief flooding her. "Who . . . who are you?"

"I am Hawk," he stated in a voice that was filled with pride and even a touch of arrogance. "What are you called?"

"Sabrina," she replied in a breathless voice, for it had just occurred to her that he stood between her and the house.

"Sabrina," he repeated. "It is as beautiful as you are."

Sabrina gathered her courage together. "Won't . . . won't

you come to the house with me? I'm sure Clay would be glad to have you."

He chuckled and his eyes appraised her with humor. "No, but I want you to carry a message for me."

"Yes, yes of course," again she was flooded with relief.

"Tell him that Hawk has been watching. Tell him that I remember my words from long ago and one day soon I will do what I have promised. Tell him that, he should remember my words. Someone he loved . . . someone to balance the debt."

"I will tell him," she replied.

He pushed away from the tree and walked to her side. She stood trembling, aware that there was no way she could escape him if he wanted to stop her.

"I have watched you since you came," he said. "Your hair is like light of the moon. It pleases me to look at it." He reached out and gripped the thick braid of her hair in a much gentler touch than she had thought his huge hand could accomplish. Suddenly she was no longer afraid, for she had seen the fleeting look of tenderness in those dark eyes.

"It was you," she whispered. "That strange call that night, the one who was there in the woods."

"I did not mean to frighten you. I only wanted to see your face."

"Why don't you come to the house yourself and tell Mr. Storm what you want to say. It is what a man of courage would do."

Again his mouth broadened in a wide smile and to her surprise his dark eyes twinkled in sudden amusement.

"You question my courage, Sabrina? he laughed. "It is a mark of your own. No one in my tribe or any outside of it would dare do so. Come, I will walk to the house with you."

He shortened his stride to match hers, and she could feel

the overpowering sense of controlled strength as he walked beside her. As they started to walk across the clearing toward the house Sabrina was surprised when Clay walked out on the porch and watched them come. She was also shocked at the fact that he held his rifle in his hands again . . . and it was pointed at the Indian's broad chest.

Both Sabrina and Hawk stopped at the foot of the steps. She was about to speak when Clay spoke first. His voice seemed stiff and somewhat angry, which was a surprise for he had never spoken to any of them so since they had been there. She was sure the man who stood at her side was the reason, yet he had a smile on his face and seemed quite relaxed.

"Sabrina . . . come here," Clay said. She obediently walked up to stand beside him. He reached out and took her arm pulling her a little behind him, but his eyes remained on Hawk.

"Hawk . . . it's been a long time. I thought maybe," he smiled, "you had forgotten."

If anything, Hawk's smile grew broader. "No, I have not forgotten."

"Don't misunderstand this situation, Hawk. Sabrina and her mother are here to care for Summer and the house."

Hawk switched to his own language, knowing Sabrina did not understand. "Is she your woman?"

"No, she is not my woman. Her coming here was not my choice. Her mother brought her without my knowledge," Clay answered in the same rapid language. Sabrina watched the exchange, and felt somehow they were talking of her. Hawk's eyes turned again to her and even though he still smiled she felt his intense gaze bore into her. She was bathed in a deep black pool that held her immobile . . . and sent a shiver down her spine. Fear of something unknown touched her and she reached blindly for the only security she knew.

Clay felt her hand grip at his arm, at the same time he saw the satisfied look in Hawk's eyes. Clay waited quietly, watching Hawk and, to his surprise, enjoyed Sabrina's touch and the pressure of her slim body against his.

"She looks at you with the eyes of a woman," Hawk said in the rapid tongue.

"She is a child," Clay replied and watched Hawk's eyes narrow. "She has nothing to do with us, Hawk."

"You speak of her as a child," he smiled, "but you know she is a woman. I watched her bathe in the stream . . . she is a woman, Clay."

"What do you want Hawk?" Clay responded, ignoring Hawk's words and the anger it built in him that Hawk had watched her.

"I have come to see the child," Hawk replied quietly. "I have only come to see and talk. I will bring no weapon."

"And if I refuse?"

"Why should you refuse? We were friends once. We share much. I only want to see her."

For a moment Clay wondered if old enmities could be forgotten, then he pushed the thought aside. Hawk was not a man who forgot what he said in the past. Much as he hoped it was true he felt there was another motive Hawk was there. He just wasn't sure where that motive was directed. He wanted desperately to believe, but he was too wary. He also didn't want Sabrina to be caught up in his problem, a problem about which she knew nothing.

He had to take the chance that Hawk was speaking his true thought. "Put aside your weapons, Hawk, and come in."

Hawk set his bow so it would lean against the edge of the porch, then he walked up and stood beside them. They were the same size, Hawk and Clay and Sabrina standing between them felt a current, a massive sense of conflicting power.

"Six years is a long time, Hawk," Clay said. "I had thought I would hear from you sooner."

Hawk grinned amiably, but Sabrina could see no light of laughter in the deep black eyes. "I am a patient man, Clay. Did you think I would come with weapons?"

"I wasn't too sure. But I knew you would come. I have been waiting for this visit a long time."

Sabrina could not understand this attitude of friendly enemies. She was confused by the strange feeling of tension that lingered between the two.

Clay's hand pressing gently against her waist drew her attention from Hawk. She preceded them into the house, noticing Clay kept himself between her and any contact with the Indian. Neither Ellen or Summer were awake yet, and Sabrina was not quite sure of what to do. She looked questioningly toward Clay for guidance.

"Go and waken Summer, Sabrina. Don't alarm her, just bring her out."

She nodded and left the room. Clay and Hawk stood for a few minutes in silence.

"What have you told the child of her mother's people . . . of me?" Hawk said gently."

"Nothing."

"Don't you think she has a right to know?"

"She is too young to understand."

"Did you ever intend for her to know?"

"Someday."

"Someday, when it is too late to learn any of our ways."

"When are you going to understand, Hawk? Summer is mine. I will teach her what I want her to know."

There was a look verging on sorrow in Hawk's eyes. "Don't cheat her Clay. Let her be all . . ."

Sabrina returned with a sleepy-eyed Summer whose sleepiness seemed to disappear when she saw the huge Indian who stood silently watching her. Then he moved a step or so toward her and smiled. "Hello, Summer."

"Hello," the child said shyly. Intelligence that glowed in her eyes told him she had recognized the subtle similarity between Hawk and herself. Her eyes brightened, then turned questioningly toward her father.

"Hawk is an old friend of mine, Summer. He has just come back from a long journey and wanted to meet you."

Hawk reached for the strange silver necklace about his neck. "I have brought a gift for you," he said, but before he could remove the necklace, Clay's words stopped him.

"No!"

All eyes turned to Clay, whose gaze held Hawk's. "No Hawk. Something less . . . important. I wouldn't want her to have something I know means so much to you."

For a minute Hawk's eyes darkened with what Sabrina thought was intense fury, then he smiled the same joyless smile of before and dropped his hands from the necklace. Then he removed a silver band from his wrist. He knelt and beckoned Summer to come to him. Without hesitation or fear she did. He placed the silver band about her upper arm and with a firm grip he closed it about her snugly. He smiled warmly at the child and she responded almost eagerly.

"Why do they call you Hawk?"

Hawk laughed softly. "One day soon I shall have to tell you the story of my name."

"You're not staying for a while, Hawk?" Clay asked, a puzzled look on his face. The look changed to another, one that pleased Hawk immensely, as Hawk smiled at Sabrina who returned it openly and warmly. It was a possessive look of jealousy Clay was unaware of.

"No, but I shall return. If," he again gave Clay the dark unfathomable look Sabrina could not read, "you do not mind. I am sure there are many things Sabrina and Summer must be interested in knowing."

"You are free to come to this house as often as you please, Hawk, and I'm sure we can tell them a multitude of stories. But," his gaze held Hawk's, "neither Sabrina nor Summer will go to the village or meet and talk with you alone."

Sabrina's resistance could be felt by everyone. Ellen tried to stop her from anger but failed.

"I don't see why I cannot do as I choose," she snapped. "I shall do so if it pleases me!"

Ellen closed her eyes and mentally groaned as Sabrina again forgot that she was no longer lady of the manor, but an indentured servant . . . for two years, bound to the man she now glared at in anger.

Clay's eyes clouded with fury. He reached out and took hold of Sabrina's arm in a none too gentle hold. He gave her a rough shake.

"You forget," he snarled, "just what and where you are. Yes! I can tell you where you will and will not go. For the next two years you belong to me! Don't forget it again."

Realization of her fragile position warred with the intense fury that made her want to strike out at him. Their eyes met and held. She could feel the force of his anger, and became aware of Ellen's frightened gaze. She knew Clay had the power to destroy her, and his anger at the moment made her believe that if forced, he just might. Determinedly she gathered her emotions under control. Frustrated tears touched her eyes, but she bowed her head and remained silent until Clay released his grip a little and again turned to Hawk whose satisfied gaze held his.

"Don't push me, Hawk," Clay said softly. "I can care for what belongs to me. Don't forget that. If you want to come as friend, then come. But don't try to touch what belongs to me."

More anger smothered Sabrina at Clay's reference to her as something that belonged to him. At that moment she could have struck his cold arrogant face.

"I know what you are capable of, Clay," Hawk answered, "and I agree. No man should take what belongs to another. I would like to return . . . to bring more . . . acceptable gifts. I should like to talk to Summer and your golden haired slave."

At this Sabrina gave a startled jerk, but again Clay's eyes, and the strong grip he still held on her arm kept her silent.

She seethed in anger, but she held herself immobile, promising herself that she would leave this house and this arrogant man as soon as her indenture agreement would let her. She wondered why she had ever felt such gentle feelings for him and promised herself not to be fooled by his kindness again, for she could see now it could quickly turn to cruelty.

Hawk rested his hand on Summer's head and smiled down on her. "I shall come again and visit, little one, and I shall bring you gifts from your . . . my people. I will tell you stories so you will remember."

Summer nodded, and only Sabrina knew of the tense trembling of Clay's body as he stood so close to her. She wondered why this strange visitor had the power to disturb Clay so.

Hawk again held Clay's eyes for a breathless moment, then he walked to the door and in a few minutes he was gone.

Silence roared about them as Clay released Sabrina's arm. Without a word or a look in his direction she ran to her room and closed the door between them.

Ellen watched Clay's unguarded face as he gazed after Sabrina's retreating figure. She smiled to herself, for she became aware of deep intense hunger in the man for the understanding of the slim girl who ran from him. It was a need she knew could develop into a far greater and deeper emotion.

He turned to her, his face closed against her. "You had best explain her duties a little more carefully, Ellen. I don't expect her to interfere in my private affairs again, or to go against my wishes while she lives in this house. Her responsibility is Summer's education. Nothing more, nothing less."

"Yes, sir, I'm sorry. Sabrina is young. I'll explain to her. She won't be making the same mistake again."

"See that she doesn't," he answered. He knelt before Summer.

"I have to go out for a few hours, Summer. I'll be back soon. Be a good girl."

"Yes, Papa," she whispered, but Clay was hurt by the unanswered questions in her eyes and the vague look of doubt that lingered there.

He kissed her gently, rose and took his rifle from the wall. He gave them one last look, then left the cabin.

Ellen stood for a moment in thoughtful silence. Then she went to Summer.

"Go in to Sabrina and tell her you are there for your lessons. Everything will be all right Summer, don't worry. Soon Sabrina will be smiling and your Papa will be back."

Summer nodded and Ellen watched her go. Again she was pleased at all she had seen. Clay Storm was lonely. He was lonely and carried a pain within. She had seen it in his eyes. She had also seen that Sabrina had the key to it. All they had to do was find each other, and she intended to do all she could to see that they did . . . as soon as she possibly could.

Eight

Sabrina sat on the edge of her bed letting the helpless anger possess her. At that moment she hated Clay Storm. A slave! Did they really think of her so? Well she was a slave to no one. He had bought her ability to work, but he had not bought her life or her soul and she intended to let him know she would never tolerate being thought of as a slave.

She let her mind drift back to Waverly Hall and her Uncle Eustice. She had not fully realized the beauty and love she had shared until this moment. Fresh tears touched her eyes and she allowed pity to overwhelm her.

After a few minutes her anger overcame her self pity. She sat up and brushed the tears from her eyes. Two years was not forever. She would do what she must do and in two years she would be free of him and able to follow her own path in life. She and Ellen could leave this wilderness and go back to the city. They would find employment in a home that did not have such dark secrets and confusion.

She thought of Summer and realized she would miss the child when she had to go. Summer would be all she would miss. They had developed an affectionate relationship in the short time Sabrina had been there.

At that moment her door opened and a small brown face appeared around it. Summer's face was so serious and her eyes so wide and worried that Sabrina had to smile. She beckoned the child in.

With a quick smile the child crossed the room and bounced on the bed beside Sabrina.

"Sabrina?"

"What?"

"You . . . you won't go away, will you?"

Sabrina heard the gentle pleading in a voice lonely for a mother's love, and again her anger at Clay Storm surged. Why did he hold this child away from memories? All children needed to know their roots. Summer was adrift with only Clay who was too often absent and too preoccupied with some spectral threat Sabrina could feel but not name. Determinedly she promised herself that the first opportunity she had to get Clay alone she was going to tell him exactly how she felt.

"No Summer, I won't be going away for a long time."

"You're not mad at Papa are you?"

"I'm afraid I am, a little," Sabrina laughed. "But I've no choice but to get over it. Summer, the other morning you told me that you went to the village of the Indians before. Have you seen this man called Hawk before?"

A negative shake of the head.

"Has anyone ever told you of him before?"

Another shake of the head.

"I wonder . . ." she thought of the tone of almost fear in Clay's voice when the Indian had offered Summer the necklace. She suddenly felt again the sense of conflicting force between Hawk and Clay, and knew it was centered on Summer . . . but how? . . . and why?

"Wonder what?" Summer questioned.

She knew there was no way to explain to Summer what she did not understand herself.

"I wonder," she laughed, "if Ellen has started breakfast

yet. I'm starved. How about you?"

"I'm hungry too."

"Good! Let's go see. Maybe we can help. Then, after we help Ellen clean the kitchen you and I can begin some lessons. Your Papa wants you to begin to learn to read and write. I guess today is the best time to start."

Summer wrinkled her nose in distaste, and both of them laughed. Together they went to the kitchen. Sabrina was not only pleased to find breakfast nearly finished, but more pleased to find Clay was not there to share it with them.

The three of them ate while Summer chattered happily on.

After the meal, Summer seemed to be thrilled with the idea of helping Sabrina and Ellen clean the house.

When this was accomplished a rapid snack was eaten quickly for lunch. Then despite Summer's reluctance, Sabrina began to open a new world to her. The world of books.

By bedtime Sabrina had Summer thoroughly captured by the wonders she could bring to life from the strange black lines on the pages of a book.

Sabrina read Summer a story then tucked the blankets firmly about her as she drifted off to sleep.

She returned to the main room to find an exhausted Ellen. "Go to bed Ellen, you're so tired. You've done a great deal of work today."

"Yes, I am tired. What are you going to do? You don't plan on waiting for Clay to come home, do you? I don't want you to do anything foolish, Sabrina. We have enough problems behind us already."

"Don't worry, Ellen, after finding his opinion of my position here, I've nothing to say to Clay Storm. At least nothing a lady would say. I just want to get a little air and I'll go on to bed."

"You're going outside?" Ellen said in alarm.

"Only on the porch, Ellen," Sabrina laughed.

"With all those Indians about!"

"Ellen, the only Indian we met seemed to be quite friendly and I doubt if he's on the porch waiting to attack me. Just a little air, Ellen, and I'll go straight to bed. I promise," she said placatingly.

"All right," Ellen muttered, "but you had better be careful."

"I will Ellen, good night."

"Good night," Ellen replied. She went to her room and closed the door.

Sabrina rose and blew out the lamp letting the glow of pale moonlight light her way to the door.

She closed the door behind her and stood on the porch enjoying the cool breeze that brought the scent of pine and blossoming flowers. Night creatures created a melody of sound and she enjoyed the serenity. The moon was huge and hung in a black star studded sky. Everything about was lit with a touch of its glow.

How peaceful . . . how beautiful, she thought, I could be happy to spend the rest of my life here. A small garden Summer and . . . she stopped the thought that blossomed to life. Clay, so tall, so handsome . . . so very mysterious.

She walked down the three steps and started across the clearing to the tall trees that bordered it. It was only a few steps to the darker shadows of the trees, and she had no idea of entering them. She was about to turn around and retrace her steps when a rustle of movement froze her in her tracks. She was just prepared to run when a deep masculine voice spoke from the darkness.

"What the hell are you doing out here alone at this time of night?"

"Clay!" she gasped with relief as he stepped from the shadows of the trees and walked to her side.

He towered over her but her relief at the sense of security his presence brought overcame any fear she might have felt.

"Sabrina, what are you doing out here alone?"

"I needed some air," she retorted, "even a slave has a right to breath doesn't she!"

She could sense his laughter before she heard the rumbling sound of it and saw the flash of his white smile.

"Sabrina, I must tell you I am truly sorry for all that happened this morning, but especially what I said to you. I didn't mean to say what I did or to do what I did. I regret it very much. Sometimes Hawk has a way of irritating me beyond reason. If I hurt you, I'm sorry. The last thing in the world I intended to do was to hurt you."

The moonlight was behind him so she could not read his face, but he read her face with unerring accuracy. Her eyes widened and her face softened. She looked up into his eyes in completely unprotected vulnerability. He knew . . . but this time he did not have the power to resist . . . or the desire to.

He reached out and touched her face lightly then traced the line of her jaw to her ear and let his hand slide into her hair. She remained motionless, suddenly vibrantly aware of every sense she possessed. They all centered on Clay. The clean masculine smell of him, like the pines that surrounded them. The sense of strength and power that held her spellbound.

Slowly, very slowly he drew her toward him until their bodies lightly touched. She was overwhelmed with the need to touch him. She reached up and pressed her hands against his broad chest feeling the slow steady beat of his heart. Now he raised his other hand and held her face between them. She felt the warmth of his body and closed her eyes as he tipped up her face and bent his head to touch his mouth to hers.

His mouth was hard and firm against hers, denying any

resistance she might have summoned. But there was none. Sabrina, completely unprepared for the sensual attack was lost in the magic that seemed to roll through her like waves of the ocean.

The hands that had pressed against his chest crept upward to circle his neck and her body trembled as he drew her tight within the circle of his arms.

Insistent pressure parted her lips and his tongue tasted the sweetness expertly drawing a low sound from deep within her. A sound of blossoming desire and need that swept everything else from her mind but Clay.

The kiss grew deeper, more and more demanding until she trembled in complete surrender.

Clay had meant only to kiss her lightly, a chaste kiss of gratitude for her understanding and care of Summer and in apology for his rough treatment. But the sweet giving of her parted lips beneath his swept every other thought away.

He held her bound against him with iron hard arms nearly crushing the breath from her. But she didn't care for she had never felt such an emotion before and she did not want it to cease.

Slowly and very reluctantly he lifted his head and looked into her eyes. Passion he saw clearly and his heart leapt with desire, but innocene he saw also and was surprised at his own reluctance to shatter that look. She was sweet and unaware of the overpowering result of the emotion she felt. She responded to him with open trust and honestly, and he knew he could not seduce her without care or thought for her feelings. That he wanted her with a fire that nearly overcame him was another thing that took him by surprise. There had been an occasional woman since Singing Bells that were used only to relieve the tension, but he had not felt this urgent need until now. He found, when he looked at his feelings honesty, that he wanted more than just a midnight mating on the ground. He did not want to face this need, not now, and not at a time when he could be putting her in a dangerous position. He had to hold it at bay, for deep inside he recognized it for what it was, and he was not prepared to handle it now. The emotion was too powerful and too consuming . . . too sweet and precious to be used lightly. And he found he could not face the thought of thurting her.

It took more effort on his part to step back from her than she would ever know. He smiled to make her assured he was not pushing her carelessly away. Again he reached out and caressed her hair.

"You are a sweet and very beautiful woman, Sabrina," he said gently. "It is a very dangerous thing for you to be out here now. You would be wise to go in and go to bed."

"Dangerous? I'm not frightened with you here."

He chuckled softly. "I'm not made of iron, Sabrina. I'm probably your greatest danger at this moment."

"Stop treating me like a little girl, Clay, or like a fool. I'm not afraid to feel . . . to care . . . are you?"

"Everything isn't quite as . . . simple as you seem to want it to be."

She stepped closer to him and laid her hand against his chest. He felt the trembling warmth of it and allowed himself the small pleasure of enjoying her touch.

"Why can't things just be simple in life? Why can't people just be open and honest with one another? Why do they hold dark secrets that make it necessary to push everyone and everything aside. Why Clay? Why is it so wrong to reach out to someone? No, Clay, I am not a child, I am a woman . . . and I'm not frightened of life anymore."

He looked down into her eyes and realized she was right, yet he could not tell her of 'dark secrets' she referred to. He was surprised at her perception and a little amused at her implications that he might be the one who was afraid.

"Maybe . . . maybe I was wrong in what I said . . . maybe you're not quite the child I thought. Maybe . . ." His words were stopped by the touch of her fingers against his lips. They did not speak for several moments, then gently he drew her back into his arms. Their lips met in a deep and consuming kiss that rocked the world in which they stood. Their bodies molded to each other as if they tried to blend into one.

When their lips parted he held her close to him in silence while he fought to control the urge to carry her to his bed and take possession of the sweet release her love offered. After he had regained some of his equilibrium he held her a little away from him, his hands on both her shoulders. Their eyes met and for the first time she read his clearly.

"Sabrina . . ."

"Don't," she sobbed in a breathless whisper, "Don't push me aside."

"Try to understand, Sabrina. If you knew . . . I can't love you! I can't. It would mean . . ."

"What Clay, what?"

"Go back in the house, go to bed Sabrina and forget this ever happened."

"Forget," she repeated in a hurt voice. Slowly she backed from him several steps. He hated the look of pain in her eyes. He wanted to reach out, to hold her again, to be able to tell someone of the deep emotions he carried. But he couldn't . . . he wouldn't. He would never let Sabrina pay the price for the painful thing that existed in his past. Things that could reach out to her . . . maybe destroy her.

Tears streaked her face, tears of a pain she could not understand.

"I can't forget," she whispered, "I love you."

She turned from him and ran back to the house. He remained where he was until he heard the door close.

"I love you," he heard the softly whispered words again and again. He gripped himself firmly to keep from following her, from going to her with the truth of the new and beautiful love that filled him. Slowly he gained mastery of himself, then he walked to the cabin. No one else was awake. He looked at Sabrina's closed door aware that he could open it, take her in his arms and past or no past make love to her until he satisfied the burning hungry need within him. He turned away before the temptation outweighed his ability to resist.

He went quietly into the room he shared with Summer. She lay on her small bed and slept serenely. He smiled down at her aware of how safe and secure she felt.

"I'll keep you both safe Summer, and because I love you but she'll never know. I'll never let my love for both of you cause you pain."

He bent and kissed the child, then he went to his own bed to face a dreamfilled sleep that left him weary and miserable the next morning.

Sabrina lay awake a long time. She heard Clay come into the house. Her eyes closed and she prayed silently. "Come to me Clay . . . tell me you love me . . . please . . ." But she heard his steps continue to his room. She rolled onto her side and cried silent tears until she slept.

Sabrina was surprised to find Clay at the breakfast table the next morning. It was not often that he was. She felt suddenly shy and a little embarrassed at the way he must have felt she had thrown herself at him last night. She knew with his charm and overabundant good looks he could have chosen almost any girl he wanted. Why should he even look at her?

He smiled at her as if nothing had happened the night before and now her embarrassment turned again to anger. It was an emotion he fully intended to use to keep himself from telling her just how beautiful she was and how much he wanted her.

"Good morning Sabrina. Did you sleep well?"

Was he taunting her, she thought angrily?

"Yes, very well thank you," she replied coldly.

It took Ellen less than a second to see from Sabrina's flushed face and downcast eyes and Clay's intense hungry look, to know that they had somehow reached out and touched each other, and the touch had been traumatic for both of hem.

They ate a rather reserved breakfast with Summer doing much of the chattering and Ellen most of the answering. There was a vibrant current between Clay and Sabrina broken only when he rose, said something about work he had to do and left.

Sabrina took Summer to the shade of the nearby trees and continued her lessons, amazed at the child's quick grasp of all she was offered. The alphabet was quickly memorized and she began on simple words. They were laughing together, their heads bent toward each other when a shadow fell over them. They looked up, laughter still on their faces, at the tall man who stood over them.

"Hawk," Sabrina smiled, "how nice to see you again."

Hawk had stood in the shadows for some time watching the two. How much they complemented each other. Summer's dark skin and black hair was a perfect foil for Sabrina's pale good beauty. He thought of how pleasurable it would be to have Sabrina in his lodge. He also thought of the effect it would have on Clay. He smiled to himself in remembrance of the poignant scene he had witnessed the night before in the shade of the trees.

He had watched and heard Sabrina reach out to Clay, and he alone knew why Clay had not taken the rare and beautiful gift she had so openly and honestly offered him.

"I have returned as I said I would. Clay is not here?" he questioned. Neither of them suspected he already knew exactly where Clay was.

"No, he's not," Sabrina answered. Hawk's astute gaze caught the flushed cheeks and the eyes that fled from him at the mention of Clay's name. So, he thought, he lives in her heart. Good! It will be felt more deeply when she turns from him.

He squatted on his haunches beside them and smiled, lifting the books from Sabrina's lap. He flipped through the pages. "It is a good book for a beginner," he smiled at Summer.

Sabrina looked at him in surprise. "You know how to read?" she said, then her cheeks pinkened in embarrassment as he chuckled warmly.

"Yes, I know how to read. I must thank Clay for that. He taught me long ago before . . ." he stopped abruptly, and his eyes swung back to Summer. "You have inherited wisdom, Summer, you will not find the learning difficult, especially with the teacher you are so lucky to have."

Both Sabrina and Summer warmed to his charm, and they chatted amiably for a few minutes. Then Hawk spoke to Summer.

"I have brought a gift for you, little one. It is in the kitchen with Sabrina's mother."

Summer leapt to her feet. "A gift? May I go see?" she said to Sabrina.

"Of course," Sabrina laughed. She and Hawk watched with amused smiles as the child scampered toward the house. Sabrina turned to watch Hawk for the few seconds that his eyes were still on Summer.

He was handsome in a dark, strong chiseled way. His features symmetrical and almost beautiful. His hair, thick and black, hung in two braids past his shoulders. His eyes were black as ebony beneath dark winged brows.

He was extremely large, Sabrina would guess the same as Clay's six foot two and at least ten pounds heavier. Where Clay was lean and strongly muscled with sinew, Hawk was massive, yet there was not an ounce of fat on him and he appeared to be in complete command.

Suddenly he turned toward her and their eyes met and held. She had the strange sensation the inner depths of her soul were being read like a book. She sensed a reaching of his thoughts to hers, and wondered what it was he searched for. She had to search for a way to break his hold.

"You . . . you said Summer had inherited wisdom."

"Yes, I did."

"You knew her mother?"

"Yes," he said, his eyes left hers and she breathed a silent sigh of relief. Then she realized he had no intention of elaborating on his answer. It touched her curiosity.

"Was . . . was she very beautiful?"

Again his eyes returned to her. He knew what stirred her thoughts. He smiled. "Singing Bells was beautiful . . . beautiful in a way much different than you."

"What happened to her, Hawk?"

Again he was silent for such a long time that Sabrina did not think he meant to answer at all. Then he spoke quietly, his gaze held by a far away memory.

"I will not speak of Singing Bells. She was Clay's woman. If he wants you to know he will tell you. If he doesn't then it is a thing he wishes to keep to himself."

He turned to her with another broad smile. "I came to bring gifts, not only for Summer but for you and your mother."

"For me?"

"Yes, will you come now and see?"

They walked along together, Sabrina deep in her thoughts

and Hawk satisfied that he had done as he had planned to do when he came. To stir Sabrina's curiosity, to push her into asking questions. Questions that Clay would know the source of. He knew Clay's anger would be roused. He also knew there was nothing Clay could do about it. He wondered if Clay would answer her questions with honesty and if he did what thoughts would be in Sabrina's mind.

Hawk smiled to himself. He was a very patient man who knew exactly what he wanted. He had waited a long time to find the right occasion. Clay's attempt to hide his attraction to Sabrina was it.

It had taken five years. Five years in which Hawk had watched and waited. Now, for the first time Hawk had found what could be a vulnerable spot in Clay's armor . . . Sabrina.

When they arrived in the kitchen both Ellen and Summer were exclaiming over the gifts Hawk had brought.

Sabrina watched Ellen and Summer while each thing was shown to her. Warm moccasins with the fur inside to keep Summer's feet warm when the snow fell, and a fine coat of beautiful fur to match. He had brought a fur blanket for Ellen's bed and a haunch of venison for supper.

When they were finished admiring Ellen's and Summer's gifts, Hawk handed a package wrapped in a fur skin to Sabrina. She opened it and gasped in surprise. Inside was a buckskin dress of pure white. It was trimmed along the arms and across the bodice with small glittering beads and tiny blue feathers. Sabrina held it up to her and both Summer and Ellen exclaimed over its rare beauty.

"Oh, Hawk," Sabrina said softly. For a moment he was touched with guilt by the sight of pleasure in her eyes. He soon brought himself under control.

"It's so very beautiful."

"It is only a dress," he replied. "It is the woman who wears it who makes it beautiful."

"Thank you, Hawk. I appreciate it very much. Will you stay and eat with us tonight. I'm sure Clay will be glad to see you again."

"No . . . I must return home. I have a short journey to take but I shall return in a few days. I look forward to learning the effect my gifts have. Maybe," he smiled, "I shall succeed in making you and your mother one of our tribe."

"I am so curious about your people Hawk. Is your village a great distance?"

"I no longer belong only to the village that is a day's ride from here. I have lived . . . somewhere else for some time. But I should like you to meet my people. Maybe . . . If you can convince Clay to let you go he will let you visit."

"I shall ask him one day soon."

"Yes . . . ask him. I would be interested to hear if he gives his permission or not."

It was a strange reply and at first Sabrina was going to question him about it, then she changed her mind. She would ask Clay, she thought he could explain better.

Hawk left and Sabrina put the dress in her room. She had decided to wait until Ellen and Summer were in bed to don the dress. She could not deny the excitement within her. She wanted to see the admiring look on Clay's eyes, she wanted to see him smile. Maybe he would reach out to her again when he knew she wanted so desperately to be part of his world.

The night he returned would be a night she would remember for a long time for it would be the beginning of a whole new world for her . . . for Clay . . . and for all who surrounded them.

Nine

Clay whistled a soft bird call, waited a few minutes and repeated it. Then he stood in silence and waited. After a short while the call was returned. Again he repeated it and waited.

He stood beneath the branches of a huge tree. From where he was he could count the Indian lodges before him. He watched one in particular and felt the silent beat of renewed pain within. He stood quietly controlling the desire to walk to it, enter, and speak again to the old man he knew sat within. But he knew too much hurt had existed, too many things had been said and done. Too much time had gone by to be able to return to the past. It had been five years since he had walked through the village in friendship.

A figure slipped from a nearby lodge and walked toward him. She was dark and slim, and several years younger than he. She walked with a free and easy stride and smiled at him when she reached his side.

"Hello Clay," she said in a gentle musical voice. "It has been long since you visited us. Is Summer well?"

"Yes, she is well. You don't question about her being left alone? I take it Hawk has already spoken to you about the women in my home?"

"Yes, he has told us."

"When did Hawk return?"

"It has been only days since Hawk returned from the land past the mountain. He has told us of the place he traveled. He says the grass is high and the hunting is good. One day soon he will convince my father that it is best to move the village beyond the mountains where no white men live."

Clay gazed at her for a few minutes, then he reached out and took her hand in his.

"Come, Swift Doe walk with me. We must talk."

She hesitated for a moment as if she knew there were things he was going to say to her that she didn't want to hear. Then she sighed and moved to his side and they walked together beneath the trees. They found a grassy spot beneath a tree and sat.

"Why Swift Doe?" Clay said gently when they had sat in silence for some time. "Why did he come back now?"

It was almost as if he had spoken to himself, and she gazed at him, her eyes filled with quiet sorrow.

"Did you believe he would not?"

"I had hoped," Clay shrugged, "Maybe I had hoped for too much. Why can he not put the past behind him? Why does he continue to believe what is wrong?"

Her eyes turned away from him and a strange hurt quality touched her voice.

"He is not alone in his wrong beliefs," she said quietly.

"You think I am wrong too?" he asked.

"In such a thing as this there is not one who is wrong and one who is right. You are both stubborn, neither will give an inch."

"He wants what is mine!" Clay exclaimed angrily. Swift Doe's head turned toward him, her eyes darkened with what was for her gentle nature extreme anger.

"Why can you not share, Clay Storm? Why must you deny Summer to us . . . to him."

Clay rose to his feet and looked down at her.

"He made his choices long ago!"

"You mean he would not accept yours!"

Clay turned his back to her and breathed deeply to keep control of anger.

"I only came to tell you that you will not have to be staying with Summer anymore when I am gone. Sabrina and her mother will be there for the next two years."

"Are you telling me I cannot see Summer anymore?" she asked softly.

He turned to look at her again. "I want you to understand Swift Doe. Summer is old enough to understand. I am having Sabrina teach her to read and write among other things. When she is old enough I shall send her to school."

Now Swift Doe rose to her feet and walked to Clay. She stood before him and placed her hand on his chest. To his surprise there were tears in her eyes.

"Clay, I will do as you say. I shall miss Summer more than you know but she is your child and I must respect your wishes. But I will say one thing to you. It will not work, this cutting Summer away from her past. This blind stubborn thing between you and Hawk might one day cost you your child's love. Listen to me only this once. You are both wrong. Don't let it destroy Summer. She can only be what the gods have meant her to be and neither you or Hawk can change that. I hope you or Hawk reach the wisdom one day that will set her free."

She turned and walked away, and he stood and watched her go. Then he turned and walked back through the woods to where he had his horse tied. He kept trying to erase the words from his mind as he mounted and rode toward home.

Sabrina felt, by midnight, Clay had no intention of coming home. The embers of the fire glowed red and she sat before them creating fantasies in her mind. The dress fit her as though it had been made for her. It made her wonder at just how closely Hawk had studied her.

She had brushed her hair loose, but the warmth of the fire made the heaviness of it uncomfortable. She drew it over her shoulder and braided it in a long braid.

As the fire began to fade more and more her eyes became heavy. She knew she should go to bed, but felt too uncomfortable at the moment. After a while her heavy lids closed and she drifted off to sleep.

Clay stabled his horse and moved on silent feet to the door of the house. Moving without noise was habitual with him. He had been thinking of Sabrina when he opened the door. The last thing he expected to see was her slim form curled in his chair asleep. What surprised him even more as he moved toward her was what she was wearing.

He walked to her side and crouched down before her. He studied her sleeping face. To him she seemed so fragile and amazingly sweet. He reached out and gently touched her cheek. Her face turned toward his hand as if seeking the feel of it. She murmured his name and sighed in her sleep. The fading light of the fire touched her face gently making her look vulnerable. It created an emotion within him he did not want but was helpless to control.

At that moment her eyes opened and he found himself immersed in a warm violet pool from which he had no desire to escape. "Clay," she whispered softly. He saw the shy inviting smile and the warmth of unselfish love as she looked up at him.

Sabrina gazed up into Clay's intent blue eyes, aware that she wanted to hold this moment forever. She wanted again to feel his arms about her and the touch of his lips on hers. She could have wept with the intense need that inflamed and consumed her.

Clay took her hand and rose to his feet drawing her with him. He was aware of everything about her.

He put his arms about her waist and drew her against him. Their bodies touched and the flame of mutual need leapt between them. He bent his head to touch the sweet parted lips that lifted to meet his.

He took her mouth lightly, savoring the willing seeking of hers, tasting, touching, blending until both were lost in the magic of it. His lips traced a flaming path from her mouth to touch her cheeks, her eyes then roamed in passionae discovery down her slender throat to the pulse that beat wildly. He lifted her against him, holding her crushed against him while he pressed kisses between the valley of her breasts.

She clung to him, her eyes closed, eager to feel the branding of his warm lips against her skin. Again his lips sought hers, this time in a demanding passion that sent molten flame coursing through her body.

His arm about her waist felt like an iron band. Her feet barely touched the floor. He held her with one arm and slid his other hand down the curve of her hip to hold her more firmly against him. Her arms about his neck, she clung to him unaware of anything but his seeking mouth that possessed hers completely and the need to press herself closer and closer to the iron hard body that molded against hers.

His lips brushed her ear nibbling gently on a sensitive lobe, and he whispered her name softly as he rocked her against him. "Sabrina . . . so sweet," he murmured as reluctantly he released her from his crushing hold. He kept her within the circle of his arm and smiled down into her eyes. His hand brushed wayward strands of hair from her face, then again brushed the softness of her cheek.

"I didn't mean to waken you," he said gently, "you looked so sweet, so childlike. I had to touch. I must admit," he chuckled, "you do not feel much like a child now." He tightened his arm about her and felt the warm welcome feel of her slim curves press against him.

"Have you fallen asleep here by accident, or can I hope you've been waiting for me?"

"I've been waiting for you. I . . . I thought you weren't coming home tonight. Oh Clay, I'm so glad you did."

"You're so damn unprotected, Sabrina," he said in an amused voice. "Don't you know you can get hurt like that?"

"I don't care, I only know how I feel. Why should I lie to myself or to you?"

"And how do you feel my sweet?" he asked softly.

"I love you, Clay, I guess I have from the moment I saw you on the dock. I cannot deny it to myself. I can't help it and I don't want to. I love you. You can't tell me anything you like but I shall not stop loving . . . whether you do or not."

Their eyes held for several silent moments, then he again bent his head to brush her lips with his. Softly like butterfly wings he kissed her again and again until she murmured a soft protest. Only then did he again take her mouth in a deep demanding kiss.

Breathlessly she clung to him while he destroyed any restraints either of them might have had. He kissed her hungrily and she responded, her hands caressing the hard muscle of his back and shoulders. A flame leaped between them, pure white and hot, a heat that could not be extinguished again.

His lips began to torment her, wandering where they would until she could have screamed with the desire that boiled within her.

Sabrina was oblivious of her surroundings now. Nothing existed in her whirling world but the hands that gently caressed her and the mouth that had ravaged her willing one.

Effortlessly he lifted her in his arms and moved toward her bedroom, not for a moment letting his lips waste the time. They sought the slender throat and the soft skin where the rounded curve of her breasts rose above the dress.

In her dark bedroom he stood her on the floor for a moment and moved to lock the door and light the lamp.

"Clay," she said shyly as he returned to her.

"Shhh love," he whispered as he brushed a light kiss across her cheek. Her eyes held his as with slow gentle fingers he began to unbraid her hair. When it hung loose and free he moved to the dress and began to untie the laces that held it. In a few minutes it lay at her feet. She dipped her head shyly, frightened now to meet his gaze. His finger lifted her chin gently and she gazed up into a gentle reflection of her own emotions. Tears touched her eyes and he smiled as he reached to touch the velvet skin. Very gently he caressed her until he could see the smoldering passion begin to build. He drew her with him to the bed where he sat and drew her down on his lap. She gasped in shock and a burning pleasure as his lips began to discover more sensitive places. Her breasts quivered and nipples hardened as his tongue played a heated path from one to the other.

She moaned in exquisite agony and pressed him close to her, closing her eyes in complete abandon. She felt the sensation of falling as he held her and lay back across the bed drawing her with him. With one turn he drew her beneath him. She lay, gazing up into his passion darkened eyes, when she placed one hand on each side of his face and drew him again to her.

He left her side only for a few minutes to rid himself of the clothes that restricted him, then he joined her again on the bed, but not before a startled wide-eyed Sabrina had gasped in surprise.

He was a magnificent masculine creature. His bronze body long, lean and well muscled with taunt sinewy muscle. Complete symmetry of movement gave him a lithe grace.

The sight of his manhood roused and throbbing shattered her equilibrium and she gave an anguished sob and began to rise from the bed . . . too late! Passion roused beyond control, Clay was beside her drawing her trembling body back into his arms. He soothed and eased her fears with gentle kisses and caresses until she seemed to forget them and again began to respond with rising passion.

Her slim body was cool to his touch and his hands sought to memorize every line and curve. A slim hip, a long slender thigh, the soft flat plane of her belly that curved into a warmer place that drew him like a magnet. To touch, gently, searchingly, to hear her soft murmured cries of pleasure as he began expertly to lift her to a plane where she had no control, where they could fly together beyond now to forever.

Aware that this first time would be difficult for her, combined with the fact that she was so slim and small and that he was more than well endowed, slowed him. He lay half atop her and pressed a knee between her legs to separate them. He caught her tightly to him as he pressed himself deeply within her. It hurt him also to hear her cry of pain and feel her stiffen in his arms.

He lay still, holding her gently, soothing her with gentle kisses and caresses until the trembling ceased. He knew the worst was past, now they were ready to touch again the sweet taste of pleasure.

Slowly, gently he began to move and he felt a surge of joy when he felt her begin to respond again. Her hands caressed him, drawing him closer and she began to lift her body to meet his.

Now they began to soar. Passion lifted them and carried them along in a stream of blazing delight. She came to vibrant life beneath him. All that had any meaning to her now was Clay. Clay with the magic of his love, that was consuming every rational thought she had and leaving only him.

They blended, moving together, giving and taking in wildly shared abandon. She held nothing from him, but gave herself to him body and soul, completely. He filled her completely, totally wiping away every ounce of control that was left.

The fiery culmination of their love left them both weak and clinging to each other reluctant to let go of the searing total joy they had found. For a long time they lay silently holding each other until mutual breathing was controlled and they again had some semblance of control over their emotions.

He lay beside her and drew her gently against him. She curved her body to his and rested her head on his shoulder. Content, they lay in silence for a moment while he drew her hair across his chest and stroked its silky strands.

Clay smiled. At this moment he felt many different emotions . . . regret was not among them.

He turned on his side to face her, and lifted her chin with tender fingers until their eyes met again. What he saw in the depths of her eyes filled him with a warmth and pleasure he had not felt in a long time. Love, complete unselfish love blossomed like a rare beautiful flower before him. It held him speechless for a moment.

He caressed the smooth skin of her cheek and then bent his head to touch her mouth with the gentlest of kisses.

Was it her innocent surrender, her sweet giving love that had taken him unprepared? He had not meant this to happen, yet he had wanted her with every ounce of his being, and in wonder, he realized he still did. He wanted to hold her close, bind her to him with unbreakable love, protect her from the hurt he knew loving him could bring. Was there a way he could make her understand without hurting her?

"Oh Clay," she whispered as she clung to him," I never

116

knew loving someone would be such a beautiful thing. I'm so glad fate brought me here."

He watched her closely, realizing if she knew everything she would feel she had been used. He also realized he didn't want to lose her. He wanted to continue to see the warm gentle look of love in her eyes.

He tightened his arms about her and smiled down into her wide violet eyes.

"Do you know, my innocent, you are the most beautiful thing that has been in my life for a long, long time? You love completely and openly without any reservations don't you my love?"

"Is there another way Clay? Can anyone love with half their heart?"

He chuckled as he bent to kiss her again, this time more thoroughly and lingeringly. "Yes my love, some people can. There are all kinds of love Sabrina, some love can even be labeled hate."

"I don't want that kind of love Clay. I love you with all I possess, with every thought I have. It is the only way I know."

"And I don't want to change that," he said, so seriously that it sent a sudden chill through her. "Promise me one thing Sabrina, no matter what ever happens, or what you ever hear, give me the chance to explain it to you. Will you do that?"

"Clay . . . Nothing anyone says could change how I feel about you. "Why . . ."

"Just promise me."

"All right, I promise. I'll come to you with anything."

"Good. One more thing."

"What?"

"Hawk gave you the dress?"

"Yes, why?"

"I . . . I don't want you taking any more gifts from him."

"But, Clay, he . . ."

"He can visit if he wants . . . when I'm here. But I don't want him giving you any more gifts."

"But why Clay? I'm sure he meant only to be kind to me."

"He meant . . . well . . . less than kindness. Sabrina don't let's quarrel," he grinned, "I like what we were doing much better."

"Oh," she laughed softly. "You mean this," she said as she drew his head down to her and kissed him softly.

"Mmmm, something like that, Sabrina . . . I'm . . . I'm sorry if all this is something you don't understand. Will you trust me . . . Will you do what I ask?"

"'I would trust you with my life Clay," she said softly. "I feel so safe, so warm and at peace when you hold me. I don't want to be anywhere else . . . with anyone else. I only need you to tell me you feel the same for me as I do for you."

"My sweet beautiful innocent," he murmured as he drew her tight against him. "How could a man be so stupid not to love you?"

He tasted her lips with gentle searching kisses, reaching to the depths of her with a searing need that lifted her beyond every thought but the magic of belonging.

Slowly their passion soared again. With slow experienced deliberation he began to lift her senses to a plane where all control was lost to her.

She responded to his lead with a vibrant passion that nearly overwhelmed him with her trusting surrender. She gave completely, and he immersed himself in the sensual pleasure blocking every thought from his mind and his senses but her. He sought the sweetness that would always fill his memories from this night on. The silken texture of her soft skin as he touched with gentle searching hands. The tentative trembling touch of her hands that sought him with the same heated passion he felt. The way her body molded itself to his, clinging with the same fiery need that filled him. He knew without doubt that this deep fulfilling hunger would be part of him forever. Each kiss, each touch multiplied the need until he knew there would never be an end to the desire to possess her. He heard her passionate abandoned words of love with intense pleasure, knowing she was lost to reality.

Only when he knew he had carried her along with him to the height of desire did he allow himself to be lost in her magic and tumble with her into a fiery cauldron of wild consuming pleasure.

Afterward he held her close to him until the trembling ceased. He caressed her gently and held her until he heard her slow even breathing and knew she slept.

But sleep would not come to him so easily. That he would love her and want her for always he knew, but would she still want him if her innocent love for him was shattered and she felt he had used her love as a convenience . . . as a balm for an old memory.

Slowly and quietly he rose from the bed. He did not disturb her sleep and dressed quietly. Then he bent to pick up the dress that, in their moment of passion, had been left on the floor. He stood holding it, knowing the significance of it, and knowing the real reason it had been given to her. A grim cold angry look crossed his face for a moment, then he turned to gaze again at the slim sleeping girl, and a look of all consuming possessive love replaced the anger.

"None of this will touch you Sabrina," he thought angrily, "None of it . . . no matter how hard he tries."

He touched her hair lightly, then bent to brush a feather light kiss on her lips. He smiled in satisfaction when he heard her murmur his name softly, sigh a deep contented sigh, and drift into a deeper sleep.

He blew out the candle and left the room, closing the door softly behind him. But he did not return to his room to seek his own bed. Instead he tied the dress into a bundle and left the house. He went to the stable and saddled his horse and rode away. He rode in the direction of the Indian village and a confrontation with Hawk.

Ten

Clay rode in a slow relaxed manner, and no viewer would have realized the tumultuous emotions that raged through him. He would touch occasionally the bundle that contained the dress, absently rubbing his fingers over it.

The moon bathed the area in a bright gold light, and the huge stallion he rode lengthened his stride and ate the miles between his home and the Indian village.

Once there, Clay tied his horse beneath a tree that bordered the village. He knew quite well exactly where Hawk's lodge was situated. He stood over three hundred yards from Hawk's lodge beneath the covering darkness of the trees. Putting both hands to his lips in a cupped fashion he emitted the same strange eerie call Sabrina had heard the night she had arrived. It was a call that went back to their childhood, and a call he knew would bring Hawk quickly.

He waited a few minutes and repeated the call. Then he leaned against the tree and waited again.

He was rewarded almost immediately when he saw Hawk step from his lodge and gaze in the direction the call had come from. Clay waited, and in a moment Hawk walked in his direction.

They stood facing each other unable to read each other's emotions in their eyes because of the darkness. For a few minutes there was a deep absolute silence.

"You wanted to speak to me, Clay?" Hawk questioned with amusement that angered Clay even more.

"You know why I'm here, Hawk."

"I'm not too sure, suppose you tell me?"

"Don't try to use Sabrina, Hawk. She knows nothing about us. Don't hurt someone who is innocent."

"Hurt? Why should I hurt her? I am pleased to think of her as friend. There are not many in the white world."

"You have changed Hawk. You never used to lie before."

There was a moment of absolute silence and Clay could physically feel Hawks anger before he regained his control.

"I do not lie, Clay," Hawk said softly.

"You don't want her involved in this?"

"No."

"Then," Clay said softly as he turned and lifted the dress and handed it back to Hawk, "why this, Hawk?"

Hawk didn't take the bundle, yet he knew what was in it. He chuckled softly. "To her it was just a dress, just a pleasing gift. I knew to you it would be more. Did it upset you Clay?" His voice regained some of its amusement. "Did it cause you to think thoughts you didn't want? Or maybe . . . do something foolish you should not have done?"

Clay's anger, blended with his guilt was almost beyond his control. He held himself firmly, knowing Hawk had done it to deliberately goad him into doing just what he had done. The last thing he wanted was for Hawk to know the complete success of his gesture.

"I'm not that stupid, Hawk. I've done nothing I regret doing."

"How did you explain to her that you were taking it from her? How did you explain to her what it was?"

"I didn't, and I don't intend to. She is . . . a servant. I don't need to explain. She will do as I say. I've told her she is to take no more gifts from you."

"She is a slave?"

"No . . . not slave, servant. She will be free in two years."

"If she is not a slave then she must have time of her own, time you do not control."

"Of course she does."

"Then . . . I will remain a friend, and unless you are afraid you must let her do with her free time whatever she chooses to do."

"Stay away from her, Hawk."

"I remember," Hawk replied in a gentle voice, "saying something to you like that once. Stay away from her Clay . . . my friend Clay . . . she is our medicine woman, she is our life blood . . . she is my future bride. Did you heed my words Clay? Did you leave things as they were? No, instead you stole what was already mine.'"

"She was not yours," Clay responded in a quiet voice. "She loved me, Hawk, and I loved her. She would not have been happy with you. You were not the kind of man to take a woman who did not want you."

"In the end she was not happy with you. She missed the way of her people. She knew your marriage was a mistake."

"She told you that?"

"No . . . she told Swift Doe."

"I don't believe you."

"You don't want to believe. If you did, you would have to admit another truth."

"What truth is that?"

"Summer . . . she is her mother's child too."

It was good then that Hawk did not see Clay's near loss of control. If he had, he might have known completely of Clay's vulnerability over Summer and his dead wife.

"Summer is mine."

"Not completely, she is Singing Bell's too . . . she

123

is Indian."

"She is white!"

"You cannot erase blood Clay. At this time we need her too. She has her mother's gifts. I have seen it, and you, if you will admit the truth, have seen it also."

"I see my daughter . . . my child, and I have no intention of sharing her . . . with you or anyone else. One day I intend for her to be educated, to have everything money can get for her."

"There are some things only the gods can give."

"Hawk, I'm going to warn you. Don't try taking from me what is mine. I'll stop you."

"I will take nothing. One day, if you do not stop walking the path you are on, it is the truth that will take away from you what you hold closest. Face the truth, Clay, or lose everything."

Clay threw the bundle at Hawk's feet. "No more gifts Hawk . . . no more."

He turned and walked away, unable to see the sorrow in the eyes of the Indian whose gaze followed his shadowed form until the deeper shadows of the night swallowed him and all that could be heard was the drum of receding hoof-beats. It was only when the sound faded that he sighed deeply, picked up the dress, turned and walked slowly back to his lodge.

Clay rode slowly home, angry at Hawk more for the memories, fear and guilt he had roused within him than what he had done. Firmly he pushed the thoughts to the back of his mind, refusing to allow them to blossom. It was nearing dawn when he stabled his horse and walked to the house.

Sabrina stirred and came half awake. She was aware of

several things. Dawn was near . . . and Clay was gone. She could feel his absence like a tangible thing. There was an empty feeling within her and the need to reach out for him and feel the warmth and security his arms brought. With feline grace she stretched luxuriously, and a small throaty chuckle sounded softly. "Clay," she murmured. She loved him. With a passion that surprised her she thought of him and the night they had shared. She sighed a deep sigth of utter contentment, rolled on her side and drew his pillow against her. She lay, relaxed, and let every moment, every touch, every sweet memory of the past night bloom again within her. Her world seemed to her to suddenly be filled with a bright rosy glow. All the torment and fear from the past was forgotten. She did not have to worry about the past any longer for Clay was her protection, and she did not have to be frightened of the future any longer for Clay would fill it with the security and strength of his love.

She thought of the fear and disgust that had nearly overcome her at Clyde or Thomas' touch then remembered with wonder the sheer intense pleasure she had shared with Clay and the extreme difference loving someone made.

Warm, secure and completely content. Sure that all problems were past, Sabrina drifted into a light comfortable sleep.

She was wakened again by deep masculine laughter accompanied by childish giggles. She smiled at the pleasing sound and rose from the bed. She fully intended to put on the dress Hawk had given her, but when she looked for it there was no sign of it. She remembered well when it had slid from her to the floor and wondered if Clay had picked it up for some reason. If he had, he must have taken it along with him for after an exhaustive search she knew it was not in her room.

Quickly she donned a plain green cotton dress and hurried to find out what was causing so much laughter.

When she opened the door of her room she looked out across the living room to see Clay and Summer on the floor before the fireplace. They were engrossed in each other and did not hear her quietly walk into the room.

Clay was allowing Summer a temporary upper hand as they wrestled on the floor. Summer was laughing as she tried to force her father to the floor. Suddenly she squealed as he gripped her and tumbled her down on the fur rug and began to tickle her.

Sabrina smiled, and at that moment Clay looked up and saw her. Their eyes met and held, and under the warmth of his gaze she could feel her cheeks flush and a trembly warmth spread through her until her legs became weak.

Clay stood up and drew Summer up beside him.

"Why don't you see if Ellen has our breakfast ready, Summer. I'm hungry, aren't you?"

"Yes Papa," Summer replied. She went to Sabrina first. "Good morning Sabrina. Are you hungry too?"

"Yes Summer, starved," Sabrina answered.

"I'll go see if breakfast is ready," Summer said. In a moment she was gone. The room was quiet, and Sabrina could not release herself from Clay's heart stopping gaze as he slowly walked toward her.

He stood so close to her that she had to tip her head up to look at him. His eyes were warm as they held hers and she quivered with the intensity of it.

"Clay . . ."

"Good morning," he said softly, and his arms came about her drawing her close to him. He tipped her chin up with his hand and kissed her with a deep searching hunger that shattered any logical thoughts she might have had. She clung to him, aware of nothing but the need that boiled within her.

She felt the powerful strength of him as he crushed her to

him, knowing there was no place on earth she would rather be now, or forever, than where she was at the moment.

Reluctantly he released her lips, but continued to hold her close to him. He smiled down into a love-filled face that filled him with intense pleasure as he read the look clearly.

"If you hadn't come out soon I would have scandalized Ellen completely by coming in after you. My patience is worn thin . . . I couldn't wait to hold you again."

"Oh Clay," she murmured softly, "I . . ."

"Tell me love. It's been too many hours since I heard you say it," he answered gently.

"I love you Clay."

"Beautiful," he whispered, "you are so very beautiful."

Again his mouth captured hers, searing her, branding her forever.

Clay released her only when Summer's excited call came to them. They watched as Summer ran from the kitchen toward them.

"Papa, Ellen says to come and eat. I told her Sabrina was up."

"Good, let's go." Clay swept Summer up swiftly and he and Sabrina shared the pleasure of her pleased laughter as he carried her under one arm toward the kitchen.

They sat about the huge wooden table eating ravenously of Ellen's good cooking. Ellen had been watching both Sabrina and Clay and it took her only moments to realize that something was different with both of them.

"Papa?"

"Yes, Summer."

"Are you going away today?"

"No, I've some work to do around here."

Ellen watched the bright glow in Sabrina's eyes at Clay's words. Sabrina was delighted that Clay would be somehow close to her for the day.

"Can I go swim in the river?"

"You'd best ask Sabrina that," Clay grinned. "She might have some studies for you to do first."

Summer's shoulders slumped and she turned hopeful eyes toward Sabrina.

"Suppose," Sabrina smiled, "we take our books to the river, study for a while then you can swim."

Immediately Summer's dark eyes brightened and she nodded enthusiastically.

"Go and get the books and papers."

"May I be excused Papa?"

Clay nodded and again Sabrina was struck by the gentle manners Clay had bred into the child, manners that did not belong to a backwoods family. Summer ran quickly and returned with the books.

Clay set about chores that consisted of repairs while Sabrina and Summer went to the banks of the river. They found a shaded spot where the water was clear and not too deep.

Summer had been taught to swim by Clay almost before she could walk. For over an hour and a half, Sabrina held her attention on her studies, then, as the sun rose higher her hungry gaze roamed toward the cool inviting water.

"All right Summer," she smiled, "suppose we rest for a while. You can swim a little if you like."

Before Sabrina was finished talking, Summer had already discarded the dress and moccasins she wore and was headed for the water. She splashed unhesitatingly into it and was swimming about with the ease of a slim silver fish, her naked body slim and brown.

Sabrina laughed at her antics in the water, enjoying the child's laughing delight. The sun was already high when Sabrina called a tired Summer from the water.

"Why don't you lie in the shade on the cool grass and rest

for a while? We'll have a little more time to study before lunch."

Summer was tired and she readily agreed. She lay in the cool shade of the tree and soon her eyes closed and she slept.

Sabrina looked at the cool water for some time before she decided to enjoy it a little too. Taking off her shoes and stockings, she gathered her dress about her slim hips and waded into the water.

She hummed softly to herself realizing how completely happy she was in this wilderness.

"Just as beautiful as the first time I saw you there."

Clay had set about his work with determination, but a slim, violet eyed golden beauty kept wavering between him and what he was doing.

Finally he put his equipment away and walked toward the river. He didn't know what he would say once there, but he knew he wanted to be with her every moment he could.

He pushed aside the underbrush and smiled at the scene before him. Summer, curled in contented sleep beneath the shade of the tree, and Sabrina with her skirts bundled about her slim hips and her legs trim and bare wading in the water. It called to mind the first time he had seen her so. He spoke softly and savored the look of pleasure in her eyes when she turned and saw him.

"Come out of the water, mermaid," he said as he reached out his hand. Unhesitatingly she walked toward the bank, took his hand and smiled as he drew her up beside him. Without a word he drew her into his arms and held her. One hand pressed against her back, the other caressing a rounded hip and holding her firmly against him.

He felt no resistance and was filled with heated desire as her slim arms came up about his neck and she lifted her lips willingly for his kiss.

Soft lips parted beneath his, not only accepting but

searching as deeply and with as much need and intense pleasure as he did.

Flame leapt in his veins, and his arms tightened possessively about her crushing her against him. He felt every soft curve mold to him and it fed the fire that threatened to consume him.

Her tongue teased him, challenging him to deeper passion, and he was not one to resist such temptation. When he lifted his head their eyes met, hers liquid pools of bemused fascinated passion. She wanted nothing more than to hold fast to the security his warm caresses brought.

There was a look of infinite gentleness in his gaze.

"Having you this close and not possessing you is certainly much more than any normal man is expected to withstand. You should have sent Summer home for her nap." His voice was a whisper against her hair mixed with the soft sound of need, and she knew surely if Summer had not been resting against the cool green grass she would have been. The thought had no aversion for her, for in fact she felt the bite of unfulfilled desire as much as he.

Strong steel sinewed arms held her close as she rested her head against his broad chest. She felt a gentle hand caress her hair and a feather light kiss against it.

"Sabrina?"

"Yes."

"Look at me," he commanded gently.

She tipped her face up and looked questioningly into his eyes.

"My father built my house when I was a boy. He built it so that every room was safe from attack from without."

"I don't understand Clay."

"Every door has a bolt capable of keeping the most determined force from entering," he added quietly.

Slowly the impact of his words came clear to her. She

smiled, filled with the warm rush of pleasure.

"There will be no bolt on my door tonight Clay, nor will there be any other night. I would never close a door between us."

She was held breathless by the quick light of pleasure that danced in his eyes and the quick smile that touched his lips.

"Always my sweet innocent" he said softly as his arm tightened possessively about her slim waist. "You ask nothing, but with your sweetness you make a man want to give you everything." He laid his large hand against her cheek and she turned her head to press her lips to it.

"I love you Clay," she said softly, "I love you."

The simple honesty of her words sent a quiver of almost painful need through him. He bent his head to again take complete possession of her mouth and sank into the warm depth of her complete surrender.

"Papa?" came a questioning small voice.

All thoughts of Summer had been driven from his mind by Sabrina's soft slim body molded to his and the warm giving lips that promised him so much. Now he groaned softly as his attention was drawn to Summer. Sabrina's soft laugh did nothing to ease his nearly physical pain. He rewarded her muffled laughter by tightening his arms about her until she gasped breathlessly before he released her. He smiled at Sabrina wickedly before he turned to Summer.

"It's time to get up, sleepy head," Clay said as he walked to her and bent to lift her body effortlessly into his arms.

Sabrina gathered the books and papers and her shoes and stockings and walked beside Clay as he carried Summer back toward the house.

Once there he deposited her on the porch with instructions to see if Ellen had any lunch ready. The child scampered happily inside the house. Clay turned to Sabrina and smiled as she passed close to him to go into the house.

"No matter how you came here my love," he chuckled as his eyes roved over her warmly, "It was the best decision I ever made to let you stay."

His hand touched her waist with gently caressing fingers as he held the door open for her to go in. As she passed him she stopped and returned his smile.

"And I . . . I am grateful that fate brought me here. You are a man of mystery, Clay Storm, and yet . . . I would rather be here, with you, than anywhere else in the world today."

She stood on tip toe, brushed a quick kiss on his lips and walked past him to join Summer and Ellen in the kitchen. She was unaware of the gaze that followed her slim figure and the battle within the darkened blue eyes that had come unbidden and completely unwelcome.

Eleven

Clay was in an exuberant mood, and he made lunch a delightful time with his teasing and his deep masculine laughter. Both Ellen and Sabrina were caught completely in his wit and humor.

Ellen, watching the glow of Sabrina's face and the way her violet eyes could see only Clay, knew that the girl had fallen helplessly in love with Clay. She didn't know that their discovery of each other had gone to completion, and she became afraid that it would not be long before it did. What worried her was that Clay might take advantage of Sabrina, as many had done with indentured servants, and discard her when their time of servitude had ended.

She watched Clay closely when he was involved in conversation with either Sabrina or Summer, and had to admit he was wildly handsome and man enough to turn the head and heart of the most experienced woman. Was he the kind to break Sabrina's heart? Was he cold and deceptive or warm, open and honest as he appeared? She promised herself to talk to him alone as soon as possible. If she couldn't find his intentions at least she would warn him that Sabrina was too sweet and good a person for him to hurt.

If she thought Clay was unaware of her scrutiny she was wrong. He was aware not only of her intent gaze but the thoughts in her mind that he easily read. He also knew that he would eventually have to ease her fears somehow. He did not intend for Sabrina to be hurt by loving him . . . but, after all he had known he should have remembered that what one intended and what happened were sometimes two different things.

Sabrina concentrated on helping Ellen and caring for Summer the balance of the day. It was difficult for her because she could not control her wayward thoughts. Vibrant memories of Clay's gentle touch made the balance of her day an agony of suspense.

She was passing an open window in the course of her work and a sharp noise drew her attention. She went to the window which opened to the back of the house. Leaning on the window sill, she looked out.

Clay stood a few yards away and the noise she had heard was the sharp crack of an ax against wood. Clay was chopping wood for the balance of the night's use and the following morning.

He stood in profile to her and was completely unaware of her warm hungry gaze upon him. He had removed his shirt and was swinging the huge ax with lithe even movements.

Fascinated, she watched the play of the setting sun across his bronzed muscular body. The ripple of muscle along his back and arms sent a shiver of expectant delight coursing through her.

Her cheeks pinkened at the thought that he might turn and see the need in her eyes, yet she could not draw her eyes away.

She watched him stop for a moment to wipe the sweat from his brow with his forearm, then he again swung the ax high and brought it down with a resounding crack splitting the log in two. He bent forward and retrieved the two pieces, throwing them on the stack he had already chopped.

She was mesmerized by the graceful movement of his slim hipped, broad shouldered body, and bent forward in breathless expectation.

Clay was accustomed to the wild and always prepared for the unexpected. It was why he suddenly sensed her eyes on him. He turned quickly and was caught and held by a limpid purple gaze that struck him physically and left him suddenly short of breath.

Her eyes alight with the same need he felt, warm and seeking. Her lips slightly parted in breathless expectancy. The rapid rise and fall of her breasts told him her emotions were the same as his.

Slowly he walked toward her. She watched him come, unable to move, even to breathe with the sheer intense joy she felt.

"You're a most distracting vision, love," he smiled as he reached to touch her cheek with gentle fingers. Their eyes held in a magnetic moment while his fingers slipped down the slender column of her throat to trace a light path across the soft rise of her breasts.

His smile faded to a deep passionate gaze as his hand slid into her hair and drew her face to his.

The kiss was lingering and gentle as his mouth caressed hers in a sensuous blending that melted her bones to liquid and sent molten flame through her veins until she thought she could bear it no longer.

She whispered his name softly and reached to touch him.

"I have never known a day to be as long as this," he said.

She laughed softly, knowing the pleasure of his need for her.

"I too would wish the hours away."

He sighed deeply, a shattered half-laugh half-groan.

"Sabrina, take yourself away from here or I swear I shall take you this minute no matter who is near."

135

Reluctantly they moved away from each other knowing in a matter of time they would be able to fill the desire that drew them to one another now. Determined, he turned away from her and returned to the job he was doing.

Supper was as pleasant an affair as lunch had been, yet all felt the intangible feel of emotion in the air. For Sabrina and Clay it was a joyous feeling nearing euphoria at the idea that the day would soon be ended.

For Summer, it was a warm comfortable feeling to see her father laughing and happy and knowing it was Sabrina, for whom she was rapidly forming a deep affection, who made him so.

For Ellen, it was tense worry, for she read signs all too well, and she had not had a chance to speak to Clay alone about the matter and it looked like she was not going to get the opportunity when Clay rose, stretched and announced he was going to tend the horses before he went to bed.

Sabrina bathed Summer and prepared her for bed. She brushed the child's long dark hair thinking of her father's thick dark hair through which she had run her fingers. She took pleasure in noting Summer's resemblance to Clay.

Sabrina knew Ellen was very tired, so she rose and took Summer's hand.

"I'll take Summer to bed and tell her a story, Ellen. Why don't you get some sleep, you look tired."

"You'll be going to bed as soon as the child is asleep?"

"Yes . . . yes, I'm tired too."

"Very well, good night Sabrina . . . Summer, good night child."

"Good night," they both answered and watched Ellen walk to her room and close the door behind her.

Sabrina took Summer to her bed and at Summer's insistence told her not one story but two. By the end of the second, Summer's heavy eyelids closed and she drifted quietly off to sleep.

Rising slowly from the bed so as not to disturb the child, she walked to the door. Closing it softly behind her she stood for a moment in the darkened hallway. Then she walked into the now empty living room where there was still a soft light from the dying fire.

She stood in the center of the room, unsure of whether Clay would return soon or not. Then she went to the door and stepped out onto the dark porch.

She gazed up at the dark velvet sky lit with millions of diamond bright stars. She was completely unaware that Clay stood in the shadows and watched her. Pale moonlight touched the softened planes of her face and glimmered in the strands of her pale gold hair.

"I've been waiting for you love," he said softly.

Sabrina was not frightened, she wasn't even startled. Somehow she had known Clay was near. She felt him without turning as he walked soundlessly up behind her and put his arms about her, drawing her back against him to rest securely in his embrace.

Gently he kissed the top of her head and held her in silent appreciation of the beauty around them, and the beauty they shared.

"It's so beautiful . . . so peaceful here," she said.

"More so now that you are here. Your coming has sort of completed everything." Clay brushed his cheek against the softness of her hair. He wanted to tell her so much, but knew he could not without jepoardizing the gentle new love that blossomed within her.

She turned in his arms and looked up at him.

"You're like this place Clay. There is so much about you I don't know, so much that even frightens me a little, yet I feel at peace with you. Content in a way I have never known before. Oh Clay, I want to love you, I want to fill your heart like you fill mine. Don't ever let me go Clay."

His arms tightened about her, pressing her closer to his lean hard body.

"There's nothing here to be frightened of, Sabrina, and I've no intention of ever letting you go. If things seem like a mystery now, have patience. Trust me and one day it will all be clear for you. Trust me . . . love me, and let me show you just how much you have filled my world since you came."

His voice softened as he bent his head to touch her lips. Slowly, sensuously he slanted his mouth across hers. She sighed in surrender and slid her arms about his waist to cling to him.

All things scattered helplessly from her mind except Clay and the magic spell he wove about her. One arm bound her tightly to him while the other hand caressed gently rounder, softer places. He braced himself against the column that supported the roof and drew her against him, off balance enough that she had to rest against him and cling to him to keep her balance.

Randomly, his mouth sought to discover every vulnerable spot as it roved from her lips to a sensitive ear and down the slim column of her throat to the valley between her breasts.

Her unrestrained surrender filled him with a joyous sense of pleasure. The passion he had wakened in her sent her seeking a renewal. She pressed her lips in random kisses against his throat and cheeks while her hands caressed his lean ribs and chest.

Their need became deeper. The deep warm kisses were not enough. The hands that sought to touch had roused a passion that burned to be fulfilled.

"God, Sabrina . . . I want you so much."

She could feel the fierce beat of his heart as she pressed against him, matching the violent throbbing of her own.

He held her a little away from him and captured her face

between his hands. Then he lifted her face to his and took her mouth again.

His hot hungry kiss demanded what she was all too willing to give. A soft moan came unknowing from her as he backed away from her for a moment. Then she saw that he had backed toward the door and had his hand extended to her. Unhesitatingly she put her hand in his and could see the instant flash of his smile as he drew her with him.

They crossed the living room and went down the hall to her room on silent feet. At her door he pushed it open quickly and drew her inside with him. When he closed the door she heard the bolt slide home. Then they stood in the moon-touched room.

He was beside her, and she closed her eyes inhaling the deep masculine scent of him . . . of leather and pine . . . of love and need. She felt his fingers nimbly loosen the laces of her dress and the touch of the cool breeze against her heated skin.

A hard, yet gentle hand caressed silken skin until her body quivered with desire. She moved closer and slim fingers began to push aside the inhibiting clothes he wore.

In breathless moments they stood, rose tipped breasts pressed against a fur matted chest, soft slim thigh against hard muscled ones. He slid his hands down the curve of her back to rest on her hips and press her closer.

With infinite tenderness, he brushed his lips against her throat then down to soft shoulders . . . on to taste the sweetness of rose-tipped aureoles that thrust up to meet his questing mouth. A low anguished moan escaped her as his hungry mouth traveled on. He knelt before her, drawing her body close to him and she twined her fingers in his thick dark hair to hold him even closer.

She could no longer control the ecstatic anguish that tore through her as his hot hungry mouth plumbed the depths of her.

Then her moaning sobs were stopped by his lips as he lifted her body and crossed to the bed. They tumbled to the blankets, aware now of nothing but the wildly abandoned passion that seared them both.

His breathing was a harsh ragged thing in her ear and she could feel with every sense she had the control he was holding over himself until she could meet him at the peak of passion.

With exploding pleasure that tingled through every inch of her, she rose to meet his thrusting hips.

Then in wild twisting abandon they climbed together until reality and breath nearly ceased.

She wanted all, and he refused her nothing. She moaned and cried out his name over and over as her hands caressed the broad muscle of his back. Then with a shattering moan she felt the deepest pleasure wash through her in wave after wave of sheer ecstasy.

Slowly, very slowly, pulses returned to normal, breathing became controlled and they held each other in a silence that spoke a multitude of words about the rare and beautiful pleasure they had shared.

Sabrina lay still, her head resting on a warm and comfortable chest, and her body held snugly and safe against his. For some time they remained silent, content to hold each other.

Again, Sabrina thought with wonder of the intense joy being with Clay brought her and compared it to the fear she had felt when Clyde had tried to rape her. Knowing the difference was an intangible thing labeled love. An emotion she had never known until Clay had reached for her. She wanted to keep this beautiful thing forever. She thought of the man who held her, the man whose touch had the power to lift her beyond anything she had ever known, but a man of whom she knew nothing.

"Clay?"

"Umm?"

"You're so quiet, what are you thinking?"

He chuckled warmly as he turned on his side to gaze down at her. Pale moonlight touched the bed in which the lovers lay. With infinite tenderness he caressed the slim length of her.

"Thinking?" he replied in an amused voice, "what rational man could be thinking of anything else but you when you are so soft, so warm and so near."

Her heart leapt with pleasure.

"You were thinking of me?"

"For the life of me, love," he chuckled, "I can't seem to think of anything else lately. I didn't plan on it, but somehow you have taken possession of my thoughts and my heart."

Content for the moment, she snuggled closer to him and twined her arms about him. He rocked her close to him.

"But it's you who are thinking, love," he said softly.

"Only of you," she whispered.

"And what about me?"

"I want to know you Clay, I want to be part of you. I feel . . ."

"What?"

"As if some part of you is not here, as if you hold it away." She felt the slight tremor of his muscles and knew she had struck a sensitive spot.

"Clay?"

"Sabrina . . . maybe there are things I'd rather you didn't know. Do you love me enough to accept me the way I am now? The past isn't important to either of us. Let's just think about each other and the future."

She sat up and looked down into his questioning gaze.

"Don't you know by now I would love you no matter what?" she said softly, and the warmth in her deep purple eyes struck him speechless. It was the first time in his life he had ever experienced such unselfish, open giving.

He smiled and reached to touch her cheek, then slid his hands into the thick silken mass of her hair and drew her to him.

"Sabrina," he whispered, "my sweet, sweet innocent. You will never know the depths from which you have lifted me. Keep that trust for me, love, let me know it will always be there . . . love me Sabrina."

He drew her down to him and kissed her with such infinite tenderness that she could have wept with the beauty of it.

Gentle loving hands reached and held, passionate lips blended in a kiss of promise.

Sabrina pushed every thought from her mind but Clay. For Clay it was not quite so easy. The soft finger of guilt spoke eloquently. He had asked for a commitment from her, but had not offered the same in return. He hoped the day would come when there was no reason to hold any secrets from her. The day when he finally convinced Hawk that there was no way he could reach Clay and take from him what was his. Until then Hawk must never be allowed to believe that Clay had another vulnerable spot besides Summer . . . his love for Sabrina.

He knew in all honesty he should stay away from her until any threat had passed . . . but he couldn't. From the first taste of her sweet love he had been captured, bound by the most fragile yet the strongest binding of all . . . deep intense love.

Passion began to soar again, to the heights neither of them had ever experience before. Like a symphony, their bodies blended in a song of everlasting love.

A hunger had been released that would never be appeased. It would claim them always. It would survive in every touch, every gaze, every movement forever.

Like eagles in the sky, they soared lifting, twisting, floating. Calling to each other with a touch, with hot moist lips, with a blending together that forged them into one.

Afterward, when they had again regained some semblance of control over their passion, they lay together clinging to one another. After a while Sabrina, secure and warm curled against Clay's body, slept. Clay lay very still for a long time content to hold her close to him.

The first pale streaks of early dawn touched the horizon when he slowly rose from the bed. Gently disentagling himself from slender arms, he secured the blanket about her, bent to kiss her gently, then dressed and left the room.

In the kitchen he stirred the banked fire to new life and brewed a pot of very strong coffee.

He sat before the fire, sipped a cup of coffee and thought of how the future could be with Sabrina, Summer and a future that held no threat.

He was still seated before the fire when he heard stirrings from Ellen's room.

After a short while her door opened and she walked down the short hall to the kitchen door. She stopped for a moment, surprised to see Clay seated there.

"Coffee is hot Ellen, have a cup before you start breakfast."

"I will, thank you," Ellen replied. She poured a cup and went to sit across from him. "While we're alone," she began, "I have something I feel I have to talk to you about."

Clay watched her for a moment, then he said quietly, "Sabrina?"

"Yes," Ellen replied, "Sabrina . . . someone I don't want to see get hurt . . . and you . . . the one who could hurt her the most."

Twelve

Clay stood up and tossed the remains of the now cold coffee into the fire, listening to the sputtering hiss as the drops of coffee evaporated in the flames. He set the cup aside and leaned against the fireplace, his intent blue gaze on Ellen.

"Say what you want to say, Ellen," he said.

Ellen was unsure of how to say what she felt. How could she accuse the man who held their papers for two years of immoral thoughts. What could she say without any other tangible proof but her own intention.

Slowly, she began to tell him of how close Sabrina had become to her. How she had had only her uncle and Ellen to love her since the tragic deaths of her parents. She tried her best to explain to Clay that she had been Sabrina's only family for a long time now and felt as protective of her as if she were her own daughter.

"She has had enough fear and pain in her young life," Ellen said gently, "and she has no one else to protect her but me."

"Protect her from what?" Clay asked gently.

"A broken heart," Ellen replied softly. "It would shatter her. She is like her mother was. Fragile, yet one who loves completely. Don't let her fall in love with you, Clay Storm. You have dark secrets in your eyes. I don't want that child to pay the price that could come with loving you."

"I have no intention of doing her any harm, Ellen,"

"I didn't say that."

"What did you say?"

"I said don't love her . . . don't let her love you."

Clay laughed a soft bitter laugh. "Love is not a thing that is that simple to control. You are right about one thing Ellen, she is sweet and honest and loving. I've been lonely and empty for a long time Ellen. I've needed her. She's like a breath of new spring after a fierce hard winter."

"What about what she needs?"

"Are you sure you know what that is? Maybe what she needs can be found right here."

"Can you answer one question with a completely honest answer?"

"I'll try," he smiled.

"Are you going to marry her?"

"Ellen," he began, then he paused, knowing Ellen would not understand or like what he was going to say. "I know you are not going to understand this, but there are several reasons why Sabrina and I can't marry right at the moment."

He saw the suspicion in her eyes accompanied by a touch of distrust.

"One of which," he continued, "is that the minister around these parts is a transient one. He won't be around this area until spring again. By then I hope anything that stands between us is resolved."

"That's the only reason?"

Clay laulghed to himself. He couldn't understand why he wanted or needed this woman's trust, or cared if she understood or not . . . but he did. He wanted her to look at him without the doubt in her eyes she had now.

"No Ellen, it's not. But you'll just have to trust me because I can't explain the other reasons to you now." His deep blue gaze held Ellen. "I can only promise you, Ellen, that I won't let anything hurt her. I happen to care as much about what happens to her as you do, even if it doesn't look that way now. And I'll tell you another thing," he added in a gentle voice to soften the words he said, "despite what you say, think, or do, Sabrina is mine and she'll stay mine as long as I can hold her."

Ellen trembled with the fear that gripped her for she knew what he said was truth. Clay's captivating eyes told her with their intense gaze that he had the power to hold Sabrina and he intended to use it, and that nothing Ellen could say or do would stop him.

"I'll . . . I'll take her away."

"No Ellen, you won't. First, where and how can you take her in this country that I could not have the authorities find you. You can't take her back to England, for as you say she would be caught and punished. No, you are bound to me for the next two years and there is nothing you can do about it." He wanted now to ease the words he had just said. "Sabrina won't leave me . . . I won't let her go . . . but I won't let her be hurt either. Don't doubt for a moment that I can keep her . . . protect her from anything . . . or anyone."

"Except you."

"She doesn't need protection from me."

"There's something violent and angry in you, Clay Storm. Will she be caught between you and whatever it is you are fighting?"

"She has nothing to do with anything from the past."

"But it can reach out to touch her too?"

"No . . . I won't let it."

"Do you care for her Clay," Ellen said softly, "or are you using her somehow?"

"I care Ellen . . . believe me, I care."

Ellen was about to answer again when a sound came to

them. Sabrina had come out of her room and started down the short hall toward them. Clay turned to look in her direction . . . but Ellen's eyes remained on his face.

She watched the hard blue gaze soften to a warmth that reached out across the room to touch Sabrina. She saw the taut lips smile and could feel him reach for her without moving. His whole body seemed to lose its stiff angry stance and soften toward the slender woman who walked toward them.

Slowly, Ellen turned to look at Sabrina and saw the reflection of Clay's warm look in her eyes. Her heart skipped a beat when she realized Sabrina was beyond any words Ellen might say. She was hopelessly caught in his intoxicating aura and she did not want to leave it. She stopped in the doorway. Her words were for them both, but her flushed cheeks and glowing eyes were for Clay alone.

"Good morning," Sabrina said softly. With a sinking heart Ellen knew that there was nothing she could say to Sabrina that would reach her. She was helplessly, hopelessly in love with Clay Storm.

She read accurately Clay's quick look that challenged her to speak. Ellen remained silent.

Clay pushed himself away from the fireplace and walked to Sabrina's side. She gazed up into his eyes and the sweet familiar feeling of love swept her up into a blue sea and left her weak. How she wanted to rest against that broad chest and feel the hard arms enclose her and hold her.

Clay gazed down on her, fascinated that she could rouse him with a look, and that she looked so completely desirable fresh from bed. It also surprised him that even after a wild tumultuous night filled with passionate love he felt a renewal of need for her so quickly. He knew now there would never be an end to his need for her, that if he tasted her sweet love again and again he would never have enough.

Her cheeks grew pinker under his warm gaze, yet her eyes

held his without hesitation. He could not resist the urge to touch.

He reached out and gently touched her hair and smiled. "Good morning."

Clay turned to Ellen.

"Why don't you get Summer up?" he said. "After breakfast I'll take her and Sabrina swimming."

Ellen reluctantly left to do as he said. In a moment Clay drew Sabrina into his arms for a long lingering satisfying kiss.

"I swear," he said, as he brushed her hair with a light touch, "you're even more beautiful today."

"Clay," she whispered softly as her arms circled his waist. She closed her eyes and surrendered completely to the pleasure she felt when he held her so.

"Well, what do you say love?" he chuckled, "after we feed Summer, let's take her swimming."

"Clay, I've nothing to swim in."

He chuckled as he tightened one arm about her and let the other hand roam gently over seductive curves.

"Love, I could think of nothing better, and sometime when Summer isn't along we'll have to look into that. For now, anything would do."

She laughed softly, but before she could reply, Ellen and Summer came out of Clay's room. Reluctantly, Clay moved away from her.

When Summer came into the room, Clay went to her and scooped her up in his arms. She giggled in pleasure as he tossed her up, caught her and squeezed her, growling like a bear as he did.

Ellen silently went on to the kitchen to begin preparations for breakfast.

Sabrina watched Clay and Summer with a smile lighting her eyes. She loved all facets of Clay, but especially his deep love for Summer.

Clay laughingly assured Summer, when he could get a word in between Summer's delighted chatter, that yes, Sabrina was going to swim with them, and yes they could take a lunch and spend the morning.

It was only a short time until Ellen came to tell them that breakfast was ready. When breakfast was over, Clay told Ellen to pack up something they could snack on for lunch. While she did, Sabrina went to her room to see what she could find that she could swim in.

She had a chemise and a pair of white pantalettes. She cut the pantalettes short and carried them with her in a small bundle.

Clay and Sabrina walked through the woods toward the river while Summer skipped on ahead impatient with them for being so slow.

Clay put his arm about Sabrina's slim waist and they talked quietly as they walked.

When they arrived at the river, Summer had already tossed aside her clothes and her slim tanned body was splashing into the cool water where she swam like a young otter.

Sabrina put the lunch beneath the shade of the tree and lifted her bundle.

"I'll change in a moment," she said as she went behind a bush.

"Need any help?" Clay laughed.

"No thank you, I can manage to dress by myself."

"I know that," he chuckled, "I had hoped to help with the other part."

"Wicked man," she giggled.

Clay wore a pair of his old pants cut off just above the knees. He stood by a tree watching Summer cavort in the water. The rustle of the bushes drew his attention and he turned . . . to stand struck to admiring silence.

The chemises and cut off pantalettes were not sheer, but the way they clung to her stimulated his memory. He went to her side and reached to touch a bare soft shoulder. There was no way she could doubt the look she read so easily in his eyes. Her breath caught as a large hand held her waist and drew her closer.

Their lips inches from each other, their bodies tense and vibrant with awakened need . . .

"Papa! Papa! Sabrina!, come on in the water!"

Both Sabrina and Clay jumped with the shock of Summer's shrill happy voice, both began to laugh in guilty humor at the same time.

"Come on," Clay grinned. He took Sabrina's hand and walked toward the water.

"Clay, I really can't swim very well," she said.

Clay drew her closer to him.

"Don't worry love, I don't mind holding you close while you learn better."

They laughed, but Sabrina soon found, to her pleasure, that Clay meant exactly what he said. He took immediate advantage of her insecurity to caress her.

The morning was spent in laughter and fun in the water. It was Clay who called a halt after a while.

"Come on Summer, out of the water for a while. I don't want you to get too tired."

Obediently, Summer came from the water with Clay behind her. Sabrina waded out behind them. In a moment, an exuberant Summer was gathering wild flowers and berries which she ate at once. Clay laughed and turned to Sabrina. His eyes widened then grew warm with deep appreciation. Sabrina looked down at herself and gasped in surprise. The material, soaked completely, clung to her like a second skin . . . and was completely transparent.

Rose tipped breasts, chilled by the cool breeze, pushed against the thin fabric that covered them. Slim hips and legs were finely molded and left nothing to Clay's already warm imagination.

Casting a quick look to see that Summer was safely still in sight, he went to Sabrina and put his arms about her.

"What a delicious treat you are," he murmured, "so sweet." His lips found her quite willing ones, and clung for a heart stopping moment, then reluctantly he moved away from her.

"You had best dress Sabrina. I'm not made of iron and you are much too inviting."

Sabrina changed quickly and they sat beneath the shade of a tree. It was then a subject came up that Clay would just as soon had not. Sabrina sat with her back braced against the trunk of the tree and Clay lay with his head in her lap and his eyes closed. For a few minutes there was a completely relaxed silence.

"Clay?"

"What?"

"The dress Hawk gave me. I wanted to wear it, but it's just disappeared. Did you put it somewhere?"

Clay remained quiet for a moment, then he said quietly, "Sabrina . . . I took the dress back to Hawk. I also told him I didn't want him to give you any more gifts."

Sabrina was shocked and sat for a moment in stunned silence.

"Clay . . . why? I . . . it was so beautiful. I thought it was something special. Sort of an offer of friendship between Hawk and us."

Clay sat up and turned to her.

"Sabrina, the dress was nothing special. It meant nothing. I asked you once before and I'll ask you again. I don't want you to take any gifts from Hawk. There was nothing special about that dress, but if you want one like it, I'll cure a deer-skin and one can be made."

How could she explain to him that she still believed that the dress had meant something to Hawk. She had no way of fighting what Clay said. She was new to this territory, to this frontier life and unsure of what more the gesture might have meant to Hawk. She felt it was a gesture of kindness and of friendship yet, Clay's attitude made it sound so different. Still she was hurt that he had taken it from her and returned it with hard words instead of letting her give it back with some kind of explanation.

"Clay . . . the dress was a gesture of friendship to me. Couldn't I have taken it back? At least I could have tried to explain why I couldn't keep it."

"No," he said bluntly.

Trying to contain the anger within her, she choked back words she would have said.

"But . . ." she began to protest.

"I don't want you to even think of going to the village. First, you would get yourself lost trying to find it, and I'd have to search the countryside for you and second, I don't want you to give Summer the idea that it's all right to go there."

"Clay . . . didn't her mother come from that village? Why shouldn't Summer go there? Doesn't she have family there? Why . . ."

She stopped talking when she saw Clay's eyes harden to a cold dark blue. He took hold of her shoulders in a firm grip and held her eyes in an unrelenting gaze.

"Sabrina, I think I want you more than anything in my life, but we've got to have one thing clear between us. Your past is yours and I'll never question it . . . but my past is mine, and I don't want it dredged up. Leave it alone Sabrina, let the past die and just reach for the future."

The words that closed her away from his past were softened by the other words . . . sweeter words, and the ones Sabrina reached for. I want you more than anything else in my life.

He watched the tear touched angry eyes soften and was satisfied that he had effectively stopped her before anything damaging could be said or done between them.

"I want Summer to have a good life. I want you to teach her all you can, and when she's old enough we'll send her East to school. I have plans for her that don't include that village."

"I'll do all I can for Summer, Clay," she answered. But deep inside she could not stifle the feeling that something was drastically wrong. Clay held something inside that he refused to let anyone touch. She was frightened by it . . . and Clay read her emotions easily, as he always would.

"I know you will, love," he smiled as he drew her closer to him. "You are a loving person, and Summer and I both need your love . . . desperately," he added softly as he bent to touch her mouth with a gentle lingering kiss.

There was no way for her to deny her need for him. She knew that she loved him beyond anything else. Caught in the magic of a kiss that would always be able to weave a spell about her, she clung to him and surrendered with a deep sigh of pleasure.

All thoughts scattered helplessly as she felt his long lean body hard and warm against hers and the flame of desire leap to vibrant life.

His mouth claimed hers in a deeper and deeper kiss that turned her bones to liquid and wiped away every thought but the strength of the arms that bound her to him and the burning need for his possession.

It was a very reluctant Clay who moved away from Sabrina when a hungry Summer returned.

They ate a pleasant meal together, then despite Summer's protests, Clay said the time had come for them to return home.

Again Summer scampered on ahead while hand in hand, Sabrina and Clay walked slowly home. Both aware of the deep desire to be together, and both aware that when the moon rose they would be.

What they were not aware of was an incident that was happening at the same time, an incident that would change the course of both of their lives.

Thirteen

Hawk sat in his lodge, motionless, as he had been for several hours. A woman had come earlier with a bowl of food as she always had. It sat beside him now, cold and untouched.

The sun was high overhead when he slowly rose and left his lodge. He stood outside and squinted in the bright sun, gazing at another lodge that sat less than a hundred feet from his, then he began to walk slowly in that direction.

When he reached the door of the lodge, he stood for a few minutes as if he was still, after so much thought, uncertain of whether what he was doing could be accomplished the way he planned.

Resolutely he squared his shoulders and called out softly to the man he knew was within.

"My Father, your son would enter your lodge and speak with you."

A deep voice called out to him to enter. Hawk pushed the door covering aside and went inside.

It was dimly lit within, both from pale beams of light and the embers of a small fire, before which sat a man. He was a man whose age could not be guessed. The skin on face and hands were dark and lined, yet the body seemed strong. The dark intelligent eyes glittered with interest, amusement and a drop of question that Hawk recognized immediately. Yet

Hawk stood, still unsure of how to speak the thoughts he had.

"Sit my son," the old man said in a firm yet gentle voice.

Hawk sat crosslegged on the ground opposite his father with the pale glow of the burning embers between them. The old man chuckled gently.

"After all these years is there still a thing of which my son is afraid to speak to me?"

"No my Father, I am not afraid to speak to you of anything. I am only afraid of words that might cause you pain."

"Pain has been felt many times Hawk, but still I survive." The dark eyes smiled, "Speak."

"Swift Doe . . . she is to marry within four days."

"Yes, it will be a good marriage. Swift Doe is a good woman."

"Yes, she is. She will be a good wife, and Sleeping Wolf will be a good husband."

"Is that why you came to speak to me this day, to tell me what I already know?"

"No, it is not."

"Then speak what is in your heart, Hawk."

"I would have guests invited."

"There are many."

"No . . . others."

"Who?"

"There is a white woman I would ask to come."

"And who is this white woman and where is her lodge?"

"Her name is Sabrina . . . her lodge . . . she lives with Clay Storm."

The words were said quietly, and for several moments their eyes held, and there was a deep expressive silence. Then the old man spoke again.

"You would ask her to come alone?"

"No my Father. I would ask her to bring Singing Bells'

child . . . and I would ask Clay to come too."

Again the old man was silent, and Hawk grew tense. Surprised at himself for the need within him for understanding, he wanted his father to understand what he hardly understood himself.

Again, as he had many times in the past few days, he allowed deep purple eyes and a shy sweet smile to linger before his eyes for a moment. Still he could not believe that she seemed always to linger somewhere in the depths of his mind, to reappear when he least wanted her to.

"He will not return here."

"Not if I ask him, my Father. He knows what is in my heart."

"Then . . ."

"I would tell him that you desire that he come and bring the child with him."

"He will not believe you. He also knows what is in my heart. He remembered my words too well. From that day he has never come to this village. Why would he come now?"

"I . . . I have seen him, talked to him. I also know Swift Doe has gone to see the child many times and spoken to Clay often. Clay has not been to our lodges . . . but he has been near the village."

"How do you know?"

"I have heard the signals we shared as children. I have talked to him, and I know Swift Doe has also."

The old man sighed deeply and his eyes lingered on the half dead fire, yet Hawk knew his thoughts were elsewhere. He remained silent.

Memories flickered in the dark eyes, memories both sweet and painful. A day past . . . words said . . . friendship and love severed.

Again the old man sighed deeply, as if the memories were a heavy burden.

"My Father . . . if we open the door, maybe the child will find her way back to us."

"Even if he doesn't want her to."

"Sometimes the gods plan things and we have nothing to say about it. What happened so long ago was wrong. Maybe the gods have found a way to change it."

"The white woman?"

"Maybe."

The old man, despite what Hawk thought, felt the unspoken words and emotions. He knew there were things in Hawk's mind he preferred not to say. He also knew Hawk had plans in his heart that were different from what he spoke.

There was no way he could tell Hawk that he could sense the strong emotions just below the surface and that he was using his father's love to help him. He wondered if this was not the way the gods had planned it also.

"If Clay agrees," he began, "what do you think you will accomplish?"

"I would have Summer know her people. One day I would have her hear our side of the story. It is obvious Clay has told her nothing, for Swift Doe says she is not permitted to come here. In fact," he added softly, watching the old man's face, "she has been told nothing about her mother and . . . she is not permitted to visit her . . . grave."

He watched the old man's face flinch in pain, and hated what he was doing, yet he felt the end would justify the means.

"Do you believe word from me will bring him here . . . and the child?"

"It's the only thing that will."

"Then tell him . . . tell him to come here for Swift Doe's wedding. And tell him . . . tell him I desire to see the child."

Hawk knew the sacrifice it took for his father to refute

words he had said so long ago and ask Clay to return. There were no words he could say to make the pain any less. He rose slowly and walked out, knowing his father's mind was caught in the past and he would not hear the soft words of farewell.

The old man sat silently. The pain was more for knowing his son was using him for some kind of revenge. He was old enough and wise enough to know that this kind of revenge often hurt the one who used it more than the one it was used against.

Hawk was on his way back to his own lodge when he stopped. Swift Doe stood in front of it, obviously waiting for him. At this moment she was the last person he wanted to talk to.

His father had refused to say the words of condemnation for what was in his mind and heart; Swift Doe would not be so gentle.

He continued to walk toward her, steeling himself for whatever she might say.

"Hawk, I would speak with you," she said before he could pass her by and enter his lodge.

He stopped and waited patiently, but his eyes avoided hers.

"Hawk, I have watched you. You have spoken to your father. Was it about Clay and the white woman?"

"It is not your concern Swift Doe."

"It is my wedding, Hawk. I will not have it used as a means for your revenge. If you want to cause more problems, please do it at another time."

"I do not intend to cause any more problems. I am not the cause of the first."

"You are as much responsible as Clay. Your combined stubborness and pride have caused great loss to many in this tribe and elsewhere. Why do you and Clay not make peace,

Hawk? Why continue this battle?"

"When he returns what belongs to us. When he admits he stole what would never have belonged to him otherwise . . . maybe then there can be peace between us."

"What is past is gone, Hawk. Singing Bells is dead. Do you expect a man to give up his child just to soften your heart. Why do you not speak to him of sharing?"

"We do not need to share. She should be part of our tribe. She should be what her mother was to us. I see it in her as you must have. She should be returned to her home and those who will need her in the future."

"How can you speak so! If Summer were yours, would you be able to give her up so easily? Think with more than your jealous anger, it is not becoming to a man of your position! You are foolish and stupid and you will never find what you want along that path!"

Swift Doe's eyes flashed in anger and her words were such that Hawk would never tolerate from anyone in their tribe. They blinded him momentarily and he reached out and struck her sharply across the face knocking her to the ground at his feet.

He regretted it the moment he did it, but he could not change what he had done.

Swift Doe knew Hawk well, maybe better than he knew himself. She knew the blow had been in anger and guilt and that Hawk within was a gentle man. She saw the hurt in his eyes, yet she knew as a young chief he would not be able to apologize without losing face, and this he would not do.

Slowly, she rose and walked away from him, knowing his eyes followed her all the way to her lodge.

Hawk pushed aside the covering of his door and stepped inside, and for the first time the emotions he felt showed plainly on his face. He took a deep breath and firmly controlled his thoughts. He trembled from the effort of controlling his anger . . . anger at himself for allowing his emotions to make him strike out at a woman who could not defend herself against him. Somewhere deep inside, a small voice told him Swift Doe was right, but he could not, would not allow it to be heard. He had carried his pain and anger too long.

After several minutes he had regained control of himself. He would not leave for Clay's home today for it would bring him to the cabin late at night. No, he did not want Clay alone when he extended the invitation, he wanted Sabrina and Summer both present. Their excitement would make it hard for Clay. Then the addition of the words of his father, Hawk prayed, would make it nearly impossible for Clay to refuse.

He made himself gather his patience to wait, and slowly the day began to fade. He stood outside his lodge and watched the full moon rise. He wondered what Clay was doing at the moment, and what effect the well laid plans he had taken so much time to prepare would have on the violet eyed woman who continued to linger in the shadows of his mind.

Sabrina and Ellen sat on the porch and watched the same golden moon rise and bathe the area in a pale shimmering light.

Clay had decided it was his turn to tell Summer a story or so and see her tucked safely in bed. He had gathered a sleepy Summer up and carried her inside leaving the two women to the warm comfortable star studded night.

There was a moment or so of peaceful silence as they sat and absorbed the rare and tranquil beauty of the wilderness about them. Only the soft trill of chickadees and night animals broke the silence.

"Oh Ellen, isn't it beautiful here? It's so peaceful. One can breathe out here . . . feel and think like you never could in England."

"Yes . . . it's beautiful," Ellen agreed, but her voice carried less conviction than her words. Sabrina became aware more of what she did not say than what she had said. She reached out and took one of Ellen's hands in hers.

"Oh Ellen," she said softly, "are you really so very unhappy here? You certainly have no more work to do than you did in my uncle's mansion, and Clay is very good to both of us. Summer is a pleasure to care for. It's not really so difficult, is it?"

"I never complained of the work, Sabrina. It's just . . . well . . . I'm worried about you."

"Me? Why worry about me? I'm happy here. In fact, I haven't been so content or happy since before Uncle Eustice died. I . . . I really don't care if I ever go home again."

"It's because of him," Ellen replied. "When I saw him on the dock, I knew he was dangerous. I tried to warn you then."

"Warn me about what, Ellen?" Sabrina said a little sharper than she meant. "I don't think Clay has treated either of us in a way to warrant any criticism."

"Sabrina?"

"What?"

"Do you love him?"

"Yes Ellen, I do. Is that so wrong . . . to love?"

"It depends. Love isn't a token thing. He's got a way with that smile and those blue eyes, of taking what he wants. But what's he give? Inside him is something angry and hurt. Until those things are gone, do you think there's room for giving love?"

"If there is hurt inside, Ellen, I'd like to ease it. If there is anger I'd like to calm it. I don't really believe love should ask absolute perfection unless one can offer it."

"Child, you're young . . . you believe . . ."

"Yes Ellen, I believe. I believe Clay loves me."

"Has he told you he did?" Ellen asked softly.

For the first time Sabrina realized that Clay had told her many times that he wanted her . . . that he needed her. But not once had he said he loved her. For a moment, that realization silenced her.

"Sabrina," Ellen said firmly, "if the man tumbles you into his bed and gets you with babe, then what? When your two years are over and he sends you home with a bastard child, what will you do?"

"Ellen!"

"Don't Ellen me. Do you think you would be the first? I would be rich if I had a shilling for every time it's happened. I need you . . . I want you . . . but no I love you and I want to marry you. No, it's climb into my bed, little girl, then go home one day and leave me alone."

"I don't want to hear you talk like this, Ellen. Clay is not like that. He's an honorable man!"

"You need to hear the truth!"

"That's not the truth, and if you want to continue, I shall go to bed. I don't want to hear anything else like that about Clay, do you hear!"

They both stopped talking and looked at each other in shock. It was the first time in their relationship they had used harsh words and anger toward each other.

Sabrina knelt before Ellen.

"Oh Ellen, don't let's quarrel. Try to understand. I love Clay, and I will continue to love him for as long as there's a breath in my body. There is nothing I can do or want to do about it. You'll see . . . one day you will see him as I do."

Ellen held her close in her arms, loving her like a daughter and distressed with the thought that she still did not believe

163

Clay would marry Sabrina. She sighed deeply knowing right at the moment there was no way she could convince a girl blinded by love that she was destined for pain and disillusionment.

Ellen rose to her feet.

"I'm going to bed, are you coming?"

"No, the night is too beautiful. I'll stay out just for a little while longer. Don't worry so about me Ellen, I'll be fine. Good night."

"Good night," Ellen said. She walked into the now dark house and soon Sabrina heard her door close.

Sabrina leaned back against the pillar that supported the roof and closed her eyes. The words Ellen had said forced their way again into her mind. Desperately she clung to her belief in Clay. She knew there was no way she could deny the love and need she had for him, but did he love her? Had he ever once told her he loved her?

She relived every moment they had shared together, and despite her resistance to it the idea came again and again . . . no, he had never said I love you, though he had heard her say it again and again.

A small seed of doubt was planted, and though she chose to ignore it, it fell into fertile ground where one day it would sprout tendrils that would tear at her heart.

Pushing all other thoughts aside, she chose to ignore them and enjoy the beauty of the night.

She rose and walked down the two steps to the ground and stood looking up at the huge full moon and the black velvet blanket of the night sky that was studded with brilliant stars. How close they seemed out here, she thought. It was as if one could reach up and pluck one.

She turned at a small sound and saw Clay leaning against the pillar of the porch watching her. When she saw him, she smiled an open welcoming smile.

164

He returned it and walked slowly down the steps to her side. Without a word he reached for he and drew her into his arms.

She came without hesitation or reserve, her arms lifting to encircle his neck.

Still he did not speak, but bent his head to lightly brush her lips with his.

"Come and walk with me?" he whispered.

"Where?"

"Down by the stream, it's beautiful there at night."

She smiled and nodded. He kept his arm about her waist as they walked toward the encircling woods.

Fourteen

They walked side by side, his arm about her waist and hers about his. They were content to remain silent and to enjoy the beauty surrounding them and the new and gentle sensitivity they had for each other.

The night sounds were soft and mellow and blended like quiet music with the gently bubbling stream. A quiet peace touched them and they did not need to speak to know they were sharing the same thoughts and emotions.

Near the stream was a soft grassy area that was arched by the branches of two huge trees. They stood together and watched the moon dapple the water with flecks of gold.

He seemed to be in an introspective mood and she was too content to rest against him and enjoy the feel of his arms about her to disturb his thoughts. Absently he rubbed his chin against the softness of her hair, and his hand captured the soft mass of it. She could hear the solid beat of his heart as she lay against him, and again the sense of security filled her. Clay would keep her safe. She firmly pushed aside all of Ellen's words, holding firmly to the belief that Clay did love her, and one day soon they would marry and be together always.

Clay's mind drifted from the sweet beauty in his arms to the idea that some dark threat could possibly separate them.

At the thought his arm tightened spasmodically, eliciting a gasp of shock from a breathless Sabrina.

"Clay!"

"I'm sorry, I didn't mean to hurt you."

"You didn't hurt me, you just surprised me."

Clay released her and took her hand, drawing her down to sit beside him on the soft grass. Bracing his back against the closest tree, he held her against him.

"Clay?"

"Umm?"

"Have you always lived here?"

"Seems like it sometimes, but no. I was born in England. My parents came here when I was about six. My father . . . well, he had a job to do in the colonies."

"Have your parents returned home?"

"Yes, several years ago," Clay laughed. "Why so many questions, love? Are you going to judge me on my background?"

"Good heavens, Clay," Sabrina laughed in return, "I wouldn't care where or when you were born. I just wanted to know you better."

Again he chuckled a warm chuckle and held her closer.

"All right . . . let me see. My parents brought me here at six. I fell in love with . . . the country. When it was time for them to return home, I chose to stay. Not too long after I married Singing Bells and Summer came along. That's all there is to my uneventful life, the rest you know."

Sabrina held him close to her, aware he was trying to laugh away her thoughts and questions and wondering why it suddenly made her afraid.

"Singing Bells," she whispered softly, and was more aware of the thundering silence. "Clay, do you think that I am frightened of the past? I am not. I know you must have loved her deeply. I would not want to change that. I only want to love you now. I only want to help fill the emptiness you must have felt when you lost her."

Clay sat up and took her shoulders, then slowly he turned her, lowering her to the ground and bending above her.

"I don't know what to think, Sabrina. You come along from nowhere, a tiny sweet child woman, and you suddenly fill my life. Now you shatter every thought I had by understanding everything I feel. You take me by storm, Sabrina, and it leaves me a little short of breath and words. All I can truthfully say is you do fill all the emptiness, and you do sooth all the pain I felt, and," he whispered, "I do need you desperately."

He bent to capture her lips in a deep and searching kiss. Her arms drew him to her and he pressed her against the warm ground.

Joyfully she felt the length of his body against hers and the strong arms that surrounded her.

"I love you Clay," she murmured as she closed her eyes and felt the hot branding mouth search avidly for more sensitive and vulnerable spots.

She could feel the fire of his intense need and she surrendered to it completely. She felt the cool air touch her warm skin as he drew the restricting clothes off.

Both were caught helplessly in the burning hungry desire that would exist forever in each touch, each kiss. Hungry mouths tasted and sought more, hands caressed, and built the flames that consumed them. Bodies touched, clung and molded together into one. They filled each other completely, moving together to the summit of their world.

Clay felt the magic of her enclose and hold him within her, and he dove to the depths of her, thrusting deep within until he heard her moan his name softly and felt her lift to meet him.

From that moment on the existing world slipped from

their grasp and they knew nothing but the surging passion that joined them.

They shuddered to a completion that left them gasping and clinging to one another as if they were the only solid reality in the world.

"Dear God," Clay whispered against her throat, "I don't believe there is more beauty in the world than you."

They held one another until they could control the turbulent world about them. Then Clay moved his weight from her, and lay on his side, drawing her safe and snug in the curve of his body. Lingering light kisses touched her sweat slicked brow, and strong gentle hands soothed and caressed her trembling body. She rested against him aware only of the deep pleasure his gentle strength gave her.

"Clay, I want always to be with you, to have you hold me and love me. Oh, Clay, don't let us ever let this slip away, don't let anything come between us. I think I should die a little if you were ever to grow tired of me and send me away."

He raised on one elbow and looked down into her face touched by the pale light of the moon.

"Sabrina, you sound frightened."

"I am."

"Why? In God's name do you believe I would ever let you slip away now that I've found you? I think you are more frightened of someone else's words, aren't you?"

"I . . . Ellen . . ."

"I knew. Listen to me, my sweet innocent. We have something very rare and very special. Don't let Ellen's dark thoughts linger in your mind. We have found something very sweet and wonderful. Don't let her words destroy it Sabrina. Stay with me . . . trust me, and one day everything will be good for us."

He lifted her chin with his hand and kissed her gently yet possessively, and she felt his reassuring strength surround her and lift her.

Ellen's words of warning faded before the warmth of Clay's tenderness and she was lost to any other reality but the need to stay with him, be with him always.

There was no return from this path. She had taken Clay's hand and walked with him to the crest of the world where they could see eternity, and now she could not, would not leave him to return to a world that would be dark and empty without him.

"I want to be with you, Clay. No matter what. I have never been so happy as I am now. I will never go unless you send me . . . never, and my heart would break if you should."

She heard the soft murmur of her name as he drew her within the circle of his arms and rocked her gently against him.

The night drifted slowly on, but the lovers were unaware as they spoke in soft whispers and caressed with gentle hands. Again they tasted the nectar of love that was sweet and heady and left them drunk with the wonder of it.

It was in the wee hours of the morning that Clay kissed her at her bedroom door and she went inside reluctant even then for separation.

Although they slept apart, their dreams touched each other's and they convinced themselves that soon this would end and they could be together forever. But the rising sun was to bring the dark clouds into their sun touched world and shake it from its course into one they had not dreamed of.

Clay stirred awake just as the sun began to crest the horizon. He rose slowly from a bed that felt decidedly cold and empty without Sabrina.

After he dressed, he went to gather wood for the fire so that Ellen would not have to. Today, he thought, he would begin some kind of campaign to win the reluctant worried Ellen to him. He did not want her to be able to upset Sabrina anymore with her dire threats. He knew it would be difficult, but for Sabrina's sake, he had to try.

By the time he came back into the kitchen and had lit the fire, Ellen was already entering the room.

"Morning Ellen," Clay smiled, "sleep well?"

That Ellen's attitude was rather chilled he sensed immediately. She sniffed and replied with a well reserved good morning, then began to putter among her pots and pans to keep her eyes from meeting the blue gaze that watched her.

He refused to allow her to ignore him.

"You'd best get it out of your system, Ellen. We live too close to each other to spend our time angry with one another."

His smile was gentle, and his eyes were kind, almost shy and childlike. He knew his magnetism well and he did not hesitate to use his full charm on her.

"You mean too much to Sabrina for us not to be friends," he said. "I don't want her hurt in any way . . . not by me . . . not by you either."

Ellen was caught up in the boylike smile and her always sensitive heart began to melt under the gaze.

"I couldn't sleep too well last night," she began hesitantly. "I . . . I heard you come back . . . late."

"We took a walk down beside the stream," he said honestly. "It was beautiful. You should take a walk there some night. You would enjoy it."

"Clay," she said quietly. "I'm afraid for her."

"Why?" he said gently.

"She believes too easily . . . she trusts. She'll get hurt. What will happen when her two years are over . . . what will happen if she finds herself . . . with babe?" she added hesitantly. "She's a gentle girl. To be cast aside would crush her."

Clay went to Ellen's side and placed an arm about her shoulder. It, and the warmth of his blue eyes and open smile did much to shatter her equilibrium.

"Ellen, contrary to what you believe, I would be more than pleased if Sabrina carried my child. I would also keep her bound to me."

"But no marriage," Ellen said distressed.

"One day . . . but not now. Ellen, I know you don't understand, but can you try to have patience? We're happy and Sabrina would like you to share it. Don't hurt her by being angry. I promise you Ellen, all the dark shadows you see will one day be wiped away and everything will be all right. I also promise that I will never deliberately hurt Sabrina in any way. Can that be enough now to make us at least try to be friends again?"

Ellen was caught helplessly in his startlingly warm blue eyes and questioning smile. Against her will she began to melt.

"I . . . I'll try."

"Ellen, another thing. Sabrina is sensitive. I don't like to see her upset by words that don't need to be said now. Let me take care of her future Ellen. I can, and I will . . . but you can make it a whole lot easier by accepting things and not saying things that might make it harder for her."

Again Ellen nodded, mesmerized by Clay's blue eyes and almost pleading gentle voice.

Seeing her acceptance, even though it was less than complete, made him smile and give her a reassuring hug and a quick kiss on her blushing cheek.

"Let me help you with breakfast Ellen," he said with a laugh. "It will give you some extra time. Maybe you can take a walk along the stream."

"Oh no sir," Ellen said aghast. "Men don't belong in the kitchen, especially since you bought my time to do this."

Again he laughed a resonant deep laugh that made Ellen join him.

"Who do you think did the cooking around here before you came? I'll have you know madam, that I can handle it quite well."

Ellen did not doubt at the moment that Clay Storm could handle just about any kind of problem that presented itself.

Despite her protests, Clay did help her and she was surprised both that the food was excellent and that she had enjoyed his presence so completely. When everything was ready for the table, Clay announced that he would go waken Summer and Sabrina, before Ellen could protest, he was gone.

Summer always wakened easily and with bright good nature. He bent over her and kissed her and shook her awake.

"Come on little one, breakfast is ready. Let's go wake up Sabrina."

With this suggestion, Summer quickly rose, dressed and she and Clay walked across the short hall to Sabrina's room.

Clay stood leaning against the door frame in silent admiration of Sabrina's fragile beauty. He watched with deep pleasure, her sleepy eyes open and light with pleasure when she looked at him. He longed for the day when he could be with her to waken her and hold her warm body close to him and kiss the light into her eyes. He felt a surge of renewed passion that took him by surprise. He would never cease to wonder at the thought that no matter how often he possessed her he would never cease to want her more. It would be a never ending source of need that he would never be able to control.

Sabrina and Summer were laughing together and he would have given anything to join them and have an hour of laughing and sharing.

Sabrina's eyes lifted to his, wide and filled with uncontrolled love. It caught his breath and stirred him to the point where he very nearly sent Summer along to the kitchen so that he could hold her for a moment. But he controlled it, for he knew a moment would not be enough.

"Out of bed," he laughed. "Ellen and I have been working for hours to make you a nice breakfast."

"I'll be right there," Sabrina answered. Her eyes were held by the mischievous look in his warm gaze that surveyed her thoroughly and she blushed when she read the desire well that he would be more than happy to help her dress.

Clay and Summer went on to the kitchen and Sabrina followed within minutes. She had tied her long hair away from her face and donned a pale blue cotton dress that accented her eyes. Clay's appreciative look told her how well she looked.

Sabrina was at first surprised then pleased when she saw Clay's efforts to charm Ellen, and that they were successful for Ellen seemed to unfold before her eyes.

The meal was a pleasant and rewarding affair and was nearly over when the sound of approaching horses filled the air. Even Clay was a little surprised, for visitors were a rare thing.

Clay rose and walked out of the kitchen and crossed the large living room to the front door with an excited Summer right behind him. Both Sabrina and Ellen rose slowly to follow. They stepped out on the porch to see Clay, who had stiffened and was watching riders in the distance. Their eyes followed his.

"It's Hawk," Sabrina said.

"Yes," Clay said softly. Sabrina was aware of the tension in his body and the strange quiet tenor of his voice.

They stood silently watching Hawk ride slowly toward them. When he reached the bottom of the steps, he reined his horse to a halt and slid effortlessly to the ground.

"Good morning Hawk," Sabrina smiled a warm welcome. As before, she was impressed with his immense size and aura of masculine power. When he smiled at her, his dark eyes lit with pleasure which extended to Summer and Ellen. It was only strained and shadowed when his dark eyes met Clay's which had darkened to a cold grey-blue.

"Good morning, Sabrina. It is a beautiful day."

"Yes it is. I . . ."

"You didn't come here to discuss the weather, did you Hawk?" Clay said coldly.

"No, Clay, I did not. I came to bring you and . . . the ones who live with you, Summer, your daughter, a message from Black Cloud."

Sabrina, standing close to Clay, could feel his body grow taut. She looked up at him in surprise. She was even more shocked at the look on his face that within seconds went from surprise, to anger and then to disbelief . . . then absolutely unreadable.

"Black Cloud has sent a message to me?" Clay said in a deceptively soft voice that spoke eloquently of his disbelief. "What would Black Cloud have to say now, to me?"

"Soon, our village will celebrate the wedding of one of our women. She is a woman close to Black Cloud's heart . . . and to mine."

"Swift Doe," Clay said softly.

"Yes, Swift Doe."

"Why does he tell me this now?"

"He would," Hawk said quietly, "ask you to attend this wedding. He would also ask you to bring the child of Singing Bells. He would look into the child's eyes and speak with her. He would also be pleased if the women who live in your house would attend as honored guests."

Hawk could clearly see the refusal in Clay's eyes. He

spoke again before Clay could put it into words.

"Black Cloud has said these words, Clay, not I. He would see Singing Bells' child. Is it too much to ask for an old man to look into the eyes of a child? Is it too great a thing for you to give, to let him speak with her?"

Again Clay was about to speak when Summer's hand slipped into his and her wide dark eyes were lifted to his in absolute trust in his kindness.

"Oh Papa, can't we please go?" she said softly.

Clay held her hand, but his eyes were on Hawk whose face was completely unreadable.

To Sabrina it seemed as if there had never been such a silence. She sensed some kind of battle between the two men who faced each other.

"This will change nothing, Hawk," Clay said in a firm voice.

"Do these words mean you will come?"

Silence again, a heart stopping silence.

"Yes, Hawk. Tell Black Cloud we will come. But tell him nothing will change unless Hawk and his people understand that I will not let anything or anyone take what is mine."

For a moment it seemed as if Hawk would surrender to the anger that boiled within him. Then with tremendous control he smiled.

"I shall tell him. We will see you in three days. It will be a good celebration."

Without another word to any of them, he turned and remounted.

He smiled at Sabrina and Summer. Then he turned and rode away, and in the same explosive silence, filled with deep curiosity, they watched him go.

Fifteen

Clay watched Hawk's retreating figure until it disappeared from sight. No one spoke, and all of them felt the tension in Clay. Even Summer remained silent.

After a few more minutes, Clay seemed to become aware of their presence. His body visibly relaxed, and he lifted Summer into his arms. Sabrina alone sensed the need in Clay to hold Summer close to him. To Sabrina, who had become sensitive to Clay's emotions, it was as if he were afraid someone or something was trying to take her away from him.

Clay turned and walked back into the house and Ellen and Sabrina silently followed. They returned to breakfast which was finished quickly in silence.

After breakfast, Clay left the house and they heard him ride away. He did not return the balance of the day, and by midnight Summer was safely tucked in bed and Ellen had long since sought rest. Sabrina lay awake, aware of the loneliness without Clay, and wondering what had upset him so . . . and where he had gone.

Slowly she drifted into a dream filled sleep. The hours ticked slowly by, and the moon rose high in the heavens before the sound of an approaching horse told of Clay's return.

To any casual observer, Clay would have looked the same, but one who knew him well would have known at once he had been drinking.

He walked straight, and carried himself with no outward sign, except the fine pinpoint light in his eyes and desperate hunge that only one person could reach and appease.

He opened the door of the house silently and walked across to his room. Inside he stood and looked down on Summer who slept content and safe.

Just as quietly he moved across the hall and opened Sabrina's door without a sound.

He stood by her bed watching a pale ray of moonlight move across her sleeping face. Her gold hair spread across he pillow and she lay relaxed and breathing slowly. He watched her for several moments as if he wanted to memorize every line, every feature.

Gently he reached down and touched her hair, savoring the silken feel of it. Then he touched her face. She sighed in her sleep and turned toward him.

He sat down on the bed beside her and bent to taste the sweet unawareness of her soft parted lips. Her eyes opened slowly.

"Sabrina," he whispered, "my sweet, loving Sabrina." It was the deep touch of pain in his voice, of urgent need that made her lift her arms about his neck and draw him close. Then lips touched, blended, and sought to fill the emptiness within.

He slid his arms beneath her and drew her up to him, holding her close and rocked her gently against him.

She could not understand why she felt she was comforting him as if he were a lost child. She clung to him and felt the solid beat of his heart as he pressed her close to him.

She did not want to question his reasons, she knew only

that he needed her and her love for him filled her and lifted her until she could think and feel nothing but him. Again, his mouth sought hers, hungry and possessive, and willingly she returned the blazing heat of awakened passion.

He lay her back against the pillows, and for a moment their eyes held in mutual question and acceptance. He smiled and reached to touch her cheek gently.

He rose and began to remove his clothes, and in the soft moonlight Sabrina lay and watched his bronzed muscular body. She enjoyed looking at him and it caused a shiver of expectant delight to course through her to know that soon she could reach to touch him and feel the hard, lean body close to hers.

Then he was beside her, drawing her close to him and again seeking her lips to brand her forever his. She tasted the sweet tang of brandy and realized he had been drinking. But she didn't care for already her senses had begun to lose touch with reality.

The nightgown caused him very little trouble for he simply drew it up over her head and tossed it aside.

Despite the fact that he had drunk considerably, he was still aware of his own desire to give her as much pleasure as she did him. He lingered over each kiss, exploring her mouth as if he had a world filled with time.

His hands gently caressed her, warming her and making her stir and press against him. To her reeling senses, it seemed as if they reached every vulnerable spot that sent the currents coursing through every nerve of her body until she could have cried out with the ecstatic pleasure. His lips followed the course his hands had begun and soon the soft sounds of uncontrolled passion reached him.

He held himself with steel reserve until he felt her slip beyond reality. Then and only then did he sheath himself deeply within her. She moaned his name softly over and over as they began to move together in a spiraling flame of desire that rose up and up.

She was a live flame in his arms, a wild passionate woman that enclosed him and burned deeply within him until he knew that he could never be content, never find fulfillment with any other woman. She was complete woman moving urgently beneath him seeking to hold him closer and closer.

His breath came in harsh rasping gasps and hers was an answering breathlessness.

With a force that rocked their world, they left all control behind muscular hips drove him deeply within. Her eyes were closed as she surrendered completely to the surging completion that tossed them like rudderless ships before a violent consuming storm.

For an eternal instant they could only cling to each other and tremble with the magic force of their love that overcame every thought and movement.

They lay entwined, exhausted, yet sated as they had never been before. Clay started to move away from her, but Sabrina clung.

"I'm heavy for you."

"You are welcome weight," she replied softly as her hands gently caressed his sweat covered back. "Oh Clay, talk to me, tell me what hurts you so, let me help you."

"Woman," he replied, "you sweet and beautiful woman. You are all the healing I need. Just hold me and let me hold you. Sabrina, your love is all I need."

His lips gently touched her mouth in gratitude and love for the sweetness of her giving.

He rolled away from her and lay beside her, then he drew her snug and safe against him.

One hand gently soothed her still trembling body while the other held her close to him. After a long silent moment he realized that again she slept.

He thought of her words, knew what she wanted to hear and was angry at his own fear. Fear of words that might change their lives. Knowing he could not make her completely his by marriage until all threat to her safety and future with him was over.

He thought of Hawk's visit, and knew he must never let Hawk or his people know Sabrina's value to him. They would use her love for him and his for her to get the one thing they wanted most of all . . . Summer.

He knew he had to face Hawk's challenging offer. But he knew he would not let Hawk use Sabrina against him.

Somehow, he thought, he would prove to them once and for all that Clay Storm took and held what was his and no one would be allowed to take it from him.

When he felt Sabrina's complete relaxation, and knew she was in the depths of sleep, he rose gently from the bed.

He stood beside it and bent to give her one last gentle kiss. Then he drew the covers over her, dressed and quietly left the room.

It would be a day before they began their trip to the Indian village. A day in which Sabrina tried to control Summer's vibrant enthusiasm . . . and her own.

She had known some virulent thing existed between Hawk, his people, and the man she loved. She was determined to try and find the source of it and do her best to destroy it, destroy the anger and hatred she had felt, by the power of love that filled her.

Again she felt Hawk himself was the largest problem. If she could, at this marriage festival, she would try to talk with him alone. Maybe he could tell her the dark secret that seemed to turn Clay into a man she could not understand.

Clay had told them they must pack enough to last for several days. She had questioned this.

"Several days, Clay?"

"Yes, my sweet. It will be several days. The wedding itself will not even take place until there's a lot of feasting, dancing, drinking and," he laughed, "a lot of other carrying on."

"It sounds exciting, Clay."

"It is. And I don't intend to tell you a thing about it. You'll enjoy the whole thing a lot more if you don't know what's going to happen next. I'm sure of one thing. You'll enjoy it, and they'll enjoy you just as much. I'll bet you are the first light haired woman most of them have ever seen."

"Where will we stay while we're there?"

"We'll be guests of honor. Ellen, Summer and you will be given your own private lodge. I will have to share the quarters of the other single men. Could I hope," he laughed, "that you will be a little disappointed?"

She went to him and pressing her hands against his chest, she rose on tip toe and kissed him lightly.

"It will do you good to practice a little abstinence," she chuckled. "It will make you appreciate me a little more."

They were alone in the kitchen since Summer was at play outside and Ellen was hanging clothes to dry.

Clay took advantage of her proximity by grabbing her quickly before she could dodge him. As his arms bound her to him, he kissed her firmly and most thoroughly.

"I couldn't possibly appreciate you any more than I do, love, and I'm willing to prove it to you at any time you care to name . . . now for instance?"

"Clay! you are insatiable!" she giggled.

"Where you are concerned . . . completely."

He kissed her again and as his mouth warmed her his hands began to roam freely. She grasped one hand only to find another seeking a softer place. Warm lips teased her and for a moment, she could have sworn he had an over abundant supply of hands she could not seem to control.

"Clay, will you stop," she gasped, "Ellen could come in at any moment."

"Then come somewhere more private with me," he suggested with an evil glow in his laughing blue eyes.

"Good heavens!" she said, as she again caught hold of a hand that had already unbuttoned several buttons on her dress and was trying to find its way inside.

"Clay! Stop please," she demanded as she finally wiggled free and started around the table. It was no use, for on the other side he was there to catch her to him again.

"Clay," she said, but the rest of her objections vanished with a deep kiss that silenced her.

From where he stood, and his height, it gave him an excellent view from the window to keep an eye on Ellen. One on her and the other occupied with a disheveled Sabrina, he took complete advantage of his superior strength to hold her tight.

"Will you please stop before Ellen comes in?" she begged.

"One true kiss, love, and I'll let you go," he laughed. "But I warn you, it has to be good."

Sabrina knew there was no escape for her from those laughing eyes that held her and melted her will to match his own. She surrendered and he felt her body stop the resistance and melt against him. Soft arms lifted to twine about his neck and a sweet parted mouth was raised to his. Deliberately, Sabrina put everything into the kiss that she possessed. It was enough to send Clay's senses soaring and fill him with a blazing need.

Now it was his turn to be caught in the magic river of her warm giving love and he let his senses surround him and fill him. Unaware that he had relaxed his hold, he was surprised when she suddenly slipped away from him. Laughing, she immediately put the table between them.

He gazed at her with an evil glow in his eyes and cocked one eyebrow.

"Sabrina."

"You," she giggled as he stalked her about the table, "must learn to control yourself." She backed away from him keeping the table safely between.

Still he stalked her and his eyes warned her that she would pay dearly for this. She knew it was only a matter of time until he caught her so she made a mad dash for the door. Too late! She was swept up into a pair of strong arms. They were flushed and laughing in pleasure when the door opened and Ellen walked in.

Ellen choked back her laughter, Sabrina blushed a hot pink, and Clay grinned in delight as very slowly and deliberately he let Sabrina's feet touch the floor. He was just as reluctant to release her waist and held her several moments before he did.

Once her feet touched the floor and she had safely wiggled away from him, she escaped quickly by claiming work to do and ran outside to find Summer, aware of Clay's deep warm chuckle that followed her rapid retreat.

Sabrina left the house and walked across the open clearing. She could see Summer beneath the shade of the trees and walked to join her.

Summer was kneeling in the grass beneath the huge tree's low overhanging branches. They were so low Sabrina had to stoop a little to get beneath them.

It was a shaded peaceful world unto itself and Sabrina was pleased to see Summer smile a welcome when she knelt beside her. Summer had slowly begun to transfer her dreams of a mother from a dark grave to a bright and affectionate Sabrina. Sabrina knew this and was happy about it. Because she loved Clay so deeply, she loved Summer too, and was overjoyed when she saw the light of love in Summer's deep dark eyes for she knew, from the intensity of Summer's relationship with Clay, that the child loved deeply.

She watched as Summer began to gather a rather odd pile of stones and place them in a deerskin sack. The stones were different than anything she had ever seen before.

"What are you doing Summer?"

"Taking my magic stones with me."

"Magic stones?" Sabrina questioned. "May I see one?"

Summer quickly stretched out her hand. In the palm lay a stone about two and a half inches long and two inches wide. It was rather flat. She took it from Summer's hand and examined it closely. It had been rubbed smooth somehow, and painted a shade of pale blue. As Sabrina handed it back, she noticed the rest of the stones were painted assorted colors.

"Where ever did you get such beautiful stones," she asked, "and why do you call them magic?"

"Swift Doe gave them to me when I was very little," Summer said seriously. Sabrina almost laughed at a child less than five referring to her past as when she was little. "They're very special stones," Summer added.

"I can see they are."

"They used to belong to my mother too," the child replied. Sabrina was quiet for a moment, then she asked gently.

"Summer . . . does your father know Swift Doe gave you these?"

Silence . . . busy hands deposited the stones slowly in the bag with complete concentration.

"Summer?"

The wide eyes rose to meet Sabrina's. They held for a few minutes, then she slowly shook her head negatively.

"Another secret from your father, Summer . . . is that fair?"

"Swift Doe said my mother would have wanted me to have

185

them, and it might upset my father. I don't want him to be mad at me, but . . . I want my mother's stones."

Again, Sabrina was distressed at Clay's determination to keep everything of Summer's mother a secret from her. Why, as sensitive as he was, did he not realize the child's need to somehow touch the mother she had never known. Sabrina felt pity for Summer.

"It's all right, Summer, you keep the stones if they were your mother's. Maybe after we visit the Indian village it will change your father's mind. Maybe he will be able to tell us more. It must have hurt your father very much to lose your mother. Maybe we can make it easier on him if we just have patience and wait until he is ready."

"I know Papa feels bad. Swift Doe said so. She said I was to be good and not ask Papa questions until I'm older. Sabrina, when will I be old enough to ask Papa?"

Sabrina did not know exactly how to answer this.

"I don't know, Summer," she said softly. "I truly don't know. But I believe your father will know the right time and he'll tell you then. Can you have patience like Swift Doe says and wait? Summer . . . I know it makes you feel bad, but I understand and I care. Can we be friends who talk to each other? Maybe that will make it easier."

Tears filled Summer's eyes and Sabrina could see clearly the hunger within. She held out her arms and in a moment was rocking Summer gently.

When she had dried Summer's tears and they had talked a little longer, making promises of trust and secrecy, Sabrina took Summer back to the house.

Everyone was exhausted from the excitement and the day's work. Everything was prepared for them to leave the next morning. Sabrina took Summer to bed where she fell asleep before Sabrina could even complete reading her one story.

She stood looking down at the sleeping child, wondering what anger and pain was locked so deeply inside Clay that it blinded him to his own child's need.

She hoped this trip to the village of Singing Bells' birth would help her solve the mystery and let her completely enter the heart of Clay Storm.

He was the man she loved, and nothing could make her love him less, yet she knew she had to find out what secrets Hawk and the village had that had caused so much tenseness and anger in Clay.

When she came out of the bedroom, both Clay and Ellen were gone. Ellen, she knew, had gone to bed. She smiled to herself, for she also knew exactly where Clay was.

She walked down the hall to her room and opened the door. She stepped inside and closed and locked it behind her. Then she smiled at the inviting blue gaze that touched her across the room.

He opened his arms and in a moment she was in them.

"I thought you would never come," he said as his mouth began an urgent search for hers.

Sixteen

The day dawned crisp and clear. Clay, as usual, was up before dawn and had already begun preparing the packs for the horses.

Breakfast was made quickly and eaten just as quickly.

By the time the sun was full and bright they were mounting their horses and preparing to leave. Ellen and Sabrina rode the same horses they had arrived on, and Summer rode before Clay.

Sabrina watched him with admiring eyes. He belonged here, she thought as she watched his lean buckskin clad form mount easily and lift Summer up before him.

Then they were on their way. Clay at the head, followed by Ellen and Sabrina. Clay set a slow but steady pace that was designed as a mile eater. Although they had to stop often because of Ellen, Clay was pleased with the ground they had covered before they stopped to eat lunch.

"When will we get to the village, Clay?" Sabrina asked.

"In time for a good late supper, I hope." he replied. "Are you all ready?"

They all agreed they were, and again they mounted and fell into the same steady pace.

The sun began its descent, and both Ellen and Sabrina were tired.

They crested a rise and Clay stopped so that Ellen and Sabrina and a wide-eyed Summer could get a good view of the village.

Sabrina was spellbound, both by the rare and beautiful view of the peaceful village that lay before them, and the look on Clay's face as they sat in silence and gazed at it.

She was aware that many emotions were passing through Clay's mind. When he did realize that she was watching him, whatever he might have been feeling was quickly submerged beneath the smile he gave her.

From where they were, they could see three riders leave the village and ride in their direction. Clay remained motionless and watched them approach. They reined in their horses close to Clay's, and Sabrina, while they greeted Clay, had time to examine them closely.

Three men, she guessed somewhere near Clay's age. Quiet, dark men whose piercing dark eyes missed nothing. One spoke in a deep voice. There was a smile on his lips and a glow of friendliness in his eyes.

He was a slim man, yet muscle rippled under his bronzed skin.

"Welcome Clay Storm," he said. "It has been too long since you have been a guest in our village. You are welcome. Your women are welcome as well," he went on. His eyes touched Ellen, then shifted quickly to Sabrina, where they lingered in deep appreciation.

The glow of appreciation was well apparent in the eyes of the other two. They did not speak English as well as the first, and so they spoke to Clay in their own tongue.

"Your woman is very beautiful," one said.

"Thank you," Clay replied in the same quicksilver tongue. He wanted to acknowledge Sabrina as his woman, but because of Hawk, he could not. He continued in the rapid tongue. "But she is not my woman, she is only the nurse to my child and her teacher."

He gritted his teeth in self-control when he saw the new light in the eyes of the three as their gazes returned to Sabrina. The first spoke again.

"We will ride back with you," he said. "Hawk has told us to make you welcome, so food and lodging have already been prepared for the night."

"I thank you, Walking Horse," Clay replied. He knew quite well why Walking Horse did not move yet. He motioned toward the women.

"This is the woman who cares for my lodge. Her name is Ellen."

"Ellen," Walking Horse repeated the strange name slowly.

"And this is the woman who cares for my child. Her name is Sabrina."

"Sa-bree-nah," he said slowly.

Clay nodded. Too well mannered to delay any longer the three fell in beside them, and they rode slowly down to the village. Sabrina was well aware of the intense dark eyes that watched her, yet for some unaccountable reason she felt no fear. Clay and the one called Walking Horse rode close together, and Sabrina heard their voices as they spoke softly and rapidly in the strange language that sounded so short and clipped to her. She would have given anything in the world to have understood what they said. Clay was quite happy that she did not, for he was quite sure if she had, her anger toward him would have been overpowering.

Walking Horse was no novice with women. He was handsome and proud, and had drawn the eyes of many. His smile was quick and easy and he was usually filled with good humor.

"There will be much feasting and dancing for the next three days."

"Umm," Clay replied. "There usually is."

190

"The woman . . . the one with the moon colored hair. She is a stranger to our ways. Maybe she needs to be taught to sing and dance the feast with us."

Clay would liked to have strangled him, but he could only smile.

"It would be a pleasure to make her stay among us as pleasant as possible."

It was nearly more than Clay could stand and he was about to explode. In anger he would have shouted to Walking Horse that Sabrina was his and would remain his and no one would take her from him . . . but he knew when he did, Hawk would take one more step toward revenge.

Despite anything, Clay was about to snap an angry answer, when they reached the outer circle of Indian lodges. Soon they were surrounded by curious women and children.

They were led to the center of the village where Clay dismounted with Summer and helped Sabrina and Ellen. He could see that Ellen was slightly shaken, but that Sabrina was fascinated by the villagers' obvious friendliness. She was also amused by the quick easy smiles of the young men who moved as close as possible. Clay groaned mentally, knowing he was going to have an immense battle on his hands to keep them away from Sabrina.

They had stopped in front of a lodge that Clay knew well—Hawks. Despite what was said, Clay knew that Hawk was behind his father's invitation. He knew the old man had sacrificed a lot of his pride to be connected with the invitation. He also knew the old man would want to see Summer more than anyone else.

Hawk stepped outside his lodge, magnificent in his finest clothes. He and Clay faced each other.

"Welcome Clay," Hawk said quietly.

"Thank you, Hawk. We are pleased to join in Swift Doe's wedding ceremony."

191

The formal words were said, but both knew the words that remained unsaid.

Clay turned to Sabrina and Ellen to explain to them.

"You will be taken to a lodge reserved for you. There is nothing to fear. They want you to be comfortable and happy and they'll do anything in their power to make you so. Feel free to wander about the village where you will. The celebration begins tonight. I think you'll enjoy the feast."

"What about you Clay?" Sabrina asked.

"I told you before I must sleep with the single men. It is the custom. For now . . . I am going to take Summer to speak to an old friend. Don't worry, I'll be near. In fact," he laughed as he motioned toward Walking Horse, "I intend to keep a close eye on all the young bucks . . . and on you," he added softly.

Sabrina nodded and she and Ellen went into the lodge they had been given.

Clay took Summer's hand and walked toward another lodge.

Again Sabrina was surprised, and Ellen stood beside her, eyes wide and a little amazed.

The lodge was very large, at least twenty four feet in length and more than twelve feet wide. Strong sturdy trees, skinned and dried formed the large square framework, which was then covered with well-cured skin. After this registered in their minds, they were also awed by the fact that it seemed well organized . . . and clean.

A small pit in the center held red coals from what had been a cooking fire. Along the far wall were boards with a back brace that was covered with fine soft fur and looked very comfortable.

Sabrina was about to speak when Swift Doe entered.

Swift Doe had been so curious about Sabrina, she took the first opportunity to come to them. She stood inside the doorway and looked at Sabrina who was just as curious as she.

Since Swift Doe had said nothing, Sabrina took it for granted that she could not speak English. So did Ellen.

"What a very beautiful girl," Ellen said.

"Yes," Sabrina agreed. "She is lovely. I wish she could speak our language. I think I should love to talk to her and have her explain everything to me."

"I would be very pleased to make you welcome in my village," Swift Doe smiled, "and I am happy that Clay chose to bring you to my wedding."

Both Ellen and Sabrina were taken by surprise, but it was made less embarrassing by Swift Doe's friendly smile.

"Your wedding," Sabrina replied, "then you must be Swift Doe?"

"Yes, I am Swift Doe. Has Clay told you of me?"

"Very little, but Summer has spoken of you. You cared for her occasionally?"

"Yes, a few times," Swift Doe replied.

"What . . . what has Summer told you of me?"

"Nothing really, except she thinks of you as a friend."

"I am happy she feels so."

Sabrina walked closer to Swift Doe. Their eyes held and both smiled hesitantly, reaching for a beginning friendship.

"I . . . I should like to be friends also, Swift Doe. I should like to speak to you of many things."

"Yes," Swift Doe replied, "yes, it is good for us to be friends. Maybe . . . maybe it is the way of the gods."

"I don't understand."

"I shall explain to you one day soon."

"You speak our language well."

"Clay taught me, when I was a child."

"Clay taught you English . . . he also taught Hawk to speak and read our language. But, why . . .?"

Before she could finish, the door hanging was brushed aside and two other women entered.

"We will talk again," Swift Doe said softly. "I have a feeling you can be the one Clay needs. For now please enjoy yourselves. You will find our customs different, but I hope you will like our village."

Swift Doe introduced the other women who smiled shyly.

One of the women reached out and touched Sabrina's dress with a light touch and admiring eyes. It was then that another idea presented itself and she turned to Swift Doe.

"Swift Doe, I would truly like to join you to celebrate your wedding. Could I . . . is there any way I can find a dress of your people?"

Swift Doe smiled in genuine pleasure.

"Come to my lodge with me. I have many from which you can choose."

"I want this to be a surprise for Clay."

"I'm sure," Swift Doe replied softly, "he will be surprised."

Sabrina, in her excitement, missed the double meaning to Swift Doe's words.

Ellen remained in the lodge with the two new arrivals while they tried hesitatingly to explain to her what everything was for and she in return with signs and words asked a multitude of questions.

Sabrina and Swift Doe walked across nearly the length of the village to Swift Doe's lodge. Even Swift Doe had to smile at the whispered words and awed looks that followed them.

Swift Doe's lodge was considerably smaller than the one allotted to Sabrina, but it was soon obvious to Sabrina that it personified Swift Doe herself, for it was filled with things of beauty that told much about the girl who lived in it.

The furs on her bed were well-cured and extremely fine. The lodge was scrupulously clean and neat. Assorted things hung on pegs from the frame and soft fur pelts were hung about the walls to create an unusual beauty.

Her generosity was soon apparent when she took what dresses she had and presented them to Sabrina.

"Please choose what pleases you and fits you and let me be honored by presenting it to you as a gift of friendship."

"Swift Doe, how kind of you."

"It would make me very happy to know all our friends and guests are happy on the day of my wedding. It is good luck."

They began to sort through the clothes so Sabrina could try them on, and were soon laughing and chattering together.

Sabrina chose an amber colored dress of fine buckskin, worked and cured until it was very soft. A row of fine worked beads formed a pattern across the bodice and back and the arms and hemlines were fringed. It fit Sabrina well, clinging and molding to her slender curves. The deep color accentuated her purple eyes and pale gold hair.

Swift Doe braided Sabrina's long, golden hair in two braids into which she worked soft golden brown feathers and strips of fine wine colored rawhide.

"I have never seen a golden haired Indian before," Swift Doe laughed, "but you do look very beautiful. All the young men will be captured by you this night . . . all but Sleeping Wolf."

"Sleeping Wolf . . . won't he like me?"

"He had best not," Swift Doe laughed again, "he is to be my husband in two days, and I am afraid he would meet with much violence should he look at another now."

They laughed together slowly and happily forming a bond that would draw them close in deep friendship. Swift Doe held most of the words she truly wanted to say deep inside her until she knew for sure the relationship between

Sabrina and Clay.

They were talking together of some of the customs and did not realize the amount of time that had gone by.

Then the soft steady thrum of a muffled drum beat drew their attention.

It was picked up by another rhythmic beat, then another and another until the night air was filled with a steady throbbing beat.

"The feast has begun," Swift Doe said as she and Sabrina rose. "I did not realize it was so late."

"Summer and Ellen . . . I must see they are ready."

"Ellen has already been cared for. The two women who came were sent by Hawk to see to her care. They will already be at the main fire and most likely eating."

"Clay?"

"Clay has gone to speak to Hawk's father. They are old friends since Black Cloud first brought Clay here as a boy. Summer is with them, but don't worry, they will soon join you."

Sabrina would have liked to ask Swift Doe many more questions but Swift Doe was already holding the door cover aside and beckoning Sabrina to join her which she did.

The night was brightened by a huge, golden moon that hovered just over the horizon. It was crowned by a million, diamond stars.

The village itself was lit by the bright glow of several large fires. In the flame colored brightness, Swift Doe led Sabrina toward the largest fire.

Many eyes followed as they did, eyes aglow with admiration for the beautiful golden haired girl who had chosen this night to be one of them.

Walking Horse and Sleeping Wolf left the fire by which they had been standing and moved toward the two women.

Sleeping Wolf was tall, slim and so handsome that even

Sabrina had to gaze lingeringly at him. As they approached, Sabrina could read Sleeping Wolf's eyes well and she chuckled softly as she whispered to Swift Doe.

"I do not need to ask who walks with Walking Horse. His eyes devour you. He is so handsome, Swift Doe. You are a lucky woman."

"He is much man," Swift Doe whispered back, "and I shall be pleased and happy to be his wife, but don't tell him so. Sometimes it is good to keep them from getting big headed."

Sabrina laughed again and the bright smile and sparkle of her deep purple eyes reached out and touched Walking Horse in a way he had never been touched before.

"Sa-bree-nah," he said as he stopped beside her, "you are part of our tribe this night. Come and eat with us and join the dancing."

"Thank you Walking Horse. I really am hungry."

Sleeping Wolf silently took Swift Doe's hand. There were no words to be said about his emotions, they lived in his eyes as he smiled down on the woman who would soon be his wife.

Ellen was already at the fire making herself known among the other women with motions and sampling every dish that was brought to her.

They were seated in places of honor on fur covered benches several feet from the fire. Walking Horse made sure that Sabrina was seated next to him, and that each bowl of food passed was offered to her.

Sabrina looked about for any sign of Clay or Summer, but she saw that three places were obviously reserved for them.

Sabrina was caught up in the laughter and excitement. Mountainous amounts of food and drink were offered to her and she tried her best to sample everything.

Walking Horse tried his best, with his limited knowledge of her language, to explain the types of food she was eating. He thought he was doing quite well until Hawk appeared and placed himself on Sabrina's other side.

"You are enjoying yourself, Sabrina?"

"Oh yes, Hawk. The food is delicious," she answered as she reached for another tidbit of meat. "What is this, Hawk, it is so good?"

"Rattlesnake," Hawk replied calmly.

Sabrina's hand froze and her face turned pale even though she tried to smile. It was when she heard Walking Horse's muffled laughter did she realize Hawk was joking with her. She wondered if she would ever be able to read that granite face and those unfathomable dark eyes.

Everyone seemed to be having a marvelous time, yet Sabrina wondered where Clay and Summer were and why they had not joined them for the feast.

Knowing Clay's reluctance even to come, she wondered if there were some problems progressing somewhere for which she was innocently responsible. Causing Clay any problems was the last thing she ever wanted and she was impatient to see him and tell him so.

Sabrina had never learned to mask her emotions, and though Hawk's face was unreadable to her, he could read hers easily and accurately.

He knew it was Clay she thought about and was annoyed with himself that that idea upset him. He had intended to try and take her from Clay as part of his revenge, and he did not want any other emotions to interfere in this plan . . . yet . . .

"Sabrina, come and walk with me. I will show you the rest of my village and try to explain some of the wedding ceremony to you," Hawk said as he rose and extended his hand to help her to her feet.

Walking Horse was dismayed at Sabrina's loss, but he would never think of interfering in any wish of Hawks. Hawk's anger and strength were already well known, and he also had too much respect for the man who one day would be his chief.

He watched the golden haired beauty rise and walk away with Hawk. Then his mind went to Clay, and he wondered how he would feel about it.

Seventeen

Clay stood before Black Cloud's lodge, Summer's hand in his. He gripped himself firmly, annoyed that he trembled like a boy about to be punished. Perspiration dampened his brow and made his hands moist.

It had been over five years since he had entered this lodge. He loved the man inside like a father, but past words had created a gulf he would find hard to cross.

Summer looked up at her father, aware and surprised that he seemed to be so shaken. She felt his hand quiver and become moist in hers.

This was her father, a man of iron, a man of which she had no doubts or fears, yet he seemed to be almost . . . afraid.

Wisdom beyond her years told her that whoever lived in this lodge was someone exceptional. She stood quietly and waited while her father, in a gentle voice, called out to the person within.

Someone in a deep voice called to them to enter. Clay pushed aside the door covering and went in, putting Summer before him.

She stood very still until she could receive from her father some kind of hint or signal of how she should react. But her eyes missed nothing about the lodge in which they stood and the man who sat across the room from them.

The lodge was bathed in a pale red-gold glow from the red coals of the fire before which the old man sat.

Then her eyes met his across the fire and she felt a new warmth within her. She felt kindness and gentleness and a slow hesitant smile touched her lips. Still she did not speak, but waited for her father to speak first.

"Black Cloud," Clay said softly, "I thank you for the invitation to Swift Doe's wedding."

"Would you have come otherwise?"

"No," Clay replied.

"It has been many years since we have seen you, my son. You look well."

"I am well." Clay put his hand on Summer's shoulder and pushed her forward gently. "This is Summer," he stated shortly, and again the gentle eyes rested on Summer.

"She has the beauty of her mother. She will be an exceptional woman some day." The gaze shifted back to Clay. "Does she also have her mothers gifts? Hawk has told me it is so."

"The answer to that question is one of the main reasons I decided to come," Clay replied.

"Come and sit by my fire," Black Cloud said. "Would it anger you if the child sat beside me?"

"No, of course not," Clay pressed his hand against Summer's shoulder. "Summer, this is Black Cloud. He is chief of this tribe. Go and sit beside him."

Obediently Summer went to Black Cloud's side. Almost eagerly he held out a hand that drew her close to him. She was not in the least afraid, and she liked the warm smile and the way the dark eyes crinkled at the corners. Without knowing why, she felt a deep affinity with this man. He motioned to her to sit beside him, and she did. As he turned his gaze back to Clay, he absently caressed Summer's hair.

"Speak what you have come to say."

"They are words I spoke a long time ago. I did not take Singing Bells away from this village against her will. She loved me, and she chose to make my way hers. She died giving birth to Summer. Do you believe that I will let anything come between me and the only thing I have left of Singing Bells?"

"Your heart is still the same, Clay Storm," Black Cloud said in a weary voice. "I had hoped the time you spent with Singing Bells would change you. She had the same hope when she turned her back on the people who needed her medicine. She came to you with the same hopes and prayers your father had. It is a sad thing that they were for nothing."

Clay fought the anger that rose within him. He tried to keep his words steady for he did love and respect the man who sat before him.

"Summer is mine, Black Cloud," he said softly. "Yes, I have seen in Summer the same magic, the same medicine as Singing Bells had. But they will go. As she grows, I will educate her in the white man's way. After a time she will forget."

"Clay," the old man replied, "because of the battle between you and Hawk, you have hardened your heart until you cannot see any truth at all yours or his. You cannot deny the call of her blood that will one day rise up in her heart. So you and Hawk will war over her until you destroy each other and the things you love most. If you feel as you do, why do you not leave this land? Go back to your people."

"I will not be driven from a place I love. Not by anything or anyone."

"Your pride is cold, Clay," Black Cloud said in gentle sympathy. "You and Hawk must both learn one day that true love is willing to sacrifice. You and Hawk may battle, but I and my people only want to share with you. Why do you close your heart?"

"You are the one who told me to leave this village years ago and never return."

"Only to keep you and my son from harming each other, or from breaking Singing Bells' heart. It was a thing I had to do."

"It is too late to relive the past now, Black Cloud. I want only to live in peace and to raise my child as I see fit."

Black Cloud was silent for some time, then he spoke gently.

"You have seen her mother's medicine in her . . . I also see her mother. We," he said in a whispered voice, "will need her one day. Do not take away her true heritage and make her an object to be laughed at in the white man's world. One day her two bloods will war as you and Hawk do. If she does not have the strength of both behind her, she may get lost. Listen to me, Clay. Put aside your pride and anger at Hawk. I will beg him to do the same. Let us share what we once had."

Clay could hear the pleading in the old man's voice and he knew how hard it was for him to say these words. He gazed at Summer who had been watching them both with a deep intent gaze that, for a moment, made him believe she understood all that was happening.

He tried to put that thought from his mind, but he couldn't for he knew the almost mystical power her mother had possessed . . . and he had seen and recognized the signs in Summer long ago.

Summer had, in fact, understood much of what was said. She remembered vivid dreams she had that her father had tried to ease from her mind. Suddenly, she felt a strange sense of loss, as if something dear were being torn from her. Without hesitation, she reached out and placed her hand in the old man's. She knew, without thinking, that it gave him comfort. She lifted her eyes to her father . . . then reached her other hand across the coals of the fire to him.

Both men were filled with the ache of remembrance. Remembrance of a sweet, quiet woman who had tried to join them before. They saw her in the dark eyes of the child.

Clay reached out and took her hand. It was as if a chain had been forged. Each man could feel it as their eyes met and held.

"I will think on your words, Black Cloud. I will carry them home and keep them in my heart for a while. I must have time to decide."

"It is good that you begin to think with your heart instead of your pride, my son. If I can get my son to do the same maybe there can be peace between us again."

"I never wanted to war with my brother Hawk. It is he who carries it in his heart."

"He believes that it was wrong for Singing Bells to come to you, to live the white man's way. He knew what she meant to her people . . . and he is still jealous and still carries the pain of her loss as I am sure you do. He blames the white man's way for her death. You were brothers. I pray to the gods that one day you will be brothers again. I will speak again with him when the wedding is over. Maybe one day we will walk the path of life together again."

"I have only said I will think about your words," Clay warned. "I never said I would change my mind."

Black Cloud smiled, "We must walk one day at a time. It is enough for now that you think. Go and let Summer play with the other children. Soon it will be time for them to sleep and the dancing to start. One day soon we will speak again."

Clay stood up.

"Summer, come along, you can play for a while, then it's time for you to go to bed."

204

Summer rose and stood looking into Black Cloud's eyes. Then she put her arms about his neck. Black Cloud closed his eyes and pressed the child close to him.

"Good night, Grandfather," Summer said. Then she moved to Clay's side. Both men were shocked, and Clay could see the old man's eyes cloud with tears. He took Summer's hand and silently left the lodge.

They walked slowly from Black Cloud's lodge toward the large one where the children would play and sleep under the watchful eyes of three older women.

"Summer?"

"Yes, Papa?"

"Why did you call Black Cloud grandfather?"

"I don't know Papa. He just seemed so lonely and . . . I thought maybe he would like it."

Clay stopped and looked down into the dark trusting eyes of the child he loved completely. In the light of the moon and the reflected fires, he could see that she spoke the truth. She had felt a bond and had responded to it with love.

He reached down and lifted her into his arms and felt the familiar warmth as her arms circled his neck and she rested her head against him with confidence. He pressed her close to him.

"I love you, Summer," he said softly

"I love you too, Papa. More than anything else in the whole world."

He walked slowly, taking the moments to hold her tight for suddenly he felt as if some force beyond the darkness of the grave might separate them.

A large lodge situated well away from the festivities was the one chosen to be used to care for the children for the celebration and the dancing would go long into the night.

Children played about it now, and once there it did not take long for Summer to join them for it was a rare thing for her to have friends to play with.

Clay made sure she would be well cared for. Then he turned to walk toward the largest fire where he expected to find Ellen and Sabrina seated and comfortable . . . and waiting for him. He stopped at the edge of the fire and gazed in surprise at the vacant seats where Ellen, Sabrina . . . and Hawk should have been seated. Ellen was the only one of the three there.

In all the confusion there was no way he could find Hawk and Sabrina without making an obvious fool of himself. Yet he knew they were together somewhere.

He walked closer to the fire and soon several people began to greet him in open and welcome friendship.

"Ho! Clay Storm," Walking Horse laughed. "You are late, friend."

"Have you eaten all the food," Clay returned with a grin, "and have you drunk all the liquor?"

"There is enough for you, friend. Come eat and drink with us."

He went closer and sat by the fire. Ellen, to his amusement, seemed to be enjoying herself completely. He could see that Sleeping Wolf and Swift Doe had eyes only for each other.

He began to chafe under the desire to get to his feet and begin to search for Sabrina.

Food remained in the bowl he held in his hand. The drink Walking Horse had given him remained untasted.

He knew there was no excuse for him to search for a woman he had claimed to be only a servant.

"Damn," he thought angrily, "where in the hell can she have gone?"

Sabrina and Hawk walked along the moonlit forest path.

A soft breeze whispered lightly through the trees and the soft throbbing of the drums could still be heard.

"Your village is beautiful, Hawk. I had not realized it was so big. I had expected . . ."

"What?"

"I don't know. A small group of tepees or . . . I really don't know."

"You miss the big cities from which you come?"

"No," she laughed. "To tell you the truth Hawk, I have been happier here than any place else in my life."

"It is good you feel so. We would keep you here," he chuckled. "From Walking Horse's face, I can tell you would have many who would hold you here."

Sabrina smiled at his teasing. She could not understand Clay's reaction to Hawk. He seemed so kind and understanding to her.

Hawk remained silent for a while enjoying the way Sabrina seemed to find so much pleasure in the night.

He was also aware that every sense he had spoke of her presence. Hawk had known many women, and only one had ever reached inside him as this tiny slim woman did who walked quietly beside him, and she was gone forever.

Now he was aware of her completely, and it caused a mild jolt to his conscience. He had felt she was an open generous person and would believe easily. He had intended to use this against Clay. But now he found that not only did he not want to use her, but he wanted her . . . wanted her with a sudden awareness that caused him a great deal of surprise.

Resolutely, he held himself in check, and concentrated on Clay. After a while he had renewed control and was again prepared to do what he had planned for so long.

"Hawk?"

"Yes."

"Would you answer a question for me?"

207

"If I can."

"I know it's not really my business, but I feel there is something between you and Clay I can only feel but do not understand. Can you tell me what it is?"

Hawk was quiet, and for a while Sabrina felt she had questioned what he could not answer. Then his voice broke the silence.

"Sabrina, Clay and I were boys together. There are many things both good and bad between us. It is a thing we can only find the answers to ourselves. I thought I might bridge some of it when he returned with you. It . . . it is a thing we will work out between us."

When he mentioned the time of her arrival, she remembered the beautiful gift he had given her.

"Oh Hawk, I must thank you again for the lovely dress you gave me."

"You liked it?"

"Yes."

"Then why did you let Clay return it to me? The gift had much meaning and I truly wanted you to have it."

"I . . . I didn't let Clay return it, he just did."

"I do not understand your position, Sabrina. Are you his slave that he can tell you what gifts you can and cannot take? We have slaves in our tribe, some of other tribes we have taken, yet we would not deny them a gift if another chose to give them one."

He knew he had touched a sensitive spot. He also realized that Clay had hurt her just a little by doing so. It was a spot he intended to irritate a little more.

"I am not a slave," she pronounced firmly.

He stopped walking and turned to her. He had chosen where he stood well for the moon was behind him and bathed her face in its light.

"Then I do not understand how he can take from you

what is yours."

"He cannot."

"Good," Hawk smiled, "then I can return the dress to you and you can give me pleasure by seeing you wear it."

"No . . . I"

Hawk waited.

"Clay said he would give me a dress like it. He said it had no special meaning. I don't want him to be angry."

"But the dress did have meaning. Did he not explain it to you?"

"No, tell me Hawk."

Hawk remained silent again. He had planted a deadly seed. He knew that in the space of two days she would see with her own eyes the meaning of the dress. It would be a blow that would turn her from Clay . . . and he would be near to comfort her broken heart.

"I am sorry that I spoke of it. Perhaps Clay intends to explain himself. If he does not before the ceremony, then I shall," he said gently. "I too, do not want him to be angry."

Sabrina wanted to argue with him, but she was unsure that he was not right. It was Clay who would explain and she would not judge until he did.

"All right, Hawk," she agreed reluctantly. "Maybe it is best we return to the celebration. Clay must be wondering where I am by now."

"Before we go back, I have one more thing to say to you."

"What is it?"

"I would like you to know you are very welcome to visit our village at any time. Since you are not a slave surely you must have time of your own to spend as you please. I know I speak for Swift Doe, myself and," he chuckled, "surely Walking Horse when I say it would honor us if you were to come often."

"Thank you, Hawk. You and Swift Doe and all your

people have been exceedingly kind to me. It would give me a great deal of pleasure to come to visit occasionally, but without Clay to guide me how would I find the way?"

"It is a thing I must think about. Before you leave I will have found a way. In case you need anything you will then be able to come to us."

"All right."

"One thing more, Sabrina," he added softly. She waited for him to speak. Her face, touched by the light of the moon had a translucent beauty that took his breath away. He found the fragile web of her beauty weaving a spell about him that he was finding impossible to break. He reached out and touched her hair lightly and watched shock and awareness fill her eyes.

"You are a very beautiful woman, Sabrina. I find great pleasure just looking at you. I would be your friend, and if you should need anything, you need only ask and if it is in my power I will get it for you."

"Thank you, Hawk," she replied gently.

"Come, let us return to the celebration. It is time for the dancing. You must dance with us to celebrate the wedding to come. It is good luck for the bride if all are happy at her celebration."

"I'm afraid I know nothing of your dances," she laughed.

"Don't worry," he echoed her laughter, "there are many who will be most willing to teach you."

They walked back through the village and to the large fire that was still being fed to keep its glow.

Clay watched them come. He saw a laughing Hawk. He saw Sabrina, beautiful in the native dress. He saw her laugh at something Hawk had said, her face aglow and her eyes sparkling in happiness. A cold, hard, jealous rage filled him, yet he knew there was nothing he could say or do for he himself had claimed to all ears that Sabrina was nothing more to him than the woman who cared for his child.

He knew Hawk was taunting him, and he would not give him the satisfaction of knowing he had succeeded in rousing Clay's anger or his jealousy.

Sabrina came to his side bubbling with laughter and excitement. He listened with a smile, yet his eyes held Hawk's with a silent reply . . . she is mine Hawk . . . and you cannot find your way to me through her.

Eighteen

Clay had very little opportunity to get Sabrina alone, for the dancing was started with an insistent throbbing of drums and Sabrina was fascinated and soon completely involved in it.

Her bright eyed laughter, and her rare golden beauty drew the young men like magnets.

Clay could do nothing but smile, and seeth in silent anger.

Sabrina also did not get much more time to spend with Swift Doe, for she was monopolized by a Sleeping Wolf who made absolutely certain everyone knew to whom Swift Doe would belong.

It was in the wee hours of the morning before they all found their way to beds.

The next day dawned bright and clear. Clay rose and went immediately to the lodge Sabrina and Ellen shared. He was surprised to be met by an early rising Summer who was just leaving to join other children in play.

"Summer," Clay smiled, "come and give Papa a good morning kiss."

He lifted her in his arms and she hugged him enthusiastically, then she kissed him several times and Clay thoroughly enjoyed it.

As he set her back down on her feet, he turned her back

toward the door she had just come out of.

"Go and tell Sabrina to come out. I would like to talk to her."

It was completely improper in the eyes of the village for him to go inside.

"I can't Papa."

"Why?"

"She is already gone."

"Gone, gone where?"

"Hawk came this morning and she went riding with him."

"Oh," he said quietly. "Hawk . . . damn!" he muttered under his breath. "Go ahead and play, Summer," he said quickly when he felt his daughter's astute gaze on him.

Clay turned away from the woman's lodge and walked slowly toward where his horse was grazing with the rest of the herd. He wondered what kind of excuse he could find to go after Sabrina and Hawk. A deep jealousy and an accompanying fear held him in its grasp. He knew there were things Hawk could say that might make a difference in Sabrina's love for him and he didn't really know whether Hawk felt he could use Sabrina against him or not—he didn't want to give Sabrina the occasion to tell Hawk her feelings for Clay.

Intent on his own thoughts, he did not see Walking Horse coming toward him until they nearly collided.

"Walking Horse," Clay laughed, "Good morning. You're out early too. Where are you going?"

"I was going to ask Sabrina if she would like to go for a ride. It is a beautiful day and I should like to show her the beauty of our land."

"You're too late too, Walking Horse."

"Too late too?"

"Hawk and Sabrina have already gone for that ride."

Walking Horse chuckled. "And I thought I was clever

enough to get up earlier than everyone else. I should have known no one gets too far ahead of Hawk when he wants something."

"What do you mean, wants something?"

"You did not see his eyes last night as he watched Sabrina? He is much interested. Especially since you have made it clear she is not your woman."

Clay cursed to himself while he tried to keep the unconcerned look on his face. He was about to speak again when he noticed the wicked glitter in Walking Horse's eyes. He grasped the opportunity.

"You have something in your mind," he grinned, "and I have a feeling it might be interesting."

"I was only thinking," Walking Horse said innocently, "that Hawk and Sabrina might welcome a little company."

Their gazes held and both smiled.

"It doubt it very much," Clay replied. "But, we should certainly go and find out. Do you have any idea where he might have gone?"

"Why Clay," Walking Horse said gently, "to the place he is proudest of. The Valley of Pines. It's . . . it's quite beautiful and very secluded."

Walking Horse chuckled softly and Clay's laughter joined him as he dropped his arm across Walking Horse's shoulders.

"Let's go."

They walked to their horses and in less than twenty minutes, rode from the village.

Sabrina and Hawk rode slowly, enjoying the clear, cool morning air. Hawk had been up very early, disturbed by the fact that despite all his efforts he could not get the golden haired woman to leave his dreams.

Of course, he knew it would aggravate Clay to find Sa-

214

brina gone, but it was not the reason he had asked her to go. He really wanted to share her company, to show her his valley and to watch her eyes when she saw how beautiful it was. He was sure Clay would have no way of knowing where they had gone.

Hawk turned his head to smile at Sabrina who returned it. Again, as he had the first day he had seen her bathing in the stream by Clay's cabin, he admired her beauty.

He felt a stir of desire within him, and as he had once before, he pictured her in the warmth of his lodge with the world shut away from them. He suddenly found the thoughts he had of using her as a way to Clay were slowly disappearing. Now he wanted her for himself and for no other reason than her own beauty and gentleness.

They crested the hill that led to the valley he wanted to show her. A place he loved, and had shared with very few.

He reined his horse to a stop and Sabrina stopped beside him. He smiled again at the roses in her cheeks, the pleasure in her eyes and the smile on her lips.

"Hawk, it is so beautiful here. It is breathtaking. I should love to stay forever in a place like this."

"You have not seen its real beauty yet. We will walk from here down to the banks of the stream that runs through my valley. When you stand by the stream you can hear music from the water and the breeze that whispers in the trees."

"You are a poet at heart, Hawk, and you don't look like one. You are a deceptive person," Sabrina laughed.

"What does a poet look like?" he challenged.

Her eyes sparkled.

"Touche," she replied. "I know you are right. Poetry is in the heart and not in how one looks."

Hawk chuckled and dismounted. He went to her side and put his huge hands about her waist and lifted her gently from her horse to stand beside him.

"Let me tie your horse with mine. Then we will walk and I shall show you a place so beautiful even the greatest poet would be silenced."

She handed him her reins and watched as he hobbled the horses so they would not stray. Then again he came to stand beside her.

Instantly, both were well aware of each other. He of the way the sun glistened in the gold strands of her hair and the way her eyes lifted to his in complete trust and friendship. She with the immense size and strength of him and the fact that he was so startlingly handsome.

"Do we have to walk far?" she questioned.

"Are you tired?"

"Heavens no, I have not enjoyed myself so much in a long time."

"It is not far."

"Then let's go," she laughed. "I find I can hardly wait to see this beautiful valley of yours."

He nodded and they started to walk down into the depths of the green valley below them.

The deeper into the valley they walked, the more spellbound Sabrina became with its wild intense beauty.

Tall pines towered over them and they walked silently on a bed of pine needles that was soft. The sweet smell of them touched their senses.

Sabrina was silent, simply allowing her senses to absorb the beauty about her. There are no words she could say that could tell of the peace and contentment she felt.

After a short time, they came to a stream that was not either wide or deep, yet its crystal clear water tumbled recklessly over smooth stones.

Hawk led her to a huge flat rock where they could sit and survey the Eden they had found.

Sabrina was aware of a depth and a sensitivity of the man

who sat next to her, and again she wondered what the mystery was that stood between him and Clay.

Hawk too, was aware that the woman who sat next to him matched the beauty of the place in which they sat.

"You have enjoyed your time in our village, Sabrina?"

"I have Hawk. I have never felt so welcome anywhere. I cannot wait to see the wedding ceremony. When will it happen?"

He chuckled, "There will be more celebration tonight. Tomorrow the ceremony will take place just before nightfall. After that the celebration will be much louder, much more colorful and much more fun. I think you will enjoy it."

"I'm sure I will. Do you always celebrate for three days at a wedding?"

"No," he grinned, "for a sub-chief like myself it will be longer."

"I am curious Hawk."

"About what?"

"About you."

"Me? Why are you curious about me? I am a simple man."

"Oh Hawk," she smiled, "I doubt very much if you are a simple man."

"What do you think?"

She gazed at him and held his eyes with hers.

"I think you are a very complex man, with secrets within you. I think you feel strongly about anything . . . maybe everything. And I wonder . . . why you have not married before this. Surely the women of your tribe cannot be blind to how handsome and intelligent you are. How have they let you slip away this long?"

She watched his smile fade, saw his eyes turn from hers and gaze out over the rippling water.

"I was to have been married once. It did not happen. I had

even given her the wedding robe."

"Wedding robe?"

"It is an old custom."

"Tell me about it."

"It is a dress of white deerskin and decorated with symbols of love. It carries luck and the pride of the man."

"It sounds very beautiful."

"It is. You will see Swift Doe when she comes to Sleeping Wolf. It means much, the dress."

"Did . . . did you lose your woman, Hawk?"

"She is dead, Sabrina . . . it was a long time ago. Maybe I shall marry one day, but not for a long time. I have another thing which must be done first."

"I'm sorry, Hawk. I didn't mean to pry."

"It is all right." Again his eyes returned to hers and they were smiling again. "I did not bring you here to make you unhappy, but to see you smile."

She knew he was shutting her out of his thoughts, and she did not want her intrusion to damage a blossoming friendship.

"I'm glad you brought me here," she smiled. "I shall never forget this place."

"Do not forget it. Come and enjoy it as often as you like. To see it when the winter snow fills it and weighs the branches of the trees, and the ice on the water. It is as new as this minute."

"I . . . I will ask Clay to bring me."

"You once said you had time that was your own. If you care to come here, then I should be happy to bring you."

"No . . . Hawk . . . I owe Clay more than that."

He was close to her, his shoulder brushing hers and he held her eyes with his. Now was his opportunity to hear her say what really existed between her and Clay. Now he would know positively if Clay were really vulnerable here.

"What," he said softly, "do you feel you owe Clay?"

She was about to speak, about to tell him of her love for Clay and his for her when a shout caused them both to turn in surprise. Clay and Walking Horse were riding toward them.

If Hawk had any emotion at all it was well hidden by the time Clay and Walking Horse reached them. He watched Sabrina smile, saw her eyes grow warm as they touched Clay . . . and was astounded at the surge of jealousy that filled him.

Clay and Walking Horse rode to their side and dismounted.

"Good morning," Sabrina smiled. Clay searched her eyes for any secrets, knowing she was entirely too open to hide them from him. He saw only clear purple-blue eyes that smiled with a warmth that made him nearly sigh with relief. He knew at once Hawk had told her nothing to upset her—still he was grateful he had come when he did.

"Good morning," Walking Horse spoke to both Sabrina and Hawk, but his eyes were only for the golden haired girl that smiled at him. Hawk grunted a greeting. "Walking Horse, I did not know you had been in this valley before."

"I have only seen it, but I thought it was your private place so I did not intrude."

"I see," Hawk replied, but his unspoken words stated clearly that he wondered why he chose today to do so.

"It's a beautiful valley, Hawk," Clay said.

"Yes. One day I might choose to build a lodge here." His gaze held Clay's. "It would be a good place for a man to raise his children."

"Yes," Clay answered softly. "It would."

"It is time for me to get back," Sabrina said. "I should see to Summer or she will play all day without thinking of eating or taking a nap."

"I have watched her," Hawk said. "The child has a great love for you."

"And I have a great love for her," Sabrina answered. "It is not difficult to love her, she is a special child."

"Yes, she is," Hawk answered.

"Well," Walking Horse laughed. "I am hungry. Let's go back to the village."

As they walked back toward their horses, Clay and Hawk fell a little behind. Sabrina and Walking Horse walked on ahead chatting together without noticing.

"Walking Horse looks at your woman with hungry eyes," Hawk laughed. "I should be more careful if she were mine. Walking Horse is a good man, and the women of the tribe find him quite handsome. He will snatch her from under your nose if he is given the chance."

"Don't try to create things that don't exist for my benefit, Hawk. Sabrina has common sense. By the white man's law, she is tied to me for two years. She is a woman of honor and will fulfill her obligations. But do not try to build it into what it is not. She is the woman who cares for my child . . . that is all."

"Is it?" Hawk said softly.

"Yes, it is."

"Then it will not matter to you if she visits our village often. I have asked her to do so. Will you stop her? She seems to think you will."

Clay was silent for several minutes, then he replied in a very quiet voice.

"As I said, Hawk, Sabrina is tied to me for two years. I don't see that it is necessary for her to visit here often, but if she chooses to come, I will bring her . . . and I will take her home. She is not a way to Summer, Hawk, so why not forget it?"

Hawk was about to answer when they reached the horses.

Sabrina and Walking Horse were too close now not to hear them.

The conversation turned to other things and they rode back to the village together.

Sabrina told a fascinated Ellen about the beautiful valley as they made preparations for the night's celebration.

"Sabrina," Ellen said slowly, "Do you feel some . . . some strange thing between this Hawk and Clay?"

"What kind of thing, Ellen?" Sabrina answered, but she knew Ellen's feelings echoed hers. "They have known each other since they were boys. I'm sure they have small, minor conflicts, but there is nothing seriously wrong or Clay would not have come here, and he would not have brought us."

"I don't know," Ellen said thoughtfully. "It seems like more."

"Ellen," Sabrina laughed, "don't let's go about imagining things. We were brought here to enjoy a wedding. Let's enjoy it. Clay seems to be enjoying it. If anything were wrong, he certainly wouldn't be having such a good time."

"Maybe you're right."

"I know I'm right." Sabrina stood back as she finished dressing. "Do I look all right?"

"You look like you almost belong here except for the hair and fair skin."

"Good. Let's go and have fun."

They left their lodge together and started to walk toward the already lighted fires.

As they passed in front of one the lodges, the two women who had cared for Ellen before stepped outside and called to her. She stopped to join in their excited conversation.

"I'm going on, Ellen," Sabrina said.

She left Ellen and walked between two lodges. The firelight did not touch this shadowed spot so that two people standing at the other end did not see or hear her coming. It was Walking Horse and another man.

Sabrina would have continued to walk toward them making her presence known. But their words stopped her and though she hated to eavesdrop, she could not seem to help it.

"She is the most beautiful woman I have ever seen," Walking Horse's companion said. "But I would not be the one to bring down Clay's anger on me."

"It is a thing we do not have to worry about."

"Why?"

"I have spoken to Clay. He says the woman means nothing to him. She is only the woman who is to care for his child."

"She means nothing to him," the second man laughed. "Clay is either blind or he is a fool."

Walking Horse shrugged and laughed as they turned to walk away.

"Still Clay says she is nothing to him. He insists when her time to serve him is over, he will set her free. If his words are true, and I have never known him to tell a lie, then I shall try to make her smile for me. If the gods choose I would make her my woman and be proud."

They continued to talk and their voices faded as they moved away. Sabrina stood frozen, tears slipping unheeded down her cheeks.

How long she stood so she did not know. She felt a thick, heavy pain that nearly smothered her.

Was it true? Had Clay lied? Had he just made her believe then carelessly used her? She did not know . . . but she intended to find out.

She brushed the tears from her face, replaced them with a smile, and continued her walk toward the fire . . . and the truth.

222

Nineteen

True to Hawk's word, the celebration was definitely more boisterous and exciting. So much so that no moment presented itself for her to say a word to Clay alone. After a while it became clear that Clay was not making any effort to monopolize her time. Slowly, Walking Horse's words pressed in upon her.

Grimly, she resolved to wait until the wedding ceremony was over. She wanted to give Clay the benefit of the doubt. Her love would be much harder to kill, she thought, than by a few words she didn't know were true.

Again it was in the wee hours of the morning that the village grew quiet, the fires died, the drums were silent and everyone slept.

Sabrina lay awake for a long time, wondering what Clay was thinking at the moment, if he slept, or if past dreams of sweet moments haunted him as they did her. Valiantly, she fought the memory of his magic touch and warm kisses. After a while she won . . . and drifted off to sleep.

The next afternoon would be the time of the wedding and again it would be followed by the final celebration.

Summer came to Sabrina's lodge while Sabrina was still in bed. She knelt beside Sabrina's bed. Sabrina pushed aside the fur robe that covered her and silently beckoned Summer to climb in with her.

"Quiet Summer," she whispered, "We must not disturb anyone. Climb in with me and I'll tell you a story. Why are you up so early?"

"I thought you wanted me. I dreamed you."

"You mean you dreamed of me."

"No . . . no, I dreamed you. You were unhappy, Sabrina. You were crying."

"I haven't been crying," Sabrina said.

"Not outside. But you've been crying inside."

Sabrina lay still, holding Summer close to her. Aware of the pain she had felt most of the night. Wondering at the child's words, and a little afraid of what she could not quite understand.

"Summer, do you dream people often?"

"Oh yes. I dream Papa a lot. I always know when he's unhappy or happy. I even know when he doesn't feel good."

"And others?"

"I can dream Ellen now, and I could always dream Swift Doe."

"Tell me about these dreams, Summer."

"I don't know what to tell you. Sometimes I'm awake and sometimes I'm asleep, and it just comes. I can feel . . . things."

"Things?"

"Sometimes if I close my eyes, Sabrina, I can feel . . . things. I just know when something good or bad is going to happen. Sometimes it scares me so I forget it and try not to let people in."

Sabrina herself was overwhelmed at the thoughts Summer was talking about. She wanted to ask someone about it.

"I see," she said softly. "Well, suppose we forget the bad dreams. How would you like me to tell you a story?"

"Oh yes, I'd like that."

They curled close together and Sabrina spent the next half hour telling fairy tales to a rapt listener.

Soon the village began to stir and everyone could feel the contained excitement. Bustling activity began as the women started the preparations for the feast. Ellen was completely involved in the preparations and excited about learning how to prepare a feast the Indian way.

Sabrina looked for Swift Doe, but was told she would not be seen again until the ceremony for she was undergoing the rite of purification.

Swift Doe was alone in the lodge that had been filled with aromatic steam. She knelt, naked, her head bowed and prayed the ancient prayers to her gods that her marriage would be a good and productive one. As she cleansed her body, so also she cleansed her spirit and her heart.

Sleeping Wolf had never felt so tense and nervous in his young life. Though he smiled and kept his face unreadable, acquiring Swift Doe as his wife had been his dream for so long he still could not believe it was coming true.

Clay had gone with some of the men to hunt for the meat that would supply the food for the final wedding feast.

It did not take long for Sabrina to become involved in the preparations. She worked with the women while they chattered happily with her and told her their wedding customs.

Deep pits were dug and lined with stones. In these, huge fires had been built early in the morning and kept burning until the men returned with the meat. Then all the coals from the fire were dug out and discarded, leaving the stones red hot. The meat was wrapped well in herbs and leaves, placed in the pit and covered over to cook until the wedding ceremony was over.

There was no opportunity for Clay and Sabrina to talk since she was so involved in learning and helping with the cooking.

Sabrina began making friends, and when the cooking was nearly done, they drew her with them to bathe and prepare themselves for the ceremony. A vibrant electrical excitement filled the air and Sabrina was as caught in it as if she belonged in the village. She had never felt so welcome anywhere in her life. Again, she thought of Waverly Hall, but realized, with complete honesty, that she had been happier in this strange wild country than any time in her past.

She dressed with elaborate care, and brushed her hair and let it fall about her to her slim waist. The women were fascinated by its pale shimmering gold. One shy girl gifted her with a band of leather decorated beautifully and helped her bind it across her forehead.

"You are so beautiful," one said. "The young men will have eyes only for you this night."

"Thank you," Sabrina smiled, but she wondered if Clay would pay any more attention to her tonight than he had in the past two. Walking Horse's words drummed stubbornly against her will to listen. Determinedly, she made excuses to herself . . . but her heart had begun to disbelieve.

The sun was low, casting an amber glow across the village when the villagers began to move singly and in groups toward the huge lodge that sat in the center and in which all important ceremonies were held.

The majority of the people would remain outside, but with a show of their perpetual good manners they made room in the ceremonial lodge for Clay, Ellen, Summer and Sabrina.

There was a low throbbing of drums and all eyes turned to the wide entrance of the lodge. Sleeping Wolf entered with his entourage of young men. He was magnificent in white buckskin, but Sabrina's eyes continued to return to Clay.

Even across the room his magnetism drew her. His bronzed face touched by the glow of the fire deepened the blue of his eyes. His lean muscled body sheathed in buckskin sent a quiver of remembered pleasure through her. She wanted him . . . she would always want him.

He seemed to feel her eyes on him, for he turned his head. Their eyes met and held for a magic moment that lit the fire of need within her. He smiled, and it was as if he had reached out to touch her.

Their attention was taken from each other when the drums increased their beat. Then the door cover was held aside by two girls. Sabrina's heart nearly ceased to beat and she felt a deep pain touch the center of her being.

In the doorway stood Swift Doe. Beautiful . . . Exciting . . . and wearing the dress Clay had taken from Sabrina. Pieces of Hawk's words came to her. "The wedding robe . . . all a man's love . . . a gift of love to the bride . . . a man's pride." Clay had taken all the love she could give, and had never had the intention of marrying her. He had given a wedding robe back . . . after he had taken her. It twisted within her until she became dizzy with the hurt of it.

All eyes were on Swift Doe, so Sabrina moved slowly until she reached the entrance of the lodge. Then she turned and ran.

Clay had seen Swift Doe enter and the dress she wore. His eyes turned to Sabrina. He read her face as he always could. He felt her pain across the room and knew what she was thinking.

He tried to reach the door before her, but was too late. He saw her turn and exit. When he finally reached the door, to the surprise of the onlookers, he broke into a run and followed her slim form across the village toward the trees on the outskirts.

Sabrina had reached the edge of the forest. She stopped beneath a huge tree, leaned against it and let the hot tears overcome her. She was completely unaware that Clay had come up behind her until he took her shoulders, turned her around and drew her into his arms.

She was stung by the sweet emotion of knowing she wanted him more than the breath of her life, and that he could use her so casually and plan to discard her when he was done with her.

She pressed her hands against his chest and pushed him away from her.

"Don't Clay," she whispered. Her voice cracked with the pain. "Don't touch me please. I can't bear it."

"Sabrina."

"No Clay, please. Don't you see," she sobbed, "I can't fight you . . . and I can't let you do this to me. I know what I am to you . . . let me alone. Let me have my pride."

"You don't understand, Sabrina. At least let me explain."

Sabrina looked up into his eyes and wanted, with desperation, to believe.

"When . . . when you married . . . did your wife wear that dress?"

"Yes, she did," he said, "but . . ."

"And the night you came home and found me wearing it," she replied, "did you think of her, Clay? Did old memories bring you to me?"

"It's not that way, Sabrina."

"And . . . and when I could have had the dress . . . the symbol of a man's wish to marry . . . you took it away . . . you took it because you are still married to a memory. A memory I was good enough to replace for a while . . . a while, but never for a lifetime."

"That's not true," he said sharply. "Come here, Sabrina, let me tell you the truth."

"I know the truth. You were lonely. Finding me in that dress reminded you of your wife. How easy to take me. After all," she laughed harshly, "where could I go? . . . what could I do? . . . and" she cried, "I loved you! What a fool! I loved you . . . God help me, I shall always love you."

She buried her face in her hands and wept.

Suddenly strong arms were about her and binding her against him so tight she could not move, could barely breathe.

She tried to fight but knew she was helpless. She was half his weight and his strength held her immobile.

Quietly she stood, prepared if not physically, at least mentally, to do battle.

Silence . . . he held her until she could not resist, she looked up into his eyes. His lips touched her forehead gently, then her cheeks. Again she tried to resist but he tightened his arms. She turned her face away, then gasped as one hand slid into her hair, gripped it firmly and drew her head back. Slowly, his mouth bent to hers.

"No, Clay! . . . Please! . . . Let me go!"

The rest of her words were silenced as his mouth claimed hers in a devouring kiss that shattered every thought and sent a flame through her that leapt through her veins and melted bone and sinew until she melted against him.

"Clay," she moaned softly when he finally released her lips, "why do you do this to me? Can't you see . . . it's not fair."

"Look at me Sabrina," he said firmly.

"No! I don't want to!"

"Liar," he said softly. "I can feel your heart beat. I can feel your body tremble, and I can taste love on your lips whether you will it or not. You belong to me Sabrina, and no power on earth will take you away from me—not even you."

"I don't want to love you!"

"But you do," he said softly. "You do now, and you always will."

She looked up at him. Tears blurred her eyes and traced

lines down her cheeks.

"Oh please, Clay, let me go. Don't play this game with me any longer. Yes, I love you, I always will. But I cannot live with less than your love. I know you can hold me, make love to me and I cannot fight you. But don't Clay. Let me go . . . please let me go."

"Little Sabrina," he said softly as he captured her face between his hands. "My sweet love, I will never let you go . . . never."

His lips tasted the salt of her tears as he kissed them away. Wet with her tears, his lips found her moist parted ones.

She moaned softly as the gentle touch drove all thought away. Her body, held close to him, resisted no longer. Her arms came up about his neck as their lips blended in a magic kiss that consumed all thought about each other.

They sank together to the warm grass covered ground. A hunger swept them both past reality to a blinding ecstasy. Hard calloused hands sought with infinite gentleness the soft warm silken skin. Slender hands gripped his broad shoulders drawing him closer and closer in urgent need.

Through passion darkened eyes, Clay gazed down at the woman he loved beyond reason. Her pale gold hair spread about her. Her eyes, half closed, were warm in desire. Moist warm lips, parted and seeking with the same need that consumed him.

"Clay," she murmured, "love me . . . love me."

He needed no more than this. His mouth sought hers again, tenderly, reaching within her to touch the spring of love that blossomed full and vibrant. Gently his lips played the sweet familiar song upon hers, slowly, tasting, seeking.

Wildly, they blended together, while hot flames burst into life searing them and molding them into one.

Sabrina responded to his touch with an abandoned pleasure that filled him again with the joy of possessing her. A joy he would remember forever.

Sabrina's whole being throbbed with an awareness and need for the flame of his touch.

Ecstatic torturous pleasure made her cry out to him. Clay, who took her will and her world and made it his, Clay with the magic touch that could tear aside all resistance.

A husky groan escaped him as he bore his weight down to her willing body and sheathed himself deep within her. He moved with a need that hovered near violence, yet she accepted him with the same need as his. Sweet, violent consummation left them holding each other in breathless wonder.

Then as the warm glow of blissful content settled their breathing, they drifted back to the earth completed, exhausted, yet filled with the remembered union.

She lay still, curled against him and enjoying the firm steady beat of his heart. She knew she would never have it in her power to leave him.

Clay sat up, resting on one hand, he reached out and gently caressed her cheek, letting his fingers trace her slender throat to the soft taut peaked breasts.

"Oh Clay," she whispered desperately, "what am I to do?"

"Is it so bad, so wrong, Sabrina?" he said gently, "to love me, is that something that causes you so much pain?"

"Clay!" she cried as she sat up beside him. She reached out and lay her hand against her cheek. "To love you? No! I shall always love you. The pain is not knowing that you love me."

"Love you," he whispered. Gently he touched her hair, then sliding his hand to the back of her head he drew her to him and touched his lips to hers. "You're the sunlight in the morning. You're the fresh smell of the pines and the stars in the sky. You're the beginning and end of all the love I ever want to know. Do I love you Sabrina? Do I breathe, do I feel?" He took her hand and held it close to his chest. "It beats with only one rhythm . . . Sabrina . . . Sabrina . . . Sabrina."

He watched tears sparkle in her eyes and slip gently down her cheeks. Saw the tremulous smile, felt her tremble like a leaf in a high wind.

"You're crying again," he smiled.

"I . . . Clay . . . is it true, really true?"

"Nothing in the world has ever been truer."

Suddenly, she threw herself into his arms. Taken by surprise, he fell backwards carrying her with him. They were both laughing.

Then their laughter was again silenced by the depth of the emotion that bound them one to another.

She lay across his chest, her hair falling about him. He reached up and captured her face between his hands and slowly drew her down to him.

"Sabrina, I asked you once long ago to trust me, and not to believe what you think you see and hear. I'll ask you again. Trust me Sabrina, and know in your heart that I love you. I love you and if you believe that and in me, one day everything will work out for us."

"I've waited so long to hear you say that," she said. "I do love you Clay, and I don't understand all the things I feel happening. But, I will trust you. Just . . . just tell me again that you love me."

"One day, I will explain to you. For now, is my love enough to hold us together?"

"Yes," she whispered, "yes, my love."

"Sabrina," he murmured as he drew her tighter in a firm embrace and joined her lips in a kiss of promise.

The night grew deeper, but the lovers knew nothing but each other and the vibrant love they shared.

It was long after the village slept that they walked back

together. Clay said goodnight to Sabrina and went to his lodge to try to find sleep.

Both were unaware of the tall dark form that stood in the darkened doorway of his lodge and watched them. He had a satisfied smile on his face.

"So," he said softly to himself. "If she was not your woman before this night, she is now my brother. Now let us see if you can keep what you have. Now let us see if the truth does not take away from you what you love most."

Twenty

To Sabrina, it seemed as if she had just closed her eyes when she was shaken awake. Bright sunlight lit the lodge.

"Wake up sleepy head," Ellen laughed, "Clay has everything ready. We're to leave this morning."

"Where's Summer?"

"Under her father's feet, begging him not to go home yet. Clay says please hurry and untangle her from him so we can get started."

Sabrina laughed, but rose immediately. The need to see Clay was the uppermost thought in her mind and heart. Dressing quickly, she left the lodge. As soon as she stepped out the door, she was met by Walking Horse who had obviously been waiting for her.

"Good morning, Sa-bree-nah."

"Good morning, Walking Horse." She smiled at him, and he fell into step beside her.

"I am sorry to see you leave us this morning. You have enjoyed yourself in our village?"

"Yes I have, very much."

"Good. Then you will come again soon?"

"I'm not sure what plans Clay has, but I do hope we will. You must come and visit us also."

Sabrina's drawing room manners meant politeness to her.

To the tall, handsome Indian that walked beside her, it only meant encouragement. He smiled.

"I shall come," he said, delighted at the invitation.

They walked toward Clay who was busy packing the horses, with Summer at his heels doing her best to argue him into staying a few more days.

When Summer saw Sabrina coming, she left her father's side and ran to Sabrina.

"Sabrina, ask Papa. Maybe we could stay for a while."

"Summer, if your father says we must go, then we must. Maybe if we ask nicely, he might consider bringing us back one day soon."

Summer's face went from disappointment at Sabrina's first words to bright excitement at the last. Clay groaned and Sabrina laughed, knowing Summer would soon begin a campaign to return to the village as soon as possible.

Sabrina went to Clay's side and smiled up at him.

"Good morning," he said gently. "I can't believe you can manage to look so beautiful with so little sleep and at this hour of the morning." He lowered his voice and his eyes held hers. She could feel her cheeks pinken with his reference to the night before and the pleasant warm sensation that began in the center of her and flowed through her.

"Good morning," she whispered.

"I've got everything packed. We'll be ready to leave in a few minutes."

"I must say good-bye to Hawk."

"Don't worry," Clay laughed, "we won't get away that easily. Hawk, Walking Horse, and several others will ride along with us for an hour or so . . . sort of give us a gala sendoff."

Clay helped both Ellen and Sabrina mount, then he mounted and reached down to lift a still reluctant Summer up before him.

As Clay had said, Hawk, Walking Horse and several

braves rode with them as they left the village.

They made it a laughing and happy occasion, the braves showing off their elaborate horsemanship and shouting flowery tributes to Sabrina and laughing jibes at Clay.

After an hour of this, they dropped behind. Sabrina turned to wave a last farewell. From this spot on, they would be traveling alone.

The balance of the trip home was uneventful. Once there, Sabrina was busy catching Summer up on the lessons she had not done while they were at the Indian village. Ellen fussed over a house she labeled completely filthy. She at once began to rip it apart and thoroughly clean it with Summer and Sabrina's help. Clay, very wisely, went hunting to restore the supply of food.

It was two days before Clay returned, and he returned when the house was dark and everyone was asleep.

Sabrina had waited every night until her sleepy eyes would no longer stay open.

Clay put the rewards from his hunt in the kitchen where Ellen could find them in the morning, then he went out and crossed the clearing to the stream where he took the time to wash the dust of travel away. When he finished, he walked toward the house with a determined step. Two days and two long nights were too long to be away from the sweet warm woman he loved. He thought of his time away when he had lain at night missing her completely and dreaming of her slim body in his arms and the taste of her sweet lips against his.

He opened the door quietly and went in, closing it soundlessly behind him. He needed no light to make his way across rooms he had known for years . . . or at least he thought he didn't. He did not take into account Ellen's penchant for rearranging rooms when she cleaned them. He promptly tripped over a bench, fell into the table which tipped and deposited him solidly upon the floor with enough noise to wake the dead.

Doors were thrown open and soon Ellen, bearing a candle, and Sabrina and Summer were looking down on him and trying not to laugh at his angry face and rather bizarre situation of being flat on his back.

"What the hell . . ." he muttered.

"Good heavens, Clay," Ellen said, "what are you doing down there?"

"I might ask you the same thing," Clay growled. "What was that bench doing there?"

Sabrina tried to stifle her laughter, and Clay glared at her suspiciously while he rose and righted the table.

Summer too was just a little too bright eyed to suit her father.

"Summer, go to back to bed," he said.

"Yes Papa," she replied. But he still heard her muffled giggles as she left the room. Then his eyes turned back to a pink faced Ellen. He continued to stare at her until she turned and quietly left the room. It was only then that Sabrina could hold her laughter no longer. She sank into a chair and surrendered to her laughter.

Then suddenly she yelped in surprise as strong arms lifted her bodily from the chair.

"I believe you're laughing at me, woman."

"Oh, Clay," she laughed as she laid her head on his shoulder, "you did look so funny flat on your back in the middle of the living room . . . especially half under the table. Tell me," she giggled, "did the table attack you in the dark? Were you afraid?" she lowered her voice in pretended seriousness.

Clay had to chuckle at what he realized must have been an amusing scene. Then slim arms about his neck and willing lips close to his put an end to all other thoughts.

He let her feet down until they barely touched the floor

and held her tightly against him. Gently, he took her warm willing lips with his.

"God," he murmured against the softness of her hair, "two days feels like forever when I'm away from you."

"I missed you too," she sighed softly.

His arms bound her to him, and she welcomed the breathless hold, realizing how empty and lonely she had been when he was gone.

There was nothing but pale moonlight to touch the room. They were shadows holding each other, yet each knew the other perfectly and for now emotions had complete control.

Lips touched, blended in a sweet gentle kiss. He tasted the love in her with a deep sense of pleasure and homecoming. Her slim body pressed against his awakened desire with a touch of searing flame.

As she always would be, Sabrina was caught in the magic spell Clay's love could weave about her. She surrendered completely to the need that filled her to overflowing at his touch.

Effortlessly, he lifted her in his arms and on soundless feet walked to her bedroom door. She laid her head on his shoulder pressing her lips to the throbbing pulse in his throat. She could feel the rapid beat of his heart that matched the thundering of hers.

When he pushed her door shut, he stood her on her feet, then went to light the candle. When he returned to her side, he cupped her face in his hands and kissed her again and again slowly feeding the flame of her passion. Then with hands that trembled he began to undress her. Her wide purple eyes lifted to his and he smiled.

"I like undressing you. It's kind of like a miracle every time, seeing something so beautiful emerge. You take my breath away Sabrina . . . you're so lovely."

His words were soft as he let the dress fall to the floor and gently caressed the smooth texture of her skin.

"You are," he whispered, his eyes warm, "a miracle."

He put his hands on her hips and drew her against him, and she willingly lifted her lips to his kiss. A kiss that rocked her world and sent it careening into the star lit void. A deep and vibrant hunger filled her, with a surge of pleasure she felt strong arms lift her and lay her gently against the pillows.

In moments he was beside her drawing her close to him. She could feel his long muscular length against her and the heat of his throbbing manhood that told her his hunger echoed hers.

"Sabrina," he whispered as his hands caressed her and lifted her passion to soar on wings of love to a world where only they existed.

Slender fingers caressed the hard muscles of his arms, sliding up to draw him closer and closer. Her body trembled to his caresses and the gentle touch of his hands sent violent shreds of excitement hurtling through her until she could bear the sweet exquisite pain no longer. She cried out to him in passion-filled words as he continued to search her being for a desire that matched his.

A husky moan escaped her as he joined them together, plunging to the deepest depths of her and driving what little was left of her senses beyond her reach.

She welcomed his thrusting weight, holding him within her, arching to meet his slow sure motions.

Her hands slid down the muscle of his back to his thrusting hips to urge his penetration deeper and deeper.

She no longer had any thought, any need but Clay . . . Clay . . . Clay.

They floated downward from the height of passion together holding to each other. Clay raised on one elbow and looked down into eyes limpid and soft, regarding him with the same warm appreciation. He allowed himself the pleasure of sinking into that deep purple pool. He bent and brushed a light kiss on rosy parted lips.

She smiled, sighed deeply as he again lay beside her and held her close to him. Her head rested on his shoulder and he absently caressed her hair as they lay in a moment of contented silence.

"As I said before, Sabrina," Clay whispered against her hair, "loving you is a small miracle. Each time is as new as the first and just as sweet."

Her body curled against his, her hand caressing lean ribs and a fur matted chest. Sabrina felt more content than ever before. Clay's words only added more pleasure to her happiness.

"Sabrina?"

"Yes?"

"I have to talk to you about something, and I want you to understand."

"What is it, Clay?" she questioned, but a tiny cold finger touched her.

"You know I love you, and you know I want to keep you with me forever. But it is impossible for us to marry until the Reverend makes his rounds, and he won't be in this area until well into the spring."

"I don't understand," she said as she sat up and looked down at him.

"It's something that is beyond my control, Sabrina. There is only one preacher for several hundred miles." He reached up to touch her shocked face and chuckled, "Sabrina, you don't still doubt that I want you . . . that I love you? If I could do something about it, I'd do it tomorrow."

"But Clay! What if I . . . I mean . . . what if I'm . . ." Her fiery cheeks and downcast eyes spoke eloquently of her meaning.

"Carrying my child?" he asked softly. "There couldn't be anything in this world that would make me happier. I love you Sabrina, and in the spring, if you're willing, we'll be married."

"Oh yes, I'm willing Clay. I want to be your wife. But what will people say if . . ."

"What people?" Clay laughed. "There are no people close enough to know. Sabrina, on the frontier this kind of thing is accepted. I wouldn't want to wait a year to hold you, to make love to you. I can hardly stand a day or two. Understand," he whispered, "stay with me. Don't close yourself away from me. It will all work out." He drew her down to him and kissed her until she clung weakly to him.

"I do love you Clay," she breathed softly. Bending close, she let her lips linger against his, savoring the feel of his hard seeking mouth and the deep masculine scent of him.

She was content as he held her close, resting against him. She closed her eyes to enjoy more fully the gentle touch of his hands as he caressed her.

"Sabrina?"

"Umm?"

"There's one more thing I would ask you."

"What Clay?"

"I don't want you involved with Hawk and his people. It would be best if they didn't know our plans."

Again the icy finger touched lightly, a fear she could not name or understand. She looked up into his dark blue gaze and for this one time she could read no emotion behind them. They held hers, waiting for her response.

"I don't understand, Clay. I thought Hawk and his people were friends. They treated us so well and welcomed us in their village. I thought . . . well . . . that we might visit and remain friends. Especially Swift Doe."

"No Sabrina. I don't think we'll go back to the village,

241

and I intend to make it clear to Hawk that I don't want him here, especially if I'm away."

"But Clay . . . why? What is there between you. Does it have something to do with your wife? Can't you tell me?"

"Sabrina, listen to me. The past . . . my past, it's a painful thing. It's a difficult thing for me to talk about. Maybe some day, but for now . . . can you believe in me? Can you trust me? Can you help me start a new life? A life just for us."

"I can understand you finding it hard to talk of your wife, but Clay, what could Hawk and a whole village of kind and gentle people have done to make you want to cut them out of your life? I thought you had once been very close friends."

"It's all tied together," he replied. "And I want to sever some of the ties. It will be easier for me in the future, and for Summer."

"Easier for Summer," she said, surprise in her voice, "but they were her mother's people. How can it be easier for Summer if you cut away half of her roots?"

Clay sat up beside her and took her shoulders in his hands.

"Sabrina, I've been raising Summer for five years. I want a whole different future for her than living in an Indian village. You've been good for her, you have the ability to help her into that future. I have plans that don't include her past or mine. I need you to help me . . . I need you both for Summer and for myself. I love you Sabrina. Stay with me, help me make a whole new future for us all."

He drew her into his arms and began to kiss her, soft gentle kisses on her eyes, her cheeks, her throat then her soft lips where he explored leisurely.

"Help me Sabrina," he whispered as their lips tasted gently, "I need you."

She trembled in his arms, letting all thought of arguing

escape her. He wiped all thoughts from her mind, even the question of why Clay would want to sever Summer from even her mother's memory.

Gently, he pressed her down against the downy pillow, following her with tantalizing kisses that made her head swim. With deliberate expertise, he began to lift her senses to a vibrant plane of excitement.

Tongues of liquid flame began in the very center of her being and flowed outward through her limbs like molten lava.

With a soft moan, her arms drew him closer, exploring as he was the infinitely exquisite pleasure. Like a symphony, their mutual love sang clear and pure.

When again their senses descended from the stars, and their breathing was controlled, they lay safe and secure in each other's arms. Clay slept . . . but Sabrina could not.

She lay close to him, her head resting on his shoulder. She watched his chest rise and fall with slow even breathing. She gazed at his profile. The strong chin and the handsome chiseled features. She loved him, completely and without reservation, yet the small nagging fear again touched her mind with feather light fingers.

Something in Clay's past had the ability to frighten him . . . to hurt him. He did not want to tell her what it was, yet she knew some dark thing between Clay and Hawk could endanger Summer's future.

Why, she wondered, would a man love a woman, marry her, have a child by her, and then after her death, try to wipe all memory of her from her own child's mind and heart. Why, if Clay wanted to sever all ties, did he stay in this area at all? Why didn't he take his child and leave?

If she were going to be part of Clay's life, and she knew she had to be, then she had to find the answers to these questions . . . no matter what Clay said.

She thought for several minutes, then made a final decision. One day, Clay would again have to leave them to tend to his traps or to go for supplies, which usually took several days. When he did, she would find a way to get to the Indian village. She had to ask Hawk some questions . . . she had to have some answers.

Yes Clay, she thought, I love you and I want a good future for all of us. You, Summer and me. Maybe if I can open that door, maybe if I can make you understand that there is nothing in the world big enough to separate us . . .

Possessively she put her arm across his waist. He stirred in his sleep, murmured her name and drew her closer to him.

She smiled, content with his love and with her thoughts. She had no idea that what she was thinking now was exactly what Hawk wanted her to think, or that he waited only to tell her the truth, hoping it would turn her from Clay. He wanted Clay to lose her love.

Neither Clay nor Hawk took into consideration the love, strength and grim determination of the girl who finally closed her eyes in relaxed sleep.

Twenty-one

Hawk sat back on his haunches after drinking from the fresh cool stream. He remained immobile watching his horse drink. His eyes scanned the area about him, filled with pleasure at the beauty and serenity his valley would always hold for him.

A faint smile touched his lips as he remembered the fair haired girl that had sat with him here. He remembered exactly how the sun had touched her hair, and how her eyes had sparkled as she gazed at the beauty about her.

It had been over a week since she had left them, and it still surprised him that he could remember everything about her. Surprised and annoyed him. He couldn't allow it to happen, yet it had. Night after night, she had returned to him, returned in dreams he could not exorcise . . . in fact, did not want to exorcise.

Again he smiled, as he realized if he could take her from Clay, he would accomplish all his purposes at one time. He could have Sabrina . . . and balance the scale with Clay.

He thought of Clay, and remembered days past. The memories were both sweet and bitter. Lost love, friendship and dreams that had changed so drastically in the past five years.

Hawk had traveled beyond the mountains to the rolling

green plains that lay beyond, and he knew one day his whole village would be forced to make the same journey. The white man had infiltrated his land. Even the valley he now enjoyed would not always belong to him.

Again he thought of the dark eyed girl who had held the secrets of his heart and of his dreams. He knew, even after all that had passed, that Clay did not fully understand what Singing Bells had meant to her tribe, nor did he understand what Summer still meant to them. He knew it was useless to dream that one day Clay would understand that they only wanted to share in the gifts the Great Spirit had given both to mother and to daughter. Clay was a very stubborn and possessive man. He refused to share anything he felt was his. Hawk could remember long years of arguments, of talks that had been useless. Clay was strong — but in his strength lay his weakness.

He pushed the dark thoughts of bitter past from his mind, and dwelt again on the fair haired woman named Sabrina. It had been a long time since Hawk had felt about another woman the way he had felt about Singing Bells. He had forced such emotions away. There had been many women since then, but he had not allowed them to touch the inner place Sabrina had walked into so casually. Now he could not force her out.

He rose and tossed aside the pebbles he had been skipping across the water. It did no good to allow his thoughts to remain in the past. There was one thing he had to do, then he had to concentrate on the future safety of the tribe that would one day be his responsibility.

Before he could defend himself against it, thoughts of Sabrina returned.

Clay had made her his woman, of that he was sure. But had he told her the truth? Did she question why Summer was held away from her mother's people? Did she know what the past held . . . would the truth change her feelings for Clay . . . he hoped it would. No matter how he tried to deny the feelings of anger, no matter how he tried to hold himself away from her, he knew he wanted Sabrina for revenge, but he also wanted her for himself, and at this moment he wasn't sure which emotion was strongest.

Slowly he mounted his horse and turned him from the valley he loved. He rode toward the village. He had hardly left the valley when he saw a rider approaching. He shaded his eyes with his hand and in a moment recognized Walking Horse.

He reined in his horse and waited. It was soon obvious to him that Walking Horse had been hunting, for a doe hung across his horse's rump. When Walking Horse saw him he raised his arm as a gesture of greeting and kicked his horse into a faster gait. In a few moments, he reined to a stop by Hawk's side.

"I see the hunting has been good," Hawk said.

"Yes, I have been lucky this day. I am also hungry. Would you like to make camp and eat with me Hawk?"

Hawk agreed and they proceeded to hobble their horses, and ate some dried meat and berries Walking Horse carried with him.

They sat by the fire in silent camaraderie.

"Hawk," Walking Horse said, watching Hawk's face with astute eyes, "I'm going to Clay's lodge tomorrow. To visit, and to bring Sa-bree-nah a gift I have made for her. Would you like to ride with me brother?"

He asked the last quietly as if he expected it might upset Hawk.

Hawk's face was as immobile and unreadable as the man he gazed at. He had to admit that Walking Horse was one of the handsomest of his warriors. A touch of jealousy struck and he was as shocked at it as Walking Horse would have been had he known.

"You bring Sabrina gifts. It is a thing Clay might not be too happy about."

"Why should it bother Clay?"

"I got the feeling that Clay was rather possessive of Sabrina. She belongs to him and he might not be pleased about your interference."

Walking Horse laughed. "It is not so, my brother. If it were I would not do such a thing. But he told me himself. Sabrina is only his servant. He said she meant no more to him than that. He also said when her time of service is over he will set her free. It is a strange custom these white people have, but if it sets Sabrina free, I will not question it."

"I see," Hawk replied. "Maybe I shall go with you."

"Good. We shall leave before the sun rises."

"Maybe," Hawk said, "we shall even stay for a few days." Hawk smiled, and his eyes sparkled with mischievous amusement.

"Yes," Walking Horse chuckled, "maybe it would be good to stay with such friends for a while. And," his eyes answered Hawk's humor, "maybe we can even convince Sabrina she should visit us again soon."

"Then let us go back to our lodges, brother. If we are to start before dawn, we had best prepare for the trip."

They rose, extinguished their fire, and rode back to the village.

Dawn was a faint light streak on the horizon when they rode from the village and headed toward Clay's home.

Sabrina stretched luxuriously and yawned, then she turned on her side and drew Clay's pillow into her arms. A contented smile touched her lips and her eyes closed in sweet remembrance of the night.

Caught in her dream, she was unaware that her bedroom

door had opened and Summer's head peeked around it.

Summer thought Sabrina slept, then she came in, closed the door softly behind her and tiptoed to the bed.

"Sabrina," she whispered, "are you awake?"

Sabrina laughed softly and opened her eyes. She reached out and took a smiling Summer's hand and drew her down on the bed to sit beside her.

"Good morning, Summer. My goodness, you're up early. I'll bet no one else is awake, why are you?"

"I couldn't sleep anymore."

"What do you mean, you couldn't sleep anymore?"

"Someone is coming, Sabrina," the child said so softly, and for the first time Sabrina realized Summer was trying her best to pretend she was not afraid, and not doing a very good job of it. Sabrina sat up and drew the child close to her.

"Did you see or hear someone coming? Did something frighten you?"

"No . . . no, I dreamed them."

"Dreamed them? Did you have a nightmare?"

"I wasn't asleep . . . I just dreamed them."

"Summer, you said this once before. Tell me now what you mean. Who's coming and how did you dream them if you weren't asleep?"

Summer reached her hand up to touch the silver band that encircled her slim upper arm.

"Sabrina, I think Hawk is coming, but I don't know who is with him. Someone is with him, but I don't know who."

"How . . . Summer . . . you . . . you actually see Hawk? I mean, you know it's Hawk who is coming?"

"It's because I have this. It used to be Hawk's. That's how I know. I know Hawk is coming, I just don't know who is coming with him."

Sabrina was shaken and she really didn't know what to

say. Summer watched her for a moment then she said softly.

"It's all right, Sabrina, I don't mind. I dream a lot of times. It doesn't frighten me anymore. Besides, Hawk is a friend."

Sabrina knew this was another question she had to find the answer to. She had to know if Clay knew this strange sense his daughter seemed to possess.

"Yes, yes, Summer, Hawk is a friend and it will be nice to see him again so soon. Maybe we should tell your father right away so he will not go away."

"No!" Summer said quickly. "Sabrina, I don't want to tell Papa. Please don't. He'll be angry. Please, Sabrina, don't tell him."

For the first time since she had known Clay, Sabrina became angry with him. This type of thing must have happened before and Clay had tried to push it aside by becoming angry with Summer, angry enough to make a child who worshiped her father afraid to speak to him of a secret that frightened her.

She promised herself to protect Summer, but she also wanted to know more about this secret thing and what Clay felt about it. Someday when she and Clay were married and she was free to question.

"Don't worry Summer, I won't say anything. Besides, maybe you might be wrong this time. After all, it's been only a week or so since we left the village. Maybe they won't be visiting this soon. Come on, let's go have some breakfast. We'll cook for Ellen this morning and surprise her."

Summer nodded and they rose, made the bed hastily and went to the kitchen. Summer never said that in her mind she knew Hawk was coming and she knew the expected visit somehow frightened her.

Her fear was pushed to the back of her mind with the pleasure she found in making breakfast for Ellen and her father.

When everything was prepared, Sabrina said she would waken Ellen and Summer could go and wake her father.

Summer ran to her father's room from which Sabrina soon heard muffled deep laughter threaded with delighted giggles. Within ten minutes, Clay came out of the room bearing a squirming, laughing Summer under one arm. He deposited her on her feet and smiled across the room at Sabrina.

"Good morning. Summer has just told me you and she just made breakfast. I can't wait to eat this masterpiece." He walked across the room and stood beside Sabrina, then lowered his voice. "I didn't know you could cook too." His eyes sparkled in humor and warm pleasure at seeing her.

"You just might be surprised at what I can do, Clay Storm."

"My sweet," he said softly, "I would enjoy being surprised any time the desire strikes you. Feel free to find areas you might like to surprise me in."

She blushed and laughed.

"Come and eat, Clay."

Breakfast was a leisurely and contented affair with Clay and Sabrina enjoying Summer's delighted chatter.

"Sabrina, come for a ride with me today," Clay said. "I have something I'd like to show you."

"Can I come too, Papa?"

Sabrina could have laughed at the look on Clay's face, but restrained herself, yet he could read the laughter in her eyes.

"I don't see any reason why you can't, Summer, unless Sabrina has some studies you need to concentrate on."

"No," Sabrina said innocently, "Summer is doing fine. She can miss a day of studies."

Clay chuckled, and Sabrina had the sudden impulse to run to him and throw herself into his arms and kiss him.

"How long will we be gone, Clay? Should I bring something to eat?"

"That might be a good idea," he said. "The three of us will have a picnic."

Summer was so excited, she could barely finish her breakfast. Then she and Ellen went to the pantry to see what could be put in a package that they could eat later.

Clay went to saddle two horses and bring them from the barn. In less than an hour, Summer was seated before Clay and the three of them were ready to leave.

The valley that held Clay's cabin was bordered on both sides by high green hills. They rode to the top of the hill in a direction Sabrina had seen Clay go before. From the top of the hill they looked down across a grass covered plain to a ridge of mountains beyond. The plain had scattered patches of bright colored wild flowers, and Sabrina and Clay both sat in wonder at its beauty.

"Oh Clay, how very beautiful your world is."

"Yes," he said as he gazed at her with a look of intense warmth that told her he included her among his beauties. "I come here often. It's a place that brings peace no matter how you feel."

Again, Sabrina was struck with the sensation that Clay Storm was no frontiersman. There was so much more to this man than she knew.

They rode slowly across the grass covered plain to the foot of the mountains, then gradually the ground began to rise. The air was fresh and clear. Soft white clouds, tied to the earth by threads of early morning sunlight, moved across a sea blue sky.

Then the sunlight was cut away from them and filtered down in bright streams through the high trees. The massive trees created a new beauty by the shadows and a coolness into which they rode. Sabrina was spellbound by a beauty so rare and so complete, it was nearly painful to watch. She watched Clay's face and knew the answer to why he would never leave this place. He loved this beauty, it held him captive and he could not bear its loss.

Sabrina was about to speak when they broke from the depths of the forest into a bright sunlit meadow. Surrounded on three sides by high green hills and the forest through which they had come, it appeared like an Eden, a shangri-la, a quiet place in which a soul could soar.

"We'll stop and have our picnic here," Clay said.

"I have never seen a place as beautiful as this," Sabrina said as she slid down from her horse and handed its reins to Clay. He secured the horses and returned to her side to enjoy her rapture with a place that also held his heart.

They stood in a sea of calf-high grass that undulated in a soft breeze, rolling and changing its color like a deep rippling ocean of shifting blues and greens. Scattered about were patches of yellow and white flowers that also waved an inviting welcome to any passerby.

Clay slid his arm about Sabrina's slender waist and drew her close to him. In shared silence and joy, they watched Summer run from one patch of flowers to another gathering armfuls of them. After a few minutes, Clay went to his horse and got the blanket and bundle of food. They spread the blanket on the ground in time for a laughing, bright eyed Summer to tumble the mass of multi-colored flowers upon it.

Amid laughter and complete contentment, they shared a mid-afternoon meal.

Summer was fascinated that Sabrina could twine the flowers together to make a crown and when Sabrina finished it she handed it to Summer, who promptly placed it on Sabrina's head.

Clay watched, held spellbound by Sabrina. Her pale gold

hair blown by the breeze and a crown of wild flowers nestled within its mass. Her violet eyes sparkling with warm laughter. Soft moist red lips he fought the urge to possess.

They were a world contained within each other and it would be a magic time Sabrina would remember forever.

Summer soon nestled close to Sabrina on the blanket and drifted into dream-filled slumber.

Gently, so he would not waken her, Clay rose and extended his hand to Sabrina.

"Let's take a walk," he whispered. He saw her eyes go quickly to Summer. "We won't go far and we won't be gone long."

She raised her hand and he drew her to her feet.

His arm came firmly about her waist, and she slid her arm about his. Together they walked slowly through the tall grass.

Their voices were soft, blown away on the breeze, gentle, as lovers words usually were.

When they were well away from Summer, Clay stopped and drew Sabrina into his arms. He held her close, content for this moment to do nothing more than feel her slim body close to his and the willing touch of her arms as they clung to him.

She looked up into blue eyes that were warm and enveloped her within them.

"I only wanted a moment to hold you love, just to feel you in my arms," he said softly. "Just to see if my heart has lied to me." He touched her lips with his. "No, it has not. You are still the sweetest thing it has ever been my good fortune to find."

"Clay," she whispered as again his lips found hers in a sweet gentle kiss that asked nothing except the affirmation that she felt as he did. Tenderly, he savored the response he felt through every fiber of his being. He held her face between his hands and let his lips discover the soft corners of her mouth, her cheeks, brushed her temples and again caught her mouth with his.

"Clay, I love you so much, so very much," she sighed as she laid her head against his chest and her arms about his waist. The solid steady beat of his heart was a firm reassurance and the iron arms that bound her to him gave her a sense of security such as she had never known before.

"Before I get carried away, my love, and do something that is rapidly getting beyond my control, we'd best go back and gather up our little girl. It's time to head for home."

She laughed, and they walked back, but each knew they would much rather have stayed there and fulfilled the promise of their kiss.

Summer still slept, so they gathered up the remains of the food and put it away then sat and talked quietly. Less than a half hour later, Summer stirred awake. Sabrina took her on her lap and held her while she reoriented herself. Clay rolled the blanket and tied it on his horse. He helped Sabrina mount then lifted Summer in his arms and mounted. Then they started toward home at a slow, steady gait.

The ride back was as pleasant and as breathtakingly beautiful as the ride out had been. The sun was beginning to set and the early evening sky was flame red with streaks of yellow and amber.

A yellow glow of lamplight shone from the cabin windows as they rode up. Sabrina dismounted and took Summer from Clay. She took her inside while Clay took the horses to see to their care for the night.

Inside the house, Ellen rose from her chair to greet them.

"Did you have a nice day?"

"It was beautiful, Ellen. One day you should ride out with us to see."

"No thank you. I'll stay right here in comfort. Horses are

not my strong point." They all laughed. "I've a warm supper ready. Are you hungry?"

They both agreed they were and Clay came in and voiced his approval and they sat together to enjoy one of Ellen's very finest meals.

After the meal, Sabrina read a story to Summer, bathed her and put her to bed. She was just re-entering the living room, when Ellen and Clay's conversation came to her.

"What all do you need Ellen?"

"I've made a list, Clay. There's quite a lot of things your kitchen's in need of."

"Give me the list. I'll leave first thing in the morning. It will only take me three or four days."

Sabrina entered the room and Clay explained to her that Ellen was short of supplies and that he intended to go for more the next morning.

"I'll be gone just a little over three days. You'll be all right?"

"Of course, Clay, we'll be fine. I'll work on Summer's lessons so she can surprise you when you come home."

"And I'll finish cleaning this house," Ellen said.

"But you won't rearrange the furniture, will you Ellen?" Clay laughed, "or at least will you put a sign out to give me warning?"

Ellen laughed, assured him everything would be right where it was when he came home.

Ellen soon claimed fatigue and went to bed. Clay blew out the lamp and in the glow of the red embered fire, he reached for Sabrina who smiled softly and stepped into the circle of his waiting arms.

Twenty-two

It was a habit of Clay's to rise before the sun. Seeing the morning sunrise was one of the things that had caught him in the magic of this new and growing country.

He rose now and dressed without light. He left the house silently and walked across the clearing to the barn. He was completely unaware that his movements were being watched by interested eyes.

Walking Horse and Hawk had arrived at Clay's house in time to see the lights go out. They had decided not to disturb the family and made camp.

Hawk woke early and while Walking Horse still slept, he stood beneath the covering darkness of the trees and watched the house. He was immediately alert when the door opened and a shadowed figure left the house. He knew instantly it was Clay. He watched as Clay saddled a horse and rode away. He knew Clay planned on being gone several days because he had a pack horse. Most likely, he thought, Clay is going for supplies.

Clay rode slowly, allowing his thoughts to drift to Sabrina. Combined with the glorious dawn of day, thoughts of Sabrina's beauty seemed to be the most appropriate thoughts.

He was well used to riding long distances; he rode easily, his body relaxed and moving with the gait of the horse. He rode without thought of anything else but Sabrina and the deep warmth within him thoughts of her brought.

When he came to the banks of the river, it was already past noon. He stopped to eat and rest for less than twenty minutes, then again he was mounted and on his way.

By late afternoon, Caleb's cabin came in sight. He had been seen by the inhabitants long before he reached the cabin. Caleb was waiting on the porch for him.

"Hello Clay," Caleb grinned. "How you been, boy?"

"I'm fine, Caleb," Clay smiled as he dismounted. "Got something good to eat and a drink in there?"

"Shore do boy. Step down and come on in."

"I can't stay long, Caleb. I'm on my way in for supplies. I don't want to be away too long. I don't want to leave the women and Summer too long."

He walked up on the porch and stood beside Caleb who cocked one eyebrow and looked at him curiously.

"The women?"

"The women," Clay laughed as he clapped his hand on Caleb's shoulder. "Let's have that drink and I'll tell you a very, very interesting story."

"Well come along boy, this sounds mighty interestin'."

They walked into the cabin together where they shared more than one drink and Clay told the story of Sabrina's arrival. He left out anything about the development of a relationship between him and Sabrina.

"So her daughter turned out to be a little older than you thought," Caleb grinned.

"Yes, but she's been a blessing for Summer. She's teaching her to read and write and in the future to be a lady of quality, I hope."

Caleb remained silent for a moment, then he said.

"Clay, I know it ain't none of my business, and it ain't good for a neighbor to nose into someone else's affairs . . .

but what are you goin' to do now Hawk is back. He ain't a man to ever forget all that happened. You seen him yet, or talked to him?"

"I've done both," Clay replied. He went on to explain to Caleb about Swift Doe's wedding and their visit to the village. "Caleb," Clay continued, "Hawk or no one else is going to run me off my property. One day he's going to have to understand and forget the past and make peace. When he does, I'll listen. Until then . . . no one . . . no one takes what is mine."

"Maybe . . . maybe," Caleb said softly, "you should try makin' the peace."

"I have nothing to make peace over."

"We all make mistakes, Clay. It takes two to make a fight . . . and two to make peace."

Clay gazed at Caleb for a moment then he replied.

"Are you suggesting I'm as wrong as Hawk is? You know what happened. Caleb, you've never said anything one way or the other, now are you saying I'm wrong?"

"Clay, I can't say who's right or wrong. It ain't my place to say nothin'. I like you, you're a fine man like your father. I liked Singing Bells and there's a special place in my heart for that little girl of yours. All I'm sayin' is . . . well, maybe I can understand how Hawk feels too . . . he loved her too. All I'm sayin' is . . . think on it Clay. Maybe the thought of makin' peace will come to you."

Clay remained silent. Then he drained his glass, set it down and stood up.

"I have to be on my way, Caleb. I've a lot of supplies to buy."

"Clay . . ."

"I'll think about it, Caleb," Clay said in a voice that made Caleb understand the subject was closed. "I'll see you on my way back."

Clay walked to the porch with Caleb behind him, unaware of the worry and pain in Caleb's eyes. Outside he mounted, waved a quick good-bye and in a few minutes, was gone. Caleb stood watching the empty trail for a long time.

"You're a good man like your father, Clay, but you're sure as hell as stubborn and possessive as he was. Before you get real bad hurt again, I sure hope you learn you got to be able to let go before you can hold on."

He turned and walked back into the house and closed the door behind him.

Clay again rode slowly, now trying his best to keep past memories from entering his mind. He forced his mind to dwell on Sabrina and the happy future they could share. But when he made camp that night and rolled in his blanket to sleep, dreams came unbidden and unwelcome and there was no way he could force them away.

Sabrina wakened slowly, vaguely wondering what it was that had wakened her. Bright sunlight in the room told her it was much later than her usual time to rise. After a few moments the low murmur of voices came to her and she realized what had brought her awake. The voices were low and rumbling . . . men! It brought her immediately, completely awake. Clay was gone. Who were the men who were talking. Then came the fleeting memory of Summer's dream . . . what had she said . . . "Hawk and someone else was coming." Was it true? Could Summer see what was going to happen?

She rose quickly and dressed as rapidly as she could. When she walked into the parlor, she, in spite of all her mental preparation, was shocked to see a smiling Hawk seated by the fireplace with a chattering Summer on his lap. What surprised her even more was, true to Summer's dream, Walking Horse, the second person she had said was coming, stood leaning against the fireplace watching the two in conversation.

Both Walking Horse and Hawk saw Sabrina at the same time, and both were caught in the aura of her sleepy eyed beauty. Neither spoke for a moment, but Hawk stood and put Summer gently down. It was Hawk who astutely read the surprise in her eyes as they lingered on Summer, and he put the right meaning to it. Obviously, Summer had told Sabrina they were coming and their arrival had shocked her.

"Good morning, Sabrina," Hawk smiled.

"Good morning Hawk, Walking Horse, it is nice to see you again, but . . . Clay isn't home."

"Yes, so Summer has told us. It is too bad we have missed him. But then," Hawk chuckled, "it will give us an excuse to come again."

"I'm sure you do not need an excuse to come here. You are Clay's friends and Summer's people. I feel, and I'm sure Ellen does too, that after our grand visit to your village we are friends too."

Both men were pleased at her words, and both were soon pleased with the way they were made welcome.

"I shall make a nice dinner," Ellen said.

"If you will come outside, Sa-bree-nah, I have brought something for you," Walking Horse said.

"A gift . . . for me?"

"Yes."

Sabrina walked with Walking Horse toward the door. Summer started to follow, but Hawk put his hand on her shoulder to gently restrain her.

"Summer," he said gently, "stay and speak with me for a while."

Her dark eyes lifted to his and he was aware there was no sign of surprise in them. He smiled and she returned it easily.

Walking Horse and Sabrina went to his horse where he untied a bundle from the back and handed it to her.

Sabrina went back to the porch and sat down to unbind the rawhide laces that bound the bundle. When she unwrapped the soft leather that held it, she gazed delightedly at the beautiful gift he had given her. She knew instantly he had taken a great deal of time and care in the making of it. A pair of beautiful, white doeskin moccasins trimmed in rabbit fur and decorated with fine intricate bead work lay in her lap.

"How very beautiful, Walking Horse."

"You are pleased with them?"

"Pleased! They are lovely. I am more than pleased. I shall wear them. But . . . how did you know the size to make?"

He chuckled and sat beside her on the porch. "I measured your footprints."

"Measured my footprints," she laughed.

"Yes, outside the lodge when you visited us. It was easy. I measured your footprints and made the moccasins."

"How very thoughtful, and how very kind."

"Sa-bree-nah," he said, "you are a very beautiful woman. It would please me if you would allow me to visit often."

It was only at this moment that Sabrina realized what Walking Horse's intentions were. Surrounded by Clay's love, warmed and held within it, she had not realized that any one else felt the same as she. She was about to explain when Hawk and Summer came out. She decided to wait until she and Walking Horse were alone. The last thing she wanted to do was to damage the pride of a man as kind and considerate as he.

The next hour or so was spent in chatter about Swift Doe, the village and other gossip that told Sabrina and Ellen all that had happened since they had left.

A warm inviting lunch was made even nicer by the open

and happy conversation.

"Are you going to stay until Papa comes home?" Summer questioned.

"No, little one," Hawk smiled, "we will return to our village."

"But," Walking Horse said quickly, his eyes on Sabrina, "we will come back soon."

"When will you return home?" Ellen said.

"We will stay the rest of the day and leave when the sun rises again," Hawk answered.

A tentative thought began to form in Sabrina's mind. If Hawk were to spend the night, maybe she would have time alone with him. She wanted desperately to know the secrets that dwelt between him and Clay. Could he — would he talk to her? Would he tell her what she wanted to know? She was frightened, yet she knew whatever stood between Clay and Hawk was something that would always linger as a shadow over their love. It was Hawk that Clay did not want to know of their future plans to marry . . . why? What difference would it make to Hawk if Clay married again?

A multitude of questions filled her mind and she knew only Clay and Hawk had the answers. Clay would not reveal them . . . maybe Hawk would. She only hoped her knowledge of the past would release its hold on Clay and leave him free to love her.

The balance of the afternoon was quite pleasant, but Sabrina did not find a moment alone with Hawk until late in the day. Summer had begged for a ride on Walking Horse's beautiful black stallion. He had taken her up before him and rode away.

Hawk and Sabrina found themselves walking across the clearing toward the woods.

"You have come from a very long way, Sabrina," Hawk said. "Tell me about the place you come from."

Sabrina found herself explaining about her uncle, Waverly Hall, and the circumstances that had brought her there. They walked as she talked and soon found themselves deep in the shaded forest. They were so engrossed in their conversation that they did not notice how far they were walking.

"And so that is how I came to be here. By law, I must be a servant for two years to Clay."

"And after that? What will you do?" he questioned.

Sabrina herself did not know why she did not tell Hawk that she planned to marry Clay and remain with him. Clay wanted it to be kept between them for now and she could not bring herself to betray him.

"I don't know. I'm not sure what I will do. I guess it depends mostly on Ellen and her brother. He will probably help her, and we will find a house and remain in the city."

"Is that what you really want to do?"

Her mind and heart both shouted no, but she smiled at him and shrugged.

"One cannot always have or do what one wants in this world."

It was only now that they simultaneously realized where they were. Hawk knew the place well from many past visits. Sabrina knew it too, but from only one visit. The day she had followed a weeping Summer into the forest. They stood on the edge of the meadow where the grave of Singing Bells was.

Hawk stopped walking and his eyes went to the spot before he could prevent it. Sabrina looked up at him, then her eyes followed his. She knew instantly that Hawk knew this place.

"Hawk, I have been to Singing Bells' grave."

He looked at her in complete surprise. It was the last place he would have thought Clay would have taken her.

"Clay . . .?"

"No, Summer."

Sabrina went on to explain how she had followed Summer to this spot, and had been told by the child it was her mother's grave.

"It must be very hard for her," he replied, "not to know her mother."

"It is. Hawk . . . Summer knew you and Walking Horse were coming today."

"I might have known she would," he answered. "I gave her the bracelet."

"I don't understand. There are so many things I don't understand."

"She is like her mother. Singing Bells has left her beauty in the spirit of her daughter. There is not much the child could do that would surprise me now."

"That explains nothing to me. It only makes the mystery greater and darker than it was before."

"Mystery?"

"I think you understand, Hawk," Sabrina said quietly, her eyes holding his, "and I think there are many things you could tell me about Summer . . . and about her mother. Things that might make it easier for all of us, but especially for Summer. She needs to know about her mother. Can you tell me?"

"It is not my place to tell you. Ask Clay when he returns."

"I cannot. It is a subject that seems to cause him pain. I don't want to do anything that will hurt either Clay or Summer. I just feel if I knew more about her mother, I could make Summer a little happier."

"Why do you think it will make her happier?"

"I saw her here, crying at her mother's grave. A mother she never knew. I know Swift Doe has told her some things. I know Swift Doe has given her a leather bag filled with colored stones Summer calls her magic stones. She says they were her mother's. I believe the child is searching for her past and won't be happy until she finds it."

"Sabrina, there is another who can tell you the truth better than I."

"Who?"

"My father."

"Then I must talk to him."

"He is old and cannot travel. You would have to come to our village. If he knew why you wanted to come, Clay might not permit you to go."

Sabrina thought his words offered the answers to all her questions, yet Clay had forbidden her to go back to the village. Was Clay afraid of what she would find there?

"Hawk, how long will it take, if we travel as rapidly as possible, to get to your village and back?"

"Two days."

Two days, and Clay said he would be gone four. It would give her plenty of time to be back before he returned. She was frightened, yet she knew she and Clay could not go on the way they were. Secrets were not a good basis on which to start a marriage, and was it fair, because of these secrets, that she had to keep her happiness and plans for her wedding a secret? She gripped herself firmly. Even if Clay were to become angry with her, she still felt, for Summer's sake, she had a right to know.

"Hawk, will you take me to your village as rapidly as possible and bring me home? I want to be back before Clay returns."

"You want to go to my village now?" he said, his dark eyes questioning. "Why this sudden trip? Would it not be better for Clay to return? Then you could tell him you chose to go."

"No, Hawk, please. I'd rather Clay didn't know I made

this visit. It would be easier on us all. I have to know about Summer's mother and her past if I'm going to help her grow into a happy person. Please Hawk. Without questions. Will you take me and bring me home?"

"What of Summer?"

"I shall take her with me. She is my charge, not Ellen's. Besides, she enjoyed herself so much the last time."

He watched her in silence for a moment, then he shrugged his shoulders and smiled.

"Of course, I shall take you if you want to go. My whole village would be pleased to see you return. Come, let us go back and tell the others. Walking Horse will be surprised too, but it will please him. It seems," he added softly, "you have captured more than one heart in our village."

She looked closely at him as they walked along, but his eyes remained gazing down the wooded path they followed.

When they reached the house, Walking Horse and Summer were sitting on the porch in animated conversation. When Summer saw them coming, she jumped up and ran to them. Before Summer could release her excitement in endless chatter, Sabrina spoke.

"Summer, how would you like to pay another visit to Hawk's village?"

This stopped all of Summer's words for a minute. She stood, her eyes gazing from one to another.

"Do you think Papa would be angry if we didn't ask his permission?"

Sabrina did not want to tell Summer that this worried her also, but she thought if Clay were angry, it would be with her and not a child who was not responsible.

"We shall be back before your father is home, and since I am here to care for you and I would like to go again, then your father wouldn't expect me to leave you, would he?"

"No," Summer said quietly, but she showed all signs that

she knew she was being maneuvered.

Sabrina did not want to look either at Hawk or Walking Horse for she sensed that they also felt the undercurrent between woman and child.

"Come on Summer, let's gather a few things. We will go and have a couple days of fun and be back in time to greet your father."

Summer ran to do as she was told, and it was only minutes from the time she went into the house until Ellen came rushing out onto the porch, surprise written clearly on her face.

"Sabrina, Summer has just told me you and she are going with Hawk. Is this true?"

"Just two days, Ellen," Sabrina smiled. "You won't be frightened here alone for a short time, will you?"

"Of course I won't be frightened," Ellen replied. "But what will Clay say?"

"As I told Summer, it's only a couple of days of fun for her while her father is gone. We will be back before Clay comes home."

Sabrina walked up to stand close to Ellen who lowered her voice and spoke so the two watching men did not hear.

"Sabrina, why do I have the feeling this is going to cause trouble?"

"Don't be silly, Ellen, what trouble could a two day visit cause? Summer can play with other children."

"And you can ask questions," Ellen said softly.

"Yes," Sabrina whispered, "yes Ellen, I can ask questions, especially since I know now just who and what to ask."

"Sabrina, don't do anything foolish."

"I won't. But Ellen, I love him, and I've got to do something to push away some of the shadows that surround us. I've got to Ellen, can you understand? I've got to."

"Oh Sabrina, maybe I do understand. But, I don't want to see you hurt. I don't want to see something come between you two. I think he really loves you."

"I believe him. I know he really loves me. But what shall I do Ellen, let him keep those dark shadows inside until it does change what he feels. How can I fight, Ellen, if I don't know what I'm fighting?"

Before Ellen could speak again, Summer returned.

"I'll get my things," Sabrina said quickly.

Walking Horse went to saddle a horse for Sabrina.

"I shall take the child in front of me," Hawk said. He mounted and reached down to draw Summer up before him.

Sabrina kissed Ellen's cheek.

"Ellen, don't worry. I promise I'll be back before Clay gets home. I will be the one to tell him what I've done."

"All right child. I hope you're right. I hope what you're doing will make things good between you two. I'll pray for you both, child."

"Thank you, Ellen. I'll pray too. I'll see you in two days. You will be all right."

"Of course I'll be all right."

Again Sabrina gave Ellen another quick kiss. Then she mounted her horse.

Walking Horse was amazed but pleased at the turn of events that would bring Sabrina back to his village, even if it was only for two days.

They rode away slowly and Ellen stood on the porch watching until they had completely disappeared from view. Reluctantly, she went inside and closed the door behind her.

No matter how she tried to fight the feeling, she still could not shake the thought that Sabrina was stirring a cauldron of trouble, trouble of which she had no idea and which she was in no way prepared to fight.

Her thoughts were more than accurate, for a situation was unfolding several miles away that was about to start the cauldron boiling.

Twenty-three

Intent on his own thoughts, Clay decided to make no more stops before town. He pushed himself as far as his horse's stamina would stand, stopping only when absolutely necessary. Doing so cut more than a day's time from what he had planned on spending.

He had always taken a great deal of pleasure coming to town for a few days at a time. He had many friends and they had always made his stay enjoyable. But this time his mind was on Sabrina. He had not realized he would miss her as badly as he did. All he could concentrate on was returning home as soon as possible.

He went to the general store and left the list of supplies he wanted with George Evans, the storekeeper, who had been his friend since he was a boy.

"You stayin' the night, Clay? Should I have these things ready in the morning?"

"No, George. If you can get them ready right away, I intend to start home before late afternoon."

"You in a powerful hurry?" George questioned and Clay could see he was obviously curious about the reasons.

"Yes, I am," Clay grinned. "To tell you the truth, George, this is the first time I've been so anxious to get back." He dropped the subject much to George's irritation. "I'm going out, I've a couple of gifts I want to buy. I should be back in a couple of hours. Can you have these things ready by then?"

"Sure Clay, sure I can." Clay could have laughed at George's obvious irritation at Clay's reticence. He was dying for information.

"Thanks," Clay replied, covering his amusement. He turned and left the store.

"Closed mouth son of a gun," George laughed to himself as Clay left.

Clay wanted to buy Sabrina, Summer and Ellen something special, but he wasn't sure exactly what. At that moment he passed a small dress shop, and stopped short. He gazed in the window at a beautiful gown that was the exact shade of violet blue as Sabrina's eyes. Instantly he could see her in it.

Hesitantly, he reached for the door handle. It would be the first time he ever walked into a dress shop. He was embarrassed and hoped desperately no other women were inside.

A young woman approached him. She was aware of his discomfort.

"May I help you, sir?"

"Yes . . . ah . . . that dress in the window, I'd like to buy it."

"Of course, sir. What size would you like it?"

"Size?"

"Yes sir. What size is the young lady who will be lucky enough to wear it?"

"Good heavens, Madam, it never occurred to me to ask. I've no idea what size she is."

"Can you describe her to me? Is she my size?"

Clay eyed the woman speculatively.

"Well . . . ah . . . ." He didn't want to insult the woman.

"It's all right," the woman smiled with a sparkle of laughter in her eyes for this tall uncomfortable man. "Is she smaller?"

"Yes," Clay replied. He held his hand even with his shoulder. "She's about this tall, her waist is small, I can span it with my hands. She's slim . . . but she's . . ."

"Curved?"

"Yes." Now Clay was smiling too, as he sensed her sincere wish to help. He used both hands to express Sabrina's slim, curved body. "She's . . . very nearly perfect," he added.

"And, may I add," the woman smiled, "she's very, very lucky as well."

"Thank you," Clay chuckled. "I guess you must have deduced by now I'm rather new at this."

"Yes," she laughed, "I have." She went to take the dress from the window. She held it up beside Clay. "I should imagine this would be about right. If it is a little large . . . anywhere, bring her in for a fitting and we'll make sure it fits perfectly."

"Thank you. Would you wrap it please."

The woman nodded and went to the counter.

"By the way," Clay added as he followed her, "do you carry dresses for young girls as well?"

"We surely do. Do I dare ask again what size you prefer?"

"If you do, I shall prove my complete ignorance and tell you again I don't know."

"How old is she?"

"She'll be six in a few weeks."

"Well, I'm sure I can find something. Do you have a color preference?"

"Something close to the other. I think that would please her."

Again the woman turned to the rack of dresses. In a few moments she lay a dress in front of Clay that was a little deeper blue than Sabrina's but very pretty.

"Excellent," Clay said. "Now, maybe a shawl for an older woman will complete everything."

This accomplished, the woman wrapped each and a satisfied Clay left the shop.

Now he had another thought in mind and he found a jeweler and went inside. Once he had described to the man what he wanted, it was only minutes before a tray of rings was set in front of him. It did not take him long to choose the one he wanted. A slim gold band with another even thinner twined around it. Two small diamonds and a small emerald nestled into the entwined gold. He tried it on his little finger and it would not slip past his knuckle. He felt it would be close to the right size.

"Put it in a box and wrap it for me, please. I shall go to the bank and get the money."

"You needn't worry about that, Mr. Storm. I'm sure if you will only make out a note, we will be quite satisfied. The Storm name will be quite sufficient."

"Thank you," Clay smiled. In a few moments, he accepted the ring, signed the note and left the shop.

Very pleased with himself, and allowing his thoughts to dwell on the look he would see in Sabrina's eyes he started down the street, only to collide with someone turning the corner.

It took a moment for both to regain their balance, then he looked down into familiar brown eyes.

"Elenora," he said, "I'm sorry. I didn't mean to trample you."

"Clay," the girl said breathlessly, "I had no idea you were in town."

"I just arrived today."

"Goodness, I hope you're staying a while. We would be delighted to have you for supper."

"I'm sorry, Elenora, but I really have to start home tonight. I didn't bring Summer along and I don't want to leave her too long."

Elenora Stewart was exceptionally pretty. Her family had been friends of Clay for a long time. He felt toward Elenora almost as an older brother, but that was the last thing Elenora thought. She had wanted Clay for a long time.

She was a dark haired beauty. Her midnight hair coiled elaborately. She was dressed with impeccable good taste. She had an exquisitely voluptuous body which she tried her best to bring to Clay's attention. Her smile was wide, brilliantly white, and wasted on an unaware Clay whose mind could conjure up only visions of a happy Sabrina.

"I heard you acquired an indentured servant to care for your house and Summer. Isn't she safe with her," she leaned close and she placed a hand on Clay's arm, "just for one night Clay?"

"I'm sorry, really sorry, Elenora. Please send your parents my regards. But I have to get home."

Elenora pouted prettily, but Clay was aware of an urgency inside him that drew him to a house many miles away where a golden haired girl held all his thoughts.

"Well, you will be coming back soon, won't you? There's to be a celebration in two weeks for the opening of the new park. Surely you will come for the festivities and the dance afterward?"

If she could have read Clay's thoughts then, anger would have replaced the sweet smile.

His thoughts were again on Sabrina. Would it give her pleasure to wear the dress he had brought her and spend a day or so in town. He could imagine holding her, watching her eyes smile up into his as they moved about the floor. The new thought intrigued him.

"Clay?"

"Oh . . . yes, Elenora, I might just do that. In fact, it

might be nice for Summer, too. She hasn't been to town be-fore."

"Yes," Elenora answered sweetly, "Summer . . . I'm sure we could find someplace to put her for a day or two."

Clay smiled, but her words had struck a cold spot deep within. No one, as far as he was concerned, would . . . put . . . his beloved Summer anywhere and expect him to play elsewhere.

"Well . . . I'll see what happens. For now, I have to go. I'm expected home by tomorrow afternoon."

"Then," she smiled again as she leaned suggestively close, "I do hope to see you again."

"Good-bye Elenora."

"Good-bye Clay."

Elenora stood for a moment and watched Clay walk away. A deep warm hunger invaded her as it always did when Clay was near. She wanted him . . . wanted him more than any man she had ever known. Reluctantly, she was even prepared to accept his child. But she decided once Clay was hers she would find a way to keep his child . . . child of an ignorant savage — from under her feet.

She could not understand how a man with Clay's back-ground and wealth could live like a frontiersman . . . marry a savage, and allow her to bear his child. Well, she thought, one day she would wipe all that from his mind and they could live a life of travel and pleasure she had always wanted.

She turned and walked down the street with a suggestive sway to her hips that drew the attention of every man she passed.

Clay retraced his steps to the general store where George had all his supplies ready. It took him a half hour to pack everything. Then he paid a boy to watch them while he ate a quick meal. Then he mounted and headed for home. He found a deep pleasant excitement within him, and a fierce need to see, kiss and hold his violet eyed Sabrina.

They crested the last hill that overlooked the Indian village. It had been a pleasant ride with both Hawk and Walking Horse trying their best to keep it so.

As they rode down into the village, word of their arrival went before them and they were met with happy enthusiasm.

Summer was delighted to rejoin the friends she had made during her short stay and soon was running to join them in the new games they had so recently taught her.

Hawk stopped in front of his own lodge and the three of them slid down from their horses.

"Hawk, how soon can I speak to your father?"

"My father has not been well for some time. I will make you comfortable and go to see him. If he is well enough, I will come for you. If not, we might have to wait a few hours."

"I don't have much time, Hawk. I must be home in two days."

"I will see what I can do. I'm sure he will talk to you soon."

"Thank you, Hawk."

"I shall take you to the visitors lodge Sa-bree-nah," Walking Horse said.

Sabrina smiled at him, handed her horse's reins to Hawk and walked to the visitors lodge with Walking Horse. She knew she had to have patience.

Hawk watched her go. He had known that Sabrina might have thought what he would have told her about the situation between Clay and him might have been some form of revenge. He hoped his father's words might make a difference. The only thing that bothered him was he was not sure what words his father might say. He would go to his father

276

first and try to find out what he would tell Sabrina.

He unsaddled both horses and put them out to graze with the tribe's herd. Then with slow reluctant steps, he walked toward his father's lodge.

He stood outside his father's lodge for several minutes, wondering why he hesitated to go inside.

Fear was an emotion Hawk had never known, yet its fingers touched him now. He wanted his father to present the story only from his side and he really was not sure his father would do that.

Determinedly, he gripped himself, then he called out to his father, whose firm quiet voice told him to come in. He gazed across the few feet of space into his father's old—and very wise eyes.

"Welcome home, my son," the old man said softly, "I did not expect you back quite so soon."

"I have brought Sabrina back with me."

"It is pleasing to know she found pleasure in our village the first time she visited us. But I am surprised she came again so soon. Has Clay returned with her?"

"No . . . no he has not. Clay is not home now, he has gone to their city for supplies."

"I see," his father replied gently. Hawk had the sensation his father could read his every thought.

"Sabrina wishes to speak with you."

"With me . . . why would she speak with me?"

"I think you know what she seeks . . . the truth."

"The truth," his father repeated softly. "And what truth does she wish to hear, Clay's . . . or yours?"

"There is only one truth."

"Is there . . . my son? Truth depends on which eyes you look from."

"I cannot tell you what to say, my Father, first because I know you would not use my words. I can only ask you to remember the grief we all felt at the loss of Singing Bells and the need we have to share in the gift of her child."

"I remember, my son, always I remember."

"Then tell her! Tell her of the gifts the child has. Tell her what Summer's mother was. Tell her how much we need just to share in her future . . . that our future and hers are linked together."

"And," his father added softly, "shall I tell her of your love for Singing Bells?"

"No."

"Why?"

"She might think it is revenge only that makes us feel so. She might think the only emotion is jealousy."

His father sighed deeply and his eyes were filled with sadness, for he knew Hawk, his beloved son, lied to himself as well.

"Very well, my son. Send her to me."

It was a command from his chief and Hawk could not disobey it any more than any other warrior in his tribe could, even though he wanted to know what he intended to say to Sabrina.

"Yes my Father," he said. Hawk turned and left the lodge. He walked across the open center of his village to the lodge that would be Sabrina's.

Sabrina had waited patiently for Hawk's return. She had no idea exactly what she would say to the chief of this village. She only knew this man had the key to the darkness within the man she loved and she had to find a way to let in the light.

She was involved in her thoughts and it startled her to hear Hawk's voice as he called to her.

She rose from the fur covered bench upon which she was seated. She walked to the door and pushed aside the cover.

"Hawk?"

"My father will speak with you now."

"Oh, thank you Hawk. I'm so grateful."

"Come, I will walk with you."

She stepped outside and they walked across the open area again.

Outside of the chief's lodge a nervous Sabrina gazed up at the tall silent man who stood beside her.

"Will you come in with me?"

"No."

"Why?"

"Because it is best my presence does not influence either your questions or my father's answers."

"Hawk, is there a special way I should address him? I am so frightened."

"Don't be frightened, Sabrina," Hawk smiled, "My father is a very gentle and a very kind and understanding man. There is no need for your fear."

He took her hand, gave it a reassuring squeeze. Then he walked away and left her to face his father alone.

In a voice shaken and quiet she requested permission to enter, and when a deep and resonant voice told her to come in, she pushed aside the door covering and went inside.

She stood in the doorway while the covering closed behind her. Across the few feet that separated them, deep, dark brown eyes filled with compassion and humor met wide violet ones filled with questions.

"Come in, my child," he said gently. "Come and sit near me. Your beauty is as my son says and it would give me pleasure to have you sit near and talk with me."

Sabrina realized immediately that Hawk's description of his father had been quite accurate. All her fears seemed to melt away. She walked to his side, then she sat down on the fur rug at his feet.

"It is good of you to speak with me," Sabrina said. "There

are so many questions I would like to ask you if you do not mind."

"I would be most willing to answer your questions as best I can, but first, may I ask you a few questions myself?"

"Yes, of course."

"Tell me how you came to be living in Clay Storm's home."

Sabrina explained the entire story of her past. He listened without interruption and his eyes and ears missed nothing, not even the words Sabrina did not say.

"It is a very strange way for the path of your life to take. Has it made you very unhappy?"

"At first, when I came to a strange country, among strange people, I was afraid. But not now. I feel more at home here than anywhere I have ever been. I'm happy here."

The old man reached out and touched the fascinating shimmer of her golden hair. His eyes were kind and his voice was gentle as he asked.

"Do you love him, my child?"

At first, Sabrina was startled at the perception in the old man's mind. Then she smiled, aware he had already read her heart like an open book.

"Yes, yes I love him. I would be happy to share his life forever. To bear his children. To try and become a good wife."

"Yet my son has told me that you came back to our village at a time when Clay was gone, without his knowledge or his permission. Love does not have any room for dishonesty."

"Love does not have room for dishonesty," Sabrina replied, "and under any other circumstances I would not have considered doing this. But love does not have any room for secrets either, and Clay holds many in his heart. So many that I am afraid one day there will no longer be any room for me."

"Why do you not ask him to share his thoughts and his heart with you?"

"I have."

"But?"

"He asks me only to trust him, to believe in him, and to wait until he feels the time is right to tell me."

"Then why do you not wait as he asks?"

"Because I am afraid. Afraid that time will never come. I am afraid the past will draw him further and further away from me until there is no hope for our future or our love. I could not bear the thought of losing him."

"What is it you want from me?"

"I want you to tell me about Singing Bells, Clay's wife. I want you to tell me what there is between Hawk and Clay. They talk like friends, but I can see the cold shadows in their eyes. Maybe if I know the truth, there will no longer be a need for secrets. Maybe I can even help bring them together as friends again."

"It would be a most difficult task, my child. Clay and Hawk find the black space between them too deep to cross."

"Then, tell me. Let me try."

"It is difficult to make boundaries in this thing. Maybe you will hear things you do not want to hear. Maybe the words I say will hurt you. Maybe you will love Clay less because of my words. Maybe . . . maybe in this case both are right . . . and both are wrong."

"Nothing," Sabrina said gently, "could make me love Clay less. Right or wrong, he is the man I love and I will love him forever."

"All right, Sabrina. I will tell you the story. Then—you must make the decision.

Sabrina sat quietly and relaxed as the old man began to talk.

Twenty-four

Clay smiled to himself. He stood by his horse and chewed thoughtfully on a piece of dried beef he had carried along so he would not have to stop to cook. It was only to rest the horses that he stopped now.

He smiled because he could not believe his own emotions. He felt like a boy with the first woman he had ever known. He could hardly wait to see Sabrina, to hold her slim body next to him, to satisfy the deep hunger that flowed within him.

He imagined her eyes sparkling in delight at the gifts he brought. Warm thoughts of her golden beauty wearing the dress, and even warmer thoughts of helping her remove it.

After Sabrina had lived in his home long enough to relax Hawk's vigilance, when Hawk had realized he could not get to Clay or Summer through Sabrina, then and only then would it be safe to marry.

He turned to his horse to retighten the cinch.

"Sorry old boy," he chuckled, "when we get home you can rest as long as you want. But I can't stand to be away a moment longer." He checked the packs to make sure they were bound tightly then mounted and urged his horse forward.

He traveled at a steady gait that ate the miles rapidly. He would, if his plans went well and he could continue to travel at this pace, be home a full day and a half earlier.

He gave no thought to the dark haired woman he had left on the street in town. If he could have known what was happening there at the same moment he might have been able to stop what fate had in store. But in the euphorious mood Clay was in at the moment, he was unaware of any dark clouds on the horizons of his life.

Elenora returned to her home, a huge white house that was very nearly a mansion. Her father was one of the richest men in town and the house he had built on the edge of town was a beautiful and none too subtle reminder to everyone.

Her buggy drew up behind another that was parked in the oval drive. The house itself sat upon a grade and the docks could be seen from there. Shading her eyes with her hand, Elenora could see the ships that rocked in the harbor. Among them was a large one that had not been there in the morning. Obviously, she thought, her father must have guests from England with whom he did a great deal of business.

She stepped down from the buggy and went inside. As she removed her hat and gloves, she was approached by a young maid.

"Father has guests?" she asked.

"Yes Ma'am."

"Is it anyone interesting Martha, or just boring business?"

"You might be interested, Miss Elenora. It's a rather nice looking young man from England. I don't think he's come here for business though. I think he's looking for someone."

"Looking for someone? Who?"

"I don't rightly know, Ma'am."

"Thank you, Martha. Where is Father now?"

"In the study, Ma'am."

Elenora walked to the door of her father's study. She

rapped lightly, then opened the door and walked in.

Her father smiled as he watched her approach. He was proud of his daughter's dark beauty. He was also proud of her resemblance to him which was her ability to keep her strong passions and iron will carefully covered by a velvet exterior.

William Gregory had always been a man who had fought and scratched for all he achieved. Elenora Gregory was a woman who would do the same — with pleasure.

"Hello, Father," she smiled, "I'm sorry to interrupt you. Were you very busy?"

William laughed to himself. Obviously, Elenora wanted to find out who was here and why.

"Not really, Elenora, please come in." He motioned to a man who was seated across his wide desk from him. "We have a guest from England who is here looking for someone. I told him you would know almost everyone in town and if anyone could help him you could."

Elenora crossed the room to her father's desk so she could get a better look at the man. He rose as she approached.

It was one of those rare occasions when kindred spirits knew and understood each other in a moment. He assessed her quickly. Willful, beautiful, stubborn and a woman who would stop at nothing to get what she wanted.

She also assessed him with the same ease. Handsome, rich, sensual and a man who knew what he wanted and would not hesitate to take it no matter who he had to step on to do it.

There was no doubt in either mind that they knew each other immediately, and that the day would come when they would know each other much better.

"Elenora, may I present Mr. Thomas Mellon. His father was an old friend of mine in England. Thomas, this is my daughter Elenora."

Elenora smiled and extended her hand to Thomas who smiled in return, took her hand and touched it to his lips.

"Had I known there was this much beauty in this new country, I should have made it a point to visit much sooner."

"Thank you, Mr. Mellon."

"Thomas . . . please."

"Thomas," she repeated softly, "and you must call me Elenora."

"A great pleasure . . . Elenora."

"My father said you were looking for someone. If there is any way I can help, I would be very happy to."

"You are most gracious, Elenora."

"As I told you, sir," William laughed, "my daughter knows everyone and everything that happens in this town."

"I must explain," Thomas began a well planned out story, "after my father died, well, we were all devastated with grief. I had a very disastrous argument with my sister. She fled from the house and went to some friends. After I had time to cool my thoughts, I realized what a grave unjust mistake I made. I went in search of my sister only to find she had come to this country with another woman. They had come as indentured servants. It is terrible to think of my sweet, young sister so alone and unprotected here. And working as a servant. I vowed to find her and bring her home where she belongs. I have a picture," he said as he drew a small picture of Sabrina from his pocket and handed it to Elenora.

Despite the poor photography, Elenora could see Sabrina was exceptionally beautiful. She also did not see any resemblance between the two. In an instant, she realized Thomas was lying. Curiosity inflamed and excited her. Why did he seek this girl? It certainly was not for the purpose of reuniting a family.

"Do you have any idea to whom she was indentured? I'm afraid I have never seen her before."

"Oh yes. I've found the name of the man who paid her passage. She was to care for his young daughter. His name is Storm — Mr. Clayton Storm."

Both Elenora and William were startled.

"Clayton Storm," William said, "yes, we know him quite well."

"Yes," Elenora said softly, "I even knew he had acquired a woman to care for his child. I just didn't know she was so young . . . or so . . . beautiful."

Thomas, who knew jealousy well, did not doubt for a minute the emotion he saw in Elenora's eyes. He smiled to himself, knowing he had acquired the best ally in his search for Sabrina, a jealous woman.

"Where can I find this Clayton Storm?"

"I'm afraid," Elenora said, "it is a long hard journey to his home, and that can be only made if one has a guide. The wilderness out there is filled with dangers . . . even Indians."

"Can I hire a guide?"

"No . . . there are very few who know where Clay's home is located. Clay has always wanted it that way. None of the guides will take you there unless they ask Clay first."

"I would rather surprise my sister. She might still be a little angry with me and decide to run away again."

"There may be a way," Elenora said. "Give me a little time to think about it."

"Of course. May I come and speak with you again this evening?"

"I'm afraid I have another engagement," William replied, "but you and Elenora can discuss it."

"Yes," Elenora said softly, and Thomas read well the brown eyes that smiled up into his.

That night after a leisurely dinner over which Thomas had entertained her with stories of exciting London society, they walked in the garden. Now Elenora found to be the appropriate time to make things clear between her and Thomas.

"Thomas," she said with a half smile, "you are a charming, exciting man. I have a feeling you and I have common goals and the strength to get them. I want Clay Storm . . . now suppose you tell me the truth . . . just why are you here and what do you want?"

Thomas laughed. Here was a woman he understood, and one who understood him. Without hesitation he explained.

"I want Sabrina McNeil. I have always wanted her. I have the law on my side to get her back to England. There will be no one to know she doesn't end up in court but with me. From then on I shall be her . . . shall I say, guardian."

"Her master," Elenora said. Thomas was aware that the thought seemed to fascinate Elenora.

"Yes. She will be my mistress. I shall command her life, her world, her body and soul. She will obey me . . . in every way. I have dreamed of her . . . and I shall fulfill each dream. I will possess her completely as I promised myself long ago."

Elenora licked her lips in controlled excitement. It was the deep touch of controlled violence she saw in Clay that had drawn her to him first. They had shared the first touch of a relationship, cut short when Clay met and married his Indian wife. Elenora had been the only one to have no regrets when word of her death had come.

"I have a suggestion," she said.

"You have my undivided attention."

"Clay has done a great deal of business with my father. In fact, father has had occasion to go and see Clay. I'm sure, if I persuaded him nicely, he would make another visit."

"What can that do for me?"

"I shall find out for sure if your Sabrina is there. Then we

287

can make plans."

"Well, you are right. If I come with the law, he may be able to get her away. I want to take her completely by surprise."

"Yes, I don't want Clay to have any idea where she has gone. Clay can be overly gallant at times. With enough time, Sabrina McNeil shall just disappear. He can be made to believe she just ran off. Servants have been known to do that. You can have her on board ship and gone before he knows."

"Delightful idea," Thomas chuckled. "How long will this take?"

"Well, there is a celebration and ball next week. Clay might decide to come. If he does his servants will be left at home to care for his half breed child. That might be the best time to go get her."

"And," Thomas replied, "just what shall I do with the next two weeks."

"Oh Thomas," Elenora laughed throatily, "I'm sure we'll find some way to keep you entertained."

They laughed together and walked back into the house.

One more valley . . . one more hill, Clay thought as he urged his very tired horse forward. The sun was deep in its descent, but Clay cared nothing for the beauty that surrounded him. His thoughts were only on soft violet eyes, gold spun hair and a slim goddess who called to him with every beat of his horse's hoofs.

When he finally did crest the last hill, he stopped for a moment and looked down on the valley. The house sat nestled in the deep green foliage. Home . . . Sabrina. They meant the same thing to him now.

Again he urged his horse forward and rode down the hill.

When he stopped in front of the house, he was surprised to at least not see Summer who usually greeted him when he came home. Then he remembered how Sabrina and Summer liked to walk in the woods.

"That must be where they are," he muttered. He decided to care for his tired horse before he would go and look for them. He unpacked the packages carefully and laid them on the porch. Then he took the reins of both horses and drawing them behind him, he walked to the barn.

Once he had cared for the horses he walked back across the clearing and up the steps of the porch. He opened the door and walked in . . . to a completely empty room.

"Sabrina!" he shouted. "Summer . . . Ellen, where is everybody?"

Ellen walked slowly from the kitchen. A twisting fear in her heart at the reaction her words might bring. He was home long before Sabrina had thought he would be.

When she appeared in the doorway, Clay was smiling, but the smile slowly faded as he saw the pale face and worried eyes of Ellen.

"Ellen?" he said slowly, wondering why he suddenly dreaded what she might say. "Where are Sabrina and Summer?"

Ellen could not find the words to say that would reach the man who gazed at her across the room.

"Clay . . . she . . . you must understand. Oh . . . I told her . . . I warned her."

Clay was beside her now, he took her by the shoulder and gave her a shake.

"Ellen, answer me. Where are Sabrina and Summer? Has something happened to them? For God's sake, woman, answer me."

"They're not here, Clay."

"Where are they, Ellen?"

"They . . . they went with Hawk and Walking Horse."

She could feel the tremor in his large body as if she had violently struck him. His hands gripped her shoulders until she cried out.

"I'm sorry, Ellen. I didn't mean to hurt you. What do you mean they went with Hawk? Why? In God's name, why would she go there now . . . after . . . why Ellen? Did Hawk come and ask her to go? What reason did he give? How long have they been gone?"

"I can't answer all your questions at once," Ellen cried. Her eyes were wet with tears and Clay realized she was frightened to death.

"Ellen," he said in a gentler voice as he stepped back from her. "Tell me what happened here."

"Well, Hawk and his friend came. Walking Horse brought Sabrina a present. Then . . . well . . . Sabrina just decided to take Summer to play with some of her new friends while you were gone. She didn't mean to do anything wrong, Clay. It was just for Summer to have someone to play with. She was lonely, Clay, and I'm sure Sabrina had no other thought in mind but making her happy."

His heart felt like lead in his chest, for he knew Ellen was deliberately lying.

"And just when are they supposed to be back?" he said in a voice so calm and cold that it made Ellen quiver in fear. His eyes were like two chips of blue ice.

"They should be here any minute. Sabrina said she's be home before . . ."

"Before I got home," he completed. He turned from her and stood by the fireplace, his back to her. From his rigid body, she could almost feel the beginnings of a deep fury.

"If you expect them back any minute, Ellen, then I suppose I must just wait. Fix me something to eat."

He said the words in cold, hard, clipped tones that set her

to quick movement.

All the time she prepared the meal, she prayed silently that Sabrina and Summer would walk through the door. She also prayed Hawk would not come in with her for the grim silent man who sat so still in front of the red embered fire gave off an aura of intense contained anger that was about to explode at any moment.

He ate the meal she prepared him in absolute silence and she cleared the table, washed and put away the dishes and still he sat in silence contemplating the dying fire.

Ellen took a seat opposite him and picked up her mending. She had to do something to keep her hands busy she thought, but they were shaking so bad she found it hard to hold the needle.

Clay's mind was playing havoc with thoughts of Sabrina . . . Sabrina and Hawk. Impossible! Yet Clay knew the fascination and charm the tall handsome Indian had for women. What would he tell her? His mind raged. What would she tell him? It was the last possible thing he had wanted to happen.

There were so many things he did not want Sabrina to know yet. Their love was too new for these words, it would not stand the force of them.

No one knew the beginning of the story, Clay thought. All they could tell her was the worst. Only he held the truth, and it was the truth he wanted one day to tell Sabrina himself. Someday when her love for him came to a fullness, when he was sure she was his. When there was no turning back for Sabrina. Then he had meant to tell her.

He stood up and walked to the door. Pulling it open, he stood in the doorway and looked out across the clearing as if mentally he could draw Sabrina back to him.

The sun sat complacently on the horizon, lighting the world with a pale red glow. Time ticked slowly by, and still

Clay stood immobile, like a statue carved of granite.

Ellen's nerves were stretched taut and several times she pricked her finger with the needle until finally, giving up all pretense of sewing she laid it aside and watched Clay.

Clay turned from the door and walked to his room. Ellen heard him moving about and knew he certainly had no plans of going to bed. Her heart leapt when she saw him come out carrying his coat in one hand . . . and a rifle in the other.

"Clay! What are you going to do?"

"I'm going after them," he said grimly.

"Clay don't be a fool. Night is coming on. You'll pass each other in the dark."

Clay smiled at her, but brushed past her on his way to the door.

"Clay, listen to me. Wait until morning. Sabrina will be home by then, at least let her explain."

It was as if he did not hear her at all. He walked purposefully across the clearing toward the barn. Ellen followed after him. Inside, he led his horse from its stall and started to saddle him.

"Clay don't go after her. It's foolish. She'll be back soon I'm sure."

"Yes, she'll be back soon. Both of them will. Just as soon as I can get to them."

Ellen watched as he finished saddling his horse and began to lead it from the barn.

She knew she had to try one more time to stop him, for deep inside she knew something within him that had been dammed up had suddenly broken loose. Outside he was pushing the rifle in its sheath and preparing to mount.

"Clay!"

Clay stopped, turned and looked at her. She ran to his side.

"I warned you once about hurting that child, and you

swore you never would. You swore you loved her."

"I don't intend to hurt her, Ellen," he said in a voice that was strangely soft. "I love her . . . she is mine . . . no power on earth takes from me what is mine. I only intend to bring her home . . . where she belongs."

Ellen was stunned at the cold silence of his words.

"She is not an animal . . . a horse or a gun. She is not a possession, Clay. I . . . I don't think you know what love is. Please Clay, wait here. Let her come home to you. Everything will be all right. If you go with this kind of anger you will destroy something fine and beautiful. You may never get it back again."

He looked at her again with the ice blue gaze and she knew with sinking heart that her words had gone unheard.

"She's mine," he said softly, "and Summer is mine. Hawk needs a lesson on trying to take what belongs to me. Maybe now is the time."

He turned and mounted his horse. Whirling about, he rode from the clearing and Ellen could only watch in helpless fear. She watched until he became a black shadow on the horizon. Then with tears in her eyes and fear in her heart, she turned and walked slowly back to the house.

Twenty-five

The old man bent slightly toward Sabrina as he spoke. Sabrina sat on the fur rug at his feet and listened to his words without interruption.

"It began a long time ago; sometimes I think it began long before Clay's parents brought him here when he was a very young boy. He was less than seven summers when he first came. His father was a strong quiet man and his mother was very beautiful. His father extended his hand in friendship to us and we were pleased to return it. Soon our children became friends. Hawk and Clay, from that day on were very nearly inseparable. One taught the other, Hawk the teacher of the ways of the forest and Clay the teacher of the ways of the city.

"As they grew in age and size so did their love for each other. They became blood brothers . . . they lived together, fought together, and shared much of the same pleasures.

"They reached manhood sharing a closeness few brothers had. Then into their lives came Singing Bells."

"Clay's wife."

"Eventually yes, but before she was Clay's wife, she was many things to many other people, and that is the root of the problem."

"Singing Bells was of your tribe; why had not Clay and

Hawk noticed her before?"

"No, she was not of our tribe. She was of a tribe that is many weeks travel from here. She was called to us because of a great sickness that struck our tribe for she was a woman whom the gods blessed with the power to heal. Singing Bells had many powers. She captured both hearts when she came and she never released either.

"As time went on, Clay and Hawk competed for her attention. It was then I began to notice the flaw in Clay. Clay was a strong, honest and determined man . . . he was also a man so possessive that when he loved he smothered what he loved."

Sabrina thought instantly of Clay's words about Summer. She is mine, no one takes what is mine. A wave of shattering sympathy struck Sabrina.

"Eventually, Clay won Singing Bells, and it was then we discovered, as did she, that he intended to take her away from all she had known and loved. They married here in our village and Clay took her to his home.

"Hawk would visit them often, but his and Clay's relationship was never quite the same. As possessive as Clay was, Hawk soon began to feel unwelcome in his home. Then . . . Singing Bells began to resist Clay's overpowering possessive jealousy. She felt . . . as if she could not breathe. She also knew the powers she possessed were needed by her people and she was wasting them. Then she made a mistake. She began to visit us when Clay was away. She wanted so desperately to share the love she had with both her husband and her people. Of course, it was not long before Clay found this out. He must have felt betrayed, for he forbade Singing Bells to come here again. When Hawk came to visit, Clay always made sure he did not leave the two of them alone. Hawk, as a brother, tried to talk to Clay, but Clay only believed Hawk still loved his wife."

The old man sighed deeply and for a moment he was silent as if the memories were almost too painful to bear. Sabrina remained silent. Then the old man continued in a subdued voice.

"Then Singing Bells found that she carried Clay's child. She was overjoyed for she did love her husband completely and she thought a child would somehow change him . . . it was not so. Clay became even more possessive. Swift Doe was her only contact with her people. One day she told Swift Doe that she loved Clay completely, but that she intended to return to her people for she could not live in such isolation . . . but it was not to be. I believe such a thing might have changed Clay. But Singing Bells died giving birth to the child. Now I believe Clay is making the gravest mistake of his life. We have watched Summer, and we know, as does Clay, that she possesses the same powers as her mother did. But Clay is determined to make of Summer what she is not. In the process, I believe he will destroy her love for him. We want to bring Clay and his child closer to us. We want to share her, watch her grow, love her as he does. We would have her know all the roots of her people, know that she is loved by many, needed by many. But there is now a dark valley between my son and Clay and us. For you see, we know Hawk is wrong also. He never stopped loving Singing Bells, and he blamed Clay for her death without being united with her people. He also never let Clay forget the child's past is half ours. Clay feels Hawk will try any method to draw Summer back to us . . . and for once I believe Clay is right. We pray for something or someone who will clear Clay's blindness, open Hawk's heart and draw the two back together. I believe the child's life and future depend upon this, and I hope one day the great spirit sees this pain and seeks to remedy it."

At first, Sabrina felt a deep, burning anger. Both Hawk

and Clay were using her and Summer like pawns upon a chessboard. This anger slowly faded into a deep sympathy. Tall, strong, and handsome, willful and self-possessive, both men had fallen prey to their darkest passions. She also realized this could not continue for a lovely child's future depended upon it. She also realized Hawk had been drawn to her and her clearing vision saw the reasons Clay had acted as he did. He felt Hawk was reaching for Sabrina and through Sabrina could reach Summer. Someone had to open Clay's heart, she knew, but she had no idea how to do it.

She realized the old man had been watching closely and was reading her thoughts with wise eyes.

"My son has begun to feel a love for you, my child. Can you return this love?"

"No . . . I cannot lie to you. I like Hawk very much . . . but I love Clay as I will love no other man."

"And Clay loves you?"

"He has told me that he does."

"Are you frightened of this?"

"Yes, I am. What if I cannot make him understand? I cannot even tell him yet that I have been here. He will believe that I have betrayed him also."

"I do not understand the ways of the gods, my child. I only know what I believe. I believe you were sent by them, and I believe through you we will unite the two men each of us love."

"I wish I could believe as strongly as you," Sabrina said.

"You," he chuckled softly, "are not as old as I. Age gives one different beliefs."

She smiled and reached to take his large callused hand in hers.

"I will do what I can, for all of us. I have grown to love Summer as my own, and I hope to bear other children for

Clay. I would have him happy and I know it cannot be unless he rids himself of this terrible black thing. I will pray and hope that all the love I have to give is enough."

"Complete love is usually enough to handle anything. I have seen it move mountains."

"I hope you are right. I am so glad I came and talked with you. At least I will understand Clay more. Maybe time will help us all."

"And I must answer to my son," he smiled. "It is best he does not know yet all that was spoken here. He would deny much of what was said. Can you hold these words within you?"

"Yes, for the peace and love we hope to rebuild . . . I will. I am grateful."

"Work hard to understand the man who loves you, for I am sure the secret of his crippling emotion is somewhere in his past and only you carry the key that might unlock that door."

"I will, I promise, I will."

"May the gods bless you."

"Thank you," Sabrina rose and walked to the door. Then she turned and looked again at the old man whose intelligent sparkling eyes followed her. She smiled.

"One day Clay and I will come to visit you. We will bring Summer to play with your other children. Maybe we will bring another child to receive your blessing."

He nodded, and Sabrina turned and left the lodge.

Trying not to look like he was obviously waiting for her, Hawk stood some distance away. It had taken some time and he was extremely tense and nervous about what his father had said. When he saw Sabrina appear he started in her direction. He stopped beside her and enjoyed the pleasure her quick smile brought.

"The talk with my father was good?"

"Yes, Hawk, it was."

Clearly he desired to know all his father had said. He was about to diplomatically ask, when her next words told him she had no intention of telling him what had transpired between her and his father.

"Hawk, I must return home at once. I want to be home when Clay gets there. It is best . . . for all of us . . . that I am there when he comes home."

Hawk was about to speak when their attention was drawn by a shout. Swift Doe was running in their direction and both of them instinctively knew something was very wrong.

Swift Doe came breathlessly to their side.

"Hawk . . . Sabrina. There's been an accident."

Sabrina's heart leapt. "Summer!"

"Yes. She has fallen from the high rocks."

"Is she badly hurt?" Hawk demanded.

"I don't know, I was afraid to have her lifted. The other children guard her. You must come and carry her back."

Both Hawk and Sabrina began to run. Hawk outdistanced her immediately and he was kneeling at Summer's side when she arrived.

She watched Hawk's gentleness as he felt for broken bones, and could feel his love for this child. Why, she wondered, did he allow past things to twist this love out of control.

"She has no broken bones," he said, "but she has struck her head. I will carry her back to my lodge."

"No," Sabrina said quickly. If Clay found this out, there would be nothing to stop the anger. "Take her to Swift Doe's lodge."

With infinite gentleness, Hawk lifted the child in his arms. Sabrina and Swift Doe followed as he carried her back to the village.

"At least I have two days," Sabrina thought. Clay need

not know of this either. It would be best for all.

Inside Swift Doe's lodge, Hawk lay Summer on the fur covered couch. Swift Doe ran for water and Sabrina knelt by the couch.

A nasty bruise on Summer's head was already swelling. The skin had been broken and blood covered the side of her face.

Swift Doe returned with water and Sabrina bathed away the blood. Then she lay the cool damp cloth across the child's forehead. Still, there was no sign of response from Summer.

After a few minutes the door covering was pushed aside and Hawk reentered with the medicine man who knelt beside the child. After a few minutes of examination, he spoke in a rapid tongue Sabrina could not understand.

"She is not injured badly," Hawk translated, "but she must be still for a few hours. Then she will be all right."

A few hours would still give Sabrina time to get home before Clay.

"I will stay beside her," Sabrina said.

"My husband is away hunting, so I can share my sister's lodge," Swift Doe said. "Then you can remain beside her until morning."

"Thank you, Swift Doe, that is very kind of you."

Sabrina turned to Hawk.

"We must start home in the morning."

"If she can travel, I will carry her. We will go at daybreak."

Again Sabrina nodded. Then she returned her attention to Summer. The others quietly left the lodge.

She refreshed the cloth with cool water and replaced it on the child's head, then she took Summer's hand in hers and spoke to her softly.

"Summer . . . Summer."

Slowly Summer's eyes flickered open, and she smiled

weakly up at Sabrina.

"Sabrina, I'm sorry, I fell."

"It's all right, Summer, you're going to be fine. You just have to lie still for a while."

"Sabrina, I saw Papa and he was angry. It was what made me fall."

Sabrina was aware now of Summer's mystic ability to reach out and touch the emotions of others. It still frightened her, but after Black Cloud's explanation, she understood a little better. She also knew it had frightened Summer who was still much too young to handle the strange things that came to her. She had reached out to her father who had tried to make her forget. Now she reached out to Sabrina.

"You saw your father?" she asked gently and saw the relief in Summer's eyes when she realized Sabrina believed her.

"He was angry Sabrina, very angry."

"It might have been something that is going to happen in the future, but I'm sure it has nothing to do with us. Your father loves you too much to be that angry with you. Don't worry, Summer, everything will be all right. If you feel all right at dawn we'll go home. Then together we will spend a lot of time trying to make your father happy."

Summer smiled and Sabrina was pleased to see warm sincere pleasure leap into her eyes.

"Try to get some rest. I'll be right here if you need anything at all."

Summer closed her eyes for a moment, then she opened them again.

"Papa always tells me stories when I'm sick. They help me sleep."

"Then, I guess," Sabrina laughed, "I shall have to tell you a story."

It took two stories before Summer's eyes closed in sleep.

The village grew quiet and Sabrina found it difficult to

keep her eyes open. She refused to lie down in case Summer might need her. She sat beside the child and allowed her thoughts to linger on Clay. She loved him with a depth she had never even known she possessed. She wanted a life with him, to share forever.

She tried to think of ways she could help change what had happened. She searched for words she could say to help Clay believe that his love for her could never be replaced or lost.

Memories, sweet and filled with tender love touched her mind and she allowed Clay's warmth to reach out and enfold her. No one could ever be able to reach within her to the depth that Clay could. She was lost to any other need but Clay . . . who with one touch, one kiss could send her passion soaring and eclipse every other sense from her mind. Her body grew warm with the remembrance of his love and she felt again the surging touch of fiery love that would always possess her at the thought of him.

Hawk stood in the doorway of his lodge and gazed across the open space to the lodge in which he knew Sabrina was awake. He longed to go to her. To tell her how he felt about her, to ask her to stay in his village.

This slim golden haired girl had shaken his world and for the first time in his life he was unsure of himself.

He knew it was the wrong time to speak to her of how he felt, yet he wanted her. If he went to her now, told her that he wanted her to stay would she listen? What if . . . what if he just did not take her back in the morning? As soon as the thought came into his head he was angry with himself. What man of honor would think such a thing?

He was about to turn back and go to his bed when a movement on the crest of the hill caught his attention. Someone approached the village.

He stood still and watched the shadowed form crest the

hill and start down into the shadows of the trees. The rider disappeared, but Hawk knew he was headed for the village.

He stood quietly and waited until the rider broke from the trees, then he stiffened in shock . . . Clay!

For a moment he was tempted to cross to the lodge where Sabrina was and be found with her when Clay came, but again his ingrained sense of honor would not allow this. Instead he walked to the clearing and stood and waited.

Clay stopped his horse a few feet from Hawk. Their eyes met and held.

"Where is she Hawk?"

"Asleep I imagine."

"Where Hawk?"

"She and Summer are sharing the lodge of Swift Doe. Her husband is away."

Hawk tried to ignore the cold blue flame of anger that simmered in Clay's eyes.

"Why Hawk?" came the soft and very controlled insistent voice.

"Why what?"

"Don't play with me Hawk. I'm in no mood to toy with words. I warned you once before to stay away, Hawk. Why did you come for Sabrina? Why did you bring her here? Did you think I would allow you to walk away . . . walk away with what was, is, and always will be mine."

"You are wrong, Clay."

"Am I?"

"Yes, you are. I did not ask Sabrina to come here, nor did I ask her to bring the child . . . she asked me."

"I don't believe you," Clay snapped.

Hawk was astounded. Even with all of their difficulties, Clay had always known Hawk would never lie, had never told a lie in his life.

"It does not matter if you believe me or not. When you are

more rational you will remember I have never lied to you . . . ever."

"Sabrina asked you to bring her here?" Clay asked in a still disbelieving voice.

"If you care for proof you need only ask Walking Horse. You will believe Walking Horse will you not?"

Slowly Clay dismounted. Without another word to Hawk he brushed past him and walked toward Swift Doe's lodge.

"Clay . . . don't wake them. Summer needs rest. There was a slight accident today."

Clay whirled about, his face pale.

"Accident . . . what kind of accident? Who was hurt, Sabrina—Summer?"

"Summer. She fell from the rocks near the falls. She is well now and all she needs is some rest."

Now Clay's anger was aggravated by worry. He was beside himself with conflicting emotions. Without another word he walked toward Swift Doe's lodge. The inside of the lodge was lit only by the dying embers of the fire. Summer lay on the fur covered couch in a sound sleep. Sabrina sat beside her, her back braced against the couch and Summer's hand in hers, and sound asleep also.

Her head rested against the dark fur and her burnished hair spread against it in golden profusion.

Emotions he could not control tumbled through him. He loved her!—his anger exploded like white searing lightning. He loved her!—betrayal of all he had thought he had found in her. He loved her! And she had taken Summer against his wishes and had come here. He loved her! and she had deceived him by thinking she would return before he did.

Would she have kept it a secret? What had Hawk told her?

Reason warred with unreason. He wanted to jerk her to her feet and strike her, yet he wanted to tenderly lift her in his arms, hold her close to him and kiss those soft parted lips.

He looked closely at his daughter. He saw the bruise on her head, but knew her soft even breathing told him she slept a natural sleep.

"Sabrina," he said quietly. She stirred, and slowly the violet eyes opened and met his. He watched emotions fall across her face. Warm accepting love which slowly, before his eyes, turned to fear. Fear, the one emotion he had hoped never to see in her eyes. Yet fear . . . meant guilt. Had she betrayed him, had she deliberately meant to deceive him?

He did not realize that his quiet voice and the cold chill of his eyes in which still lingered the emotions he was trying to control, frightened her.

"Clay," she whispered. She rose to her feet, unsteady because of her exhaustion and the sudden fear that had struck her when she had seen anger on his face.

She held out her hand to him, but he did not take it at once and the moment was lost as her hand dropped to her side.

"Clay, please talk to me," she whispered painfully. "Let me explain."

"There's no explanation needed right now. We can talk when we get home. Get your things and wrap Summer. We're going home."

"Clay, Summer has been hurt. Why wake her now? Let us stay the night, here together, the three of us. Tomorrow we can talk."

"Sabrina," he said coldly, "wrap Summer. She is going home. You have a choice. You can go with me now . . . or you can stay."

Sabrina gasped as if he had struck her, and Clay regretted the words. He knew he would never let her stay. He did not even know why he wanted to hurt her except for the fact that he had been hurt and struck back without thinking.

He watched the light in her eyes die, and tears replace it. She turned away to do as he said.

When they stepped out of Swift Doe's lodge they found a very surprised Hawk outside.

"Hawk, will you bring Sabrina's horse," Clay said.

Hawk saw the tears in Sabrina's eyes and could sense her trembling body. He cast Clay an angry look, but he would not make it worse for Sabrina.

Without a word he went to get Sabrina's horse. When he handed her the reins, their hands touched and her eyes lifted to meet his. They held momentarily then she dropped hers and mounted. Clay mounted with Summer in his arms. Without a word, he moved his horse before Sabrina's to lead the way. Sabrina gazed down into Hawk's sympathetic yet angry face.

"Thank you, Hawk for bringing me to speak with your father. I'm sorry it had to end like this."

"Are you all right, Sabrina?"

"I'm fine. Don't worry, I'll be all right. Hawk," she added softly, "help me stop this. Come to visit us soon."

"It is useless. Too much has happened. Clay holds too much anger in his heart for me."

"I will never be defeated, Hawk," she said softly. "One day you will see. Love can cure all things." She rode after Clay and Hawk watched her go.

"Not this time, Sabrina," he said softly. "Hawk does not forget so easily either."

Twenty-six

They rode in absolute silence. All Sabrina could see was Clay's broad stiff back ahead of her.

She let her thoughts dwell on the words Hawk's father had told her. She knew that both Clay and Hawk were wrong in what they were doing just as surely as she knew this tug of war between the two was a thing that could kill both Summer's future — and the new and sensitive love she and Clay shared.

For hours they traveled. Sabrina was exhausted, so exhausted that she did not at first realize that the sun was rising and that they were nearing Clay's house.

A worried Ellen was standing on the porch when they rode up.

Clay dismounted and handed a still sleeping Summer to her.

"Take her in and put her to bed. Keep her there all day. She fell and has a nasty bruise and I don't want her running about."

Ellen took Summer, but her eyes were on Sabrina who slumped wearily in the saddle in a state of complete exhaustion.

"Sabrina child," she began, but Clay interrupted her firmly.

"I'll take care of Sabrina, you take Summer and do as I told you."

"Yes sir," Ellen replied, as she reluctantly carried the child inside.

Clay went to Sabrina's side and gently lifted her down into his arms. Mentally, he flayed himself for his cruelty, but he could not seem to stop it.

Her head rested on his shoulder and she moaned softly as her weary body protested every move. He carried her to her room and lay her gently on the bed. Then he closed the door and returned to sit by her side.

She watched him out of tear dimmed eyes. When he sat beside her, he lifted her hand in his and held it gently. But his words were not quite as gentle.

"Sabrina, I don't know why you did what you did. I don't even care to hear your reasons. We will not talk of it again. From this day on I forbid you to go to that village again. I do not want Hawk invited here. They are not part of my life any longer and I do not want it to be part of yours. Do I make myself clear?"

Anger flooded her and gave her strength she didn't know she still possessed. She sat up and pulled her hand from his.

"No, no it is not clear. If you forbid me to do something, at least you owe me a reason for not doing it!"

His eyes glinted a crystal blue as he tried to control his anger. "I forbid you to go there, Sabrina. You are still indentured to me."

"Are you telling me if I do so again you will send me away?"

Why couldn't she listen? he thought. Why did she twist what he said? He knew he could never send her away.

"No, I'm not saying that. I'm only telling you what is best for you and Summer."

"Is it Clay? Is it best for Summer and me, or is it best

308

for you?"

"I don't know what you're talking about. Now you're tired, go to sleep. We'll talk later."

He rose and walked toward the door, but her next words stopped him.

"Are you running away now Clay?" she said softly. "Are you afraid to face the truth?"

He turned, and his eyes deepened as they burned into hers.

"You said you loved me Clay," she whispered, "but you shut me out. Is it love, Clay, or are you using me?"

"Don't be a fool Sabrina," he snapped.

"Don't make me one, Clay," she cried.

"I've tried to protect you. I don't want something you have no concern in to reach out and spoil our lives."

"You want me just to be silent while you and Hawk play your little games. Can't either of you see what you're doing to Summer?"

"What has Hawk told you?"

"Nothing. Hawk and I did not speak of you or the past at all. I only know that Summer is old enough now to sense the struggle that is going on. She is the daughter of Singing Bells, Clay, and whether you will it or not, part of her calls out to her mother's people. She needs to be part of them like she needs to be part of you. Don't continue to tear her apart Clay, or you will lose her one day."

"Quit meddling in what you don't understand!" he said angrily.

"I don't understand because you refuse to talk to me."

"It's not your affair. Stay out of it Sabrina."

"I can't," she sobbed. "Clay, I love you. Let me into your life, let me understand you and help you."

"I don't need your help, and I don't need your interference in something you cannot understand!"

"You asked me to trust you Clay. You said one day you would tell me all the truth. Perhaps today is that day."

"No, Sabrina," he said softly, "no . . . let it go."

"When Summer fell," Sabrina said, "she said she fell because she saw you. She saw you and you were angry. Oh, Clay, can't you see what you're doing?"

Clay stood very still, yet Sabrina felt as if some part of him had gone from her.

"Summer," he said very gently, "is mine. No hand from the past will ever take her away from me, even though they try to use you to do it."

Before she could answer, he opened the door and was gone, closing it firmly behind him.

Sabrina lay back against the pillow and gave way to the tears that burned her eyes. She wept deeply and brokenly. She had fought to reach him and he had placed a barrier between then she could not shatter. She felt her heart had been brutally battered, and she longed to return to the strength and warmth of his arms.

Clay stood outside the door and listened to her cry. He wanted to go back into the room and crush her to him and kiss the tears into silence. But an old fear held him and refused to release him. After a few minutes, he walked away.

Ellen, after she had tucked Summer safely in bed, had come out of Clay's room in time to see him close Sabrina's door and walk out.

She watched him ride away, then she went to Sabrina's room. She opened the door to find Sabrina weeping bitterly. She sat down on the bed beside her and placed her arm about her.

"There, there child, don't cry so. It is always darkest before the dawn."

"Oh, Ellen," Sabrina sobbed, "I've lost him. He's so angry with me I feel he almost hates me."

"No, child. I don't think he hates you. You just threw a scare into him. I imagine Clay Storm has not been scared of many things. I think, when he found you had gone to the village, well, I think he thought he might have lost you. Losing something he loves does not come easy to him. He just replaced his fear with anger. Anger was an easier emotion for him to handle."

"What can I do, Ellen?"

"Rest for now. Get your strength back. I have a feeling Clay will be back soon and when he does, you can certainly face him better if you're not exhausted."

Obediently Sabrina lay back against the pillows, and within minutes was sound asleep.

Ellen fumed, and if Clay had returned then she too would have jeopardized their safety again by shouting exactly what she thought at him. But he did not return.

Sabrina rose in the early afternoon. The first thing she did was look in on Summer. She laughed to find her sitting up in bed and playing with her dolls. She went to her and sat on the edge of the bed.

"How do you feel this afternoon, Summer?"

"I feel fine, but I'm hungry."

"Hasn't Ellen brought you any lunch?"

Summer's eyes twinkled mischievously, "Ellen still thinks I'm asleep and I don't want to make her mad at me. She told me I was supposed to sleep all day."

"Well, I'm sure if you sleep all day you will be up all night. Why don't we both get washed and dressed and have something to eat?"

Summer readily agreed to this and got out of bed with such alacrity that Sabrina had to laugh. She was sure now Summer was quite over her fall.

They rose, washed and dressed then went to the kitchen. At first, Ellen was alarmed but when they both assured her they were all right she proceeded to produce a rather large hearty meal to which they did justice.

Sabrina entertained Summer and began to refresh her lessons, but her mind was with Clay, wondering if he were still angry with her, where he was, and if, when he returned to her would things be the same?

The three of them ate a solemn supper which was made quite late because they had eaten such a late lunch.

Sabrina let Summer stay up later than usual in the hope that Clay would return. But the hour grew later and later and with a heavy heart Sabrina put Summer to bed.

She and Ellen sat before the fireplace and talked, but Sabrina would not discuss Clay any further and Ellen stayed away from a subject that seemed to hurt Sabrina so badly.

The hour grew later and Ellen's eyes grew heavy.

"Ellen, do go to bed. You're so tired."

"What of you?"

"I slept too late. I'm going to read for a while then I'll go to bed. I'll be fine. Go get some rest please."

Ellen went to her room and soon fell into a deep sleep.

Sabrina tried to read, but the words blurred before her eyes and visions of Clay's cold blue angry eyes wavered before her. Her love for him and the pain of his rejection swelled within her, each battling for supremacy. The love won out as it always would. Again hot tears filled her eyes and escaped to trace paths down her cheeks.

Almost angrily, she wiped them away. She loved him, and she would do battle with the ghosts of his past until there was no strength in her body.

She knew it was possible Clay could be gone for days. As angry as he had been, he might just stay away longer. She worried that he might have returned to the village, that he and Hawk might have met again.

Visions of conflict flashed before her eyes and she had to

control a tremor of fear. Resolutely, she rose and went to her room. She undressed for bed and blew out the candle and climbed into the bed.

She lay for a long time fighting the visions of Clay's anger before she was finally able to drift into a troubled sleep.

Clay stabled his horse and walked across the clearing to the house. The moon, high in the sky, told him it was already the wee hours of the morning.

Guilt and remorse filled him and he wanted nothing more than Sabrina's forgiveness. He knew she would be asleep, and for tonight just to look at her would be a soothing balm for his frayed emotions.

The door to her bedroom opened soundlessly. He walked across the floor just as silently, and stood looking down at her.

Sabrina lay on her side, her knees bent slightly, one hand under her cheek and the other rested on her hip.

The pale gold of her hair spilled across the pillow and shafts of moonlight washed her in its glow.

She looked so vulnerable, so helpless that a new rush of guilt touched him, yet from the words she had cried to him before he had gone he had begun to realize his shy woman-child was much more woman than child.

She stirred restlessly in her sleep and turned on her back, then she stirred again as if subconsciously she was aware that he was watching her. After a few minutes her eyes opened.

With the room lighted by an almost daybright moonlight there was no mistaking who stood by her bed. She slowly sat up, her eyes never leaving him, unsure of what to expect from him now.

He sat on the edge of the bed and lifted her hands in his, pressing them to his lips.

"Sabrina, I'm sorry. I never meant to say the things I said

to you. I never meant to hurt you."

Ellen's words returned to her. "Clay Storm has not been scared of many things . . . he thought he might have lost you . . . losing something he loves does not come easy to him . . . he loves you . . . he loves you."

"I know Clay," she said softly, "I know."

"Sometimes I don't understand myself this blackness that gets into me. I just know that I don't want to lose your love. I need you Sabrina . . . I need you, my love."

It was a poignant cry of need from the depths of his soul, and it reached out to touch her heart with fingers of flame. There would be time for them, she thought. They would spend the balance of their lives together and day by day she would build his faith and trust in her until he felt so secure in her love that he would be able to let go of the dark shadows of the past. Then he would be able to talk with her, to share the pain and let her love heal him.

"And I need you Clay," she breathed. "I need you."

"Sabrina," he whispered her name as he gathered her to him. Gently his mouth claimed hers. The kiss was deep searching, and found the warmth of her love burned bright enough to sear his mind and body.

Their mouths separated for a moment and he looked down into warm translucent eyes that had open invitation within. Then again their lips mingled, tasted . . . tested.

"When I left you today," he whispered against the soft flesh of her throat, "I went dead inside. I realized how black my world would be without you. Sabrina, don't leave my world."

Then her arms were about his neck and her lips met his with a brilliant warm desire. Half parted moist lips sought to blend with his hard seeking mouth in a feverish need.

His hungry mouth searched hers leisurely now and most thoroughly. Now she was lost to any sense of reason. There were no questions or thoughts in her mind now but the warm gentle hands that began expertly to search her warm willing body.

He did not hurry now, but sought to give as much pleasure as his own flaming body was enjoying.

The nightgown she wore was slipped with no resistance over her head and found its way to the floor forgotten and in moments his clothes followed. Ecstasy and pleasure blossomed within her and began to grow to a need that she knew now, if they shared forever, would always be Clay.

She was not even aware of their blending yet they joined in mutual need. She rose to meet his consuming passion and her throbbing senses responded to his every move with a fire that raged like a tempest.

Each thrust, forceful and hard, lifted her to a new sense of joy and fulfillment. Now she could not seem to get enough of him. Her breathing, hoarse and labored, matched his. Twin heartbeats throbbed the insistent beat of almost unbearable passion.

They were one now, one need, one pounding heartbeat, one flame. She felt there could be no more, but their wild consuming passion had no boundaries.

He lifted her higher, beyond reason, beyond knowing, beyond any control. Higher again until she cried out in the ecstatic pleasure. Higher again until her world shattered to a million glittering pieces and she could only cling to him. A kaleidoscope of whirling pleasure consumed them both and they clung to each other as they floated downward from the pinnacle of ecstasy.

Their senses slowly returned from beyond the universe and they lay quietly, holding each other until the pounding heartbeats could quit and the ragged breathing could be brought under some semblance of control.

He held her close to him, as if he were still afraid that

some force could separate them. Her head lay against his shoulder and lightly she caressed a hard fur matted chest.

Sabrina knew she could not use this flaming emotional experience they just shared as a way to get him to reveal the things he held inside. It had to be a thing which flowed from him with security and trust. They had taken the first step toward the opening of all doors that existed between them.

Clay knew only that Sabrina was his again, and he vowed silently to himself to be more careful in the future for he had no intention of ever losing her again.

He rolled on his side and rested on one elbow to gaze down into her warm eyes.

"I do love you Sabrina," he said gently as he brushed wayward strands of hair from her cheek. "And I am sorry for what I said to you today. I'm afraid where Hawk is concerned, I'm a little irrational at times. I don't want to lose you Sabrina. Will you have patience? . . . Will you stay with me?"

"I never intended to leave you Clay. I love you. I only wanted to be closer to you, to be part of your life. I wanted to understand you, share all your dreams and hopes both for us and for Summer."

He smiled. "You love my daughter."

"As if she were a child of my own. She is part of you Clay, and I love all that is you."

"Oh God, Sabrina," he sighed as he drew her close to him and buried his face in the sweet fragrance of her hair, "there are no words in the world to tell you how very precious you are to me. We'll leave the rest of the world out of our lives."

She knew from these words that Clay was still not quite prepared to open the door and let her walk through memories of the past.

But now she knew at least part of the story, for it had still not occurred to Clay that someone other than Hawk had told her all that had happened. She would retain her secret too, and use it to help build a bridge over the dark chasms to the past.

Sabrina closed her eyes and allowed her senses to enjoy the hard solid length of him against her. Gentle hands that sought to familiarize him with every curve, every valley of her body.

With no sense of time, he explored leisurely and with infinite care until again he could taste the sweet surrender on her lips and in her seeking body that lifted his pleasure.

He knew there would never be a time when the magic of her would not be able to reach within him and touch the places where no one else could live. He would always need this vibrant filling love that sent his passion and his need soaring.

Yet two minds still held one separate thought. He, that she was safely his and that he could close off anything that could touch her and change their love. She, that one day all the past would be open and they would have no unspoken things existing between them.

But before any of these thoughts could come to fruition, Fate would interfere and send the testing fates to see if the promise of these lovers could survive the testing and receive the reward of forever.

Twenty-seven

Ellen was amazed at a bright-eyed smiling Sabrina when she came to breakfast the next morning, but it didn't take her long to realize the reason.

Clay had been out caring for the horse and bringing wood inside for the fire. Sabrina was already seated at the table when Clay opened the door and walked in carrying a load of firewood in his arms.

The way his eyes searched out Sabrina's, the way Sabrina's turned warm and bright under the warmth of his gaze told Ellen as no words could have.

"Good morning Sabrina," he said softly. His speaking of her name was a caress. "Did you sleep well?"

"Yes, very well," Sabrina replied. Rosy cheeks and downcast eyes spoke eloquently of the night's passing.

Clay dropped the load of wood near the fireplace and went to sit beside Sabrina. The table was a long wooden one with two benches on either side. Sabrina smiled as Clay slid close to her. A gentle hand touched her waist and caressed its slimness, then rose to touch the silken strands of her hair.

"It's a beautiful day Sabrina, would you like to go for a ride?"

"I would, but what about Summer? She'll be disappointed. Besides, I hate to see her miss any lessons; she's doing so well."

Ellen watched the warm loving exchange and wondered why it no longer alarmed her. The feeling that these two belonged together and that Clay was strong enough and his love deep enough to protect her from anything washed through her.

"We'll take her with us. That way," he chuckled, "we can kill both birds with one stone."

Sabrina quickly agreed and before long, Summer joined them for a breakfast that was leisurely and filled with laughter. The day itself progressed in the same vein and it flowed from one day to the other. Sabrina felt as if they were all one loving family. Clay and Summer's joyful sharing of their days with her and Ellen and the magic of the nights she spent in the safety of Clay's arms.

She was so caught up in Clay's love and the beauty of their moments together that she was quite unprepared for the first touch of trouble to appear. In fact, it took her some time to recognize it for what it was.

It had been a week filled with a sharing of each other, and now they sat in the parlor in front of a red embered fire. Ellen was mending one of Sabrina's dresses. Sabrina sat with Summer on her lap on the rug in front of the fire. They were engrossed in a book Sabrina was reading. Clay was engrossed in watching the firelight play on her golden hair, and the way her ivory skin picked up the pale glow of the fire. Vividly he could remember the touch and the taste of her and the need to reach out to her was so strong he very nearly went to her side.

Resolutely he held himself in his chair knowing this was a need that would never die. If he possessed her every moment of the life he intended for them to share, it would never be enough. He would always have the desire to reach out and touch her, to hold her, and to love her.

The sound of an approaching wagon must have been on

the edge of Clay's senses for several minutes before he realized what it was. Visitors were a very rare thing and he was surprised that whoever it was came in a wagon.

It was really Summer who reacted to it first. Her head came up and she gazed at her father.

"Papa someone is coming."

"I know sweet, I know," Clay rose and walked to the door. Summer was quickly off Sabrina's lap and following him.

He opened the door and his face must have registered his surprise for it drew a curious Sabrina to her feet.

"Mr. Gregory," Clay said, "and Elenora. How . . . how nice to see you again. Is there something wrong? It must be important to bring you this far."

William Gregory walked into the room and Sabrina smiled for she thought only that this man was a friend of Clay's. The smile wavered and very nearly died when the beautiful Elenora Gregory came in behind him. Elenora's next words did not make things any better.

"Clay dear," she smiled, "I'll bet you are surprised to see me again so soon."

"Elenora," Clay said with a mental groan at what Sabrina might be thinking. He looked at her and his consistent ability to read her thoughts served him well for though the smile on her lips did not, the one in her eyes died. "This is a surprise. I never expected to see you two out here."

"I've a little business to discuss with you and Elenora decided I might be lonely, so she came along."

"You'll spend the rest of the night of course?" Clay invited, but he would much rather had sent Elenora and her father to the other end of the world.

"I've told my guide he could sleep in your barn. Is that all right?"

"Of course. Ellen can take him some blankets later," Clay replied. "Have you eaten? I'm sure Ellen can rustle something up?"

"No, I'm not hungry. Are you Elenora?"

"No," Elenora replied sweetly as she turned to Sabrina, "but I could use a drink. Would you mind please?"

She had immediately placed Sabrina in the position of servant. Clay's anger built but his face remained shuttered. Sabrina turned to go.

"Sabrina," Clay's voice was firm and commanding, "stay here. Ellen, would you get our guests something to drink? Elenora, Sabrina is as much a guest here as you. She is Summer's teacher . . . not a maid. I won't have her treated as one."

"I see." Elenora's voice and arched gaze spoke eloquently that she was beginning to believe Sabrina's position here was much more than Clay intended to say.

"And . . . just what do you . . . teach?"

Sabrina's cheeks pinkened with her own suppressed anger, and she decided to speak before Clay could.

"'I teach Summer reading, writing . . . and deportment. You do know what that is, don't you . . . proper manners and genteel treatment of others?"

Sabrina's voice was also sweetly soft, but Clay chuckled to himself. His little kitten had claws.

Elenora's smile wavered for a moment but held steady as her eyes filled with rage.

Summer had missed nothing that had passed between her beloved Sabrina and the dark haired lady she did not like.

"Well Clay," Elenora said as she moved close enough for her body to brush against his arm, "now you don't have to worry about someone taking care of the child. You can come into town for the ball and have a good time and know that she's being safely tucked into bed at night. Maybe," she said softly, "you could even spend the night with us."

"I'm afraid not, Elenora. I've already made reservations

at the hotel. Both Summer and Sabrina will be coming to the ball with me and we will bring Ellen to help us . . . tuck Summer safely into bed."

"One doesn't usually bring their servants to a ball Clay, and really, it's no place for a child."

"Well," Clay smiled, "I consider Ellen and Sabrina part of the family, and Summer will go with me if I choose for her to go and I'm sure no one will be too upset about it."

Before Elenora could voice any more of the arguments that were apparent in her eyes, Clay turned to her father.

"You did say you had some business to discuss with me?"

"Yes Clay, it's rather personal. Could we talk alone?"

"Of course. Would you like to walk outside, we could have a smoke and talk."

"That would be fine . . . just fine."

The two men left the room to a sharp and very deep silence.

Elenora walked to Summer and reached out to touch the child's dark shiny braids.

"Really," she said in a disgusted voice, "someone should do something with this child's hair. She shouldn't be wearing it like a savage. After all, she is a Storm."

Summer shrank from the touch of her hand and her eyes glistened with tears she refused to shed. They turned to Sabrina in helpless need.

"Summer's mother was an Indian. I am told she was very beautiful and very kind. It is a beautiful thing to see a child remember her mother's ways. She would be very proud of Summer as I am . . . and I'm sure Clay is too."

Gratitude sparkled in Summer's eyes, and Ellen smiled contentedly at Sabrina's defense of not only Summer, but Clay's dead wife as well. Pride in Sabrina came out in her voice as she spoke.

"I'll read Summer a story and put her to bed. I think it's

322

late for her to be up and," she glared at Elenora, "I wouldn't want her to come in contact with something that might make her sick."

Elenora flushed at the insult, but before she could vent her rage, Ellen took Summer's hand and left the room.

Sabrina and Elenora were left gazing silently at each other. Sabrina had no way of knowing that Elenora knew much more about her than she could imagine. Thomas had told her most of what had happened. Elenora smiled, realizing it would be Thomas who would rid her of this golden haired nuisance. She also knew she would help him do it in any way he chose. For now she had only to bring back word of the situation here. And help Thomas plan Sabrina's imminent downfall.

"So Clay plans on bringing you to the ball? I had no idea servants could dress that well . . . or," she said suggestively, "has Clay been buying you clothes . . . among other things?"

Sabrina was now filled with rage, but Elenora was the last person she would let see it. Instead she smiled again.

"You have not been too observant. Clay does not strike me as a man who would have to buy anything . . . or anyone. Of course, you would know better than I about that."

"Little tramp," Elenora hissed, "Clay will never marry you. Why should a man have to purchase a cow when the milk is being given free? You will regret coming here my girl, when he tires of you and dumps you back in the garbage heap where you belong."

"Again you are not very observant," Sabrina said softly, "or don't you recognize honor when you see it. Of course, one can hardly be able to recognize a quality one does not possess."

Elenora would have struck Sabrina and a royal battle might have followed had not the door opened and Clay and

William returned.

Clay saw sparkling violet eyes, pink cheeks and trembling lips and body and he knew something had been said that had shattered Sabrina's control.

"Sabrina, where's Summer?"

"Ellen has taken her to bed."

"Why don't you join them? The three of you can share my room tonight. Elenora can have yours and William can have Ellen's?" His voice was calm and gentle and he could feel Sabrina reach for its strength and calmness.

"What of you Clay?"

"Oh," Elenora said, "I'm sure Clay will find some comfortable place to sleep."

"I'll sleep in the barn Sabrina," Clay said firmly. "It's quite warm and comfortable in there. Besides, I have some things to talk over with the guide." He lowered his voice to a gentle touch. "Go to bed Sabrina . . . get some rest."

"Very well, Clay," Sabrina replied. She turned and went into his room, feeling all the eyes on her as she did so. Inside she explained to Ellen and Summer that the three of them were to share the room for the night.

"Is that awful, ugly lady going to stay here all night?"

"Summer, that's not a nice way to talk," Sabrina admonished, "Besides, she is not ugly. She happens to be very beautiful."

"No, Sabrina, she has a pretty cover but inside she's all black and ugly. She's not like you. You're pretty inside too, just like your cover."

Sabrina wanted nothing more than to agree with Summer about Elenora, but she knew she could not for Summer's sake. Jealousy held her in a firm grip and she could feel the painful touch of it deep within. How close had Clay and Elenora been? In the depths of her mind that question was answered before it was asked. Elenora's words still stung, but Sabrina refused to mistrust Clay. When the reverend came to this area again, she and Clay would marry. Then she could forget about Elenora Gregory forever.

She firmly put everything from her mind but getting Summer to go to sleep. She read Summer a story, and watched her heavy eyelids close.

"That woman is just what the child says she is," Ellen whispered.

"Ellen, they are friends of Clay's and we have nothing to say about it. I don't want Summer to hear you saying such things."

"After what she said to you!"

"That doesn't matter Ellen. Summer has to learn to act like a lady, and she can't do that unless we act like it first. I want you to watch what you say in front of her."

"All right. I'll be careful. But I can think as I choose. That woman has her hooks out for Clay and she's going to try to get him by hook or crook."

"Ellen!"

"Well it's true. You can see it in her eyes. The way she falls all over him. She is black inside. That child sees more than you think she does."

"I know Ellen. Sometimes it frightens me. She seems to be able to do things . . . see things that are beyond most grown people."

"You've got to protect yourself."

"From what?"

"You're not used to fighting that kind of woman."

"I have no intention of fighting her. Clay has to make his own choices. I can't force him to love me more than someone else. It has to come from his heart."

"Love! That woman doesn't know love. It's lust she's counting on."

"If that can change his mind," Sabrina said softly, "then

maybe it's best I know that now."

"And what of the child? What if that woman gets hold of him?"

"You're not giving Clay any credit. I don't think he'll do anything to hurt Summer. He loves that child more than anything in his life. He'll protect Summer against anything."

Ellen made a soft distressed sound and climbed into the huge bed beside Summer who instantly nestled against her.

Sabrina blew out the candle and walked to the window. She pushed open the wooden shutters and inhaled the soft night breeze.

Again she felt the deep pleasure of the beauty and peace of her surroundings. She knew she would always be happy here with Clay.

She watched the black star lit sky and allowed the gentle memory of Clay's love to flow about her and hold her. It was enough to fill her world, she thought, and she would ask for nothing more than to reach inside the man she loved and open all the dark places so she could fill them with the bright magic of her love as he filled her.

She was about to close the window and go to bed when a slight sound from the porch drew her attention. She stood still and watched a figure step down the porch and walk toward the barn.

By the light of a large white moon there was no mistaking who it was . . . Elenora Gregory.

She watched her slip into the barn and pull the door closed. There was a deep stifling pain within Sabrina and she could hardly breathe.

Then resolutely she drew the shutters and went back to bed . . . only to find that sleep was impossible and the dreams that came were uninvited and unwelcome.

Twenty-eight

Elenora had sensed someone was watching her as she crossed the clearing. A quick glance told her the shadowed form in the window had light hair. She smiled to herself knowing what Sabrina must be thinking as she watched her cross to the barn. Surely Sabrina would believe she and Clay had a rendezvous planned.

At the barn door she slipped inside and shut it quietly behind her. In the dim light she could only make out two forms that stood on the other side of the wide barn in quiet conversation.

It took her no time to identify Clay's tall broad shouldered form as he turned to see who had come in.

Clay had been speaking to the guide who had brought the Gregorys to his home. Of what Elenora didn't know for she only heard his last words.

" . . . not ever to happen again."

"Don't worry Clay, it won't," the man replied.

Clay had turned then and saw Elenora enter. With a light cautionary touch to the guide's arm to speak no more, he turned and walked to Elenora's side.

"Elenora what are you doing out here?"

"I want to talk to you, Clay . . . alone please."

The guide shrugged under Elenora's glance and walked to

the door. Despite the fact that even in the dark he could read Clay's annoyance, he left.

"Wouldn't your father be a little upset to find you out here?"

"He doesn't need to know," she laughed softly. She threw her arms about his neck and pressed herself close to him, a body that could, at one time, have aroused Clay to passion . . . now he felt annoyed. "Oh Clay, I've missed your visits to town. Why haven't you come to visit me . . . we . . . we had so much together."

Clay caught her wrists and drew her arms from around his neck. Her clinging and the heated passion in her eyes made him wonder why he had ever found her in the least appealing. He wanted now only to be rid of her, for the only woman who would be able to touch his senses was a violet eyed girl who, even now, lingered on the edge of his consciousness.

He moved her a little away from him.

"What we had together was a shared pleasure. We both enjoyed it for a time, but we knew . . . both of us . . . what it was right from the beginning."

"But I love you Clay," she pouted.

"Love was never discussed between us Elenora. We both knew what we were doing."

He appraised Elenora, realizing for the first time that her voluptuous beauty was slowly beginning to dispute with sexual freedom and overindulgent living. She tried now to look young and abused, and only succeeded in looking a little ridiculous.

"You said you loved me," she protested.

"No, Elènora, I never said I loved you. I thought, from the way you accepted me, that you knew exactly what you were doing and what you wanted."

"I . . . I was too innocent to know."

"Elenora, for God's sake don't take me for a complete fool. Do you think I don't know when a woman is a virgin? Don't you think I knew there have been others before . . . perhaps since?"

"And that little whore who's living with you," she snarled angrily, "was she a sweet little virgin?"

"Leave Sabrina out of this. She has nothing to do with us."

"Can you leave her alone, Clay?" she replied, "or is she a teacher for both you and your child?"

"Sabrina happens to be a very good teacher for Summer, and she happens to be the example I want Summer to follow."

Elenora was shaken at this obvious idea that he had never thought of her in connection with Summer.

"How can you say these things to me?" she said, her wide eyes filling with tears . . . tears she hoped would soften him. She had no idea he was filled with fury at her slurs of Sabrina. "I come from one of the best families in this part of the country. My father is also one of the wealthiest. Oh Clay, I didn't mean to make you angry, or for us to argue." She again moved close to him and rested her hands on his chest. Forcing her anger and jealousy into submission she gazed up at him with tear-filled pleading eyes. "I know you didn't mean what you said and I forgive you. Please Clay," she whispered as her arms crept about his neck, "let's forget everything . . . make love to me Clay . . . and send her away. You don't need her." She pressed herself against him and lifted her wide pouting lips for his kiss . . . a kiss that never materialized. Instead, she was startled when he gripped her by the shoulders and pushed her roughly from him.

"Clay!" she cried when the final realization came to her that Clay was rejecting her completely.

"Elenora, go back to the house. Don't make this any

worse than it is. There's nothing between us any longer, if there was much to begin with. As far as Sabrina is concerned she stays . . . for the two years she is indentured to me . . . and for the rest of life if I can convince her to stay."

"Stay . . . stay!" she gasped, "you would marry that stupid little nobody when you could have a bride with more wealth than she has ever seen?"

"I would marry her in a minute if she never had a chance of having a penny to her name. As soon as Reverend Willoby gets back in this area, I intend to do just that."

There was a sudden stillness in Elenora that should have warned Clay she would never be an easy loser. They stood as the few inches between them changed to miles.

"I had no intention of hurting you Elenora," Clay said, "but I've no intention of letting you or anyone else hurt Sabrina either."

Elenora was not stupid. She had said too much to Clay already. Soon, she thought Sabrina would be in Thomas' hands and she would have Clay to herself. She didn't want to burn her bridges behind her. She controlled the urge to lash out at him with bared claws, instead she smiled and moved away from him a little.

"I'm sorry I said the things I did Clay. It was just the shock. I wish you both a lot of happiness. There is no need for us to part as enemies. You will still come for the ball . . . you and Sabrina?"

"Yes, we'll be coming."

"Good. Maybe I can make amends for the foolish things I said by becoming friends with Sabrina. After all, if she is to be your wife, then we will see each other often."

Clay doubted very much if he would allow Sabrina very close to Elenora in the future, but he had no intentions of rousing her anger again.

"That would be fine Elenora."

"Good," she smiled. She went to Clay and kissed him lightly. "Good night Clay."

Turning quickly she slipped out the door and walked back across the yard. Seething with hatred and anger she vowed to speak to Thomas as soon as she returned to town.

She was aware Sabrina's window was now closed. It was the only thing that had pleased her in the last hour, for Sabrina would have no way of knowing just how long Elenora was in the barn with Clay. In the future she might just have to use it.

Clay stood watching the closed door for some time after Elenora left. He was sure in his heart he had not heard the last from her. She was not the kind to take rejection very easily.

He remembered well, wild nights of lovemaking with Elenora, but he had also known her favors had been well distributed to others. He knew he had never encouraged her to believe for a moment there was anything serious between them. He also wondered if he had said too much when he had told her about his plans with Sabrina. Knowing Elenora's vindictive nature, for a moment he was worried about what she might say or do to Sabrina.

"Damn," he muttered. "It's not bad enough I have to keep an eye on Hawk, now I have to keep an eye on her too."

He found a pile of hay and spread a blanket upon it, then lay down and sought sleep. He missed the soft warm curves of Sabrina to nestle against him and made himself another vow. It would not be long until he would make Sabrina permanently his. Then there would be no more nights of separation.

At breakfast the next morning, Clay was taken by surprise by two things. Elenora's bright cheerful and very friendly attitude and Sabrina's withdrawal and averted eyes.

He was impatient for the Gregorys to leave and the moment their wagon disappeared he sought out Sabrina who seemed to be trying to avoid him.

He found she had returned to the kitchen and was helping Ellen clear and wash the breakfast dishes.

Ellen sensed something was drastically wrong when Sabrina continued to work and refused to look at Clay.

"I want to talk to you, Sabrina," Clay said firmly.

"Later, Clay, please, I'm busy."

"Right now," he demanded. "Besides, this is not your duty. Summer is all you have to think about."

"Summer is playing for a while and there is quite a lot for Ellen to do."

Clay had reached the end of his patience. He went to Sabrina and grabbed her wrist in a grip that she could never have a chance to break. Dragging her behind him, he walked out of the kitchen, sending Ellen a look that silenced anything she might have thought of saying.

He dragged a resisting Sabrina from the kitchen into the parlor before he released her. Defiantly she turned to face him.

"Now that you've shown me what a brute you can be, what is it you want to speak to me about?"

"What in the hell is the matter with you?" he said angrily.

"If you want to drag someone around, why," she asked sweetly, "don't you choose someone who might enjoy it, like your little barn mate."

"What?" he blinked in surprise.

"Wasn't your little romp in the hay enough for you? Why didn't you follow her wagon, maybe you could have found some soft grass somewhere and tumbled her again."

Clay's stunned look slowly changed to a smile and his eyes grew warm as he went to Sabrina and despite her protests bound her to him with steel like arms so that she could not move. Clay chuckled.

"Why love," he said softly, "I do believe you're jealous."

"I'm not!"

"I'm glad," he whispered against her hair, "but don't you think you are jumping to conclusions. You may have seen her come to the barn, but if you had taken the time to check, you would have seen her leave a few minutes later . . . quite angry with me for telling her just how much I love you and that we plan on being married as soon as the Reverend comes back."

Her eyes lifted to his, bright with new hope.

"Really Clay . . . you told her that?"

"I did, love . . . my sweet innocent," he laughed. "You wear your heart in your eyes, love . . . I'm glad you were jealous though," he said softly.

Her arms slid about his waist and all struggle ceased. With a gentle touch he brushed a soft kiss across her mouth.

"Going to the ball was the only good suggestion Elenora had. It will give me the chance to show off the two most beautiful women in the world."

Now her eyes filled with genuine distress.

"The ball," she said.

"Don't you want to go?"—

"I do Clay, but I can't."

"Can't . . . why can't you?"

"Oh Clay, it's impossible! I've nothing to wear to a ball, and if it's this soon, I can't even make something. And Summer . . . " She was thoroughly frustrated now. "I would never let her go unless she had a proper dress. She's so pretty I would want her to be at her best."

Clay smiled then stopped her chatter the most pleasant way he knew. He kissed her into silence.

When he released her lips he knew resistance was about to begin again.

"Sabrina, go and get Summer and come back here. I have

something to show you both that will surprise you and please you I hope."

"But Clay . . . "

"Nope, no arguments," he grinned. "Do as I say, will you? It will be worthwhile."

Sabrina knew it would do no good to argue any further. Reluctantly, she went to find Summer and bring her back to the parlor. By the time she did, Clay was returning from his room with two large boxes in his arms. He told both Summer and Sabrina to sit down, which they did side by side watching him expectantly. Clay silently handed each one of them a box and sat back to enjoy the look he hoped to see in their eyes. Another small box rested in his pocket to give Sabrina at a time that he felt would be more appropriate . . . and more private.

"Summer, why don't you let Sabrina open hers first. It will be less confusing and we can enjoy both gifts better."

"All right Papa," Summer agreed. Father's and daughter's eyes turned to Sabrina who, when the dress was revealed, gasped in surprise. Then she lifted the dress tenderly from the box and stood to hold it against her.

"Oh Clay, how very beautiful."

"Will it fit?"

"I believe so, but . . . however did you know the size?"

Clay grinned realizing how much pleasure it gave him to see her face flushed with pleasure and watch her eyes glow.

He held out both hands expressively.

"I just told the girl what I could remember . . . and I remember very well," he added softly.

"Can I open mine now Papa, please," Summer cried in an excited voice.

"Yes Summer, go on open it."

Rapidly Summer opened the package and drew out the dress that was so very close in color and design to Sabrina's that she squealed in delight. It was the first party dress she had ever seen.

"Sabrina! Sabrina!" she cried excitedly, "it's just like yours." Summer ran to Clay and jumped into his lap and Clay laughed as he gathered her to him.

"You are going to a very fancy ball with Papa and Sabrina. Would you like that?"

"Oh yes Papa! Yes I would. Papa?"

"What kitten?"

"What's a ball?"

Both Sabrina and Clay had to laugh at this.

"Sabrina can explain it to you."

"Can I go and show my pretty dress to Ellen?"

Clay nodded and Summer gathered the dress up and ran to the kitchen where they could soon hear excited chatter and laughter.

Sabrina lay her dress aside and went to Clay. She knelt in front of him and smiled up into his eyes.

"Clay, how very much I love you," she said. "And how very considerate and kind you are. I do love the dress."

Clay captured her face between his hands and kissed her with a deep, hungry and most satisfying kiss.

"Do you know how easy it is to be good to you," he said gently, "you make loving the easiest thing in the world to do." He kissed her once again and reluctantly stopped. It would have been much too easy to continue and this was not the time or the place. He held his thoughts for later.

"The dress matches your eyes, you know. It was why it caught my eye in the dress-shop window."

"I can just imagine you trying to tell the girl what size I am," Sabrina giggled softly.

"I'll have you know madam," Clay responded, "I did a fabulous job of that. I simply told the girl you have the slimmest waist, the curvaceous hips and the nicest . . . "

"Clay!"

"Well," he chuckled, "I sort of showed her more than told her and I have to admit it was a little difficult and somewhat embarrassing."

"What a brave and fearless man you are," she laughed.

Summer returned and soon the two women in his life were so engrossed in dresses and hair and balls that Clay chose the time to finish his daily chores.

It took Sabrina some time to get a very excited Summer to bed that night, and it was only after she agreed to hang the beautiful new dress where Summer could see it.

Sabrina tiptoed from the room to find a tired Ellen had already gone to bed.

Clay sat in the parlor before the fireplace. Quietly Sabrina went to stand beside him. He looked up at her, smiled, then took her hand and without a word drew her down onto his lap and into his waiting arms.

Their lips touched, tasted and lingered to savor the sweetness of the love they shared. Sabrina sighed in utter contentment as she felt the gentle strength of the man who held her.

"I have something else for you Sabrina. It's a gift I saved for now because it's something very special and something I'd like you to wear with the dress."

Sabrina remained silent, watching the firelight reflect in Clay's eyes. The crystal blue depths were warm with love for her.

Clay reached into his pocket and took out the small box. Without another word, he handed it to her and watched in silence as she slowly opened it.

The ring glittered before her and took her breath away with its simple pure beauty.

Tears filled Sabrina's eyes and she was speechless with the joy she felt.

She lifted the ring gently from the box, her eyes blurred

with tears.

"It's so beautiful Clay, I love it."

Sabrina began to place the ring on her right hand before Clay stayed her hand.

"No, Sabrina," he said gently, "it doesn't belong on that finger."

He took the ring from her hand, lifted her left hand and slid the ring on her third finger.

"It belongs here."

Their eyes met in beautiful promise of love given and returned in full.

"Clay," she whispered softly, "you have given me so much, made me so very happy. All I can return to you is all the love my heart possesses, and the promise that I shall try to make you as happy as you have made me, to fill your life with as much joy as I can."

Clay smiled and drew her back into his arms. He held her bound to him with iron hard arms while again his lips savored the sweet giving love of hers.

"Clay," she said as she rested her head on his shoulder and enjoyed the warm caress as his hands drifted lightly over her slim body, "I wish I could give you something to show you how much I love you and how happy I am."

Clay rocked her in his arms and laughed. "Sabrina, my sweet precious, do you realize you have given me the greatest gift of all? Your sweet love is all I need to make my world complete."

Contentment touched them both for a spellbinding moment and they existed in a state of euphoric pleasure that was only interrupted as Clay suddenly stood and, still holding Sabrina gently in his arsm, carried her silently to the seclusion of her room.

Sabrina and Clay reached for each other in heightened pleasure that night, and it wasn't until she drifted off to sleep that Sabrina began to wonder where a man who was supposed to be a woodsman . . . who had no obvious means of support . . . could afford the gifts he was buying and the excellent house he had built and all the luxuries contained in it.

Twenty-nine

The expected day for them to leave finally came much to the relief of both Ellen and Sabrina, for Summer was so filled with questions and enthusiasm that it nearly drove the two of them to distraction.

After the explanation of a ball was given her, and the dress her father had brought was hung before her, Summer could hardly contain herself.

They started after an early breakfast, and had reached their first stop before supper.

None of Clay's friends had, as yet, seen Sabrina. He smiled to himself in expectation at their surprise.

Caleb was on his porch watching them approach, and when they were close enough for him to see them clearly his eyes widened in appreciation and curiosity. In fact, he could barely take his eyes from Sabrina.

Clay could see the humor in Caleb's eyes as he stopped the wagon beside the porch.

"Step down and come in," he offered, as was the universal custom of the area. But his eyes never left Sabrina.

"Can't right now, Caleb. We'll stop on the way back."

"Hello Uncle Caleb," Summer called.

"Hello Summer. Goin' to town are you?"

"I'm going to a ball with my Papa," Summer an-

339

nounced proudly.

"That's good. Have a nice time. By the way Clay," his smile widened, "that little girl you brought out here sure has grown some."

Clay chuckled, "We'll stop on the way back Caleb and I'll explain everything."

"Shore would appreciate that Clay," his eyes twinkled with humor. "Kinda leaves me curious about your knack for havin' good luck fall all over you."

"This is Sabrina. Sabrina, this is one of my best friends, Caleb Maguire."

"Pleased to meet you Mr. Maguire," Sabrina said.

"And I'm pleased to see such a pretty face around here. Been lookin at Clay's ugly puss for too long. Be sure you stop back on your way home."

"We will," Clay said. "See you then."

Caleb waved at the receding wagon and held his curiosity for the time they would return.

They continued their trip at a slow but steady pace.

The Daugherty's house came into view and after a few minutes Clay pulled the horses to a stop in front of the house.

The door opened as Clay jumped down, and walked around the wagon to lift Sabrina down. He stood Summer beside her and reached for Ellen to deposit her safely on the ground. All this was done amid a profound silence. With a broad smile on his face, Clay turned to face Mrs. Daugherty who stood staring in shock. Then her face broke into a smile.

"Clay Storm, you scalawag. Come in here and do some explaining. Where in heaven's name did you get that pretty young thing? You sure are close mouthed, young man, and you're not leaving this house until you do some explaining."

Clay laughed, but before he could speak an excited Summer ran up to Mrs. Daugherty.

"She's Sabrina, and she's going to stay with us forever and ever," Summer chattered. "We're going to a ball and I've got a pretty dress. It's the same color as Sabrina's almost."

Now Clay and the others laughed together.

"I'm sure," Mrs. Daugherty answered, "you've got a little to add to that Clay."

"I do, and if you'll provide some coffee, I'll provide the explanations."

"Come in and sit. I had supper all ready for Hank and the boys anyway. T'wont be a thing to set a couple more plates."

The supper, or so Sabrina thought, was enough food to feed a small army, and Irene Daugherty kept insisting Sabrina eat more.

"You're much too thin," she insisted.

"I can't eat another bite," Sabrina laughed.

The conversation had finally exhausted every other subject except the one Irene wanted to know.

"Now," she smiled as she sat back in her chair, "suppose you tell me how this lovely young creature happened into your life, Clay Storm, and you'd best make it a good long story, because I want to know all the details."

Clay took his time and explained exactly how Sabrina and Ellen came to be there. He had Sabrina explain as much as she could about what had happened to her in England. Irene was shaken and angry about all that had happened to Sabrina. But Clay was to change her thoughts in moments.

"Irene," he said, "Sabrina will not be staying just for the two years of her indenture. She'll be staying as my wife when we can get married."

"How wonderful!" Irene exclaimed and Sabrina and Clay were soon enthusiastically and heartily congratulated.

The Daughertys wanted them to stay the rest of the evening and night. Clay thought this over for a time. If they kept going it would be quite late but they would arrive at their hotel and be settled so that the next day could be spent in shopping for any trifles Sabrina and Summer might need for the ball.

"We'd best go on Irene. But I promise we'll stop and visit a little longer on the way home."

"It's a long way to town yet Clay."

"I know, but I'd rather make it even if it's late. We'll be fresh in the morning and Summer and Sabrina can do some shopping."

"All right. But don't you forget to stop here on the way back."

"I won't."

When they could finally get away, Clay increased their pace to all the horses could reasonably stand. Still it was very nearly midnight before they arrived at the hotel. It was less than an hour before all the exhausted travelers slept.

The next day Sabrina and Ellen were given some money and told to take Summer and buy anything she or they might need for the night's festivities.

"But Clay," Sabrina protested, "this is too much money. We really don't need that much."

"I don't want you to spare the expense. I want you and Summer to be the finest women at the ball, and," he smiled, "I want you to buy Ellen something nice."

"Me, why me," Ellen said.

"I want you to come along so that you can bring Summer back to the hotel when she's tired. I," he grinned at Sabrina, "intend to keep Sabrina dancing till an outrageous hour. Then we may take a long buggy ride in the moonlight."

Ellen watched Sabrina and Clay exchange a warm and loving look. It made her realize again the deep and vibrant thing that existed between them. Both Summer and Ellen seemed to be enclosed in the warm glow that held the two lovers.

Ellen and Sabrina obediently took Summer shopping and they returned later that afternoon completely exhausted.

The ball would be held in the huge ballroom of the hotel, and since they were already there, Sabrina and Summer would have more time to prepare.

Sabrina stood before the full length mirror and examined herself. She had gathered her hair in a mass of curls atop her head with fringes of curls framing her face and her slender neck. The violet blue dress matched her eyes exactly and it was most flattering to her slim curves.

Draped at the edge of her shoulders it was low enough to expose the creamy rise of her breasts. Unadorned by any frills or lace, it complimented Sabrina's tiny figure. From the waist it flowed outward in layer after layer of violet blue lace.

She carried an ivory and green fan in her lace gloved hands and had draped an ivory lace shawl becomingly about her. She needed no jewelry for she seemed to glow with an inner light that needed no enhancement.

Summer burst in from the room adjoining Sabrina's and whose door stood open so that Sabrina and Summer would be close.

Sabrina had brushed Summer's long shiny dark hair until it glistened, then tied it with a ribbon that matched the dress. The dress itself was nearly a duplicate of Sabrina's except for the round collar that encircled Summer's neck.

"You look so beautiful, Sabrina," the child breathed. "Like one of the ladies in the fairy tales you read to me."

Sabrina went to Summer and knelt before her and took both the child's hands in hers.

"And you look beautiful too," she smiled.

"You smell good. Like the flowers in the fields at home."

Sabrina laughed and gathered Summer into her arms to give her a resounding hug. She felt the pleasure in Summer as the child's arms clung.

This was the scene that held Clay as he walked into the room. The two people he loved most in the world, sharing a love for each other that could bind them as a family forever.

Sabrina looked up, sensing Clay was there. Their eyes held for a caressing moment, then he moved to their side and extended a hand to draw Sabrina up beside him. Sabrina's amazement at Clay's adapting to any place he seemed to be grew as she gazed at the handsome man who stood beside her.

Bone colored pants that seemed to mold themselves to his long legs, a dark blue jacket that boasted broad shoulders and a lean tapered waist. A shirt of white silk with a froth of lace at front and cuffs. Clay's dark skin combined with the jacket brought his crystal blue eyes into startling contrast, blue eyes whose mesmerizing gaze she seemed to be drowning in. He raised her hand to his lips and kissed her slim fingers softly.

"You are so very beautiful, love," he said. "I shall be the envy of every man in this town."

An insistent tug on his sleeve drew his attention to Summer, who was impatiently waiting for him to see how she looked.

"Summer, I've never seen you look so pretty, or so much like a lady. It will be a pleasure to escort two such beauties to the ball."

He bent to kiss a very pleased Summer.

"Are you both ready?"

"Yes," they said in unison.

"Where's Ellen?"

"She's still getting ready in her room Papa. Shall I go get her?"

"Yes, and tell her to please hurry. I can't wait to show you both off."

Summer ran quickly and Clay took immediate advantage of her absence to draw Sabrina into his arms.

Gently his lips touched hers in a slow tender kiss that melted every bone in her body and drew a sigh of contentment from Sabrina as he reluctantly released her.

"And would madam be interested in a long moonlit buggy ride after the ball?" he whispered.

"Madam would be interested in being anywhere you are," she replied in a low murmur as her eyes warmed with the stirring need within her.

"Stop looking at me like that Sabrina," he chuckled, "or I shall say damn the ball and take you to my bed and ravish you."

At that moment Sabrina would have been quite willing, but both were saved the choice by the return of Ellen and Summer.

As they reached the top of the staircase the sound of a Strauss waltz drifted up. Clay tucked Sabrina's hand in his arm, took Summer's hand and slowly they descended the stairs.

They entered the ballroom and stood framed in the doorway, creating a picture everyone in the room admired. Everyone except Elenora who stood by her father and watched them enter.

Elenora had returned from Clay's home in a cold murderous rage. She immediately told Thomas all about Sabrina and Clay's plans to marry her.

"It will never happen, Elenora. I shall see to it," he had told her.

"After the ball," Elenora demanded, "take her then."

"I don't want to do that yet."

"Why?"

"There is not a ship leaving for England for three weeks. I shall take the law with me, have her arrested at Clay's home and bring her back just in time to leave and before Clay can do anything to stop me."

"I want her away from here!"

"Don't be a fool woman. Do it my way or Clay will put a stop to it. We have to be able to leave as soon as I get her."

"You promise it will be soon."

"As soon as the ship is ready to leave, have patience, soon I will rid you of all that stands between you and Clay Storm. Then," he laughed, "we will both have what we want."

Elenora held her hatred for Sabrina in control, with a bright smile on her face she approached them. But another sensed her enmity at once. Summer's hand gripped Clay's in a grasp that startled him. He looked down to see her face grow pale and her eyes grow wide. His gaze followed hers to Elenora.

Then Clay said something that made a startled Summer realize her father understood her emotions more than she had known. He gave her hand a reassuring squeeze and spoke softly bending near her ear.

"It's all right, Summer. I know her spirit. I will be careful to protect Sabrina."

Summer looked up at Clay and smiled realizing for the first time in her life that her father knew the secret that had frightened her for so long.

"We'll talk about it when we get home," he said. "All right?"

"Yes Papa," she whispered while her eyes glistened with pure deep love.

"Clay! Sabrina! How nice to see you," Elenora said. Her eyes appraised Sabrina with a touch of envy. "How very . . . nice you look. Did you make that yourself?"

"No," Sabrina smiled, aware that Elenora was trying to

346

goad her. "Clay bought it for me."

"I see," Elenora replied icily. Then her eyes fell on the ring that glittered on Sabrina's finger.

Clay wanted no more confrontation with Elenora. He turned to Ellen.

"Take Summer and get her something to eat, then let her watch the dancing."

"Yes sir."

Clay turned back to Sabrina with a warm smile. "And would you give me the pleasure of this dance?"

Sabrina placed her hand in his and he led her to the floor while Elenora's gaze followed them in burning fury.

Clay's arm about her slim waist and his hand confidently and firmly holding hers he swept her out onto the floor. Despite his size, Clay moved gracefully and with ease, and in moments, Sabrina was swept into the magnetic blue gaze that held hers while they moved about the floor.

They moved like one in a graceful sway to the music and many stopped in mute fascination to watch these two who seemed to be made for each other.

Young men vied for the pleasure of dancing with the beautiful newcomer, and under Clay's watchful gaze, Sabrina laughed, danced, and thoroughly enjoyed herself.

Summer was beside herself in pleasure at the surrounding beauty and watched, fascinated, the dancers and the beautiful people. She assured herself over and over that her papa was the handsomest man in the room, and her beloved Sabrina was the most beautiful woman.

Despite her enthusiasm, Summer began to tire, and before midnight Ellen informed Clay she was taking the child to bed.

Thomas had not allowed himself to be seen for fear of warning Sabrina that he was near and thereby alerting Clay. He had not stayed at the hotel for that purpose, but had been given a room at the Gregorys where no one would know him.

He was in the hotel because he and Elenora had arranged a rendezvous for later where they could share erotic pleasure safely in a room of the hotel that had been paid for by another of Elenora's friends.

But now he wanted to see Sabrina, for he had held visions of her in his dreams for so long that he could no longer resist.

The ballroom was bordered by balconies that surrounded the area. Heavy draperies were hung and drawn back so that those who cared to share a more secluded supper could have a table and close the draperies to insure their privacy.

Thomas now stood in the shadow of one of these balconies while his avid gaze scanned the dancers below. Then his eyes fell hot and hungry on the golden haired girl who swayed in the arms of Clay Storm.

He watched her slim body move gracefully about the floor. Saw her soft white shoulders and the curve of her breasts that rose beneath the soft fabric of her dress. The silken mass of her hair that made his hands shake with the desire to sink them into its depths. He saw her smile, and then tilt her head to listen to what Clay was saying then laugh in delight at his words.

A hot angry pain of need shot through him almost making him cry out. Lust touched him with flame and he hungrily bent forward to savor more closely the object of his need. From the shadows he moved forward, following her every move . . . until the light of the ballroom touched his face. Unaware that he could be seen by anyone who chose to look up, he remained motionless, greedily devouring the woman who danced below him.

Sabrina had been dancing all evening, her cheeks were pink with the exercise and her eyes glittered with the pleasure she was enjoying for the first time in her life.

Clay was getting as much pleasure in watching her enjoy herself so much as he was in holding her slim body while they danced.

"You're happy, Sabrina."

"Oh Clay, I've never enjoyed myself so much."

"We must come into town more often."

"I could dance all night," she declared happily.

"I hope not," he chuckled evilly, "I have other plans for later."

Their eyes caught and held and she knew the desire within her was ready to meet his and taste again the joy they shared. She was about to answer when a shadowed movement from the balcony caught her eye . . . her heart froze. Thomas!

Her face went white and she stopped dancing. The buzzing in her ears began to intensify and she gasped as dizziness struck . . . then everything turned black, and Clay caught her as she fell into his arms.

Clay had seen the direction of her gaze and as he lifted her in his arms he looked up, but Thomas was already gone and he saw nothing.

Elenora had seen what happened and knew Sabrina must have seen Thomas in that moment before he vanished. She watched coldly as deep concern written on his face, Clay gently carried Sabrina from the room.

Clay lay Sabrina gently against the pillows. With a wet cloth he bathed her forehead until her eyes fluttered open. Suddenly, they filled with terror and she sat up. Clay took her by the shoulder.

"Sabrina what's wrong?"

"Thomas!" she cried. "Thomas is here! I saw him! Clay, I saw him!"

Clay knew she was frantic with fear. He drew her into his

arms and held her, comforting her until the trembling ceased.

"Sabrina, be still. I'll go check."

"No!"

"Sabrina! you are safe here. I'll be back in a minute."

Clay left and made a thorough search, questioning everyone about Thomas. Then he returned to Sabrina who greeted him with wide-eyed fear.

"Sabrina, there's no one there, and no one in the hotel by that name. Are you sure you weren't imagining things? Someone might just look like him."

Sabrina gripped Clay's arm and he knew the terror was real and deep in her.

"Clay, he's here! He's after me! I'm not imagining things!"

Clay drew her into the safety of his arms and comforted her until her trembling ceased and she relaxed in his arms.

"I love you Sabrina," he said softly, "and no one will take you from me. You're safe love . . . you're safe."

She looked up at him and read the love and the promise in his eyes. Warm safety touched her and her arms encircled his neck as she lifted her lips to his and sank into the magic world Clay's love offered.

Thirty

"Clay," Sabrina whispered, "don't leave me. Stay with me please."

"I had no intention of leaving you my love," he replied gently. "Not now, not ever again."

His arms surrounded her with a warm strength she never wanted to leave. His kisses forced everything from her mind but Clay and the peaceful security he gave.

With slow deliberation he began a gentle rousing of her senses. Tender, yet firm hands removed the gown she wore and began to caress the soft trembling body, lifting it to warmth and response.

His open mouth found her warm moist lips. They parted to share his passion willingly now she existed in a whole new world where no threat existed and no fear could dwell for passion had driven it away.

Their lips blended with a fierce urgency. His hands began to search every valley and plain of her body as if each touch and caress were to be committed to memory forever.

Wave after wave of intense pleasure rolled through her like the crashing waves of the ocean against the shore.

Clay rose only for a moment to quickly cast aside restricting clothes. Through half closed eyes Sabrina drank in his long lean body, knowing the touch of it would sear her and brand her his.

A ragged moan escaped her as he returned to the bed and swept her into his arms. Breathless with the intensity of the heat of his passion, she quivered as his seeking mouth found a hardened crest of her rounded breasts and traced a path of flame on each.

She gasped as his hands roved freely from breast to belly, to rounded hip and silken thigh, and more, to a deeper place that sparked a need that could be quenched only with true blending.

Clay knew surely, as a man who had tasted many times, that this was an eternally new and unchangeable need that would consume him forever, always filling, yet always leaving the need to reach again, taste again the sweet nectar of her woman's softness yielding to his hard driving need.

He lifted himself to rise above her and lower himself within her. Diving to the very depths of her being.

He heard her shattered words, her cry to him to fill the aching desire that consumed her.

With wild abandon and complete giving, they met with a force that tore all thought from their world and left them with the one diamond brilliant flame.

She rose to meet him with a passion that met his without faltering, without thought to anything but fulfilling this need. It was a blending that left them caught in a rapturous union that burst about them like a million flaming stars.

Each knew beyond doubt that they had been blessed with that rare and special love that was a blending of wild flame and all consuming joy. They reveled in the thought that this would be theirs to share forever.

They clung weakly to one another, knowing there were no words that could express the vibrant fulfilling thing they had shared.

Clay held her, caressing her hair and easing her with gentle words. Forcing the nightmare to keep its distance.

Soothed by the magic only his love could bring, Sabrina finally slept . . . but Clay did not.

He held her safely against him while he thought about Thomas. Had she seen him or had it been someone who looked so much like him that it revived old memories? Anger filled him that something or someone could frighten Sabrina so badly that she would faint. He intended to do much more investigating into the mystical presence of Thomas. If he was here in Stirbridge he would find out. His arms tightened about Sabrina protectively at the thought. Whatever he did from now on he would do without Sabrina's knowledge for he wanted to erase all thought of Thomas and the past from her mind.

He tried to slip soundlessly from the bed but it stirred Sabrina to half wakefulness and she clung to him.

"Clay . . . don't go . . . don't leave me," she whispered. He knew the nightmare still lingered on the edge of her consciousness.

"I won't love. Rest easy. I'm here," he said softly as she sighed contentedly and nestled closer in the safety of his arms.

Habitually, Clay was awake as the sun touched the horizon. The room was shadowed and Clay lay still. Warm, comfortable and aware of the soft form that curled close to him.

To start every morning the balance of his life like this would be a completion to a dream. He rolled on his side and looked down into the sleeping face of the girl who slept beside him. She seemed to him to be so child-like it was hard to believe this was the same wildly passionate woman who had sent his senses soaring and had claimed all his love in a wildly sensuous night that would always remain in his memory. His body still remembered every touch, every moment of the passionate night they shared.

He reached out and gently touched her hair that lay in a tangled mass about her. Then caressed the soft cheek and slim throat. Slowly letting his hand roam to warmer rounder places whose softness recaptured him again.

Violet eyes fluttered open, and recognition brought a flush of warmth and a glow of renewed love that nearly took his breath away.

Sabrina had that rare and vital beauty that adapted to any circumstances without loss. She had a breathless expectant beauty with the first flush of early morning as she had been the night before, and Clay was held within it a willing prisoner.

"Good morning," Clay said softly as he drew her closer.

Sabrina sighed. "Clay, I could stay here forever. If we could just keep the world away and share this heaven for always."

"You'll get no argument from me, love. I could be quite content holding you like this."

"Clay."

"What?"

"Let's go home."

The words sounded sweeter to him than anything else she could have said. She considered him and the house he lived in her home.

"You're still frightened?"

"Not here with you . . . but . . ."

"But you're still sure it was Thomas you saw?"

"Clay, I was not imagining things!" she said. "I know I saw him! I know." She sat up in the bed as if she were afraid he was deliberately refusing to believe her.

Clay reached to pull her back down against him.

"Don't be upset. If it was Thomas, I'll find out."

"Clay, I don't want to stay here! I don't want to see him. Clay please, please just take me home. He'll never be able to find me there. I'll be safe with you."

"Don't you want to stay a day or two until I find out for sure?"

"No, Clay, please, let's just go home." It was pleading, and her wide eyes were moist with unshed tears.

"All right, Sabrina," he said gently as he caressed her hair, "we'll go home."

"Today, today Clay?"

"Yes, today."

She relaxed and he was more totally aware of how truly frightened she had been. When he found Thomas . . . if he found him, he intended to make sure he would never be a threat to Sabrina again.

Sabrina was tense until they left the town and were well on their way. Clay knew she had said nothing to Ellen about Thomas so he remained silent also.

When they reached the Daugherty's he quickly took Irene aside and explained to her why they could not stay and that he would make everything clear later.

They did not stay at the Daugherty's long for Sabrina could not seem to put enough distance between herself and the threat of Thomas.

Clay passed Caleb's house completely. He did not want to get involved in lengthy explanations with him either.

Sabrina breathed an audible sigh of relief when Clay's house came into view. For the first time since they had left town she smiled freely.

Summer had been as reserved as Sabrina, but Clay did not question her. He had known her mother's phenomenal gifts and he was reluctant to open that door in Summer's mind . . . yet it was to be opened.

They had unpacked the wagon, and were about to go into the house when they heard riders approaching.

Clay turned to gaze in the direction from which the riders

came. He could not yet make out who they were. But a quiet voice beside him made the identification.

"It's Hawk, Papa," Summer's quiet voice said. "He comes to tell us something bad."

Clay remained still . . . yet he knew Summer was right. The old possessive emotions swept through him. He could not fight the anger, pain . . . and fear that his daughter's words brought him.

Sabrina watched Clay's face, watching warring emotions she did not understand sweep across his face. She did not know if it was Hawk's arrival or Summer's words that upset him so.

They stood in silence until the riders could be seen more clearly. It soon became apparent that the riders were Hawk, and another member of his tribe.

When they had reached the porch they pulled their horses to a stop. For one silent heart-stopping moment, there was complete silence.

Hawk's face held a strange stillness and Clay and the others knew without doubt Summer had been right.

Before anyone else could speak, Summer stepped down from the porch and looked up at Hawk.

"Is Grandfather very sick, Hawk?" she asked softly.

Hawk looked down into her questioning eyes. There was no surprise either in his eyes or his words.

"Yes, little one. He is very sick," Hawk's eyes returned to Clay. "He asks a favor of you Clay."

"A favor of me?" Clay answered.

"Yes."

As if she had long understood what was going to be said and how her father would feel about it, Summer went to his side and slipped her hand into his.

"What does he want, Hawk? None of you expect me to come back to the village now? There's been enough problems Hawk. I'd rather just let everything be. Nothing has really changed, has it?"

"He might die Clay. That changes much," Hawk said softly.

Clay was shaken by these few words.

"What does he want of me, Hawk?"

"He wants to see the child again. He has some things that he must say to her and something he wants to give her."

"What! What does he have to say to her . . . what does he want to give her?"

"That was not for me to ask. I come only to bring his words to you . . . and to bring the child back with me if I can."

"You know that's out of the question," Clay replied softly.

Sabrina looked at Clay in surprise. It was impossible for her to believe Clay was so heartless he would refuse a dying man a few words with a child. Was he so afraid of what he might say to her?

"Clay," she said in a disbelieving voice, "if . . . if he is dying, surely a few words with a child is not too much to ask."

There was a challenging glitter in Hawk's eyes but he did not speak again. He merely held Clay's eyes with his.

Clay's eyes turned to Sabrina whose look of disbelief and doubt touched him. He sighed deeply.

"All right Hawk, you win. But she doesn't go with you. Sabrina and I will bring her."

"You will come now?"

"Yes, we'll come now. Will you wait while we change our clothes and saddle some horses?"

Hawk nodded and he and the silent Indian who had come with him dismounted to wait.

Clay, Summer and Sabrina changed their clothes quickly

and ate some food Ellen had made ready while they did so. After this, Clay saddled two horses. He helped Sabrina mount, then took Summer up before him.

Ellen stood on the porch and watched them ride away wondering why a dying man would send for a child and what problems could come of it.

The village seemed to be nearly deserted when they rode in, but they soon discovered most of the people in the village were gathered about the old chief's lodge.

A path among them seemed to suddenly appear as they dismounted and walked toward the chief's lodge.

At the doorway, Hawk stood aside to let Sabrina, Clay and Summer enter first. He followed behind them and closed the door covering.

The old man lay on a fur covered couch, braced into a half sitting position. Beside him a small fire burned.

The lodge was lit only by the touch of the fire, still the eyes of the old man saw and recognized Summer. He smiled.

Summer made no sound, but Sabrina could see her wide dark eyes were locked on the old man. To Sabrina, it suddenly felt as if a strange new presence, one she could not see, had entered the lodge. She cast a quick look at Clay. His face had a resigned look as if something was happening that he knew had always been inevitable.

The old man weakly extended his hand to Summer. No one missed the soft whispered sound as Summer moved slowly toward him.

"Grandfather," she said softly, as she went to kneel by his side and take his weathered old hand in hers.

"My child," the old man said. His eyes lifted to Clay's and they were filled with a deep sadness, and Sabrina thought . . . pity.

"I am grateful, my son, that you brought her. I would

look into her eyes again, and I would give her a gift before I pass into the other world."

"No!"

Everyone was shocked as Summer said the word strongly and with more authority than a child nearing seven.

"No, Grandfather," she repeated, only this time the voice was gentle. She lifted his huge hand with both of hers and pressed it close to her heart. "You are not to pass into the other world. You are not to leave us . . . not yet."

Sabrina's eyes wavered between Clay and the old man. To her shock neither of them showed surprise . . . or doubt. For a moment, Clay closed his eyes then they opened quickly and remained impenetrable.

The old man's eyes grew a little brighter and he and the child exchanged a look of complete understanding. Sabrina realized there was no one in this room who did not believe her.

There was complete and utter silence as Summer held the old man's hand close to her. Her eyes closed and beads of sweat touched her brow, yet there was a contented and peaceful smile on her face.

The old man watched her with a deep penetrating gaze for a long while. There was no movement, no sound. Everyone seemed to have suddenly stopped breathing. Even Sabrina, who could not understand what was happening, felt a strange and yet peaceful presence.

Summer continued to remain silent, her eyes closed, and rocking gently back and forth with the old chief's hand still pressed close to her.

Then, after interminable minutes, Summer opened her eyes, stopped the strange rhythmic movements. The old chief and the child gazed at each other . . . then Summer smiled, and the old man smiled in return.

It was an unbelievable thing, and if it had not been for the strange quiet look on everyone's face, Sabrina would not have believed what she was seeing with her own eyes.

When the old man smiled it was as if a heavy burden were lifted from everyone. A ragged sigh whispered through the lodge.

Summer bent forward and kissed the old man's weathered cheek.

"I love you, Grandfather. You must stay with us for a very long time."

"Yes child," the old man answered, as for a brief moment he held the child close to him.

Sabrina could not doubt that the old chief looked visibly better. She knew it was some type of mystical mental thing. Slowly pieces of the puzzle began to slip into place. Could this strange rare thing be the cause of all the problems? These people believed, their chief believed, that Summer had inherited some power from her mother.

What had her mother really been to these people?

Sabrina knew, from her extensive reading, that there were some cultures who believed that some people had rare healing qualities. Were these people believers? And was Summer the inheritor of this tremendous overpowering thing?

She wanted to ask Clay question after question. But Summer had gotten to her feet and returned to her father's side.

Again she read Clay's actions and his face quite well . . . as he put his hand on Summer's shoulder and drew her against him as if challenging someone to contradict his priority.

He gazed about him with a cold blue gaze that chilled even Sabrina. In no uncertain terms, without a word, he made it clear that no matter what their needs were, Summer was his, and he had no intention of giving any part of her away.

"You will spend this night with us, my son," the old chief

360

said. "Your horses must be tired as you and yours must be. Spend the night with us. Rest . . . then if you choose to go in the morning . . ."

If it had been Clay alone, he would not have stayed, but he knew Sabrina and Summer must be exhausted from the day's travel. Resigned to the fact that he could not drag them all the way home, he conceded to stay.

"I'll stay, but we will leave first thing in the morning," Clay stated. He took Summer's hand and turned and walked from the lodge.

The people had faded away when word had spread and there was silence as Sabrina left the lodge to join Clay.

The three of them stood outside the lodge, but before either of them could say anything, Hawk came out to join them.

Clay turned to face him, realizing the scene Hawk must see. United, one hand on Summer's shoulder and the other on Sabrina's slim waist.

"Hawk," Clay said quietly, "don't try to use this. It makes no difference."

"You are a fool if you think it does not. Her heart and her mind are open and you cannot change it. Why will you make her choose when you know one day choosing will cause her as much pain as it caused her mother," Hawk replied.

"No, Hawk," Clay said with finality, "I will take her away."

Hawk seemed so startled at this that for several moments he was silent. He, of all people, knew the love Clay had for this place, his home, and the people from which he had chosen his wife. He knew that Clay had chosen to stay in this place because he had been happy nowhere else. The surprise passed when another realization struck him. Clay was at the last line of battle, he could retreat no further. He knew he could not stop what fate had planned.

"Do you think that running away will change what has happened . . . what will continue to happen? If she has no explanation of the past then the future will confuse and frighten her."

Clay turned to Summer and Sabrina.

"Go to the women's lodge and get some rest. We will be leaving in the morning."

Sabrina knew that this was not the time or place to ask questions, but she knew that for Clay's sake and for Summer's she had to have these answers.

Sabrina took Summer to the women's lodge and put her to bed. It was only a few minutes before Summer slept.

Sabrina stood by the lodge door and watched Clay and Hawk in conversation. After a short time, she saw them separate. Hawk went to his lodge, and Sabrina watched Clay walk slowly toward the lodge in which he would spend the night.

Quietly, she slipped from the lodge and walked across the clearing to the door behind which was Clay and the answers she knew she had to have.

She did not call out to him as was the custom. Instead, she pushed aside the door cover and walked in.

Clay knew he would not be able to sleep so he did not even attempt to undress and lie down.

Instead, he sat down beside the low burning fire.

He was startled when Sabrina stepped inside the door, but he read her face as he would always be able to do.

"Sabrina . . ."

"No, Clay," she said softly, "I won't go away, I won't go to bed. For this time we will talk. I must know all the truth, good or bad . . . I must know, Clay, and only you can tell me."

Thirty-one

Clay could see something in Sabrina's eyes that he had failed to notice before. Sabrina was a soft and gentle woman . . . until she was pushed too far. Then her stubborn determination took over. This was one of those times.

"I have put Summer to bed. She was exhausted. Clay . . . I saw something tonight I can still hardly believe. I need to have you explain this to me."

She went to Clay's side and dropped to her knees beside him. With gentle hands, she reached to touch him.

"Clay, I know something is so terribly wrong. I know that you are afraid." She felt the muscle of his arm jerk at the word fear. "But I remember being afraid, and I remember your strength and understanding that made everything right. I don't know if I can make everything right for you. I only know I want to give you the comfort you gave me." Her voice died to a whisper as Clay's eyes turned to her. "I love you Clay, and I want to help you. Don't shut me out."

"Maybe," he said grimly, "you won't be so anxious to help me . . . or love me when you know the truth. Maybe I can hardly face it myself let alone tell you about it."

"There is nothing in this world that could make me love you less. You are my life, Clay, and my love will always be here."

"You're so sure of that Sabrina? I once told you that you could get hurt with that sweet unprotected love of yours. Maybe this is the time."

Her eyes held his without faltering.

"I love you. The only thing that hurts me is when you shut me away from you. Open your heart and let me inside, Clay," she said softly. "I'll stay."

Clay's eyes returned to the fire, and for quite some time he was silent. It was as if his mind were going back to try and find the beginning.

Sabrina remained silent too, and let him choose the moment to speak.

"It's a very long and very difficult story. Sometimes, I can't even remember how it all began," he said softly. Again he grew silent, and again Sabrina waited.

"I guess it would be best to start with my father. I was born in England. My father was sent here to negotiate a peace treaty with what was then a warlike tribe of Indians. He came here with my mother and I when I was a little less than six. Of course my father saw to it that his retinue contained teachers, teachers that were changed when my need increased.

"When I was seven, I met Hawk. We became inseparable friends, and we became each other's teachers. For many years it remained so. My father had been successful in his mission and Hawk's tribe became peaceful. And I'm sure Hawk too, thought that beautiful time would never end . . . but it did.

"My father decided I was ready for college, so he sent me back to England with my mother. It was only then that my world fell apart and I discovered a dark side of my nature I had not realized existed.

"You see, my father loved this country and he wanted to spend the rest of his life here. He was a very strong . . . and a

terribly possessive person. A trait I seemed to inherit. My
. . . my mother did not feel exactly the same about this place
as my father did. While I went to school in England . . .
while my father stayed here to build this place . . . my
mother met and fell in love with another man. I never knew
. . . but someone else did. Someone who was not too fond
of my family. They wrote to my father and told him.

"My father was always cursed with possessiveness . . . but
he was also cursed with jealousy . . . and violence. This is
where my fear lies, Sabrina . . . for I am touched by the
same faults. I never realized this until . . . until the tragedies
happened.

"When my father received the letter, he went mad with
jealousy. He took the first ship home without telling us he
was coming. When he arrived home, he caught my mother
with her lover. They fought . . . and my father killed him."

"Oh Clay, how terrible for you."

"That is not the terrible part Sabrina. If it were only that,
maybe things would be different."

"What happened Clay?"

"My mother was beside herself with grief. I . . . I believed
she really loved this man. No matter . . . she committed sui-
cide."

"Oh my God," Sabrina said softly.

"My world seemed to be shattering to a million pieces before my eyes. My father began to drink heavily. Maybe he
felt guilty for both deaths and he tried to wash it from him
with whiskey. I was miserably unhappy in England, and after a year or so I returned here. A year later my father died. I
guess deep down inside, I blamed the man who had stepped
into our lives uninvited and destroyed it. I vowed if I ever
found the woman I wanted, no power on earth would take
her from me. I became possessive about everything and anything that belonged to me. This is what created another

tragedy. A tragedy I guess I am as much to blame for as anyone."

Clay stood up and walked away from Sabrina to a more shadowed place. He stood, his back to her, and tried to continue his story.

"I came back here. Because I loved this place, and because it is the only place I have ever found peace.

"Hawk and I renewed our friendship, but I knew and Hawk knew that I had changed. Then . . . into our lives came Singing Bells."

"Singing Bells," Sabrina said softly. She rose to her feet and went to Clay. Slipping her arms about his waist, she lay her cheek against his broad back.

"We had heard of a great medicine woman from a nearby village. We had heard of her strange powers and rare beauty, but we did not know what she would bring.

"There was a great sickness. Hawk's people were desperate. So she was sent for. When she arrived, both Hawk and I realized just how beautiful she was. We both fell in love with her."

Clay turned to face Sabrina. "I don't mean to hurt you, Sabrina."

"Because you say you loved her? It was before I knew you. She became your wife, I expect it was because you loved her. I can understand."

Clay drew her into his arms and held her as he went on with his story.

"Singing Bells had a very strange power. She could sometimes see what was going to happen before it did. She always knew who was coming to the village and from where. Sometimes I believed she could see inside my heart . . . maybe that is why she was so unhappy at the end.

"I wanted her Sabrina, I wanted her for myself, because I loved her, and I wanted her more because I knew Hawk loved her too."

"Clay!"

"That's the truth you wanted to hear. Do you want to hear the rest?"

"Yes . . . yes I do."

"I had taken her from Hawk. She was mine, and I would allow nothing to touch us. I very deliberately took her away from all she knew and loved and tried to make her what she was not. But how can a man take such love, such compassion, such healing power and smother it? It was wrong. I can admit it now for I know I have lost the battle. Hawk and his people have won. They have taken the thing I love most from me."

"Summer?"

"Summer."

"Tell me the rest of the story Clay."

"Singing Bells came to me one day. She told me she was carrying my child. I was elated . . . she too would be mine. But Singing Bells wanted to go and visit her people. I refused to let her. In my stubborn possessive pride I told her neither she nor the child were to ever go to the village again.

"Every day I watched her try; every day I saw her fail, and every day I saw her grow more and more unhappy. I thought when the child came all of that would change. She would have the baby, me and our home. It would be enough. Again I did not count on her power. She . . . she knew that when the child came she was going to die."

"How terrible," Sabrina whispered. "She must have been a woman of great strength."

"She was, and I held that strength and love in my hand and calmly crushed it. Swift Doe has tried to tell me, and I deliberately refused to see. Again, I refused to let Singing Bells see her people, but this time she disobeyed me. There was a sick child, and somehow she knew. While I was away, she went to care for it.

"When I came home, she was not there. Later that night, Hawk brought her home. I was in a black rage of which now I am deathly ashamed. I told Hawk to leave my home and never to come there or to see Singing Bells again. They both tried to explain but I wouldn't let them. Then Hawk said something to Singing Bells I will always remember. He said he would be happy for Singing Bells and I when another such as she was born . . . for maybe then they would be able to share her with us.

"Then is when I made my vow that no such thing would happen.

"When Summer was born, Singing Bells told me that she knew the child would have her powers. It had been so in her family for generations. She begged me to allow the child to use them wisely and for healing. She died believing I would . . . but I fought. I saw things in my child I knew were true, but I refused to let it happen. I refused to talk to Summer of her mother. I refused to let Swift Doe tell her anything, and I . . ."

"You refused even to let her see her mother's grave for even then you were afraid that bond had never been broken."

"How did you know?"

"Summer followed you to her mother's grave long ago. I found her there one day crying."

"I have tried to fight it, but every day I saw her mother's power grow stronger. I saw her confusion and her fear at first. Tonight I saw her accept what she still does not understand but what she knows exists. Now . . . now I cannot fight anymore. They have won . . . and I have lost."

"Oh Clay," Sabrina said gently, "don't you understand that tonight is the first time you have won?"

"Won," he said raggedly, "how can I have won when I

have lost Summer to them, and . . . maybe lost a little of your love too?"

"Clay, your child worships you. She loves all, but you she loves more than anything." Sabrina bent down and picked up a handful of sandy dirt from the floor. She took one of Clay's hands and held it open and put the dirt in it.

"When you hold love in your hand, and give it freedom, you never lose it." She squeezed his hand closed and watched the sand drain out from between his fingers. "It is only when you hold it too tight that you lose it. Did you think I believed you had no faults, Clay? We all do. But you can only see them. I see a man who loves strongly, who has been hurt, who has been lost. I see a man who can learn to share, and I see a man whom I shall love to my last dying breath not in spite of his faults but because of them. Let me be the one to prove to you, Clay, that you are loved deeply and completely, and let us share our love and Summer's love with those who need us. I want to make you happy Clay, and I believe this is the only way."

Clay captured Sabrina's face between his hands. Tenderly, he kissed her brow, her eyes, her cheeks, then her trembling, waiting lips.

"You understand this terrible ugly thing I have carried inside for so long, Sabrina. Maybe your love is what I needed all this time to exorcise all the hatred and possessive anger I have held within. I have blamed Hawk and everyone . . . except myself. Maybe your sweet gentle love is what I have needed all this time. I once told you it was dangerous for you to love as deeply and completely as you do. Maybe that was because I couldn't until now."

Sabrina trembled violently when she felt the surging need in the depth of his kiss, yet she clung to him in complete and total surrender. He needed her now as he had never needed anyone before, and she wanted to be the source of strength he cried out for.

Their lips blended in that same blinding magic that lifted them in unison and carried them to the height of shared pleasure.

It was a kiss of peace and shared joy. Sabrina's eyes filled with tears that escaped from under her closed lids and moistened her cheeks and lips with their salty touch. Clay tasted them and knew she wept for him and for the pain and unhappiness he had known. She also wept for the promise of the future her kiss gave.

"Clay," she murmured softly as his gentle touch kissed away the grief, "we can begin a whole new life together. We can join with Hawk and his people in loving Summer. There is always enough love to share, Clay."

"I have always thought you would be hurt by your unselfish love, my precious Sabrina, now I know it's my selfish possessive love that gets hurt. I can't promise you I can change, but I will try Sabrina, I will try. It won't be an easy thing to learn to let go. I need you, love," he whispered, "I need you."

Sabrina's heart sang with the intense pleasure his words brought her. She clung to him, feeling the vibrant current of need that flowed like a tumultuous river from him to her. Her heart was filled to a capacity that was almost too much to bear.

For the first time in a long time, Clay felt himself surrender completely to a love that had no boundaries, knew no source and no ending, that filled him and left no room for any other thought.

The past was washed away in a flowing warmth making a path for a bright and promising future. It was a moment that held no taking but only giving.

They dropped to the fur covered couch together, seeking to find in each other all the new depths of their promise.

A hunger to know each other, even more completely than they ever had before slowed them and heightened their senses to a brilliant degree.

They were flame and light, engulfing, enclosing each other and reaching to the very center of their being to touch the spring that sent forth a brillilant explosion of passion and ecstasy.

They had no need to talk, there were no words to be said that could touch the beauty they had shared. He held her close to him as they tumbled back to reality.

Clay buried his face in the scented depths of her hair and savored that rare moment when two people were so completely attuned to each other that each move, each kiss, each touch was a magic blending thing.

Slim arms held him close and he could feel every inch of her slim body as she lay close to him.

After a few minutes, when their breathing was again under control, and they had regained some semblance of rationality, Clay rose on one elbow and looked down into Sabrina's eyes.

"I guess I should have told you all the truth a long time ago. I can again only blame my blind jealousy."

"You were jealous of me, Clay? I don't understand."

"You know now how the situation was with me. I believed Hawk was trying to use you to get to Summer. Then I realized another truth. He stopped trying to use you . . . he fell in love with you."

"Clay?"

"It's true. I watched it happen."

"But he never said anything to me."

"No, but he urged you to come here hoping you would see the truth in Summer. It would make you turn from me to him."

"Oh Clay, you are wrong. Hawk has never done anything

to make me believe wrong of you or to make me believe he cares for me that way. I'm sure Summer was what was in his heart. He just wanted to share this strange thing Summer seems to have with his people."

Clay chuckled and bent to kiss her gently and lingeringly, tasting her lips as if he could not have enough of the sensuous pleasure they produced.

"Go on believing as you choose, love. This night has opened a new page in my life and I don't intend to mar it in any way. Maybe Hawk does not love you, but in my mind any man would be a fool not to."

"Then I shall go on believing in our love. It is enough for the balance of my life."

"Sabrina?"

"What, Clay?"

"I know it has been on your mind, this business of us not being married."

"I understand the reasons, Clay, if there is no one to marry us. But I would lie if I told you I wish it weren't so."

"Do you want to do something exciting?"

"What?"

"Until the time comes and we can be married by Reverend Willoby, would you consider marrying me here and now?"

"Here? You mean in this village?"

"Yes. Their wedding ceremony is the most beautiful thing. You will like it. Then at least we will be married in the eyes of the people who live near us. Then when the Reverend does make his appearance, we can be married again. Then I will have you doubly tied to me."

"Oh Clay, what an exciting idea. When! When can we be married?"

"Is tomorrow too soon?" Clay laughed.

Sabrina threw her arms about his neck and kissed him several times.

"Clay Storm, you do have a way of making a woman's life mysterious and interesting. I am so happy, I never missed you in my life."

"I take it you agree?"

"Oh yes I agree. I want to make you permanently mine before someone comes along and turns your head."

"Impossible. I can only see you, no matter where I am." He kissed her again, then brushed warm seeking lips across her cheek and down the slim column of her throat to the pulse that beat a rapid acknowledgment of his ability to rouse her senses. "Tomorrow you and I will request a marriage ceremony. Then, to prove my good faith to you and to Hawk, I shall leave Summer here while you and I share a few days alone."

"I'm happy not only for me, but for you and Summer. Now you can talk to her freely. Now you can explain her past and her mother to her so that she is no longer frightened. We'll be a family, Clay," she whispered, "and I shall try with every ounce of love I possess to make you as happy as you have made me tonight."

Clay's eyes deepened with the intensity of the deep love within him. Slowly he bent to take renewed possession.

"Tomorrow . . . is tomorrow. For tonight, there is only us."

"Yes," she whispered as she lifted her parted lips to meet his. "Yes, my love."

Thirty-two

It was long past the midnight hour when Clay walked Sabrina to the lodge she would share with Summer for the night. He kissed her good night and returned to a bed that was resoundingly empty.

The village slept quietly until the calling birds and the first rays of morning sun stirred it awake.

Both Sabrina and Summer slept much later than usual, and neither were awake when Clay walked across the village to the chief's lodge. After permission was granted for him to enter, he went in to seat himself before the chief. He was amazed to find the chief so much better.

When he voiced his request for a marriage ceremony, it was quickly granted. Then he broke the news that he would allow Summer to stay with them for a few days while he and Sabrina shared a short honeymoon.

"And," he added gently, "if it will please you, Father, I will bring Summer here often to share in your wisdom and to give to your people whatever gifts she has inherited from her mother."

"You have made a great change in your heart overnight,

my son. Not that it does not please me greatly, but after all this time, I am a little surprised."

"I have faced some of my fears, some of my darker thoughts. I suppose some of it was because of the truth of Summer I saw last night and becoming aware of what I was doing to her. Most of it I will credit to the love and understanding of the woman I wish to marry."

"The golden-haired Sabrina."

"Yes."

"Then she knows all?"

"I have told her everything, even my own darkness. I have told her of Singing Bells."

"Clay . . . I would speak to you of one more thing."

"Hawk?"

"Yes. I have another fear."

"That Hawk is in love with Sabrina."

"You have seen this?"

"Yes. I have told Sabrina so, but she does not believe it because Hawk has not spoken to her."

"What are you going to do? You will not let this become another thing between you? Old wars must cease."

"That is the thing I desire most. I do not know if it would be better to speak to Hawk myself or to allow Sabrina and him time to understand. I would not want him to think it is my jealousy speaking again, though," he chuckled. "I admit I am wary of letting him talk to Sabrina alone."

"Will you be receptive to a suggestion from me?"

"Of course."

"Let the truth come from your woman. Then Hawk will not lay the blame at your door."

"You know Hawk will speak?"

The old man smiled, "My son is a man who usually tries to get what he wants. He does not step aside easily. He will speak if he feels his time is running out on him."

"When will the ceremony be?"

"Tonight, when the ceremonial fire is lit. Then we will perform the ceremony."

"It will not be permissible for me to see Sabrina again until then."

"You remember well."

"Hawk knows this, too. He will choose today to speak to Sabrina. I only hope he understands, and we can end this."

"You have admitted both to yourself and to your woman that most of the fault was yours. Now will you also admit that you know if my son is a man of honor? Do you think if Sabrina refuses him he will not be man enough to accept it and to finish your battle forever?"

Clay was silent for a moment, but his memory of Hawk went too far back. He knew what the old chief said was true. "You are right; I will admit it is so."

He rose and walked to the door, then he stopped and looked back at the old chief.

"Where will you go now?" the old man questioned.

"I am going to the grave of a woman whose forgiveness I should have asked a long time ago. I am going to explain to her that what she had hoped for her daughter will come true. Then both of us can be at peace. Will you ask Swift Doe to go to Sabrina and explain the ceremony and why it is a custom that I do not see her again until then. Maybe it would be best to tell her where I have gone."

"I will do as you ask."

Clay left the chief's lodge and went to where the horses had been kept for the night. He saddled his and rode away.

Hawk had just walked out of his lodge. He stopped and watched Clay ride away wondering why he had gone and left Sabrina and Summer here.

Again he started to walk toward his father's lodge when he saw Swift Doe leave it and walk rapidly toward the lodge in which Sabrina and Summer slept.

He stood, puzzled at both occurrences. After a few minutes, Swift Doe came out of Sabrina's lodge and started toward her own. Hawk walked to where her path would cross his and waited. She walked toward him; and when she saw him, she smiled.

"Good morning, Hawk."

"Good morning, Swift Doe. I have seen you go from our chief's lodge to Sabrina's. Is something wrong?"

"No, Hawk, nothing is wrong. Our chief sent for me so that I could explain the wedding customs to Sabrina. She and Clay are to be married here in our village this night."

For a moment Hawk was stunned. Then his mind began to move rapidly. He wanted to speak to Sabrina. Now and alone!

"I'm glad nothing is wrong," he smiled.

Swift Doe agreed. Then she went on her way to begin preparations. Hawk walked toward Sabrina's lodge.

Outside of Sabrina's lodge, he called to her and waited. After a few minutes, her bright head appeared.

"Good morning, Hawk. Did you want to see me?"

"Yes, Sabrina. I thought you might ride with me this morning. It is a lovely day, and I would like to talk to you."

"I think that would be delightful. Will you wait for me for a moment?"

"I shall prepare both horses and wait for you there," Hawk replied.

Sabrina agreed and Hawk walked toward the horses. He was turning over in his mind the words he could say to make her believe in his love for her. He was going to try his best not only to persuade her not to marry Clay, but to remain in his village and maybe to help persuade Clay to leave Summer with them also. He waited by the horses until saw Sabrina walking toward him.

She had braided her long golden hair Indian style and wore a tan buckskin dress she had borrowed from Swift Doe. She wore a bright smile for him and walked with a free and easy stride to where he stood.

"I'm ready," she said.

"You look very pretty this morning. Your cheeks are pink, and your eyes shine."

"I'm happy, Hawk, very happy. I guess I do not need to ask where we are going?"

He laughed, "My valley is very beautiful in the early morning light. I would like for you to see it."

"Then, let us go," she replied.

They mounted and rode from the village. They rode along in silence for some time while Sabrina enjoyed the beauty around her and Hawk enjoyed her.

They crested the hill that led to Hawk's favored place. Hawk stopped and they dismounted. He tied the horses, and together they walked down toward the stream.

Their conversation was sporadic and consisted mostly of the weather and the beauty of the place as they walked along.

It had not taken Sabrina long to feel that Hawk had something on his mind that he wanted to say to her.

When they stopped by the stream, Sabrina found a flat rock and sat upon it. Then she looked up at the tall, handsome Indian that stood beside her. "Come, Hawk," she said softly. "Come and sit beside me and tell me what is on your mind. I can sense something is troubling you. Come and talk to me."

"You know what I feel?" he smiled.

"You are a dear friend. I shall always know if you need to talk to me. And," she said softly, "I shall always be willing to listen."

Hawk walked to her side and sat down on the rock so

close to her that their shoulders touched. His eyes were on the scene around him, but he sensed her presence completely.

"Last night, Sabrina," he began, "You saw a very rare and strange thing."

"Yes, it was very strange, but since last night, I have thought of Summer and now I remember many strange things."

"It is a thing that should be explained to you."

"I think I already understand."

"You do?"

"Summer has received a phenonemal gift for perception and healing from her mother."

"You know about Singing Bells?"

"Yes, Hawk, I do."

"Sabrina, our village will need Summer in the future. There are dark days in our future, and we will need her as she develops her gifts."

"There is no doubt in my mind that the gifts Summer possesses should be shared with her mother's people."

"You agree with us then?" he said as he turned toward her.

"Yes, I do," Sabrina replied.

"Sabrina, I have something in my heart I must say to you. Will you listen?"

"I will listen, Hawk," Sabrina felt Hawk wanted to speak to her of Summer and her value to his village. She was completely unprepared for his words.

"Listen to my words well before you answer, Sabrina," Hawk began, "Once, long ago I loved a woman very much. She chose another, and that choice was a mistake. I felt I would never love another woman as I did her; and when she married, I left my village for awhile."

"Singing Bells," Sabrina said softly.

"Yes. When she died, I felt a part of me had died also.

Now I feel a difference in my life, in my thoughts. I have seen and felt another woman for the first time in a long time. I waited and watched for I did not believe this new thing that happened. Now . . . Now I would speak to her of my feelings. I would speak to her before she says the words that will make her another man's wife."

Sabrina's eyes widened in surprise as she realized just who and what Hawk was talking about.

"You are speaking of my marriage to Clay tonight," she said.

"I am speaking to you before you marry, for once you have said the words it is too late. Before you marry a man, you should know not only the good side of his nature, but the bad as well."

Sabrina knew what Hawk was going to say, and she wanted to stop him before he said them and regretted them.

"I have listened to your words. Will you listen to mine?"

"I will."

"With an open and understanding heart, Hawk?"

"I will try."

Slowly and carefully she explained how Clay had told her all the past, even the dark misery he had held inside. She also told him of Clay's decision about Summer which brought a look of surprise to Hawk's face.

"He will share her with us?"

"Does that surprise you?"

"Yes, it does. I never thought it could happen."

"That Clay would finally see the truth?"

"Yes."

"As Summer grew, something like last night was bound to happen. Clay could not deny the truth forever. One day Summer would have been forced to leave him, and that would have broken his heart. Now he realizes love is a thing that must be shared to survive."

"You have taught him much," Hawk said.

"No, not really, Hawk. I believe Clay had reached the point where he could not live with the past. He would have come to you sooner or later."

"You believe that?"

"With all my heart I believe that Clay is a strong and loving man. He would never have lost Summer."

"Last night he threatened to take her away."

"It was a last desperate thought."

"You do not choose to believe it?"

"No."

"You believe in his love for you?"

"Yes," she whispered, "as I believe in the love I have for him. I love him with all I possess, and I shall believe for as long as I live."

Hawk's eyes held hers, and she could feel the warmth of his reaching.

"You are a very understanding woman, Sabrina. There are not many who would not believe they had been used."

"Hawk, if I believe Clay used me, what am I to believe of my friend, Hawk? I choose to believe he is our best friend and will remain so for the rest of our lives."

Hawk smiled, "At first I did intend to use you to get Summer. That changed as you worked your way into my heart. Now I find my days and nights are filled with the violet eyes of the golden-haired Sabrina." Hawk reached to lightly touch Sabrina's hair. "Now I read in your eyes the love for my friend Clay. I will say these words to you only once before you become Clay's wife. I love you, Sabrina, and I will always have a place within my heart for you. If you should ever need me, you need only ask; and I shall come."

"I am grateful that you understand and feel the way you do. In a way, I love you, too, Hawk; and I would remain in your heart and keep you in mine—as friends."

"Yes," he said quietly, "as friends."

Hawk rose to his feet and held his hand out to pull Sabrina to hers. They stood together, and he looked down on the slim golden beauty beside him.

"Sabrina," he said softly, "I would hold you once — kiss you once — before you go from me."

She smiled and put her arms about his waist. Gently he held her close to him, then even more gently he kissed her. And he knew in all finality her love belonged to his brother, Clay. For the kiss was of good-bye, and he accepted it so.

Without speaking again, they walked back to their horses and rode back to the village.

It was the custom that a groom and bride would not speak to each other on their wedding day until the moment of the ceremony.

Clay knew this, and he knew he had to abide by it. But he chafed under the restriction.

He had returned to the village only to find that Sabrina had gone riding with Hawk. He knew Hawk loved Sabrina, and he worried that Hawk would be able to find words that might change Sabrina's mind. It was the greatest test of his new-found control of his jealousy and his possessiveness. No one would ever know how difficult it was for him and how desperately he wanted to ride out and snatch Sabrina away from Hawk.

It was with an elated heart that he watched the sun begin its descent. He saw the lighting of the ceremonial fire and knew the time was coming soon when Sabrina would be his.

In his lodge, he began preparation for the ceremony, while in hers, Swift Doe helped Sabrina prepare.

She had bathed in warm scented water. Swift Doe had loosened her braids and was brushing Sabrina's hair when a voice called to them.

"I will go, Sabrina," Swift Doe said. "It is not the custom for you to go from your lodge until they come for you."

Sabrina nodded, and Swift Doe stepped outside to see Hawk there with a bundle under his arm.

"Give this to Sabrina, Swift Doe. She will know and remember. It is good she has it this night."

He handed Swift Doe the bundle and walked away without waiting for her answer.

Swift Doe carried the bundle inside, handed it to Sabrina, and explained what Hawk had said. Sabrina smiled, for she realized what the bundle must be. She opened it and held the white wedding dress Hawk had given to her once before.

"How beautiful," Swift Doe said.

"Yes," Sabrina answered, "and I shall be so proud to wear it for it represents the love of two wonderful men."

The drums throbbed a slow rhythmic beat. All the village was gathered at the ceremonial fire where a great feast had been prepared.

All was ready. The old chief, still weak from his illness, had been placed in a seat of honor by the strong arms of his son, Hawk.

The medicine man who would perform the ceremony stood motionless near the fire.

Clay was amazed at the fact that he was more tense and nervous than he had ever been before.

He had dressed in finest buckskin and had come to the fire, as was the custom, to await his bride.

Hawk, too, arrived wearing his best clothes and soon Swift Doe came.

Everyone was there except Sabrina, and Clay's eyes continued to stray in the direction of her lodge.

He was prepared for anything except the vision that

stepped from the lodge and walked slowly toward him. He stood spellbound. He had seen Sabrina hundreds of times in the past months, but never had she seemed to glow with such beauty as she did this night.

He watched her walk to him, her eyes holding his, filled with the warm promise of a future filled with love.

The ceremony was a thing Clay barely heard, for his eyes, his mind, his heart were filled with the slim woman who stood by his side.

Loud shouts, and the heavy throb of the drum signaled the end of the ceremony and the beginning of the celebration. It was a joyous celebration both Clay and Sabrina would remember for the balance of their lives.

Clay had known of a cabin that had been built by trappers, then abandoned a long time ago. He had gone that day and prepared it, planning to spend a few quiet days with Sabrina alone before they went home.

The celebration continued on and on, and Clay tried several times to get Sabrina away only to have her snatched from his grasp.

It was well past midnight before he finally succeeded, and that was only because most of the dancers were exhausted, and many of the men were intoxicated from the drink they brewed for such occasions. He took her up before him on his horse, and they heard the celebration recede as they rode into the night.

Outside the cabin, Clay dismounted and lifted Sabrina down beside him.

"It's not much, Sabrina," he said, "but I wanted to be alone with you for a few days, and it is the only place I knew."

"Clay," Sabrina said softly, "I don't care where we are as long as we're together."

Clay laughed and swung her up in his arms and walked

to the door.

"Then welcome into my life, Mrs. Storm," he whispered.

"Where I intend to spend the rest of my life, Mr. Storm," she replied.

Clay walked into the cabin and kicked the door shut behind him.

Thirty-three

Thomas leaned across the table and laid a packet of papers in front of Elenora. His face was wreathed in a smile of pleasure at what he had accomplished.

"What is this?"

"The law, my dear," he chuckled, "the law."

"I don't understand."

"With these papers, I shall take Sabrina from under Clay Storm's nose, and there's nothing he'll be able to do about it."

"Clay's not a man to give up easily."

"What can he do? You see, Ellen was his indentured servant; but, by law, an escaped criminal cannot be. Therefore, Sabrina is not in his control. I shall take the law with me, and there's no way he can fight. He shall have to give her up."

"He'll try to do something."

"He won't have the time. Her Majesty's ship, *The Golden Fleece,* leaves within two weeks, just enough time for me to pick up Sabrina and bring her back. There will be no time for Clay to do anything."

"You are a very clever man, my dear," Elenora laughed.

"You have no idea, Elenora, you have no idea."

Elenora would have loved to question Thomas more

closely, for she would have liked to have something to hold over his head and gain control of him. She knew his wicked temper and held her tongue.

"When do you go?"

"I'm going to Storm's place in three days. That will give me just enough time to get Sabrina and bring her back. Just think, Elenora, Clay will have to have someone to console him when his little mistress is yanked from his arms."

"Oh, I shall console him," Elenora smiled, "but that's later. Right now," she said, "I find I need someone to console me."

"I shall do my very best to make your time of waiting more bearable, my dear," Thomas said softly. He bent to kiss her with a violent crushing demand to his hard mouth. He knew Elenora well by now. Violence and brute force were two things that heightened her sensual pleasure.

The three days before he left for Clay's cabin were spent together, and they enjoyed each other for they were two of the same kind of people. Both could enjoy sensual pleasure without giving one moment of real love. Both hearts were hard and always intact — never offered, never given.

The morning of the third day Elenora watched as Thomas, in the company of the magistrate and two of his men, rode toward Clay's cabin.

Ellen had been sent word by Hawk of Clay's and Sabrina's wedding and told they would be returning to Clay's home in a day or two.

Ellen was pleased at the turn of events, but she knew the wedding would not be legal in the eyes of white law, yet she was glad Clay had made some observance of their situation. Now Ellen knew it would not be long before Clay and Sabrina would be married by a reverend, and all their problems would resolve themselves.

Ellen and Lester had both known Sabrina's indenture papers had been illegal, but they had never thought anyone would ever question the fact. Now it would not matter. She would be Clay's wife, and they would never have to return home. No one would ever know of Sabrina's past. This pleased Ellen more than anything else had ever done. She would be content to stay here now if Clay and Sabrina were to ask her to.

It was a beautiful place to live, and she would love to be around when Clay and Sabrina had children. She tried to visualize how beautiful the children would be.

She also had visions of becoming a kind of godmother to them, to care for them as she had cared for Sabrina.

Ellen thought of Summer and realized she had developed a deep love for the child. She wished she knew the strange events that had led to the situation that existed now between Clay, his child, and a past of which he would not speak.

She wondered at the strange ability of Summer to see things that had not happened yet and would have loved to question Clay more closely, but she knew he would not speak of it. She had done all the work for the day and had eaten a light supper. Now she sat on the porch and watched in quiet pleasure as the sun neared the horizon.

The sunset was red and lit the world in a rosy glow. She was so involved with it that she failed to notice the two riders who rode toward the cabin until one called to her.

"Ellen! Ellen!" the figure called and waved.

Ellen shaded her eyes from the glow of the sun and finally recognized Sabrina and Clay.

In a few minutes, they came to the porch. Sabrina jumped down and ran up the steps to throw herself laughing into Ellen's waiting arms.

"Ellen, how good it is to see you again," Sabrina said.

Clay walked up the steps to stand beside Sabrina, a broad

grin on his face.

"You scalawag," Ellen declared. "You should smile. Getting married all of a sudden and without inviting me."

"It happened just like that, Ellen."

Clay laughed as he slid his arm about Sabrina and drew her close to him. "All of a sudden. There was no time then, but when we get married by the reverend, we'll make it a bang-up affair and you'll be the most important guest."

"Ellen, I have so much to tell," Sabrina said.

"Well, come on inside. Are you both hungry?"

"Starved," they declared in unison, both laughing. Ellen was caught in the warmth and love in their eyes as the two exchanged glances.

They sat together and ate a small supper while they explained to Ellen all that had happened. Clay was both amused and pleased at Ellen's obvious pleasure at the marriage, even though it was done in an Indian village. He assured her several times that he would arrange another ceremony as quickly as possible.

Ellen was amazed at the story of Summer's past and her abilities.

"Where is that child now? I think she ought to be home with her parents."

"I told Hawk he could bring her here in a couple of days. That way we would have time to be home. But if he doesn't come tomorrow, I shall go and get her. I guess I'm a little anxious to bring my family all together," Clay added softly as he reached across the table to take Sabrina's hand in his.

They were so lost in each other that they hardly heard Ellen's good night. She smiled to herself as she went to her room to give the lovers a chance to share their evening alone together.

"Sabrina," Clay said gently, "do you realize this is the first time we have shared this home as man and wife. It's a very special night."

"All nights I spend with you are special, Clay, no matter where we spend them. I want to be with you . . . anywhere."

Clay rose from the table and walked around it to reach for Sabrina. She rose with an inviting smile and stepped willingly into the circle of his strong arms. They closed about her with a warmth and strength that would always make her feel loved and wanted.

His lips found hers in a kiss that was more than a homecoming. Her arms encircled his neck, and her slim body pressed close to him in the sweetest surrender that filled his senses with the wonder that would always be his Sabrina.

She remembered well the past two nights of shared pleasure and the bright days filled with learning each other. Of all the times they had been together, those two nights would stand brilliantly in her heart.

Always, the nights they had shared before, because of Summer, Clay had come to her. Now they planned how they would change Sabrina's room into one for Summer. From this night on, Clay stated firmly, Sabrina would share the large double bed in his room.

"Summer will be upset sleeping in that room alone after sharing yours all this time," Sabrina said.

"Well then, love," Clay grinned wickedly, "why don't we give her someone to share it with."

"That sounds like a most inviting idea, my dear husband," Sabrina whispered. She did not tell Clay that she already suspected a life grew within her. She wanted to be sure.

Since their marriage and Clay's reunion with his past, Sabrina felt their love had reached a new plane of ecstatic pleasure. There was nothing shadowed between them any longer. They loved, and they were willing to shout it for all the world to hear.

He held her close to him, one hand pressed against her

back while the other explored a softly rounded hip. His mouth played a melody of sweet pleasure on hers and in satisfaction, he heard her warm murmured encouragement. She could feel his need as his lean, hard body bonded itself to hers.

"Sabrina, Sabrina," he breathed as his heated lips branded the smooth skin of her throat.

"I shall never get enough of you if I love you forever. You're like the air I breathe. I need you to keep existing . . . I need you, my sweet love. I shall always need you."

Whispered words of love were captured by his lips as he took her mouth in a deep exploring kiss that would always have the power to rock the foundations of her world.

They separated for a breathless moment, their eyes locked in deep warm desire. Clay took Sabrina's hand and drew her with him to his bedroom.

Inside he lingered over the pleasure of removing her clothes, taking the time to caress and kiss her until he was rewarded by her clinging arms and seeking lips.

They tumbled to the soft quilt-covered bed together. It was the close comfort they found as man and wife, and Clay was not to waste a moment of it.

There was no longer any rush, and Clay took the time to taste every drop of burning pleasure Sabrina could rouse in him. Now they were two people who had blended into one being, one need.

The flame of her touched him, licked along his senses, enfolded him until he knew only the desire to possess her.

For Sabrina, there was no thought but Clay, Clay with the strong seeking hands, Clay with the hard hungry mouth that possessed hers with an urgency that whipped her senses beyond her control.

His hands stroked a body that felt like silk beneath his questing fingers. She grew weak and trembly at the touch.

Together they sought the magic thing that would always blossom to life with their blending, a vibrant beautiful thing to which they could put no name, but each knew it would only happen with each other, and each knew they would never seek another.

They soared together in ecstatic beautiful flight to a culmination that left them holding each other as the only stability they had in their world.

Clay kissed Sabrina's sweat-slicked brow and caressed her hair. Their ragged breathing calmed, and the wild beating of their hearts regained its even-tempoed control.

He rolled to his back and drew her close beside him to nestle closely.

For several minutes, he was content just to hold her, and she was content to lie in the safety of his arms.

"Sabrina," he laughed softly, "you're like a miracle for me. There has never been anything in my life quite like you. I always thought I could control my needs, but you—you leave me weak as a child and still filled with the need to have you again and again."

Sabrina laughed in pleasure and pressed her lips against his throat.

"Clay, I love you so much. There is no word to say—that can tell you just how much. You make everything I want and need so complete."

Clay rolled on his side and looked down into her deep, violet eyes.

"And so, my love," he said gently, "I can offer you this," he waved his arm to include the house, "a child who loves you, and me . . . who loves you beyond reason. Is it enough to keep you happy, because above all else I want you happy. I want you to need us because without you this home will be nothing but a house. We'll be empty—both of us."

Her heart caught breathlessly at the poignant beauty of

his question.

"Clay, I lived in a beautiful mansion. It was probably all a woman could wish for. Yet I never felt as happy, as warm, and as loved as I do when I'm here in your arms. I do need you—to love me, to fill my heart and my life. As for Summer, she is like a child of my own, and if she will have me, I would be pleased and proud to be her mother. I am happy here, happier than I have ever been before."

"Summer will be pleased," Clay smiled as he bent to brush her lips with a gentle kiss, "but not nearly as pleased as I, for I intend to keep you here and keep you happy for as long as there is a breath in my body."

With a deep contented sigh, Sabrina curled against him, and he held her.

"Clay?"

"Ummm?"

"Do you know we don't really know much about each other."

Clay laughed. "I know all about you."

"You do not."

Clay again turned to look at her. "My sweet innocent, you've been well cared for and protected all your life. You're like a very rare and beautiful flower that should continue to be protected and loved. Everything about you speaks of honesty and generosity. You're perfect, and I wouldn't change one thing about you."

"Oh you think you're so clever," she protested with a laugh.

"But I am. I've captured you, haven't I? And that, my sweet, makes me not only brilliant for seeing what you are, but damn lucky that you feel as I do."

Sabrina could not help but laugh with him, and Clay was quick to take advantage of her mood to kiss her again most thoroughly.

She soon lost any thought of renewing her questions, and they spent the next hour proving their words were true.

The next morning Ellen had breakfast already prepared when they woke up. The three of them shared the meal.

"Let's work on Summer's room, Clay," Sabrina suggested. "Let's make it very special so she won't feel I'm usurping her place in yours."

Clay agreed it was a good idea, and the three of them set to work.

Summer's small bed was taken from Clay's room and put in Sabrina's. All her playthings were transferred, and the room was cleaned spotlessly. They were well pleased with the finished effect.

While Ellen prepared supper that evening, Clay and Sabrina walked near the stream. Their arms about each other, they enjoyed the cool breeze and quiet conversation.

After the meal, they sat on the porch until Ellen claimed she was tired and went to bed.

"She is so sweet," Sabrina said. "She intends to give us as much time alone as she can."

"I'm glad. I've the feeling when Summer gets home, there won't be too much time to call our own."

"Then," Sabrina smiled, "since she is coming home tomorrow, why don't we take advantage of this lovely night."

Clay came to her quickly and took her hand in his. "Your word is my command, love," he said softly. They walked back into their haven of solitude together and closed the door on the world.

The next day the three of them watched expectantly for the return of Hawk and Summer. By the time lunchtime rolled around, Sabrina was amused to see Clay begin to fret and watch the edge of the clearing. He wanted his child home. Sabrina, of all people, knew how difficult it was for Clay to control the emotions that must be plaguing him. She also knew this was the first time he had allowed her to be away from him, and in the company of Hawk and his people. She realized his sacrifice and was filled with love and pride for him.

Finally he began to pace. From the living room, to the porch, and back again. In the early afternoon, Sabrina knew his control was faltering.

"Clay," she laughed, "why don't you ride out to meet them. It will give you something to do, and it will certainly ease your mind. Besides, you're making me a nervous wreck with all this pacing."

"That sounds like a good idea," he replied. Relief was strong in his voice.

He saddled his horse quicker, she thought, than he ever had before. He put his arm about Sabrina and kissed her lingeringly.

"Thanks for being so understanding, love. I will feel much better when I have all my women safely under one roof where I can reach out to touch them."

"You know she's safe with Hawk."

"I know," he grinned, "but you don't mind if I let go slowly, do you? It's hard enough to do it even that way."

"I know, Clay, but you're doing the right thing. Summer's world will change; she will be happier, and in return, she will love you more."

"You know, Sabrina," Clay smiled, "before you came along, I had everything planned. I knew just what I wanted. Now, I only have room in my life for love, for you and a whole new world we can share. I don't know what I'd do if you were ever gone from my life. It would be a mighty dark world without you."

"I love you, Clay, and this is my world. You need never

worry. I intend to stay here forever."

He smiled, kissed her again, and mounted. She watched him ride away.

It was a long, drowsy afternoon; and by the time the sun was near the horizon, both Sabrina and Ellen were beginning to wonder why Clay had not returned.

"Surely he has met them by now. They were to be here," Ellen said.

"Maybe Clay had to ride all the way to the village. There might have been a reason for Hawk and Summer not to have started yet. If that is so, they might not be home until tomorrow," Sabrina replied.

It seemed to be that way for the sun touched the horizon with no sign of the three of them. Ellen and Sabrina shared a quick, light supper, for neither of them were hungry.

Ellen found her bed early. Sabrina went to the room she and Clay would share hopefully for the balance of their lives. This was the first time she had really been able to acquaint herself with the room. She drifted about it, realizing that Clay lingered in every corner.

The shelves that held his books drew her attention. She leafed through several, surprised that Clay's interests seem to run from history to poetry. The books were well chosen; and from their condition, they were well read.

Again as she had before, Sabrina was well aware that there was much more to the man she loved that she did not know. With a slight smile, she vowed she would spend time learning and understanding him.

She dressed for bed and climbed into the huge bed that felt very large and very empty without Clay to share it with her.

She drew the thick quilt over her and thought of how much warmer it was to curl in the security of Clay's arms than in the quilt. With thoughts of Clay to accompany her, she drifted off to sleep.

The next morning she rose before Ellen and decided to let Ellen sleep as long as she chose. Ellen had been so good to her she decided to make breakfast herself.

She prepared the food and the table and walked to Ellen's room. She opened the door and stuck her head inside.

"Ellen . . . Ellen, wake up," she said softly.

"Sabrina? Is something wrong?"

"Good heavens no, Ellen. I've made you some breakfast. Do get dressed and come and eat with me."

"I'll be right out."

Sabrina drew the door closed and started down the hall to the kitchen. It was then she heard the sound of approaching hoofbeats.

"Clay!" she cried in delight. She ran to the door as she heard footsteps across the porch, and flung the door open with a wide, welcoming smile on her face only to have it die and a look of fear and panic replace it.

Slowly she backed up as a smiling Thomas walked inside and stood gazing at her with a look of satisfaction . . . and lust in his eyes.

Thirty-four

Clay rode slowly, prepared to meet Summer and Hawk at any moment. It surprised him when time passed, and there was no sign of them.

Well accustomed to a horse, he rode with an ease that did not need much of his attention, so he allowed his thoughts to dwell on all that had happened in the past few months.

He realized he now viewed just about everything in a new light, and he was grateful to the powers that had brought him Sabrina, Sabrina whose gentle sweetness and little girl charm had reached into the dark places of his life and brightened them with the pure light of unwavering love.

He allowed himself one last look over his shoulder into the past before he closed the door on it with finality. He looked at it clearly, realizing he had let the tragedy of his parents jade his emotions and his thinking until he could not control them. He also was shaken to think again that if he had continued to walk the path he had been on, the one who would have paid the price for it would have been the one he had never wanted to hurt in his life—Summer.

He had seen the touch of Singing Bells in her daughter when she had been little more than a baby. He had watched it grow with her . . . and his fear had grown rapidly.

Clay had to wipe his heart clean of the ache that had lived

there for years so he opened it completely to the presence of Singing Bells.

He had known that Singing Bells was unhappy, yet he knew she had still loved him in the end. It shattered him to think he could have made Summer as unhappy, maybe even unhappy enough to leave him and search out her past herself when she was old enough. The thought that he might have lost Summer, and the friends he had made in the village made him wonder at the blessed fate that had brought a slim, violet-eyed girl into his life, into his arms, and into his heart.

Thoughts of their being together as a family brought his mind back to Summer and again he began to wonder why he had not met Summer and Hawk by now.

Time moved along, and when the moon stood high and white in a black night sky, he began to move into the territory of the village. It was nearing midnight when he did arrive.

Although night guards of the village saw him arrive, he cautioned them not to waken anyone else.

He made his way to Hawk's lodge and went inside quietly. He smiled to himself with a recurrent memory. As boys, it had always been a challenge to catch the other unprepared.

He stood just inside the door until his eyes adjusted to the dim light. Then he began to move stealthily across the room. He was brought to a quick halt when he heard a soft chuckle from a darkened corner.

"You have lived too soft, my brother. You have lost the silence of the cat. Now you move like a child searching for his mother."

Clay laughed as a new feeling of warmth rushed through him. It had been a long time since he and Hawk had lived as brothers. He welcomed the thought as a new beginning of a new life.

"Get up from that bed, Hawk," he said. "I expected you at my place by now, and you lie asleep like an old woman too tired to travel."

Hawk laughed, but rose and threw some twigs on an almost dead fire. When they caught, he put some wood on it and motioned Clay to sit opposite him.

"What brings you here?"

Clay sat across the fire from Hawk and they both realized this was the first time they had been alone and talked as brothers for a long time.

"I guess I got a little impatient."

"You weren't worried?"

"No, Hawk, I wasn't worried."

Hawk watched Clay closely for a few minutes then he smiled, knowing Clay spoke the truth.

"I thank the gods for this change, my brother," he said softly, "and for bringing you the golden-haired woman who caused it."

"No more than I do, Hawk. Let us speak once of things past, Hawk, and then let us put it away and never think of it again."

"Speak."

"I was wrong in a lot of things, Hawk, wrong to take Singing Bells from her destiny and wrong to make the same mistake with Summer. I was also wrong in putting the blame on you for many things that were my fault. I am willing to put all the past away if you can say the same."

"I am more than willing. But first I must say one thing to make sure nothing stands between us."

"What?"

"You knew I loved Singing Bells, but I could not turn her eyes from you. Will you be understanding if I tell you I tried to turn Sabrina's eyes from you, also? I was just as unsuccessful. I know now how much she loves you, and I will tell you, my brother, that I will be the friend of both of you if you will permit. I will never test our friendship again by saying a word to Sabrina that might make her unhappy or might make you look toward me in anger again."

"Nothing more needs to be said, Hawk. That is enough for me. One day I shall ask you to be godfather to our children."

"I would be more than pleased."

"And now, can you tell me what came up that kept you here? I was expecting you this morning."

"The sister of my father has been away for a long time visiting her children. She was to come home today, and my father wanted her to see Summer. One day, Summer will learn much medicine from her. She is a very wise woman."

"Summer behaved well?"

"She behaved as any child of seven and asked a multitude of questions."

Clay laughed.

"You do not plan on waking the child and taking her home tonight?"

"No, I had just not planned on traveling all the way here. Since I am here, I may as well spend the rest of the night and take her home tomorrow. I'm sure since it's so late, Sabrina does not expect us home until then."

"Good, you can share my lodge with me. It will be good for us to refresh old memories."

"Sounds fine to me," Clay answered.

They spent the next two hours talking about old times, laughing at old memories, and renewing a friendship that had very nearly been lost.

It was in the wee hours of the morning when they finally closed their eyes in much-needed sleep — Clay to dream of his return to Sabrina.

The next morning he was brought suddenly awake as a

laughing, exuberant Summer landed upon him, hugging and kissing him with vibrant enthusiasm. "Papa! Papa! Did you come to take me home?" she bubbled. "Where is Sabrina? When did you get here? Do we have to go home right away? What . . . "

"Whoa," Clay laughed as he caught her to him and hugged and kissed her soundly.

"One question at a time."

"Where's Sabrina?"

"Home waiting for you."

"When did you get here?"

"Last night. You were asleep."

"Do we have to go home right away?"

"Well," he said quietly, "I miss you, pumpkin, and Sabrina has created a whole pretty new room for you, and she is anxious for you to get home."

Summer smiled, and her slim little arms circled Clay's neck and she kissed him.

"I missed you too, Papa, and Sabrina. But I had so much fun here. Can I come back?"

"As often as you like, Summer," Clay said seriously, "and Papa has a lot of things to tell you as you grow up."

Summer's eyes sparkled up at him, filled with bright intelligence.

"I love you, Papa."

"And I love you, pet. Suppose we eat some breakfast and get on our way?"

She nodded and got to her feet. Together they ate breakfast. Then, to Summer's delight, Hawk informed them that he intended to ride back with them. They prepared to leave, planning on traveling light and fast, so they could be home by sunset.

Summer, with her child's innocence, kept both Clay and Hawk amused on the ride home. They stopped for a very short time to eat when the sun was high, and kept a steady pace the remainder of the day.

The sun was just at the edge of the horizon when they crested the hill that led to Clay's home. They stopped just for a minute to look at the pleasant valley. It sat in deep shadow, and that was when Clay felt the first touch of intuitive thought . . . something was wrong.

"Clay, what's the matter?" Hawk asked as he read Clay's face.

"There's no light."

"What?"

"In the house. It must be dusk there, and there's no light."

Hawk gazed at the cabin for a moment, then they both nudged their horses quickly forward.

They rode up to the cabin, and now a sense of alarm shot through both of them. The front door stood wide open, and there was absolute quiet . . . and no sign of life within.

Sabrina gazed at a smirking Thomas in stunned disbelief. She stood immobile, frozen by fear.

Thomas's eyes raked over her, enjoying the voluptuous womanly look of her. He had thought he remembered her beauty well, but now she looked even more appetizing than she had at Waverly Hall. There she had been a vulnerable girl . . . now she was a seductive, inviting woman; and he wanted her more than he ever had before.

He stood framed in the doorway; and if that did not frighten her enough, two very large and very strong men stood behind him.

"Thomas," she whispered in anguish.

"Did you really think you would get away with murder, Sabrina? How foolish. I have brought the law with me. You will return to England with me and stand trial for the murder of my father."

"No! No!"

"Oh yes, my dear," he smiled. He went to her side and lowered his voice. "I have a cabin prepared for us. I shall enjoy the return trip to England very much. I have waited a long time to taste your beauty, and I shall have days and nights to enjoy you at my leisure."

Sabrina knew she had no chance to escape Thomas. There was nowhere to run, and they could stop any move she made.

At that moment Ellen came from her room. She stopped, frozen in disbelief at the scene before her.

"You mucky scoundrel," she said angrily, "what are you doing here?"

"No need to call names, Ellen," he grinned. "I'm taking you both with me. You cannot help a criminal escape and not pay the price for it."

"Criminal! She's no criminal. We've no intention of going anywhere with you."

"No?" Thomas laughed. He turned and motioned to the two men. "You take this one. Go to the barn and use Storm's wagon," he turned back to gaze at Sabrina. "Wait for me in the barn. I'll be there in a few minutes. I'll bring this one."

No matter how she fought, Ellen was dragged out by the two men. Thomas and Sabrina stood gazing at each other, "Don't think your friend, Mr. Storm, can do anything to protect you. The law is on my side, and we'll be halfway to England before he can do a thing about it."

Sabrina came fully aware of Thomas's true intent.

"You don't intend for me to stand trial, do you?" she said softly.

"Good Heavens, my sweet," he laughed. "You are too tasty a tidbit to be hung. I intend to keep you for myself.

When we get to England, no one here will even remember you. No one in England will even know you have arrived. I have a place to take you, and no one will hear from you again—not even your Mr. Storm should he be foolish enough to follow us."

Suddenly Sabrina sprang to life. She whirled about and ran for the back door. Too late! Thomas had sensed she might do so. He was only a step behind her. Before she reached the hallway, a hard arm came about her waist, and she heard his harsh laugh in her ear as he held her helpless.

She tried to fight, but she was not even half his weight; and his hard, muscled arms held her in an iron embrace.

"My dear Sabrina," he whispered against her hair, "I have dreamed of you all these months. Now I shall have you."

"Clay will kill you for this," Sabrina gasped. She struggled as his hands slid possessively over her, groaning with the anger and disgust that filled her.

Then slowly he began to drag her toward the door. She fought fiercely all the way, gripping everything and anything she could find along the way. Still he continued to move her toward the door.

Her hands caught the edge of an oak table, and she clung to it desperately. She prayed any moment Clay would come and put an end to this nightmare.

Relentlessly he broke her hold on the table. With one arm about her waist, he lifted her from the floor and carried her outside where the wagon was waiting.

He tumbled her within and climbed in after her. Quickly he bound her hands and ankles with a piece of rope, taking the time to caress her slim legs as he did.

Anger filled her, and she kicked out at him bringing laughter at her helplessness. Tears of rage filled her eyes, and at that moment she would gladly have killed Thomas if she had had the means.

Sabrina gazed in anguish over Thomas's shoulder and watched the house . . . then the valley disappear from sight.

Ellen tried to get close enough to console her, but Thomas kept himself between them.

Sabrina felt numb with the shock. She had been shown the papers by a gloating Thomas and knew there was no escape for her. When she was taken to town, the law would send her back to England. Once she got off the ship with Thomas, no one but Clay and Ellen would wonder where she went, and they would not be able to find her once Thomas had disposed of her wherever he planned on putting her.

She wanted Clay with every breath she took and would have wept in open despair except Thomas's eyes were on her, and she would not give him the satisfaction of seeing how afraid she was.

She remained quiet, knowing deep within she was carrying Clay's child, and she had to find some way to protect it. She wondered what Thomas would do if he knew. The wagon bumped along slowly with Thomas and the other two horses tied behind. They had taken not only Clay's wagon but two of his horses to pull it as well.

She knew Clay would be furious, and she wondered if he would be able to control it now.

She determinedly gripped her emotions, held them in control, then deliberately channeled all her thoughts and hopes on Clay. She prayed he would follow and catch up with them before Thomas had a chance to get her on board the ship — before she was lost to him completely.

Clay stared in disbelief around the empty room. Without looking, he knew the rest of the house was just as empty.

He had no idea where Sabrina and Ellen might have gone,

but all his senses told him something was drastically wrong.

Summer still stood in the doorway with Hawk behind her. He was the first to sense the strange stillness that had come over Summer.

Slowly she walked further into the room until she stood near the heavy oak table. She put out a trembling hand to touch the table, and a soft, painfilled sound came from her. It caused Clay to turn and look at her. He was about to speak when a silent Hawk who still stood behind her cautioned him to silence.

Even though Clay had seen this eerie phenomenon before in her mother, he was still unprepared for it in a child. Yet he saw it happening before his eyes.

Summer stood with one hand gripping the edge of the table, her lips slightly parted and her eyes wide, she seemed to be looking at another place and time. Beads of sweat touched her forehead, and her slim body trembled as if in expectation of a blow.

"Papa," she whispered.

"What, Summer?" he replied in a low, gentle voice, "What do you see, Summer?"

"Sabrina . . . Sabrina."

"What about Sabrina?"

"She's so afraid, Papa. She's crying."

"Why Summer? Why is she so afraid? Why is she crying?"

"Someone is holding her . . . pulling her . . . she's holding on to the table, but she can't hold on. He's dragging her away. Oh, Papa, she's so afraid."

Summer was silent for a moment, but Clay knew she was feeling Sabrina's fear. He knew because he watched the tears well in her dark eyes and slide down her cheeks.

"He's taking her away, Papa . . . to a boat, a big boat." Again Summer grew silent. Then her voice was so quiet Clay could hardly hear her. "The dark-haired lady, the one who came here—she knows. She hates Sabrina. She told the man, and he came to take her away."

"Elenora," Clay said grimly.

Now Summer seemed to draw back again to where she was. Her dark eyes rose fearfully to Clay's.

"Oh, Papa, you must hurry. You can't let them take her away. You will do something, won't you, Papa? You won't let them take her away?"

"You can bet on that, Summer," he said as he bent and lifted the weeping child into his arms. "You can bet Papa will go and get her, and I won't let anyone hurt her."

Summer's slim arms went around Clay's neck, and she buried her face against his shoulder. Clay's eyes met Hawk's over Summer's shoulder.

"What has happened, Clay?" Hawk asked.

"I should have listened to her. I should have known she had been too frightened for it not to have been true."

"What Clay, what?"

"Thomas."

"Who is this Thomas?"

In as few words as possible, Clay quickly explained to Hawk what had happened in Sabrina's past. Hawk listened without questions.

"Hawk, it could only have been hours. If I go now and travel fast, maybe he won't have had time to get aboard a ship and get away."

"She is your wife Clay. He has no right to come into your home and take her."

"You don't understand Hawk," Clay said in an anguished voice. "In the eyes of the white law, she is not my wife. She is only an indentured servant. In fact, she is not even that—she is an escaped criminal, Hawk. They will put her on trial for murder."

"Then you must go quickly," Hawk said.

"You will take Summer back to the village with you?"

"Of course. She will be all right."

"She's frightened now of what she has seen. Maybe it is time it was explained to her. Take her to your father. He will know how much to explain to her to ease her fear without saying more than she can understand. Besides, she and your father seem to already understand each other."

"I will take her. I will see she is cared for. Clay . . ."

"What?"

"Bring Sabrina home safely . . . or make him pay for taking her."

Their eyes held, then Hawk smiled. He knew Clay's rage. He also knew his loves.

"I'll bring her back, Hawk, don't worry about that. And don't doubt for a minute he will regret the moment he walked into my house and took my wife."

Hawk had no doubts at all. He took Summer from Clay's arms and held her close to him while Clay went to the barn to get a fresh horse. He returned in moments even angrier.

"The bastard has taken the wagon and both the other horses. My horse is tired, but I must use him. I only hope it does not slow me up so much that that ship will sail without me." Clay's anger was violent. "When I get my hands on him, he will regret this, I swear, he will regret this."

Clay took Summer in his arms again and held her close for a brief moment.

"Papa is going to get Sabrina, Summer. Don't be afraid. Hawk will take you to his village where you will be safe and can stay until I get back."

"Please, Papa, bring Sabrina home."

"I will, Summer. I will," he said with more assurance in his voice than he really felt.

"Take care, Clay," Hawk said as he took the child back. Clay nodded, reached out to touch Summer, then strode from the house.

Hawk walked out on the porch with Summer in his arms and watched Clay's receding figure.

Clay rode at the top speed his horse would go, yet he knew the animal could never keep up a pace like this. Then, as if his mind was suddenly cleared, he thought of Caleb and the Daughertys. He knew he would be able to get fresh horses at each place.

He drove his horse to near exhaustion. It was lathered and heaving when he arrived at Caleb's.

Caleb, who opened the door of his cabin when he heard the arrival of a horse and stepped out on the porch, was surprised to see Clay, who had always given his animals great care, treating his horses so.

"Clay! What is wrong?"

"Caleb, I don't have time to explain," Clay panted, "Sabrina's been kidnapped. I've got to have a fresh horse. I'll explain when I come back."

"Good God! Sure, take what you need. Do you need any help?"

"No, there's nothing you or anyone else can do. I've got to get to her. All I need is a horse. Will you take care of mine?"

"Don't worry, Clay. Take what you need and go. I'll take care of yours."

Quickly Clay unsaddled his horse and resaddled one of Caleb's. Within minutes, he was on his way.

He rode at breakneck speed, praying he would be in time, forcing the thought out of his mind at what would happen if he was not.

At the Daugherty's, he made another switch with the same quick explanations and the same promise to explain on his return.

Now he had to make town on this horse, for there was no place to get another.

He paced the animal at a fast, steady pace.

He crested the hill above the town on a horse that neared exhaustion, but he did not stop.

He headed into town . . . and he headed directly toward Elenora Gregory's home. From the distance, he could see the ship rocking in the water and knew it would not leave until the next tide which was several hours away. Now he had to find out where Sabrina was being held . . . and he knew now that Elenora would know.

Thirty-five

Elenora and Thomas sat across a table from each other and shared a drink together. The elder Gregory was away on business so the house was theirs.

"And when do you leave?" Elenora asked.

"I've had all the papers made ready. The magistrate will hold Sabrina in jail for a few more hours until the ship is ready to leave. Then, he will turn her over to me. We shall be aboard soon and on our way. From that moment on, Clay Storm will never see or hear from her again."

"You don't intend for her to have a trial? You don't even intend for her to see the courts of England in any way, do you?"

"Let us say, my dear . . . ah . . . it would be better for me if she did not. Eventually I shall dispose of her completely and make sure none of the unwelcome past comes to light."

"She must know something you don't want known."

"She knows, but she doesn't know she knows. And I intend to see she never does. There is a great deal of wealth here, and I don't intend to let her do anything to jeopardize it."

"I must come to England one day to visit," Elenora smiled.

"I shall entertain you well at Waverly Hall. You would enjoy it. But I thought you had plans for Clay Storm?"

"I do," Elenora said seductively, "but one must have many interests to keep from being bored, mustn't one?"

Thomas chuckled, "Yes, my dear, you must come to England soon. I'm sure you would enjoy your stay."

"This Waverly Hall—is it where you intend to hold Sabrina?"

"Good heavens, no," Thomas laughed. "I have a friend who owns a house of rather poor repute. He will be glad to get his hands on a choice morsel like Sabrina. When I am through with her, he will take her off my hands and see she does not cause me any problems in the future."

Their eyes met, and both smiled for they knew and understood each other completely.

Thomas rose and was about to walk around the table and take her in his arms when the door opened. Both of them turned in surprise to see Clay standing in the doorway.

"Clay!" Elenora gasped. She was more upset at the fact that Clay had found her with Thomas than that he was so angry.

A cold, blue gaze held Thomas, and for a moment, the sensation of deep fear held him paralyzed.

"So you are Clay Storm," Thomas said stiffly.

"And you are Thomas," Clay said.

"Where is Sabrina?" His voice was even colder than his eyes which were hard enough to make Elenora take a step back from him.

"Sabrina? Sabrina McNeil. Why?" Thomas laughed. "She's in jail where murderers of her kind belong . . . and . . ." his face grew cold, "where you can't get to her."

"If you've hurt her," Clay said softly, "if you've even touched her . . . "

"Now, Mr. Storm," Thomas chided innocently. "I've done nothing but see that a criminal has been brought to justice. I will return her to England where she will be tried and hung for the murder of my father. The law is holding her, and you have nothing to say about it."

"We will see about that. What kind of a cold-hearted person are you to lock up a gentle creature like Sabrina?"

"That gentle creature committed murder!"

"Funny," Clay said quietly, "but I just don't quite believe that."

"Well it doesn't really matter what you believe. You see, the papers have been filed. She will not be released until I take her on board that ship in a few hours. You, Mr. Storm, will not be able to stop what is going to happen."

"Clay," Elenora said, "I'm sure you didn't know Sabrina was a criminal when you took her in. Surely you have no intention of marrying a murderess and making her the mother of your child. Why," she laughed "she might decide to kill you some day, or Summer, should you do something she doesn't like. Wouldn't it be wiser just to let her be taken back to pay the price for what she has done?"

Now Clay's cold blue gaze fell on Elenora, and she was shaken by the intensity of his rage.

"I will never let Sabrina away from my protection. I love her; Summer loves her. I'll find a way."

"There is no way," Thomas said angrily.

"We'll see . . . we'll see," Clay said. He turned and left, and both Elenora and Thomas stood in silence.

Clay went straight to the magistrate who looked up from his desk in surprise when Clay came in and closed the door sharply behind him.

"Clay," he said as he rose from his desk and walked toward Clay. He had known Clay from boyhood and this was the first time he had ever seen such blank cold rage in his eyes. "What is the matter?"

"You're holding Sabrina McNeil here?"

"Why yes, I am. She's due to be returned to England. She's an escaped murderess. How in heaven's name did you know?"

Clay explained quickly how Sabrina came to be brought to his home.

"I want her Martin."

"Clay . . . I . . . I can't give her to you. The papers are all legal and binding. She . . . she has to be sent back to face a trial."

"Martin, for God's sake. She's my wife."

"What? How?"

"We were married at Hawk's village."

"An Indian ceremony?"

"Yes."

"Clay, that ain't legal, and you know that as well as I do."

"But can't it soften the rules, Martin? Can't I go back with her?"

"Well . . . I suppose you could. But what good is it going to do Clay? She still has to stand trial."

"But I'll be with her. She won't be alone, and maybe she won't be afraid."

"That Thomas, he's arranged to take her back."

"Martin, do me one favor."

"I owe you and your father more than one."

"Put her in my custody. I'll take her back to stand trial. I swear on my honor."

"Clay, I've known you since you were a boy, and I've never known you to break your word. I'll do just that. I'll put her in your custody, making you my representative. You can take her back!"

"But you've got to swear she'll be given over to the court."

"I swear. I think it best we fight this battle together. Maybe we can get her cleared of all the past. I'll take her home. But I'll get her the finest lawyers money can buy."

"All right."

"Can I see her?"

"Sure, come with me." Martin picked up a ring of keys from the desk and turned to walk down a long, narrow hall. He stopped by a door and put the key in the lock. It took all the reserve Clay had not to break the door down, take Sabrina, and run.

The door swung open, and Clay stepped in and closed it behind him.

Sabrina had been sitting on the edge of a low cot, her face buried in her hands. Clay could sense that she had been crying. When the door closed, she withdrew her hands and looked up. The angry defiance on her face turned first to wonder, then to joy. With a soft cry of his name, she flew from the cot to the safety of his open, welcoming arms.

"Clay, oh Clay," she cried. Her body trembled so badly that Clay's rage at Thomas and Elenora was renewed. He held her close to him and caressed her hair.

"It's all right, Sabrina," he said softly. "Don't cry. We'll be together."

"I'm so frightened, Clay. I was afraid you would not come."

Clay captured her tear-stained face between his hands and gently kissed her into silence, tasting the salt of her tears on his lips.

"Did you really believe I would let anyone take you away from me? We belong together, Sabrina, and we'll face anything the world has to offer together."

"They're going to take me back to stand trial for Clyde's murder."

"I know, and they thought it would be so easy that you would have no defense. But you do love, you do, and I'll find a way to get you free, believe in me love. I'll never let you go no . . . never."

Sabrina smiled tremulously, and her violet eyes filled again with trust and warmth.

"Clay . . . you'll be with me?"

"All the way, love."

"What of Summer?"

"She's safe with Hawk. You have Summer to thank for me being here in time."

He went on to explain what had happened, and how he had made the rapid trip to town.

"I've had them put you in my custody."

"How did you manage that?"

"My father's name still carries a lot of weight in this town. I gave them my word I would deliver you safely, and I will. But when we get to England, Thomas has a few more surprises in store for him."

"Thomas . . . he . . . he said when we were on board the ship, you would never hear of me again. I don't believe he meant for me to stand trial. He meant . . ."

"I know what he meant," Clay responded angrily, "but he won't touch you Sabrina. Trust me. He'll never touch you, on board ship or anywhere else. Besides that kind of gives me the idea there's more about this situation than we know, and when we get to England I intend to find out."

"I'm just so glad you're here, Clay. I can face anything as long as I know you are here."

"Don't ever worry," he whispered softly as his lips caressed hers gently and tenderly. "I love you, Sabrina, and I'll be with you no matter what. When this is over, we'll go home. Summer needs her new mother—and I need you."

Again his lips lingered lovingly on her, catching her breath with the undemanding tenderness that told her as nothing else could of the love he felt for her.

A light rap on the door, and the jailer opened it.

"Clay, you got to come out here."

"What's the matter?"

"Come on out," the man repeated. His eyes touched Sabrina, then came back to Clay.

"All right, I'll be right there," Clay said. Clay knew what the man wanted to say must be about Thomas, and he didn't want Sabrina to hear. He nodded and closed the door.

"I'll be here, Sabrina, so don't worry. I have to take care of my passage. When it's time for that ship to leave, we'll be together."

Sabrina nodded. Clay kissed her again, smiled reassuringly and left the room. Almost at once, Sabrina felt the desolation and loneliness he left behind. She knew there was no future for her except Clay.

Clay came out of Sabrina's room and found the jailer waiting for him.

"Clay, you know Captain Jenners well?"

"Yes, quite well. He was a good friend of our family for years."

"Well I found out something you ought to know."

"What?"

"Captain Jenners just stopped by to tell me the ship will be leaving within the hour."

"I knew that."

"Well, while he was here, he asked me if I knew that the girl was ordered by this Thomas to be put in the same cabin with him."

"The rotten . . . " Clay began. "Well, there will be a change in that."

"I thought you might like to know."

"Clay, something about this whole thing don't smell so good. Why didn't he just send the law for her if he knew where she was? Why does a wealthy man travel all this way just to bring one little thing like that girl back?"

"That's one of many things I intend to find out as soon as

we reach England. I'm going down to talk to Captain Jenners. Don't even let him in to see her until I get back."

"All right," the man grinned, "it will do me good to tell that arrogant bastard where he can put all his high and mighty orders."

Clay left the jail and went to the docks.

Captain Jenners welcomed him and was more than surprised to hear the story Clay explained to him quickly. The captain listened to Clay's story without interrupting him.

"Well, you're right. He did book one cabin. He intended to share it with the girl on the way back. God Clay, I didn't know she was your woman. I just thought she was a runaway, and he was someone pretty close to her."

"We were married in an Indian ceremony. We intended to be married by the reverend when he came here on his rounds. We could have you marry us on board ship."

"I'm afraid not Clay. I can let you and her share a cabin, but it's against the law for me to marry a criminal until they are tried and free."

"She's no criminal!"

"You say that boy, but the law don't. My hands are tied."

"Well, at least I'll have her with me until we get to England."

"I'll take care of it. You go back and get her. It's nearly time to leave."

Clay shook hands with the captain and left the ship. When he arrived at the jail, he found a very angry Thomas. He was shouting at a jailer who sat with an amused grin on his face.

"This is against the law! I have the jurisdiction! I have to bring her back."

"Well, sir, I done made Clay Storm my representative. I ain't going to turn her over to you. I'm going to have my representative take her back for trial, and," his grin grew broader, "they ain't nothing you can do about it unless you want to go back to England and get some legal paper that says I can't. But by that time, I'm afraid I'd have to let the lady go."

Thomas turned to Clay, his face mottled with rage.

"You have your way now," he said angrily, "but nothing's going to change the fact that when we get to England, she'll be locked away, and that is something you can do nothing about. I'll see her hang! And I'll see that you pay some way somehow for this interference."

"Don't worry," Clay said calmly, "I understand you. In fact, I understand you so well that I never intend to turn my back on you. I have a feeling that's where you usually strike from."

Thomas was so angry his face grew pale. He would have liked to kill Clay where he stood, but icy blue eyes held him immobile. He knew Clay would have liked nothing better than for Thomas to attack him. He could see death in the depths of those blue eyes, and he had no intention of giving Clay the opportunity.

Without another word, Thomas left the room slamming the door behind him. Clay and the jailer exchanged mutual looks of amusement.

"The ship is ready to leave," Clay said. "I'll take Sabrina with me now."

"Go back and get her Clay, and Clay?"

"What?"

"Take good care of her. She seems like a sweet, loving girl. I'm sorry I had to be part of this. Bring her back so's I can make my peace with her."

"I'll do that," Clay smiled.

Clay went back to get Sabrina. He unlocked the door and went in to find her nervous, but waiting for him.

"I's time to go, Sabrina," he said. He watched her do her

best to control her fear. She came to his side and smiled up at him. He was caught in the trust and love that lit her eyes. Silently he prayed he could fulfill that trust.

"I'm ready, Clay," she said softly.

He took her hand and they walked out together.

They rode to the docks in silence. He knew Sabrina was trying to control her fear so he simply held her hand and let her know in every silent way he could that his strength was near to support her.

When they walked up the gangplank, they were met by Thomas who stood in silence and watched them approach. Clay could feel the tension in Sabrina and the fear as she gripped his arms in clutching fingers.

"It's all right, Sabrina," he said in a voice just loud enough for Thomas to hear, "I'll see that none of the vermin on this ship can do you any harm, be they four-legged rats or the two-legged kind."

Thomas's eyes narrowed, but he said nothing until they were beside him. Then he looked at Sabrina and said softly, "Enjoy your ocean voyage. It will be the last for you. I'll see you hang."

Sabrina's face went white, but her chin lifted in defiance as she walked past Thomas with her head up.

The captain had a man lead Clay and Sabrina to the cabin they would share for the journey. Inside the cabin, Sabrina collapsed into Clay's arms and wept. There was nothing he could do but hold her and reassure her.

He kissed her, and caressed her until he had wiped the thoughts of Thomas from her mind. He knew that now she needed him to help her keep the fear at bay. He lifted her in his arms and carried her to the bunk they would share for the next few weeks.

He took an infinite amount of time to undress her, warming her with kisses and seeking gentle hands that stirred her senses. He felt her need as she clung to him and sought him with a passion that soon consumed him as it did her.

He was stability and safety. He was love and warmth. He was the only world she wanted to live in, and he took her within him and comforted her and gave her the faith and love that would carry over the dark days to come.

His hungry mouth sought hers in long and leisurely kisses. He did not hurry, but attacked her senses with a knowledge that left her blinded to every other thought but him.

Warm hands that caressed the silken skin of rounded breast, flat belly, and slender thighs. Heated lips that followed their burning path.

Then he was within her, filling her and emptying her of any thought but the magic of the love they shared.

Sabrina gripped Clay with hands that told him of the flame that licked to life within her. She drew him closer and closer, urging him to fill her more, and rose to meet his thrusting body more than half way.

Her world now consisted only of Clay and her fiery need of him. She was free of any fear and lost to the threat of the world about her. He heard her soft voice call to him and answered with passionate words of his own.

The consummation of their love was a blinding soul shattering thing that left them gasping and clinging to each other as slowly their careening world righted itself. They held each other and floated downward from the olympic heights like two weightless beings.

When rationality returned and their breathing returned to normal, they lay together in a bonding silence.

After awhile, Clay rose on one elbow and looked down into her eyes. He was pleased to see only love and contentment. All fear had been firmly put aside for now. He smiled, and she returned it with no restraint.

"I am so glad you're here, Clay. I have to tell you something, and I want it to be now when everything is so perfect with us. Whatever happens, I want you to know that I love you and will always love you 'til the day I die."

"And that will be when we're old and gray, my love," Clay said, "What is it that is so very important that you have to tell me?"

Sabrina put her arms about his neck, smiled up into his eyes, and spoke softly watching his reaction.

"Clay, I'm carrying your child, and it has made me happy just to know I can give you part of me even if I am no longer here."

She watched sheer intense pleasure leap into his eyes to be followed quickly by an agony just as intense.

"Sabrina," he whispered, "Sabrina, my dear sweet innocent. How much I love you. We will go home together and our child will be born where he belongs — in our own home."

"Yes, Clay," she replied, "kiss me and I'll believe."

He kissed her in a way that told her he would fight the devil himself if he had to.

"For now, forget everything else. We will share this time together." He placed his hand against the flat smooth flesh of her belly, "I'll take you both home love — I swear, I'll take you both home."

Thirty-six

Clay and Sabrina lived in their own private world for the rest of the trip. With determination they put aside all thoughts of the future. They would face it when the time came to.

In spite of Thomas' obvious hatred, they did their best to keep their distance from him. On the confines of a ship, it was difficult to do, and when they were in his presence they did their best to ignore his hold over their lives.

It was inevitable that he would one day cross Sabrina's path when Clay was not with her.

Sabrina left their cabin to meet Clay on deck, she stepped out her door and literally collided with Thomas. At that moment it did not occur to her that he had been waiting for this opportunity.

He gripped her arm in a hard ruthless grasp as she tried to retreat into her cabin.

"Let me go Thomas, or I shall scream. Clay is only waiting for such a chance."

"You're a fool, Sabrina."

"I am, why?"

"What do you think he can do for you? He will only have to watch you convicted and hung."

"No!"

"That's true. He can't help you . . . but I can."

"What?"

"I can," he whispered as he drew her closer to him. "I can see you're not convicted. I can help get you free."

"But you have your price?" she said softly.

He smiled with a new self assurance and tried to draw her even closer, but she held herself stiff and resistant.

"My price," he smiled, "of course you know exactly what that is."

"Me?"

"You," he repeated. "Think about it, Sabrina. He'll have to sit in that courtroom and watch us convict you. He'll have to hear the sentence, and he'll have to live with your memory when you are hung."

"You are a cold hearted monster, Thomas. Why, if you have evidence that will set me free, why don't you use it. Why would you let me stand trial if you know I'm innocent?"

"You disappoint me Sabrina. Surely you know if I can't have you . . . I shall see to it he does not have you either. Make your choice Sabrina. Freedom with me . . . or death with Clay Storm. It would almost seem to be an easy choice."

He smiled as if he were sure of what she might say. But the smile faded when she spoke firmly and clearly.

"You have nothing of interest to me Thomas. I would rather have a few short hours with Clay than a lifetime with you. I love him and I trust him to find a way for me to freedom and a life we can share. I will believe in him always and no matter what, if the worst happens, I shall die knowing I love and am loved. You will never know the joy of that."

She jerked her arm free of him and ran to the deck where Clay waited for her. Thomas watched her go, his eyes blazing in helpless rage.

"Bitch," he muttered, "you'll pay for that Sabrina McNeil. One day you'll beg me. One day . . . "

Sabrina stood at the companionway and looked across the deck. Clay stood, leaning against the rail watching the wind fill the huge white sails above him.

She watched the sun glisten in the ebony of his hair as the wind lifted it. He seemed so large and so safe. His broad shoulders in the white shirt he wore renewed the memory of the wild strength of the lean hard body that could possess hers so magically.

As always he seemed to sense her gaze and turned to look at her. His smile was quick, his square white teeth bright in his dark face. The amazing blue eyes could be felt by her as they drew her irresistibly to his side.

His arm slid about her waist and he drew her close to his side. For a moment, she closed her eyes as she rested her head against his broad chest and her arms clung to him. It was that moment he sensed there was a new tension within her.

"Sabrina," he said quietly as he brushed a light kiss against her hair.

"What?"

"What's the matter?"

"With me? Nothing, why?"

He turned her to look up at him and gazed down into her eyes. His gaze was warm and compassionate.

"Don't lie to me, love. Don't you know I can feel anything that hurts you? Now, you tell me, what's the matter?"

She dropped her head, but his large hand lifted her chin till their eyes met again.

"Look at me, Sabrina." His eyes held hers in a grip she could not seem to break.

"Thomas?" he said.

"Yes," she whispered.

"Tell me."

Quietly she explained all Thomas had said to her. She watched the warm blue gaze turn to a cold shimmering ice.

Clay didn't do anything for the moment except to draw her into his arms and hold her. His mind was storing the idea that Thomas had just made the mistake of saying . . . there was some evidence that would set Sabrina free . . . and he had every intention of finding it.

He allowed time to slip by. Allowed Sabrina to relax under his laughter and pleasant conversation until she had forgotten Thomas . . . but he hadn't. He could not forget that Sabrina had trembled in fear when she came to him. He could not forget that her eyes had clearly shown the uncertainty and anguish she must be feeling. And he had no intention of letting Thomas get away with it.

That night their love making was a sweet gentle thing that erased completely all thought of Thomas from Sabrina's mind.

Clay held her until she slept, then slowly he eased himself from the bunk. He made his way with the stealth of a wild untamed animal to Thomas' cabin and slipped inside.

Thomas came suddenly awake as a hand gripped him and yanked him forcefully from his bunk. He was slammed bodily against the wall nearly knocking the breath from him.

He was helpless beneath a superior strength of the shadowed form that held him against the wall. He couldn't even tell who it was until Clay's voice came quiet and deadly from the dark.

"I have to talk to you my friend, and I want your complete attention."

"What are you trying to do, kill me?" Thomas gasped, "it won't do you any good."

"Oh I don't intend to kill you," Clay said in a gentle deadly voice, "I only intend to give you a warning, one very final warning."

"You're crazy," Thomas said as the hand at his throat threatened to shut off his air.

"I'm only going to tell you this once, so listen to me well. You stay away from Sabrina the balance of this trip or I shall see to it one dark night that the sharks have a large piece of meat for their supper. Do I make myself clear?"

Thomas gasped a ragged yes, and Clay gave one final squeeze then released him. Thomas gasped the air and with trembling fingers loosened his collar to breathe more freely.

Clay did not say another word as he turned and left the room.

When he returned to their cabin, Sabrina still slept. He entered the room as quietly as he had left. He undressed without a sound and slid under the blankets drawing a warm Sabrina close to him.

She stirred in her sleep and came to hazy half wakefulness.

"Clay," she mumbled sleepily, "you're cold."

"Well," he chuckled, "why don't you warm me up?"

He was even more amused when she snuggled close to him, sighed deeply and drifted back into a deep contented sleep. Clay chuckled and held her even closer.

"That," he whispered, "is not a very just reward, love, but I'm a patient man. There's always another night."

Sabrina expected confrontation with Thomas again, and quickly became aware that not only did it not happen, but Thomas seemed to actually be avoiding even eye contact with her. When she became aware of that, she was aware of the still watchfulness in Clay. She sensed something had happened but couldn't figure out what. All she knew for sure was that Thomas kept his distance, and she was going to grab these last few days of happiness before her world was darkened again with reality.

Clay made it just that, a warm interlude. A time of awareness of each other in a new and very vital way. They shared intimate meals of poor quality, yet to them they seemed a feast. They spent hours talking of plans both of them were unsure would ever be.

The most precious times they spent together were the quiet hours in the warmth of each other's arms. They talked of the child she carried, and the days they would share in the warm summer sun when their family was again intact. They refused to let the thought touch them that the child she carried might be born in a prison . . . and its mother might be hung for murder.

They stood in the early afternoon a few days later and saw in the furthest distance the darkened rim of the horizon that told them land was near.

"What will happen now Clay?" she said softly. "Will they take me from the ship to . . . "

"No Sabrina. I intend to take you straight to my home. Thomas has been informed. I will take you down to surrender yourself tomorrow. Then, I shall set about hiring the best lawyers and getting you free."

Sabrina turned to look up into Clay's eyes.

"What if . . . "

"Don't Sabrina. Don't even think it. After what you told me about Thomas, I'm sure there's a lot more to this story than anyone else knows. I'll find the truth if I have to turn England inside out. We will get you free. Don't doubt it, don't ever doubt it."

429

"Clay, I . . . I want you to know. I've been happier than I have ever been before, happier than I ever expected to be. If anything happens . . . well, I want you to know that, and to know how very much I love you and you've filled my life."

"You're not giving up on me now are you, love? Don't you know you'll be taking all the light out of my life. Stay with me Sabrina, together we'll be all right."

He held her close to him, and she lifted both hands to hold his face between them.

"No, I won't give up. As long as I have you, I'll never give up."

"Good girl," he smiled.

They watched land grow closer and closer. When the ship docked, Clay took Sabrina ashore and hired a carriage. Sabrina had no idea where Clay's family home was but it would be welcome for her because it saved her from her first night in prison.

They rode through the streets of London to the outskirts. Then to an exclusive area in which only the wealthiest families had been able to live.

Her eyes widened as they drew to a halt in front of one of the largest and most beautiful mansions she had ever seen.

"Clay . . . this is . . ."

"This is home, love," he smiled. "Although I'll admit I hadn't thought I'd ever return to it. I had even planned to sell it at one time."

"But it's . . . Clay, it's a mansion!"

"Well, my father had a taste that was a little ostentatious, I admit."

"I . . . I didn't know you were wealthy," she said, "but I should have. I always felt there was more to you than anyone knew."

"I never spent much time here, Sabrina," Clay said as he

climbed down from the carriage and helped her down. "I guess after I finished school, I'd had enough of this life. I liked it better at home. That was the only place I've ever found peace, and," he smiled, "I found you there."

He tucked Sabrina's hand under his arm and walked to the front door which was abruptly opened. A man stood in the doorway with a broad disbelieving smile on his face and the glint of tears in his eyes.

"Mr. Storm," he said.

"It's me, Paul, the proverbial bad penny," Clay laughed.

"I never thought these old eyes would ever see you again. Welcome home."

"Thank you Paul."

"No one was expecting you sir. Why didn't you send word? We would have made the house ready."

"Knowing you and your wife, Paul, I know the house is probably in fine shape." Clay entered the magnificent edifice drawing a spellbound Sabrina with him.

"Paul, this is the young lady who will soon be Mrs. Storm."

The old man's eyes turned to Sabrina, lit with warm welcome . . . and wisdom.

"Welcome home, Miss."

"Thank you."

Again Clay laughed as he clapped the old man on the back.

"I know you're dying of curiosity Paul, and it's a very long story we have to tell you, so how about a warm meal to start with."

"Yes sir, I'll see to it at once. Shall I show the young lady the house first?"

"No, I'll do that."

The old man bowed and quickly disappeared. Clay

turned to Sabrina who was still stunned at the turn of events.

"Well Sabrina, do you want to look around before we eat and get settled? I'll show you where I spent the first happy years of my life, and some years that were not so happy."

Sabrina took Clay's offered hand and he led her on a tour of his childhood home.

The house was even larger than she had imagined, and she was fascinated, yet she felt something cold and unhappy lingering in this house for Clay. She felt it in the words he did not say and the firm hold he kept on her hand as he guided her about and explained each room to her.

He kept the room that had belonged to him for last as if he too were reluctant to open doors to the past.

It was a completely masculine room and Sabrina could sense Clay in everything in it. The furniture was large and solid. Oval rugs were laid in strategic places on a glittering hardwood floor.

Bookshelves lined two walls, and were filled with books that Sabrina was sure had been well used.

One wall had several quite beautiful sketches framed and hung in a rather random pattern. The other had two large oil paintings, one of a very handsome man whose appearance was so much like Clay's that she knew instantly he was Clay's father. She gazed at the woman whose likeness hung beside the first.

She was beautiful, with ebony black hair and the same startling blue eyes as her son.

Sabrina turned to look at Clay and before he could mask his thoughts she read the painful memories there.

She slid her arms about his waist and looked up at him.

"I love you, Clay. You're my strength and all my hope for a future. You're all those things to me and I want to be that for you. Don't look back, Clay. When this is over we'll go home. Back to the place that holds only good thoughts for us. Back to the place we found each other. We'll start over," she rose on tiptoe to kiss him lingeringly, "and I'll give you a son, Clay, to replace any past hurt you might have had."

She was rewarded by the warm glow of love in his eyes and the tightening of his hard arms about her. He bent his head and took her mouth in a warm breathless kiss that told her as no words ever could that the words she had said had effectively chased away any ghosts of the past that had lingered.

"My innocent," he murmured, "always my sweet loving innocent. You have the sweetest way of sending the ghosts scurrying. I love you, Sabrina, and you're right. One day soon we'll go home."

"And I'll have our son there," she said so positively that he had to laugh.

"I suppose if you say it's going to be a boy it'll just have to be. But after knowing the wonder of Summer, I don't care if it's boy or girl, just as long as it's ours and we're together."

Her pleased laughter was silenced by a hard seeking mouth that captured hers in a fierce demanding kiss.

"Come," he said huskily, "I don't want to scandalize Paul and his wife by holding up the meal they've prepared while I tumble you into my bed, and my self-control can't take anymore anyway."

They laughed together as they again descended the stairs.

The meal, though prepared quickly, was quite good, and soon after it both she and Clay realized Paul and his wife had set the scene and discreetly left.

A low burning fire had been laid in the drawing room, and Clay and Sabrina sat comfortably before it and talked. But soon talking was not enough for either of them.

Arms about each other, they walked the steps to Clay's

room.

Tonight seemed to both of them, to be something rare and very special. They slowed the pace of their rising passions to linger over each sweet kiss, each gentle touch until they could control it no longer. With a blinding surge of white hot passion, they came together. Each filled the need of the other to overflowing, surrendering completely to the joy of sharing a love so fulfilling that it left them breathless and weak and clinging to each other.

They slept, completely sated and content. Even in such sleep, Clay held Sabrina close to him. Because even in sleep he was touched with the fear of losing her.

Clay woke the next morning to find Sabrina, resting on one elbow, gazing at him.

She had been awake for several minutes and had been content to lie so.

She had allowed her gaze to stray hungrily over him, framing a picture for her mind to hold.

She watched the steady rise and fall of his broad chest. He lay on his back with his face turned toward her and she had the unrestricted freedom to examine him.

His features, usually firm and hard, had softened in sleep and gave him a vulnerable little boy look that made her reach out a gentle finger and touch his cheek. His thick black hair fell over his forehead in a tousled mass.

She let her gaze move slowly down. Broad strong shoulders, heavily muscled arms, a slim waist and long lean muscular hips. It roused a deep warmth within her and she knew she would always feel this deep longing hunger.

Gently she laid her hand on his hip and slid it up along his lean ribs until it rested on his chest.

It was only then that she lifted her eyes and was again startled by the intense blue fire that reached within her and filled her with the reassurance of a true and fulfilling love.

"Good morning, love," he smiled. "You needn't stop just because I'm awake. What you were doing is quite interesting."

She laughed and rested against him, a soft warm curvacious woman who stirred him to again reach for the magic only they would know.

It was another hour before they went down to breakfast.

They were silent now, knowing this new day meant separation for a long time.

Both gained their strength from each other, yet within both tasted fear and uncertainty of the future.

Thirty-seven

They rode in the same silence toward the office of the magistrate. Clay held Sabrina's hand tight, giving her the only reassurance he could. There was no other way. If he did not have her surrender herself they would come for her and Clay knew how that would look at her trial, as if she had tried to run away again.

In front of the large stone building the carriage halted and Clay helped a white-faced, trembling Sabrina from the carriage. She clung to his arm as they walked inside.

Both were surprised, not only to see Thomas already there, but a magistrate that was not the one Clay's family had known, a complete stranger.

"Well," Thomas said in a smug pleased voice that immediately roused Clay's anger, and his suspicions. The suspicions were soon to be realized as Thomas continued.

"It is good you are here. The magistrate was about to send someone to find you."

"You know damn well that wasn't necessary. I had already given my word Sabrina would surrender herself."

"Yes, of course," Thomas replied in a voice that spoke eloquently of his disbelief. He and the magistrate exchanged a look that annoyed Clay and stirred again his deep feeling that something was very wrong.

Clay did his best to ignore him as Sabrina's hand tightened on his arm. He turned to the magistrate.

"The usual procedure is to sign the papers and pass a bond, which I shall do. Sabrina will be at my home until the trial."

"Well . . . ah . . . I'm afraid, Mr. Storm, that will not be possible this time."

"What are you talking about?" Clay demanded.

"It has been brought to my attention that this woman ran away from the crime she committed. That negates any such procedure. She will be incarcerated in the prison until her trial."

Clay's eyes switched to a satisfied Thomas.

"I'll just bet it's been drawn to your attention," he said coldly. "The word of a Storm and a high bond should be enough. You can't expect to lock a woman up in that place when it's not necessary. She'll be here for her trial."

"No, Mr. Storm," the magistrate said firmly, "she will be put in prison until her trial. There will be no bond. Please don't do anything foolish, Mr. Storm," he added as he read Clay's rage-filled eyes. "I have plenty of men here to enforce my rule. A short time in prison for her shouldn't be a thing you would choose to die for."

Clay started toward the magistrate who stepped back rapidly. But Sabrina held Clay's arm and called out to his blind anger.

"No, Clay, no!" she said. "It's all right, Clay. I'll be all right. If you get the lawyer and defend me, I can bear a short time in there. Please Clay, I need you. Don't let them do anything to you. Please Clay!"

He turned to her, anguish in his eyes.

"A prison, Sabrina, for God's sake it's not necessary. You could stay with me. It's been done before. I can't let you! I can't!"

"Clay," she whispered, "it's what he wants, for you to fight. Don't you see, you're my only defense and he wants to be rid of you. Please, Clay . . . don't give him the chance."

Clay realized she was right, but it took all the control he had not to fight back.

The magistrate called in two of his men who were to take Sabrina to the prison.

"I will go with her," Clay said firmly. "And don't tell me there's a rule against that."

"You can go . . . but you cannot stay."

Clay accompanied Sabrina, refusing to look at Thomas again for fear he would lose what control he had and attack him.

It was only a matter of a mile or so to the prison. Clay remained quiet, as did Sabrina. Once inside the huge stone edifice they walked down the long silent stone hall, their feet clicking sharply on the hard floor. It was the hollow echo of that sound that accompanied them to the door of the cell in which Sabrina would be locked.

The door creaked open and Clay and Sabrina went inside. The two men waited outside the cell for Clay.

The cell was eight feet long and six wide. It contained only a low bunk on which to sleep and an evil smelling hole in a far corner to use for physical relief.

One small window six feet from the floor was the only light for the day, and the stub of a candle that sat on a stone niche cut into the wall would be the only light by night.

"Sabrina, for God's sake," Clay breathed as he looked about him. "I can't leave you here for long. I shall go immediately and find someone who can pressure some sense into that magistrate. He'll soon find out the Storm name still carries some weight in the courts here."

Sabrina moved into Clay's arms and felt them tighten securely about her.

"Clay, I have a feelilng that Thomas has done something, somehow to sway the court. Please, I'll be all right. You need to help me more in court than here."

"Dammit Sabrina, I just can't leave you in a place like this."

She pressed her cheek against his chest and listened to the thundering anger of his heartbeat as he held her close to him.

"Don't you know yet, Clay," she whispered, "that I'm never alone. You are with me always. Your strength and love will stay with me. I'll be all right. You must do what has to be done to get me free."

Clay looked down into wide purple eyes as he cupped her face in his hands. Tears touched her long dark lashes and he brushed her cheek and tasted the salt of them.

"I know you are right, Sabrina, but it is so hard to leave you."

"I won't say that I am not frightened for you know I would be lying. But I have faith. We'll find a way to be together when this terrible nightmare is over. I just must tell them the truth. Surely the jury will understand I was only defending myself when I struck Clyde. I did not mean to kill him."

Clay was well aware of Sabrina's deep belief in the goodness of people. His sweet innocent had no way of absorbing the real truth of people like Thomas and their influence on others. She believed, and for now he could not shatter that belief. He knew he had much work to do to defend her properly and see her free and safe again.

"Sabrina, I'm afraid I have to leave you now, but it won't be for long. I'm going to go and see that Ellen is safely settled with her brother. Her testimony is important. I'm also going to see if I can find a way to make this place a little better. I'll be back as soon as I can."

"Yes . . . I know," Sabrina replied in a voice that searched for strength and lost. Her arms tightened about him and he held her until he felt her regain her equilibrium. She looked up at him again, her eyes swimming in tears, yet a tremulous smile on her face.

Gently he touched his lips to hers in a kiss of promise.

"I'll be back soon," he whispered, yet he found it the most difficult thing he had ever done in his life to loosen his hold and step back from her.

She stood in the center of the dark cell, her hands clasped together before her, tears on her cheeks. To him she looked so helpless and vulnerable that he had to fight a terrible battle just to smile reassuringly at her.

"I love you Sabrina. Remember that always. I won't let anything separate us for long. Some way I'll get you free. Just always remember . . . I love you."

She nodded, aware that her throat was so constricted by the agony of separation and the fear of the future she could not speak.

Then suddenly the room seemed cold and empty, for Clay was gone. She winced at the resounding slam of the large heavy door. At that moment she felt more alone and frightened than at any other time in her life.

She walked to the low cot and sat down. Then she buried her face in her hands and wept tears she had refused to shed while Clay was there.

Clay walked down the long hall and out into the midmorning sun. He gazed up at the bright sky and his heart ached with the thought of Sabrina in the dark place he had left her.

At that moment, he desired nothing more than to return to their cabin with her and walk by the stream together. Grimly, he called for a carriage and set out for the offices of the man who had been Eustice Waverly's lawyer.

When he walked into Mr. Chapin's office, a young clerk looked up expectantly.

"May I help you sir?"

"Yes, I must see Mr. Chapin immediately."

"I'm sorry sir, but that's impossible. Mr. Chapin is in conference with a client. You can make an appointment to see him . . . ah . . . day after tomorrow."

"I'm afraid that won't do," Clay said. "I have to see him today . . . now."

"But . . . that can't be done sir, he's really much too busy."

Clay walked close to the young man and his eyes were so frigid and filled with threat that the young man backed away.

"You, my young friend, will go in and inform Mr. Chapin that I am here to ask him questions about the death of Eustice Waverly. Tell him also that I'm the husband of Sabrina McNeil and I need some answers if we're to save her life."

"Y . . . yes . . . s . . . sir," the young man mumbled as he hastily retreated before the threat of violence he saw in Clay's face.

The clerk disappeared into the inner office. Clay waited only a few minutes to see him reappear followed by a large portly man.

The man gazed at Clay with both shock and pleasure in his eyes.

"Please," he said, "please come into my office. I am so grateful to hear about Sabrina's whereabouts. I have been worried to death about that child. Come in, come in and let us talk."

Clay accompanied Mr. Chapin into the office and watched as the man closed the door. He waved toward a seat opposite his desk.

"Sit down please. I've a million questions to ask you.

Would you care for a drink?"

"Yes," Clay said, "I know it's a little early, but I could use a drink."

Mr. Chapin poured a drink and handed it to Clay who took a deep swallow and sat back in his chair.

"Now, can you tell me what happened to Sabrina. I never knew anything except that she disappeared not too long after the will was read. Then I heard Thomas shouting murder."

"Which you didn't believe?" Clay said.

"Good heavens man, that child could never have committed murder. I would have defended her with my life if I could have found her."

Clay was watching Chapin closely and somehow he knew the man spoke the truth.

"Mr. Chapin, it might be best if we start from the beginning. You tell me all that happened before and I'll tell you all that happened after she disappeared. Maybe if we put the two stories together, we can come up with the answers."

Chapin agreed and soon was telling Clay how Sabrina was orphaned young and Eustice had taken her in to raise her.

"Eustice loved that child like his own daughter. That's why I can't understand him leaving Waverly Hall to his brother-in-law and Sabrina in his care. He knew the child was afraid of both of them."

"Why didn't you help her contest the will?"

"Dammit man!" Chapin said, his face reddening. "I would have if I'd had the chance. I never got another opportunity to talk to Sabrina. I was going to ask her to let me do just that, but Clyde was killed and she was gone before I had a chance. I cared for that girl too, and my wife and I would have been more than pleased if she had decided to leave Waverly Hall and come to live with us."

"Well, I can't tell you what happened that night or the

next few days, but I can tell you how she got to me," Clay said. He went on to explain to Chapin all that had happened.

"Now she needs someone to defend her in court. The trial will mean her life and she needs all the friends she can get."

"You need say no more young man, I would defend her with my life. I shall go and see her tomorrow. There must be a way out of this and if God wills it, I will find it," Chapin replied.

Neither man had touched on the one occasion that might have cleared the mystery. Clay had no reason to ask if Chapin had been witness to the changing of the will and Chapin did not think of it.

They talked for quite some time, then Chapin assured Clay he would do everything in his power to get Sabrina free.

Clay rose when Chapin was finished and extended his hand to Chapin who took it in a firm grasp.

"I have one more thing to tell you," Clay said. Chapin waited.

"Sabrina is expecting a child."

"Good God, to be in a place like that at such a time must be dreadful."

"There's no way you can get her out temporarily?"

"I doubt it. You can see a fine hand in this that wants to keep her there. I shall see if I can get a quick date for a trial. The sooner this is over the sooner you two will be together again."

Clay smiled at Chapin's effort to show confidence.

"We'll be together," he responded.

"What do you plan to do?"

"There's a law against taking Sabrina out of there," Clay said, "but . . . is there a law against someone else going in?"

"Why, no," Chapin's eyes began to glow in a smile of deep

respect. "You intend to join her there?"

"I certainly don't intend to leave her alone. If I can't get her free at the moment, I can at least make her know she's not alone."

"Young man," Chapin replied, "Sabrina has done well for herself. She has what few people ever really have, a love that knows sacrifice."

"It wasn't always so. Sabrina, in her own sweet way, has taught me a lot. I just want her to always know I'm grateful and that I'm beside her."

"I'll bet," Chapin chuckled, "it is one thing Thomas has never thought about. He is in for a rude awakening. Her friends and you will rally around her and he will get the surprise of his life."

"I'm going to my home to get some things to make Sabrina more comfortable. If there is anything you need, you can find me at the prison. Spare no expense. We have a fight on our hands, and it's a fight I intend to win. I have too much at stake to even think of losing."

"I'll do that my boy, I'll do that."

"Good-bye for now, Mr. Chapin."

"Good-bye."

Clay left, and Chapin sat for some time at his desk in silence, wondering what it was that he felt he should remember. It nagged at his memory but he finally had to put it aside and concentrate on some kind of plan.

Clay returned to his home. The first thing he did was to send a detailed message to Ellen and her brother telling them all that had transpired. Then he set about gathering things he would take with him. Warm blankets and food, a change of clothes for himself and Sabrina and a purse filled with coins he knew he could use to bribe the jailer to get anything else they might need. A few hours later he was again on his way to the jail.

He had been right. Although the jailer was amazed that anyone would want to spend any time in the jail of his own free will, he was easily bribed. Clay gave him enough money to widen his eyes with a greedy look, and a promise of more to come. A few minutes after he had arrived at the jail, Clay again walked down the long stone hallway to Sabrina's cell.

He stood while the jailer unlocked the door, impatient with his slowness.

"Don't forget to have all the things I brought carried in here."

"I won't sir, they'll be along in a little while."

The man turned to go, but Clay stopped him. He looked up at Clay in surprise. Clay held out his hand.

"I'll take the key."

"Sir?"

"I'll take the key. We'll lock ourselves in. That way there won't be any mistakes made."

The man would have argued, but a cold blue gaze sent a shiver of fear down his spine. A coward by nature, he had no intention of angering a man who looked as if he not only could break him in two but would if given the slightest provocation. Besides, he relished the thought of more of the gold coins the tall cold eyed man carried. He dropped the key in Clay's hand. Clay watched him walk away, then he turned and pushed the cell door open, stepped inside and closed it behind him.

Even in dimmer light, Sabrina would have recognized the tall broad shouldered form that stood just inside the door. She rose slowly from the bunk.

"Clay," she whispered in a choked voice.

Without a word he went to her and drew her slim form into his arms. He felt the cold chill of her body slowly warm. Felt the trembling cease and the aura of despair fade as she clung to him and let the warmth and security of him fill her with peace.

"Oh Clay," she said softly, "only a few hours and I have missed you so desperately. When you left, I felt as if my heart had ceased to beat. Hold me, Clay. Even if it's only for a little while. Hold me, and I can keep the fear away."

"Not for a little while, love," he said softly as he kissed the top of her head lightly. She looked up at him, questions in her eyes. He smiled.

"I'm staying here with you until this is over."

"Clay, this horrible cell."

"Don't you know love, I'd rather share a cell with you than to be in that mansion alone knowing you are so alone too? A little money can do a lot of things. I've brought some things along to make it a little easier."

She tried to smile, but he saw fresh tears fill her eyes and escape to trace lines down her cheeks.

"I love you, Clay. I don't suppose I really knew just how much until this moment."

"And I love you, Sabrina. You've taught me something about loving I had never known before. It's not just the feel and taste of your sweet loving. It's the unselfish giving . . . it's the sharing . . . it's so many things I had never known before you. We'll see this through together, then we'll go home and begin again. I want to start a whole new life and fill it with all the meaning I never understood until now."

"Clay . . . what if . . . ?"

"Shhh love. We don't speak of what if. It will be, just have faith. I've found too much to lose it now. We'll make it, love . . . we'll make it."

Before she could speak again, the jailer and another man returned with all the bundles Clay had brought with him.

The bundles were dropped inside and the two men left. Clay immediately went to the door and locked it.

Then he began to undo the bundles, and Sabrina was surprised at all they contained. Candles to light the cell, food and wine. Clothes for her to change into. A large container of water and cloths for her to wash with. What delighted her was that he even remembered to bring a brush for her hair. He watched her pleasure as she washed her face and hands and picked up the brush for her hair. She was surprised when he came to her and took it from her hand. He took her hand and led her to the cot where he sat and drew her down on his lap. Then he proceeded to brush her hair until it was tangle free and he could slide his fingers through it. He sat back with his back braced against the wall, then he turned her around until she rested in against him. He cradled her in his arms and they sat so in silence, content just to be together and to hold each other.

Clay was aware now, for the first time in his life, that loving was so much more than just physical possession. It was not what one took but what one gave that was the most important. He thought of all he had taken from Singing Bells, and vowed he would never make that mistake again in his life. He had acquired the ability to share and he knew it was the greatest gift Sabrina could have given him.

The night passed slowly. They ate seated on a blanket on the floor. When it was time to sleep they lay together on the bunk and he held her. He refused to try to possess her in this evil place and was content just to hold her while she slept, praying for a future together that they could share more completely.

He lay his hand gently against her belly, knowing his child, the treasure of their love, was slowly evolving within. Boy or girl? It didn't matter. He thought of Summer and all that he had taken from her. Silently he promised the one power that could feel his thoughts, that if he could get Sabrina free he would rebuild all their lives and try to give each of the ones he loved what they needed most, the freedom to love him in their own way.

Sabrina sighed deeply and contentedly and drew closer to him as if somehow she could feel his thoughts and they had reached within her to touch the well of her love.

She stirred and murmured his name. He held her and brushed a light kiss on her half parted lips.

"I love you, Sabrina," he whispered, "and somehow I'll get you free. I swear."

After a while, he too slept.

Thirty-eight

It was a week before Chapin could get the date of the trial and he was surprised that it was a little more than another week away. Surprised until he informed Clay who scowled and replied.

"He's afraid. Somehow he wants to hurry this thing up. There's something we haven't found out and he's afraid we will."

"What? In God's name man, what? We have so little defense as it is. We've got to find out what it is he's afraid of."

"I'm trying. I've got a lot of people searching for any clue. They've come up with some pretty nasty things about old Clyde and Thomas but nothing that would help Sabrina prove her innocence.   How is the child doing? Does she need anything?"

"No, I've provided everything except her freedom, and that's the only thing she needs now."

"Clay, if you're going back there this afternoon, will you ask her again about visitors? My wife and I would like to visit her as friends instead of the two times I've seen her as a clilent."

"It's better she's not getting a lot of visitors. She seems to prefer it that way, and I don't want to do anything to upset her. She's going through enough now."

"Clay . . . ah . . . I must ask you something."

"What?"

"I want you to understand what I'm going to say."

"What is it?"

"Do you intend to testify in her behalf?"

"Of course! What kind of question is that?"

"I wish you wouldn't."

"Why?"

"Clay, don't pace like that and don't look so angry. You make me fear for my safety."

Clay sat down and tried to keep the look of wild anger from his face.

"Why shouldn't I testify for her? I love her. What should I do, just stand around and helplessly watch?"

"Clay . . . I'm going to question you as the prosecutor would. You must answer my questions without explanations . . . and remember, you will be under oath."

"All right, go on," Clay replied.

Chapin stood up and walked to Clay's chair. He looked down on Clay with a rather suggestive smile on his face.

"Mr. Storm . . . how do you know Sabrina McNeil?"

Clay answered that he had bought her services as an indentured servant.

"I see. Is that your only relationship?"

"What are you suggesting?"

"Just answer the question."

"No . . . it isn't."

"Well then just what is your . . . relationship?" Chapin said in a voice that suggested what he thought might be.

"She is my wife," Clay said angrily.

"Oh? And when and where were you married?"

Clay's face began to register what Chapin hoped he would understand.

"In an Indian village near my home," he said quietly.

"I see," Chapin said again. "Tell me, did you sleep with

her before you were married?"

"Chapin!" Clay said angrily.

"Answer the question."

"Yes."

"Was she pregnant when she entered this . . . so-called marriage," Chapin leered.

"No!"

"Is she now?" he retorted quickly.

"Yes!" Clay stormed, his face dark with anger.

"I suggest Mr. Storm that the girl was promiscuous before you knew her."

"Chapin," Clay resisted.

"I also suggest she had relations with her very own uncle. I also suggest she thought that the Waverly wealth was hers and when she found it was not, she tried to seduce her uncle into sharing it. When he would not she killed him!"

"Dammit!"

"She killed him in cold blood!"

"No!" Clay said as he leaped to his feet, his face filled with rage.

They stood face to face and Chapin's face grew sympathetically gentle.

"I'm sorry Clay."

"For God's sake. That man wouldn't ask questions like that?"

"No?" Chapin said softly, "try to testify and see."

"But Sabrina . . ."

"I'm going to try to keep her off the stand too. I shall try to use witnesses for her character."

"I think," Clay said softly, "this is the first moment I've really become afraid. I thought I had only to defend her from murder, not the assassination of her soul."

"He wants to convict her," Chapin replied, "and he will use any means to do it."

"I would like to kill that man myself. How can he subject a woman like Sabrina to a thing as foul as that?"

Chapin sighed. "Because he is as he is. It is not the first time I have recognized the animal in the disguise of man."

"Still . . . we must get her free."

"Yes, we must. I shall do everything in my power. Clay, I must say one more thing no matter how much you dread to hear it."

"Say it."

"If she's convicted . . . "

"She won't be."

"If she's convicted," Chapin continued, "you will be given permission to take her child when it is born."

Clay laughed angrily. "Convict her of murder, then take her child from her. Tell me, Chapin, can we do any more to her?"

"We can pray that somewhere, somehow, we, together can find all the answers to this and save her."

"I'm sorry, I didn't mean to condemn you, Chapin, it's just that I'm so worried."

"Of course I understand."

"We have eight days, Chapin, eight days. In that time I have to find some key, something to help us get her free."

"I shall do everything in court that I can to protect her. You must do the rest, you must go in search of the truth."

"I'm going to talk to Ellen and her brother again. Maybe they can remember something."

"I hope so," Chapin replied. He watched as Clay left the room.

Clay took a carriage to Lester's house so that he could talk to him and Ellen again before he returned to Sabrina. It hurt him to return to her night after night with no news and no new hope.

He was welcomed into Lester's home, but another hour

of questions without answers left them all more miserable than they had been before.

The only thing Clay had discovered in his quest so far was the character of Clyde and Thomas, but it was no proof that Sabrina was innocent.

No matter how he tried to hold the time back, no matter how poignantly sweet their nights were, the night before the trial finally came. They spent it together each trying to appear brave, each trying to hold the specter of fear at bay, and each needing the love of the other as they never had before.

The day of the trial opening brought spectators who had relished the rumors of the wealthy heiress who had killed her own uncle for a fortune.

They also came to see Clay, the man of mystery. The handsome dark man who was rumored to be the lover of the heiress. The courtroom was full when Sabrina was brought in. Clay had been refused permission to stay with her, in fact, was not allowed to be near her during the trial. He sat with Ellen and her brother. But he watched Sabrina and was proud of her straight slim body and lifted chin. She told everyone by her calm beauty that she was innocent and was sure the jury would find her so.

She sat alone in a small enclosed area. Thomas sat less than eight feet from her, but she refused to meet his satisfied questioning gaze. She had also refused to let Clay know of the note she had gotten from Thomas telling her she could still have her freedom if she would come to him in complete surrender. She had torn it into as many pieces as she could.

The trial proceeded slowly. Witnesses Clay was sure were hired for the occasion swore to the sterling character of both Clyde and Thomas. The prosecution attorney began to form his case by asking a clerk to stand as a representative for Chapin's office. He had been a witness at the reading of the will and told the damning story of how Sabrina had been disinherited and Clyde and Thomas had been willed Waverly Hall and all its wealth.

Witness after witness and slowly the case against Sabrina had begun to build. By the end of the first day, Sabrina was exhausted from keeping her facade. She lay in Clay's arms that night and wept with fear and weariness. When she slept in exhaustion he continued to hold her, but sleep was an elusive thing for he too was finally afraid he would lose her.

One day—two—three—each worse, more damning than the one before. Then the prosecution called Thomas to the stand. A hush fell over the crowd and Sabrina's face became even paler than before. Thomas walked to the witness box and was sworn in.

"Your name sir?"

"Thomas Mellon."

"You are related to the defendant?"

"Yes, I am her cousin by marriage."

"You lived in the same house with the defendant, your father, Clyde Mellon, and Eustice Waverly?"

"Yes sir, I did."

"Can you tell us, sir, the relationship between Eustice Waverly and the defendant?"

"I object," Chapin said, "he cannot know the exact relationship."

"Objection overruled," the judge replied.

"They were . . . ah . . . very close," Thomas replied. His slight smile and knowing look made the situation look soiled.

"How close?"

"Well, she spent a great deal of time in his bedroom alone with him. Of course," he added quickly, "I have no idea how they spent all those hours."

The crowd was pleased and a low murmur circulated slowly about.

"Would she have reason to believe she would inherit the Waverly fortune?"

"Eustice said it often enough. Although in private he assured my father and me it was quite a different story."

"He told you he had intentions of disinheriting her?"

"Yes, sir. In fact, he told us that he felt sure Sabrina would stay at Waverly Hall because the money was there. He also assured both of us that she would make whatever we spent on her well worth the money."

"That's a lie!" Sabrina shouted as she leapt to her feet. But she was soon silenced by the judge and forced back into her seat.

"Can you tell us to the best of your ability what happened the night your father died?"

"The three of us had a rather cosy dinner at home. Sabrina was drinking a little too much wine and she seemed determined to seduce both of us. She kept making seductive suggestions all evening, and she couldn't keep her hands from touching. She actually acted . . . hungry. Finally she sent all the servants home. She stood on the bottom step and asked both my father and I to come and share her bed that night. She was lonely since Eustice had died, she said, and she needed love. Then she went upstairs. At the top she turned and laughed and told us both to hurry for it promised to be a warm and exciting evening.

"My father seemed captured by her, but I was not. I warned him not to go, but he refused to listen. He walked up the stairs and put his arm about her. She kissed him and they walked down the hall together toward her bedroom. I went to bed, and the next day I found my father dead and Sabrina gone."

Clay clenched his fists, refusing to give the sensation-hungry crowd more gossip to savor. The prosecutor turned to Mr. Chapin.

"You may cross-examine."

"I have no questions at this moment, but I would like to recall this witness at a later time."

Such permission was granted and Thomas left the stand.

The prosecution rested its case, and the judge adjourned until the next day. Clay watched as Sabrina's dejected form was led away.

That night Sabrina could not eat. She was so silent that it disturbed Clay, and she seemed to only be at ease when he held her. He did just that. Held her and tried his best to soothe her.

The next morning he was awakened by the jailer who told him a message had come from Mr. Chapin to meet him early.

It was still several hours before court convened that Clay and Chapin had coffee together and again discussed the case.

No matter which way their thoughts and ideas went they seemed to run up against the same wall. Thomas's testimony.

"That bastard," Clay gritted, "if I ever get my hands on him I shall take great pleasure in strangling him. How can he say such things about her like that?"

"To see an end to his purpose. Clay, no matter how I turn this thing, I read the will and I know it was left to the Mellons. I still get this feeling that it is still the culprit."

"You knew Eustice Waverly well. Why did you not try to dissuade him the day he changed the will?"

"Don't you think I would have if I could?"

"Why couldn't you?"

"I wasn't there."

"What do you mean you weren't there?"

"Just that. He called for me to come out to Waverly Hall. He said he had some new ideas to put in his will. I was sick and couldn't go so I sent an assistant of mine. When he returned, he filed the new will. I did not get a chance to read it for some time. When I did, Eustice Waverly was already dead."

The two of them sat looking at each other as the same thoughts filled their heads. Was this will a forgery of some sort? Did the Mellons tamper with the law to acquire a fortune . . . and if so . . . how did they do it? Chapin spoke again with a touch of mixed anger and shock in his voice.

"The man who was my assistant at the time is no longer with me."

"What was his name?"

"Jacob Poltice."

"Where is he now?"

"He came to me a few weeks ago and told me his wife was ill and wanted to be near her parents. It was his reason for taking another position with a firm in his own town."

"I think it would be wise if I looked up this Jacob Poltice and asked him a few questions. Do you have the address where I can find him?"

"Yes, I do, but Clay, it will take you a day to get there and a day to get back. You will have to find him and get some answers fast if you want to be in time to save Sabrina."

"Let's get that address quickly. I shall leave immediately. You go and tell Sabrina where I'm going and what I'm doing. Tell her I love her and I'll get her free of this."

Chapin nodded and they both rose and went to Chapin's office where he found and gave the address to Clay. He returned to court just as procedures were starting. When Sabrina was brought in, he saw her gaze search for Clay and when she did not see him, he watched panic touch them. He went to her side and bent to whisper to her. He explained where Clay was going and why.

"I know you are frightened child, but have faith. If there

is a way, Clay will find it."

"Will he find it in time? How long can we keep these animals at bay?"

"Don't worry about that child. I shall call half of London as witnesses. I can drag my feet for as long as necessary."

Sabrina sat numbly for the balance of the day. She no longer cared to listen to the witnesses who were called one after another. Without Clay beside her, she felt her courage begin to drain away. She closed her heart to the wicked suggestive stares of the people in the courtroom and closed her ears to any words that were spoken. She allowed her memory to go back to sweeter moments. Times when she and Clay laughed together and reached to touch one another. The only defense she had without Clay was to reach for his memory and strength and allow it to surround her like a warm protective shield.

The day drew to a close and Sabrina was returned to her cell. Chapin visited her for a time, but even that had to come to an end. He was reluctant to leave her for she was so pale and entirely too quiet to suit him.

He sat beside her and took her hand in his.

"Sabrina child," he said sympathetically. She tried to smile.

"Why Mr. Chapin, what have I ever done to Thomas and those others to make them hate me so?"

"It's not what you've done child. It is what you are. You are sweet, kind, and beautiful both inside and out. They not only cannot understand such things they are too evil to tolerate it."

"Do you think Clay will find this Mr. . . . ?"

"Poltice, Jacob Poltice. I'm sure Clay will not leave any stone unturned until he does."

"Mr. Chapin . . . what if . . . even if the will was forged, what if he refuses to testify?"

Chapin laughed shortly. "Would you face an angry Clay Storm and refuse him anything?"

Sabrina tried to laugh but lost control, the laughter quickly turned to helpless tears and soon he was holding her while she wept.

"I'm sorry."

"No apologies, my dear, you are going through a terrible ordeal. You have a right to your tears."

I love Clay so much."

"And he loves you, child."

"I have caused him so much trouble."

"And given him so much love. I'm sure he feels the scale is more than balanced. Especially since you will give him a child. We are not defeated my dear. Have hope."

"Mr. Chapin," Sabrina said, alarm clear in her voice, "if . . . if I am convicted what will happen to my child?"

Her eyes were wide with renewed fear.

"If Clay will say he is the father it will be given to him. But we will not speak of such a thing. You will not be convicted and you will go home with your husband and child and live the rest of your lives together in peace."

He held her hand a little tighter.

"Sabrina, I must talk to you about tomorrow."

"Tomorrow?"

"I tried to keep you from the stand, but I cannot. If I am to get you free you must testify. You must be able to tell the story of what happened that night. Do you feel you can do it?"

"If I must, I will tell the truth. I never meant to kill him. I struck him in panic."

"Struck . . . once?"

"Yes, once, but his head was all bloody and I know I had hurt him badly. I did not think I had killed him. I only ran because I was afraid of what he could do when he regained

459

consciousness."

Mr. Chapin's brow was furrowed as if he were trying to remember something elusive.

"Sabrina, I must go back to my office and go over some reports. I hate to leave you alone, but it is of the utmost importance to your case. Will you be all right?"

"What is it Mr. Chapin?"

"I'm not sure yet, not until I read those papers over."

"It will be all right."

"Are you sure? I truly hate to leave you. Would you like me to send for Ellen, she could stay with you at least for a few hours?"

"No, Ellen is going through enough just being in that courtroom every day."

"She's to testify tomorrow."

"Poor Ellen."

"She's anxious to make her feeling known. She has such a violent dislike for Thomas that I have to keep her under some control."

"I know. She was always my protector when it came to Clyde and Thomas. I don't know what I would have done without her all this time."

"Keep remembering that, my dear. You have a lot of love on your side. If Clay is any measure, he has enough love to win the cause. We're all here to help you, and we will."

"I know . . . I guess Clay is my strength. He has always held me together. I miss him. But," she touched the still flat plane of her abdomen, "I know his love is here, and I shall always have faith in him. I'll be all right."

"Good girl," Chapin stood up. "Try to get some rest."

"I will."

"I'll see you in the morning."

Sabrina smiled and nodded and Chapin turned to leave. At the closing of the door Sabrina's smile faded and she sat in silence knowing she could not sleep until she again felt the warmth and security of Clay's arms.

The next day there was no sign of Clay. Ellen was called to the stand and sworn in. She told of the relationship between Sabrina and Eustice. She also told of the times she had intervened between Clyde, his son, and Sabrina.

It seemed to Sabrina that the jury was unreadable — even that they did not quite believe Ellen.

Lester was next to take the stand. He could say little except about Sabrina's fear when she came to him for help and her distress at the idea of having to defend herself against Clyde's advances. Still Sabrina was not sure if the jury accepted it. Thomas's testimony had been very effective.

Then came a heart stopping moment for Sabrina. A gasp sounded, then an excited murmur spread through the crowd as the next name was called.

"Sabrina McNeil."

Sabrina rose unsteadily and walked to the witness box. She was put under oath. Then she sat, her hands clasped in her lap to keep them from trembling.

She knew now that she wanted Clay more at this moment than she ever had before.

Mr. Chapin rose from his seat and walked to her. He smiled reassuringly, hoping to give her courage for he knew the cross examination was going to be difficult for her.

He questioned Sabrina about the deaths of her parents.

"How old were you when Eustice Waverly took you in?"

"I was nine or ten."

"What was your relationship with Eustice Waverly from that day?"

"He was like a father to me."

"Did he ever tell you he meant Waverly Hall and the Waverly fortune to be yours one day?"

"Yes, but I didn't care. I didn't want the money. I loved

Waverly Hall, but I loved my uncle more."

"After your uncle's death were you surprised to find he had given everything to his brother-in-law, Clyde Mellon, and his nephew Thomas?"

"Yes, I was. But I still didn't care about the money. I loved my uncle. I wanted him to live. He could have given the money to anyone, I didn't care. He understood how I felt. He knew how Clyde and Thomas treated me."

"Will you explain to us just what happened the night Clyde Mellon died?"

Sabrina went on to explain all that had happened from the reading of the will until Clyde attacked her in her room.

The jury and all the spectators remained silent, listening intently to her story.

When she finished there was a breathless silence. It was clear the audience had thoroughly enjoyed the story and hoped there would be more. To Sabrina, it felt as if they were all licking their lips like huge cats waiting at a mousehole.

"I did not mean to kill him," she said in a tired voice. "I was only defending myself. I could never kill anyone. If he had just let me alone . . . if he had just let me alone."

"Sabrina, I have one more question for the record."

"Yes?"

"You struck Clyde Mellon once with a glass decanter?"

"Yes."

"Then?"

"Then . . . then I ran for I was so terribly frightened."

"But you struck him once?"

"Yes."

"I have no more questions."

Chapin sat down and the prosecutor rose. Sabrina felt a tingle of real fear as he walked toward her.

Thirty-nine

Clay stepped down from his carriage in front of the rather shabby looking brownstone building. He took the piece of paper from his pocket and looked at it, comparing it to the number on the building.

The two numbers the same, he walked to the door. He rapped sharply and waited a few minutes, then he rapped again.

The door was opened by a woman of about fifty. She held herself rigidly erect. Her face was long and thin, the eyes narrow as if she were perpetually suspicious of everyone.

Her mouth, pulled taut, was thin and fine and the nose pinched and thin. She gave Clay the impression she would be disagreeable. Her first answers confirmed this.

"I'm looking for a Mr. Jacob Poltice. I was told at his office I could find him here."

"Shouldn't be surprised," she said arrogantly. "He's probably been drinking again and he most likely had no clients to keep him there."

"He does live here?" Clay questioned patiently.

"He does."

"I should like to see him. It is very important, in fact a matter of life or death."

"You can go on up to his room and knock. If he lets you

in, then you can talk to him."

Glad to be away from this stringent woman, Clay moved to pass her. Once inside, he waited while she closed the door. She turned and looked at him expectantly.

"The room," he reminded gently, "what room is he in?"

"Oh. Go to the top of the stairs, he's at the end of the hall on the right."

"Thank you."

He turned and walked up the stairs without offering any information. He could feel her eyes on him.

He walked down the hall and found the right door. He stood for a minute wondering just how far he would have to go to get the information he needed from Jacob Poltice.

He knocked. He did not know just what to expect. He wondered why a man who was a trained lawyer, who had worked with a prestigious man like Chapin, found himself in a position such as this. It was obvious he had fallen on hard times.

The door was opened a few inches and a face appeared in the aperture.

"Mr. Poltice?"

"Yes, what do you want?" the ragged voice said.

"I'd like to speak to you Mr. Poltice, may I come in?"

"No! No you may not come in. Who are you and what do you want with me?"

"Please Mr. Poltice. A young woman's life is at stake. I must talk to you."

"Young woman . . . who . . . what do I have to do with her?"

Clay had not wanted to mention Sabrina's name until he was safely inside, but now he had to.

"It's about Sabrina McNeil and the Waverly estate."

The man's face grew pale and he tried to slam the door but Clay's hand was too quick — he reached out to hold it open.

But there was a restraining chain that would not let the door open.

He watched as Jacob tried again to force the door closed, then Jacob turned and he heard him start to move rapidly away. He knew he could not let him get away, Sabrina's life depended upon it. He threw his shoulder against the door and it flew open, torn from its hinges.

He caught sight of Jacob's form fleeing through an adjoining room and quickly gave chase. His long, heavily muscled legs gave him an advantage and in moments he caught up with Jacob. He grasped him firmly by the shoulder and spun him about. Jacob lashed out feebly against Clay with no hope of matching the tremendous strength that held him.

"Dammit man," Clay panted angrily as he held Jacob firmly, "there's no sense or reason to run from me. I only need a few answers."

"Leave me alone. I don't know who you are or anything about what you want. I don't know any Sabrina McNeil!"

"Then why do you run?"

Jacob again tried to wiggle free but Clay was much larger and much stronger.

"You have my answers," Clay said, "and you can save a life, maybe make up for the harm you have done."

"I don't know anything!"

Clay spun Jacob about. His face was a thundercloud of violent anger, his eyes a glittering blue threat of more violence to come. At the touch of that relentless ice blue gaze, Jacob seemed to wilt. His face screwed into a pain filled look, and for a moment Clay thought he might weep. But he regained control of himself and resigned himself to the fact that there was no longer any escape.

"I told him," he rasped, "I knew something like this would happen. I warned him he never should have done it. Greedy he was . . . always greedy. He wanted the money, and he wanted the girl."

"Come back and sit down," Clay said as he pushed the trembling Jacob before him. "We have a lot for you to explain."

Jacob sat down in a chair before Clay. Now he seemed to be completely subdued.

"What . . . what do you want to know?" he asked Clay in a weak unhappy voice.

"You were employed in Chapin's office?"

"Yes, I was."

"How did the Mellons get to you?" Clay asked softly.

"Money," Jacob laughed shortly, "money. I needed a great deal of it."

"Why?"

"I . . . I had . . . altered some funds. Chapin would have sent me to prison. I needed money and Clyde Mellon found out. I don't know how."

"Tell me the rest of the story."

Jacob sighed deeply, clasped his hands before him, and began to tell Clay just how Clyde and Thomas had exchanged one will for another.

"The will he exchanged, everything was left to Sabrina?"

"That old man loved that girl like his own daughter. We had been invited to dinner many times, and you could see it. She felt the same for him. He would have given her everything while he was still alive but she wouldn't take it. She asked him for nothing, but she gave him everything. She made him happy . . . that's something very few of us ever know."

"So when he died, he left everything to Sabrina, the house, the money, everything?"

"Yes, he did."

"How did they manage the forgery?"

"I'm not sure," Jacob went on to tell him about the exchange that occurred in the buggy a few miles from Waverly Hall.

"I'm sure," Clay said. "When we get the will examined a little more closely we'll be able to prove just what it is, but it would be easier to find who did the forgery."

"I don't know," Jacob repeated. "I just don't know who did the forgery."

"You have to come back and testify," Clay said levelly.

"If I testify that he forged the will . . . that he cheated that girl . . . it won't do any good. You said she was on trial for Clyde Mellon's murder?"

"Yes."

"You want her free?"

"Yes."

Jacob looked up into Clay's questioning eyes. Suddenly he seemed to come to a decision. His face seemed to regain some semblance of the man he might have been.

"I can do something," Jacob said softly, "that will save . . . both of us."

Their eyes held each other for a quiet moment.

"You come with me to find another man who is involved."

"We haven't much time. The trial is going on now. There's not much to protect Sabrina."

"Come with me. It will only take a few hours. This man will have to be taken by force, but believe me my testimony and his will change everything."

"What does he know that's so important?"

Jacob began to speak again and Clay's eyes widened in shock as he heard the rest of his words.

Edgar Swishbury was a prosecutor who boasted a record

for convictions of felons. When he thought he was justified he was as relentless as a bulldog. He had known Eustice Waverly's reputation for being a good and upright man, and he felt justified trying to bring Sabrina to face the consequences for what she had done.

He walked toward her now, prepared to rip her testimony to little pieces.

"Miss McNeil," he smiled, but Sabrina was well aware that it was not a friendly smile. "Eustice Waverly adopted you legally?"

"No, there was never a formal adoption. I was the child of his sister and he took me in to care for me when tragedy struck my life."

"The death of your parents?"

"Yes."

"Tell me Miss McNeil, did you believe your uncle intended for you to inherit his estate?"

"Yes, I did, but . . ."

"Thank you," Edgar replied quickly, "now, why did you believe so?"

"He . . . he told me."

"Why would he disinherit the rest of his family?"

"He . . . he didn't like them . . . he didn't trust them."

"He told you this?"

"Well . . . not exactly, but . . . I knew, I felt . . ."

"You felt. You were very sensitive to Eustice Waverly's emotions?"

"I understood him. I loved him."

"I see," again he smiled, and the jury read his innuendo well.

"Now Miss McNeil, when you heard the will read, you were very upset. Did the will make you angry with your Uncle Clyde?"

"I wasn't angry; I was just . . . disbelieving."

Miss McNeil," he said softly. The people became silent, everyone waited expectantly for the next question. "Are you pregnant?"

There was a stir . . . an excited murmur. Then Sabrina answered.

"Yes, I am."

"Who is the father of your child?"

"Clayton Storm."

"Are you married to Clayton Storm?" he said, his voice filled with feigned surprise. "I'm sorry, I've been calling you Miss McNeil. Should I be calling you Mrs. Storm?"

"Well . . . s . . . sort of."

"Sort of," he chuckled in a fatherly fashion. "How can one be married sort of? Where were the nuptials performed?"

"In an Indian village near Clay's home."

Now soft laughter touched the crowd.

"Well *Miss* McNeil. Since that is not legal in the white community . . . then you are not married to Clay Storm."

Sabrina's head bent, and her hands twisted nervously in her lap. She wanted Clay.

"You fled from this country after killing your uncle. You ran to a man you were willing to sleep with without benefit of marriage. You carry his child now. Are we to believe, Miss McNeil, that you were innocent of any evil thoughts toward your uncle? Are we to believe you were so pure you had to resist the advances of your uncle by killing him, yet you went to a man's bed willingly who was no more than a stranger to you."

"No, it wasn't like that!" Sabrina cried.

"You admit you lived in his home?"

"As an indentured servant."

"Then he took you against your will?"

"No . . . no . . . I . . ."

"Come Miss McNeil. Did Clayton Storm rape you?"

"No," she replied softly.

"Then you went to his bed of your own free will?"

"Yes," came a soft whispered reply.

"And yet you resisted your uncle?"

"Yes."

"I submit, Miss McNeil, that you did not resist."

"I did!"

"I submit that you not only did not resist, but you led him on."

"No."

"You wanted your uncle's money."

"No, I didn't."

"You wanted it enough to plan murder."

"I didn't . . . I didn't!"

"You led your uncle to believe you liked him . . . were interested in him."

"No! no! no!"

"You led him to believe if he would share the money, you would share his bed."

"I never did that."

"Then that night he came to you."

"He tried to rape me," Sabrina cried.

"He came to you believing he would be welcomed."

Sabrina shook her head negatively while tears ran down her cheeks and her voice choked into silence.

"Clyde Mellon's body was found in your bedroom. How do you account for that, Miss McNeil?"

"I . . . I was getting ready for bed."

"Why didn't you lock your door if you did not want anyone to enter your room?"

"Somehow . . . someone broke the lock on my door. I couldn't lock it."

"How convenient."

470

"He must have broken it earlier. He must have planned what he was going to do long before that night. He knew I wanted nothing to do with him. He knew I would never let him into my room so he broke the lock. He came into the room when my back was turned. I did not know he was there until he attacked me."

"Why did you not scream?"

"I tried. He said it would do me no good. All the servants were gone for the night."

"Then, there was no one there to say now if you are telling the truth."

"No," Sabrina replied quietly.

"Then you are asking this jury to believe Miss McNeil, that you were such an innocent child that you resorted to killing a man who attempted to touch you, yet a few weeks later you willingly went to bed with a man who was very nearly a stranger. A man who had bought! Bought you Miss McNeil."

"It's true . . . all I have said is true?"

"I shall suggest, Miss McNeil, that you thought your uncle intended his fortune for you."

Sabrina shook her head.

"You were angry, for you felt your seduction of him had been enough."

"I did not seduce my uncle! You are making this sound so awful."

"Murder is awful, Miss McNeil," Edgar replied. "I suggest when you found out where the money was to go you placed your sights on your uncle."

"I didn't."

"I suggest you invited him to your room that night with the full intent of doing murder. I suggest it was not an accident, but a deliberate pre-planned murder. You wanted to rid yourself of your uncle because you felt your cousin would be a conquest who would share the remaining wealth with you."

"I did not! I would never have had any relationship with Thomas Mellon! I hated him! I hated him!" Sabrina cried. Then there was an abrupt and deadly silence. Sabrina realized what her wild declaration of hatred had done to destroy her defense and make the jury believe she was capable of murder. She buried her face in her hands and wept quietly.

"And I would suggest Miss McNeil," Edgar said in a deep quiet voice, "that you harbored a hatred . . . yes . . . for your uncle and for your cousin. I believe this jury will find you guilty of the murder of Clyde Mellon and give you the justice you so richly deserve."

"Yes," came a commanding voice from the rear of the courtroom. "I think we should make sure that justice is done here today."

Sabrina's head jerked up with a look of bright new hope in her eyes.

"Clay," she cried.

All heads turned toward the back of the courtroom where Clay stood flanked on one side by Jacob Poltice and on the other by a large man whose hands were bound and who stood with a policeman at his elbow.

At the sight, Thomas's face turned white. Quietly, amid the confusion, he stood up and slipped quietly from the courtroom by a side door.

Clay walked toward Sabrina whose wide eyes and pale face alarmed him. He was only a few steps away when he realized she was about to collapse. He covered the short distance between them and caught her as she fell. He lifted her in his arms and turned to face Edgar.

"Your truth is standing there," he said angrily. "The truth that Sabrina is innocent of all this . . . and the truth that Thomas Mellon and his father are the guilty ones. I'm taking Sabrina out of here. I'm taking her to my home where she belongs."

Without another word, Clay walked out of a crowded and highly excited courtroom.

Outside he lifted Sabrina gently into the carriage he had kept waiting and climbed in behind her. He lifted her onto his lap and cradled her gently in his arms. He was worried about her pale face and continued unconsciousness. He worried also about the child she was carrying. Was the trial too much for her? Would she lose the child both of them wanted so badly? He tipped her head back and looked down into her face. Gently he touched her cheek and let his finger trace the delicate line of her jaw. She seemed so fragile to him.

Slowly her eyes fluttered open. Warm blue eyes met searching purple ones, then to his joy, she smiled.

"Clay . . . Clay," her eyes filled with tears and she reached up to touch his face with a trembling hand. "I was so afraid."

"Don't be afraid any more Sabrina. It's all over. You don't need to be afraid any longer. I'm going to take you home and keep you safe for the rest of your life."

"Clay, what happened? I don't understand."

"I'll explain everything to you just as soon as I get you safely home, call the doctor to examine you very carefully, and know you are well. There will be a lot of time for us Sabrina, don't worry about it now."

"But Clay . . . "

With a light chuckle Clay drew her securely against him and silenced any other words she might have said.

The kiss was gentle and rewarding for both of them. It was a renewal of the sweet giving love she had always so freely offered him. For her it was a warm strength that surrounded her, filled her and told her again of the vibrant love she could always depend on.

Secure in his embrace, warmed by the hard seeking mouth that claimed hers in kiss after kiss until her senses soared, Sabrina surrendered herself to the pleasure of belonging in Clay's bright loving world again.

The trip to Clay's house was entirely too fast for both of them.

When they arrived, Clay put her promptly to bed, called a doctor. Although the doctor pronounced her weak and recovering from stress, he told a pleased Clay that the child was well and seemed to be progressing normally.

Still it was the end of the day, when Clay sat on the edge of her bed, held her hand, and told her the story she had waited patiently to hear.

Forty

"You mean," Sabrina said in a shocked voice, "that Uncle Eustice was murdered? But I thought he died of a heart attack."

"But you didn't go up to see him when he died," Clay answered. "It was murder. Well thought out and well performed . . . by Clyde Mellon and his equally vicious son Thomas."

"They expected Uncle Eustice had left them everything?"

"They made sure of it."

"How did they manage that?"

"He had a contact in Chapin's office," Clay went on to explain the forgery of the will, its exchange.

"Then," she said softly, "I'm not really sorry that I hit him . . . and I'm not sorry that it killed him. Uncle Eustice was a beautiful, kind, and generous man. He did not deserve either of them."

"Well my sweet, you didn't kill him."

"Clyde? Of course I did. I struck him. There was blood all over. He looked dead when I ran."

"Looked dead, but wasn't. You see the doctor told the prosecutor and Chapin that Clyde died of a blow on the head. It was Chapin who rechecked to find that Clyde was struck . . . twice."

"Twice! But I . . ."

"Only struck him once. I know. Thomas and the large

friend I brought back with me struck him again. Just to make sure he was very, very dead."

Her eyes began to sparkle with renewed pleasure.

"Then I'm . . . I'm free."

"You are. You are guilty of nothing but defending yourself."

Clay slid his arms beneath her and lifted her up against him. Her slim arms twined about his neck and soft warm parted lips met his in a joyous need. He could feel the warm surrender and he sank within it.

"Oh Clay," she murmured, "take me home."

"You want to leave Waverly Hall? There's a lot of money for you here Sabrina."

"I want to go home Clay. I don't want to stay here. Waverly Hall has too many bad memories, and as for the money . . . I . . . I just don't want it. It has blood on it, and I don't need it. I have everything I ever need in you and Summer and the child we will share."

"I love you, my angel," he smiled as he bent to kiss her again. "You've made my life a miracle of love and I had no intention of letting you go. I just had to know how you felt . . . what you wanted."

"Now you know. I want to go home and make a happy life for you and our children. How soon can we go?"

"Well, I imagine it will be after you have gotten some of your strength back and are able to testify. When Chapin gets the loose ends safely tied up and Thomas taken care of, we'll arrange the balance of your business and we'll take the first ship home that we can find."

"Clay?"

"What?"

"Do you suppose . . . I mean . . . "

"What's troubling you Sabrina?"

"Could we get married here Clay . . . soon? It was so terrible, all the things they were saying . . . all the nasty things they implied. I know in our eyes we're married, but I truly want to be married in the eyes of the world."

"That is the first thing I'll arrange," he replied. "But for tonight you need to rest. I'll go and let you get some sleep."

"No, Clay, no, don't go!" Her arms were again clinging to him and he knew it would be a long time before he exorcised Sabrina's fear and made her feel safe again. "I need you, Clay," she whispered. "I need you to hold me, to love me. I will never feel safe without you. Don't go."

Clay, whose heart and dreams were always filled with Sabrina, needed no more encouragement. In a few moments, he had joined her in the large canopied bed. He held her close to him, caressing her gently. He could feel the tension in her and knew Thomas had left a mark in her heart that would take a long time and a lot of gentle loving care before she was free of him.

He held in check the urge to go and find Thomas and take revenge on him for every tear Sabrina had shed. He had to be content knowing the law would care for him.

They talked for a while. He tried to ease her fears with promises of the future they would share. Soon conversation ceased as passion grew.

Clay was unsure for the first time in his life. He was unsure if Sabrina was well enough, unsure whether he was rushing her too quickly. Yet he wanted her completely.

Clay let his hands explore well remembered softness until one hand rested gently on the faintly rounded belly. He felt a surge of deep love as again he realized the seed of their intense love for each other grew to fruition inside. Sabrina drew closer to Clay. There were no words she could say to tell him how content she was or the depth of the love she felt for him.

These precious hours were too sweet to lose, even as the

clock ticked away the minutes, Clay grasped and held them, slowing their beat to savor the loving more perfectly.

He bent his head to brush a kiss on the smooth skin of her belly. She sighed and let her fingers twine in his thick black hair to press him closer.

He looked up into melting purple pools of love. Gone were any past fears, and welcome passion filled her eyes. He rose beside her and his open hungry mouth took hers in a kiss that lifted her beyond the place where fear could touch her again. To that place of magic, the center of each other's love, a place where they could erase the past and build new memories that would carry them into tomorrows. Again they were one, moving together, seeking together their own special union.

Passions soared like eagles in flight, and they left behind all the pain they had ever known to greet again the love that sealed them forever together and forever one.

Sabrina stirred awake and realized in an instant Clay was not beside her. She sat up in the bed wondering where he had gone, but before she could get out of bed the door opened and Clay came in wearing a broad smile and carrying a tray.

"Just put yourself back under those covers, Madam," he laughed. "You are staying in bed for a while longer, and you're going to eat a good breakfast."

"Clay, I feel fine. I could come down for breakfast."

He stopped by the bed, set the tray on the table next to it, then he bent to kiss her lightly . . . then lingeringly.

"Let me spoil you for a while, love, just to show you how happy I am to have you back safe."

Obediently she sat back against the pillows he braced behind her.

He set the tray on her lap and urged her to eat while he sat beside her.

"Clay, what are we going to do now? When are we going home?"

"Well, I've been doing a few things while you were sleeping. In two days we'll be married here in this house if that's all right with you."

"Two days? Clay, I can't get married in two days — I don't have a stitch to wear."

"I don't mind," he grinned. "I kind of like you like that."

"Clay!"

"Sabrina you can go shopping today and tomorrow and buy anything you need. It's fast, Sabrina, but I want to take you home. I'm worried about Summer, and besides, I want you all to myself at home where we can all be together again."

Her eyes softened and again he was caught in the deep purple pool.

He reached to gently touch her hair.

"I love you, Sabrina," he said quietly.

She was about to speak when a knock came on the door.

"Yes?" Clay called.

"Mr. Storm, Mr. Chapin is here to see you sir. He says it's urgent he talk to you immediately."

"I'll be right down."

Clay turned back to Sabrina whose eyes were shadowed with renewed worry.

"Clay?"

"I'm sure it's just to tell me everything is over, love. Thomas should be securely behind locked doors by now. Don't worry. You eat, I'll go down and talk to him and I'll be back soon."

"I'll bathe and dress while you're gone."

"Why," he said suggestively, "don't you wait until I get back. I think it should be a husband's right to share the pleasure of watching his wife in her bath."

"I'll wait if you'll hurry," she laughed.

"I'll hurry," he said quickly. He was pleased to hear her contented laughter follow him as he closed the door behind him.

His smile faded as he walked down the hall then the stairs. He went to his study and opened the door to find Chapin awaiting him there. He knew the instant he walked into the room that something was wrong.

"Mr. Chapin, I imagine a lot of things happened in that courtroom. Sit down and I'll send for some coffee."

"Yes, Clay, send for some strong coffee. I think we both need it."

"Something has happened . . . what?"

"Well, I've a lot of news."

Clay sent for coffee then he and Chapin sat opposite each other.

"Sabrina is completely free?" Clay questioned.

"Yes, yes indeed she is. Jacob confessed his part in everything, and that brute you brought back with you explained his and Thomas' spart in the murders both of Eustice and of Clyde."

"Then I don't understand. Everything looks bright, yet you seem to be upset."

"Thomas has disappeared."

"What?"

"It's as if the earth opened up and swallowed him. He must have slipped out the day you came, when he knew everything was over. Anyway, he cannot be found. The police have an all out search going, but there has been no sign of him."

"Damn!" Clay said angrily, "how could he have gotten away?"

"I don't know. Waverly Hall is being watched but he has not been there. Of course he might have been and gone in all the confusion the day you returned with the evidence that damned Thomas."

"Sabrina," Clay said quietly.

"Yes, Sabrina. This man is mad, Clay. He has no sense of reason. He might try to do her some harm. He must have some friends, to be able to hide so well."

"He'll never touch her life again. Not while there's a breath in my body."

"What do you plan on doing?"

"Take Sabrina home as soon as possible. I can protect her much better there than I can here."

"She'll ask questions."

"I'll try not to tell her if I can, but if it's necessary I will."

"Well, I know you'll keep her safe, Clay. I think you are the best thing that has happened to that girl in the past year or so."

"Thank you. I hope you're right."

"I know I am. Well, I must go."

"First, let me invite you to our wedding day after tomorrow. Both of us would be pleased to have you there. It would be especially important to Sabrina."

"I should be delighted."

"Then we are taking the *Morning Star* that night and we'll be on our way home."

"Clay, what about Waverly Hall and all that money?"

"I think Sabrina will give you power of attorney to sell Waverly Hall. The money . . . well, she'll have to tell you what she wants done with it. It's hers, as it rightfully should be."

"Well, I'll talk to her when you think she's ready. In the meantime keep a close eye on her. That madman might think of some devious way to do her some harm."

"Don't worry. I don't intend to let her out of my sight."

"Good," Chapin smiled and extended his hand to Clay

who took it in a firm grip. "There was a time there, Clay, when I was afraid I was going to fail her . . . that they were going to convict her. There were the makings of a real tragedy."

"I'll tell you the truth, Chapin," Clay smiled, "there was a time there when I was planning to break her from jail and escape with her. I was a little afraid myself."

"Well, it all worked out for the best. Take her home, be happy and enjoy your home and your children."

"I plan to do that," Clay replied. "I thank you for all you have done for us. We'll keep in touch. Maybe you could find your way to come and visit us one day in the future."

"You never can tell," Chapin chuckled.

Clay escorted Chapin to the door. When he closed it behind him, a worried frown darkened his brow. He walked slowly up the stairs wondering just where Thomas Mellon might be and what he was going to say to Sabrina about Chapin's visit.

He opened the door of their bedroom to find Sabrina comfortably seated in a huge wooden tub of warm water.

She turned and smiled at him as he came in. Clay dismissed a pink cheeked young maid with a suppressed laugh and a wave of his hand.

Then he went to Sabrina. He bent down and braced one hand on each side of the tub and gazed down into her warm eyes. His eyes seemed to devour her and she was breathless with the intensity of it.

"Clay, what did Chapin want?"

Clay moved away from the tub. He took a chair and drew it close. He sat on the chair and braced one foot against the tub to tip his chair back a little.

"Not much. Just to tell us everything's over. The law knows who's guilty. You are free to marry me and go back home with me. You don't have to worry anymore."

Sabrina continued to gaze at him. She was aware that for the first time in their relationship, Clay was lying to her.

"That's not all he came for, is it?"

"He came to say that he would take care of the details of Waverly Hall and the money whenever you felt well enough to tell him what you want done."

"I see. Clay . . . ?"

"What?"

"What are you keeping from me? Something's wrong, isn't it?"

"Sabrina, it's nothing important. The only thing for us to worry about now is the wedding and the trip home."

"Clay, tell me please," she said softly.

"Come out of that tub, mermaid, and I'll tell you anything you want to hear."

Aggravated, Sabrina struck the water, splashing both herself and Clay.

"Clay Storm," she said, her chin jutting stubbornly, "tell me what's going on."

Clay realized he was not going to be able to laugh her out of her questions. He put his foot back on the floor and bent toward her. He reached out and took her hand in his.

"Thomas has escaped. He's loose somewhere, and no one knows where."

He felt her hand tremble, saw the shock slowly begin to turn to fear.

"Don't Sabrina. Don't let it touch you. He's being sought by the police and they will find him anytime soon. You are safe, and within a day or two we'll be on our way home. No one can touch you again."

He watched the battle in her eyes, then relief flooded him as he saw her love for him win the battle. Finally she smiled.

"You are right, Clay, I won't be afraid any longer. We'll marry and go home. I won't let memories of Thomas into my mind again."

"Wonderful," he grinned. He rose, bent over the tub and kissed her soundly. "Now if you want a gown to be married in, I think we'd better go buy it."

He lifted a towel and beckoned her from the water. She rose, and he wrapped the towel about her, taking the time to hold her close and kiss an enticingly bare shoulder.

He watched her dress, enjoying it thoroughly. When she finished, they walked downstairs together.

They spent the afternoon shopping for all Sabrina would need. Sabrina would not allow Clay to see the dress she chose to be married in.

She was so excited and filled with pleasure at all the new finery she had bought, and the pleasure of being with Clay all day that all thoughts of Thomas seemed to slip from her mind.

They ate a late supper together in front of a glowing fireplace, and afterward they lay before it and made love. A relaxed and sensitive joining that was a rare beauty for both of them. After a while, Sabrina slept. She did not know when Clay gently lifted her in his arms and carried her to his bed. He put her beneath the covers and joined her there. He drew her into his arms . . . then he too slept.

It was in the wee hours of the morning when Clay came abruptly awake. He lay still for a moment, searching with his senses for what had wakened him. Then he heard it again, a soft moan.

He sat up and looked at Sabrina. The pale moonlight washed over her and he could see her clearly. Obviously she was caught in a nightmare.

She moved and sighed raggedly, then she began to fight some unseen thing.

Then she began to seriously battle whatever force held her. She thrashed about and cried out. A muffled scream escaped her as Clay caught her close to him. For a moment she fought him until his calming voice reached her. Her eyes opened.

"Clay," she sobbed as she relaxed against him.

"You were dreaming."

"Yes."

"Do you want to tell me? Maybe if you do, it will go away."

"It was Thomas. Oh Clay, I could feel his hate. He . . . he wanted to hurt me."

Clay held her close, caressing her hair.

"It's all right, Sabrina. I'm here, love, and I'll never leave you. You don't have to be afraid."

"I know," she sighed. "I know."

He held her until she slept again, but it was nearing dawn before he slept. He had known Summer and her mother too long not to know that sometimes dreams had the ring of truth in them.

He wondered just where Thomas was hiding at this moment, and he realized Thomas carried enough hatred with him to hurt Sabrina, and he also knew Thomas knew that in hurting Sabrina he would be hurting Clay too.

The next day was spent much like the first, in finishing up what shopping Sabrina needed to do. Clay was with her every moment and Sabrina was well aware Clay refused to leave her alone even for a moment.

The wedding was to be that afternoon. Clay had asked only a few people to come.

When they were all gathered, Sabrina entered the room and Clay was captivated again by her rare and special beauty.

She wore a dress of pale rose, the neckline high and the sleeves long and fitted. The skirt was voluminous and the layers of rose colored lace were caught here and there with clusters of small flowers.

Her violet eyes aglow made her seem to shine and Clay thought he had never seen her so beautiful.

"It's because I'm so happy," she replied when he mentioned the fact later.

"And," he whispered, "I intend to keep you this way."

There was a great deal of of well wishing, and after a late supper, Clay and Sabrina were taken to the dock where the *Morning Star* waited for them.

It was only when they stood at the rail and watched the coast of England recede, did Sabrina truly relax and begin to believe that she was finally safe.

They stood close together, his arm about her waist and her head against his shoulder.

"Happy, love?"

"Yes Clay, happier than ever. For the first time I feel safe . . . really safe. I can't wait to get home."

"Yes, home. It will be good to get back," his arm tightened. "At least I'll have you all to myself."

"With Summer?" she laughed.

"We can deal with that," he chuckled. "We'll just slip away once in a while."

She turned in his arms and slid her arms about his waist.

"I love you, Mr. Storm."

"And I love you, Mrs. Storm," he whispered as he took her warm willing mouth with his.

Both were at the height of happiness. Neither knew of the form that sat curled in a dark corner of the deep hold of the ship. A form that sat in brooding hatred . . . and waited like a spider in its web to reach out and touch the two lovers who stood above him.

Forty-one

The trip home from England to America was a delight both for Clay and Sabrina. She enjoyed the freedom from all the strain she had been under. She laughed easily and he would hear her singing. She loved easily too, and Clay was completely intoxicated with the new and remarkably beautiful Sabrina.

She seemed to blossom, her eyes glittered with contentment and her skin glowed. A healthy pink on her cheeks and the new color to her sensitive mouth filled Clay with the continual desire to reach out and touch her.

Her slim body still did not show much trace of the child within. Clay was well aware of the looks that followed her wherever she went. He was amazed at himself that the hungry possessive jealousy that had always possessed him was not present. Instead he felt a glowing pride and a relaxed contented knowledge that she was his and she loved him as he loved her.

The nights were a pleasure beyond Clay's wildest dreams. Free from fear Sabrina had become more open. He was amazed that at times she was even sweetly aggressive. Though it surprised him it also filled him with joy that she reached for him more willingly than ever before. He reveled in it and regretted when they finally saw the American coast appear out of an early morning mist.

When they arrived, Clay made arrangements for transportation, and after a few hours they were on their way home.

Of course, they stopped by Irene's and were heartily welcomed. Irene was overjoyed at the news of the expected child. They found it quite difficult to tear themselves away.

The next stop was Caleb's, whose astute eye caught Sabrina's condition. He went to every length he could to make her welcome.

It also did not take him long to notice the difference in Clay. He was so much more open. It pleased him to see how solicitous he was of Sabrina and he enjoyed feeling the love that flowed between the two.

While Clay was reharnessing the wagon for their final leg of the trip home, Caleb had a chance to talk to Sabrina a few minutes alone.

"Sabrina, you been good for that boy. He kinda lost himself for a while there. He's a good man, a good friend, and I'm glad to see him so happy. He shore does love you girl, you kin see it in his eyes every time he looks at you."

"I love him too Caleb, very much. He's certainly made a lot of changes in my life. I never knew so much happiness existed in the world."

"I'm sure glad this business with Hawk has been settled. I was afraid those two were split forever. That would have been a terrible thing. It's amusing that a sweet young thing like you was the one to bring them back together again. I wish you both the best of luck."

"It was a sad thing, but it's over. I hope we can open all the doors again both for Clay and Hawk. Summer's life will be good when she has both of them to supply her roots and give her the love she has needed for so long."

"Well missy, I hope everything goes well. If ever you

should need anything, you need only send for me and I'll come."

"Thank you Caleb. I'll remember," she smiled.

Caleb reached out and patted her shoulder affectionately. Clay came then with the wagon and again they were on their way homeward.

It was very nearly dark when they reached the cabin. Sabrina stood on the porch and gazed about her at the beauty she remembered so well, while Clay put away the wagon and cared for the horse.

She watched him leave the barn and walk toward her. Again she had to admire the perfect symmetry of his long lean body and the cut of his handsome face as he smiled at her. He stood beside her on the porch and slid an arm about her waist.

"It's so beautiful here, Clay. Just as I remembered. I'm so glad we're back here and together."

"I," he said softly as he drew her close to rest against him, "hold the beauty here, and no one in the world could be happier than I am at this moment."

"Let's go in. I want to have a fire in the fireplace and cook you something to eat."

She turned toward the door, but with a soft laugh, Clay spun her about and caught her up in his arms. He lifted her against him and she put her arms about his neck.

"We do this properly, Madam," he smiled down into her eyes, "this is our home and you are my wife. I'll carry you over the threshold so there will be no bad luck."

"I love you Clay. Let's keep it always like this. I want us to set roots here and grow. I want us to share our love with Summer, Hawk and his people. We have so much Clay, let's hold on to it always and never let it slip away."

Clay kissed her, a warm promising kiss that told her her sentiments were echoed in him.

"We'll hold it love," he replied. "We'll hold it. I know what I've got now and I never intend to let it slip away."

Again he kissed her lightly, and she rested her head on his shoulder while he carried her inside and kicked the door shut behind them.

Clay built a fire while Sabrina put together what little food had been stored in the house.

They ate a leisurely meal and cleaned up the remains together. Then Clay built a fire in the fireplace and they sat before it and talked in low whispers. Soft laughter and gentle kisses slowly blossomed into a warm night of joyous lovemaking. It was the wee hours of the morning when they went to their bed, a bed they would share for a lifetime.

It was two glorious days they spent alone and sharing the pleasure of their love, yet both felt incomplete. It was Sabrina who first suggested the reason.

"Clay?"

"What?"

"I think we both had best admit something?"

"What's that?" he smiled as he went to her and slid his arm about her waist.

"We both miss Summer. I know you are trying to make the first days of our marriage pleasant, and I deeply appreciate it . . . but, . . . don't you think we'd both be happier if our daughter was home and our family was together?"

Clay gazed down on her, silent for the moment, but his eyes spoke eloquently of the emotion he felt. A wave of poignant all consuming love filled him to overflowing.

"God, I love you Sabrina. Somehow you seem to know every thought I think and everything I feel. Are you a witch, my beloved?"

"Tis only because I love you that I can feel your need."

"My need is you, Sabrina," he whispered, "always you."

Their lips touched lightly in a gentle blending.

"We shall go and get Summer tomorrow. For tonight, we will be content to share each other alone."

"Yes," she whispered, "yes."

Again his strength surrounded her and she was lost to the magic of his possession.

The next day, Clay rose early and began to make preparations. Sabrina rose and dressed. She stood gazing about the home and made a decision. She went to Clay at once.

"I'm not going to the village with you," she stated.

"Not going? Why?"

"It will only take you one night to be back with Summer. I want to prepare the house and Summer's new clothes and her room. Then I want to bake her a cake. We will have a birthday party and a welcome home party when you get back."

"Sabrina, I don't want to leave you alone."

"It's only one night. I shall miss you, but I will be fine."

"I'd really feel better if you were with me. I hate to be without you."

Sabrina smiled and put her arms about his neck.

"As I said once before, Mr. Storm," she laughed, "it will do you good to practice a little abstinence."

"Sabrina," he growled humorously, "I have no intention of practicing abstinence with a remarkably lovely and inviting creature like you about."

"Go and get our daughter, Clay," she said softly. "We have a lifetime to share together."

"Why is it," he grinned, "that I thought I was running my life until you came into it? Now you command and I listen. What happened?"

"Love, Mr. Storm," she giggled. "Love, and I find myself in the same boat. Bring our daughter home and we'll spend some time discussing what has gotten us into this predicament."

"You're sure you'll be all right?"

"I'll be fine."

"All right," he sighed. "But we'll make this the fastest trip ever. I'll wrap Summer and she can sleep on the way home. That way we'll be home by early morning."

"You'll be so tired."

"Don't worry," he leered happily, "you can tuck me into bed at night and help me overcome my tiredness."

She laughed and he kissed her soundly holding her bound against him as if he would never let her go.

"Bolt the door securely," he warned.

"I will."

"Don't go wandering about. Stay in the house."

"All right Clay, don't worry. Go. I'll be fine."

Reluctantly he made preparations and in less than an hour she stood on the porch and waved good-bye.

Sabrina returned to the house and began on Summer's room. It took her quite some time and she was pleasantly tired when she finished. She felt it would be good to have a cool drink, and rest for a while before she set about making the cake.

She walked into the living room and stopped. She had thought she had shut the front door, but it stood part way open. Again she started to walk toward it when a familiar voice froze her in her tracks.

"Don't bother to close the door Sabrina. My friend will be returning soon."

She spun about to see Thomas leaning against the fireplace, a satisfied smile on his face.

"Thomas!" she gasped.

"Surprised?"

"What . . . what are you doing here? I thought you . . ."

"Were captured by the police . . . maybe hung? No, my

dear. I had something very important to finish . . . and I intend to finish it," he said.

Suddenly Sabrina spun about and ran for the door . . . too late, as she flung open the door another man stood just outside it. She screamed and backed away. The evil intent in his face could be well read.

Thomas came to her and caught her wrist, giving it a vicious twist and jerking her close to him.

"I've been waiting and watching for two days. Waiting for that bastard lover of yours to make a mistake. He just made it. He left you alone. Now he'll regret interfering in my life and my plans. He'll never see you or the child you carry again," Thomas snarled.

"Please Thomas, don't do this, please . . . not my baby! Not my baby!"

Thomas spoke to the silent man who stood watching Sabrina with such a look of evil lust in his eyes that she shivered with fear.

"Are the horses ready?"

"Yep."

"You remember what to do?"

"Sure, we split up here. He won't know which tracks to follow. I'll meet you at sundown. Then," he grinned at Sabrina who shrank away from him, "we'll split up the profits later tonight."

Sabrina read his intent well. Fear struck her so deeply she could hardly breathe. She writhed and struggled in Thomas's grasp, she wept and pleaded, yet Thomas dragged her easily to his horse.

She fought him, and in exasperation at his inability to get her on his horse, Thomas slapped her several times until she became dizzy with the blows. She felt strong arms lift her. Then she was braced against Thomas's body and the horse was kicked into motion.

Summer was on her knees by the stream watching in fascination: The tiny fish darted about so rapidly. Summer was fascinated with all parts of nature. She had already confounded the medicine man with her ability to learn. He was also somewhat in awe of the rare gift of prophecy and insights into the future she possessed.

She chose quite often not to play with others, but to wander about alone, caught in the daydreams and visions she often had.

She sat back on her haunches now and let the soft breeze touch her uplifted face. She closed her eyes and let her mind reach for her father. She could sense him, almost feel him. She knew the contentment and peace he felt and how his heart was filled with love. She smiled when she knew in her inner mind he was coming for her.

Now she released him from her mind and reached for the one other person she loved so deeply . . . Sabrina.

Suddenly she gasped, and her face grew taut with fear. She wrapped her slim arms about herself and rocked back and forth as a low moan escaped her. Beads of sweat touched her brow, but still she searched. Searched for the fear and pain she felt. She was terrified yet still she let herself seek the cause of it. Deep inside she knew some terrible thing had happened . . . she had to know what it was.

Grimly and tenaciously she clung to the darkness and pain . . . then it came to her and she gasped breathlessly at the evil that had reached to touch her.

Yet still she clung to the vision until everything came clear . . . she saw him! And she saw Sabrina . . . and she knew.

She leapt to her feet and raced back toward the village. The first person she saw was Swift Doe. Breathlessly she ran up to her.

"Summer! What is wrong? Are you all right?"

"No! Swift Doe, where is Hawk? I have to see Hawk!"

"I saw him only a few minutes ago."

"Where?"

"Near his father's lodge."

Swiftly Summer flew toward the chief's lodge.

Hawk stood in front of it in earnest conversation with Walking Horse. He turned with a startled look on his face when Summer called to him.

He caught her, as she nearly collided with him, and he steadied her on her feet. He heard her rasping breath, saw the fear in her eyes, and knew it was a serious thing.

"Summer," he commanded, "calm yourself before you try to speak. Something is wrong, what is it?"

Summer tried to control herself, but the fear drove her. Words tumbled out and Hawk had to listen carefully before the story tumbled into place in his mind. His face grew grim and cold with anger.

"Walking Horse, come with me," he said.

Walking Horse had heard Summer's rattled explanations. His feelings for Sabrina had not changed they had only been buried deep within him to change into a deep and binding loyalty between him and the two whites. It took him only a few minutes to run for his and Hawk's horse.

Hawk called Swift Doe and told her to care for Summer. It was not long until they were racing toward a meeting with Clay, who, they knew now, was on his way toward them completely unaware of the events that were taking place in his home.

Clay rode slowly, but keeping a steady pace. He planned to get Summer and return immediately. He knew if he kept a steady pace both ways and traveled during the night, he could make it back home by morning. He did not want to be away a day longer than he had to.

He was amused at himself, and sifted back over the events that had drawn him and the remarkably lovely woman who was now his wife together.

Thoughts of what Thomas had tried to do to her filled him with dark emotions and he was glad an ocean separated them from Thomas and the ugliness of the past.

He had made a promise to himself that if it were in his power, Sabrina would have a happy life and he would not let anything touch her again that would cause her as much pain as Thomas had.

He crested a hill and looked down into the next valley. In the distance he could see two riders coming in his direction.

After a few more minutes his experienced eye recognized Hawk and Walking Horse. They were not the kind of men to push their horses so and he wondered what emergency pushed them. His first thought was Summer and he kicked his horse into a more rapid gait.

Soon they saw him approaching, and after a few more minutes they reined their horses to a stop within inches of each other.

"Hawk! Something is wrong. Is it Summer? Is she all right?" Clay said in a worried voice.

"It is not Summer, Clay, it's Sabrina," Hawk replied and saw Clay's face pale and his eyes deepen in worry.

"What Hawk, what? Did Summer see something?"

"Yes," Hawk replied. In rapid words he explained what Summer had told him. When he finished, without a word or question, Clay spun his horse about and headed for home . . . praying he would be in time.

Forty-two

Sabrina listened in fear to Thomas's rambling accusations during the ride. She knew without doubt his greedy evil mind had been twisted beyond repair. It contained only one thought now—revenge on her and Clay for all the things he felt they had taken from him.

She was surprised that Thomas seemed to know where he was going. They had been riding for so long that she had no real idea of how much time had passed. She realized only that her body ached and was stiff.

It was nearing dusk, the sun just bordered the rim of the horizon. Everything about them was lit in a pale gold haze. Both Sabrina and Thomas were unaware of the beauty that surrounded them.

They finally stopped and Sabrina looked about her. A lean-to was already built, and she could tell this camp had been prepared long ago, most likely at the same time she and Clay had arrived home.

Thomas dismounted and reached to lift her down beside him. Her legs were so stiff she could hardly stand and sagged wearily against him only to push herself weakly away as he put his arms about her.

"Let me go! Don't touch me!" she said brokenly.

"You may as well get used to my touch," he laughed.

"Where you are going your husband will never find you. I shall enjoy both you and caring for the child you carry. It will give me great pleasure if it is a boy who looks like his father. Every day my revenge will taste sweeter."

"You are an animal!" she cried helplessly. "How can you take revenge on an innocent child who has never harmed you? You are too cowardly to face his father. Clay will track you down, he will kill you for this."

"I've already taken care of that. My friend is hiding our trail and making an obvious trail of his own. He will follow until he finds him . . . he will wait for him . . . and he will kill him. Then he will join me and we will take you to a place where we will have much more leisure time to enjoy your company."

"I will die first! I will kill myself and the child before I let you do this."

"No my dear, we will keep a close eye on you. You will not have another chance to ruin my revenge. I intend to enjoy you for a long, long time."

He pushed her toward the lean-to where she sat huddled and watched him build a fire. He prepared some food, ate first, and gave the remains to her as if he were feeding a dog. She struck the tin plate from his hand and glared silently at him. He smiled and shrugged.

"If you want to remain hungry that is your choice. When you are hungry enough you will eat whatever I feed you even if it is just for the health of the child."

"You are insane!" she raged.

He shrugged, with an amused smile that infuriated her even more, and walked away from her. He sat by the fire and took a bottle of brandy from a bundle near him. Her fear deepened as he slowly and methodically began to drink from it.

As the sun's rays died slowly, the trees surrounding them

became dark shadows. Sabrina shivered from the cold, but would not move closer to the fire. She was afraid to draw Thomas's attention back to her . . . afraid of what he might do.

He sat contemplating the flames, and Sabrina was not aware that indeed his thoughts were already upon her. He was making plans for what he would do in the next few days. Once the man who had guided him into the wilderness had helped him kidnap Sabrina and guided him out he had full intention of doing away with him. He did not plan to share Sabrina with anyone.

Thoughts of Sabrina began to stir the need within him. He thought of all the times at Waverly Hall she had denied him. He thought of her rare exquisite beauty that he had desired for so long. Slowly the thoughts began to twist and turn inside him until they grew into a white hot need.

Sabrina's hands, still bound before her, grew numb with the lack of circulation, still she was afraid to move. Her legs were cramped and her body ached with the cold and the strain. But she refused to move for fear Thomas would turn in her direction. She leaned against a rough hewn pole and closed her eyes fighting the hot tears that threatened to choke her.

Fear such as she had never known before made her tremble. She was afraid for the child she carried more than for herself. She knew Clay, she knew he would try to follow her, but would Thomas's words be true, would the false trail lead Clay away from her instead of to her?

She was unaware that Thomas's eyes had turned toward her slim form huddled in the shadowed corner of the lean-to.

Even though it was dark, in his mind's eye, he could see everything about her.

He got to his feet silently, and walked toward her. He was

only a few feet from her when she sensed his presence. Her eyes flew open and she shrank as far as she could away from him.

He reached within and grasped her rope-bound wrists and dragged her out.

She came up beside him and his arm came about her, binding her close to him.

"No," she gasped, "don't . . . please don't."

"Do you know," he rasped, "how long I have wanted you?" His breath was harsh and ragged in her ear as he fervently kissed her cheek and the slim column of her throat.

He bent her back as his mouth searched for more softer vulnerable spots.

She began to writhe in his arms and fight, but her slim body was no match for his.

She could feel the passion within him as he pressed her against him. She moaned in helpless anguish as one of his hands entwined in the thick mass of her hair and the other began to explore the slim curves he held.

Vainly she fought, and slowly she lost. He began to drag her down to the ground.

She cried, kicked and fought in every way she could, and as she heard the tearing sound of cloth, she knew it was a battle she could not hope to win.

The soft moist earth against her back made her realize more the hopelessness of her situation. With desperation, crying and choking on her sobs, she continued to fight, knew she would continue to fight until she could no longer.

Cool air touched her skin as he ripped the fabric of her dress. She screamed Clay's name as she felt his hand touch her skin.

Then, suddenly, he was lifted from her and tossed aside. Through tear-blurred eyes she saw a large form drag Thomas to his feet. She saw deadly fear in Thomas's face as he gazed at the man who looked at him with the eyes of death.

Clay, Hawk and Walking Horse thundered to a stop in front of Clay's house. They leapt from their horses, and ran inside . . . to meet an empty room.

With sinking heart they knew they were too late. Thomas had already been there. The only question was . . . where had he taken Sabrina.

It took the three of them only minutes to begin to search the area about the house for any trace of tracks that would tell them which way the abductors had gone.

They were alarmed when they found two sets of alien tracks they knew were the abductors. One set of tracks had strategically been covered, yet Hawk's astute gaze caught it.

"We have no choice," he said. "We have to split up. Two will follow one set and one the other. We will make smoke for each other if we discover anything."

"Hawk," Clay said in an anguished voice. "It is nearly dark. It will be hard to track. We have to find her soon. No one can tell what that maniac will do to her."

"I know, brother," Hawk said seriously. "But you and I have tracked before in the shadows. We will find him."

"I'll kill him . . . I swear, I'll kill him. If he has touched her, hurt her in any way, I shall make it a long time for him to die."

Hawk and Walking Horse exchanged silent glances. Hawk's finger pointed to one set of tracks.

"Clay, you follow these. Walking Horse and I will follow the other. One of us will find them and do whatever is necessary. In the morning, we will make smoke to signal the other where we are."

Clay nodded and the three of them split up and soon disappeared into the shadows.

Their trails grew wider and wider apart. Clay followed minutely the trail before him. He prayed silently with every moment that Thomas and Sabrina would be on the other end of it.

It was some time before he saw the pale glow of a fire through the darkened shadows of the trees. He stopped, dismounted and tied his horse. He removed his rifle from its sheath and began to move toward the light of the fire.

When he grew close enough he was again taken by surprise to see no sign of anyone near the fire. He grew closer and closer, but still there was no sign of anyone near. He stood now just within the ring of light and stared in disbelief at the emptiness about him.

Clay, had he been a man with less training in the wilderness, would have been unprepared for attack, but he had been trained by his Indian family, so his senses absorbed the soft crack of a twig and the fact that someone was approaching from behind him.

He spun about as the large shadow of a man leapt at him. He caught him and they both tumbled backwards.

The man had been prepared to attack a surprised and defenseless man. A coward by nature, he did not want to fight a man who was prepared for him.

A knife glittered in the glow of the fire, and automatically Clay reached for the knife he had sheathed at his waist.

They clashed, sending fluttering shadows leaping in the glow of the fire. Without a sound they battled and slowly the expertise of Clay began to win out over the villainous surprise of the other.

Clay's rage had complete control of him now. It knew no quarter, and gave none. He buried his knife between the ribs of his attacker. Heard him grunt and felt his hold slip. Then the man's body sagged to the ground. Clay stood over him panting. Then he groaned aloud with the knowledge that he had followed the wrong trail. A worse thought came to him. Now all he could do was wait until morning and pray for Hawk's signal that he had found Sabrina.

Hawk and Walking Horse followed the slight well covered trail in absolute silence. They were well trained hunters, and now they knew they had to use all their expertise because one they loved depended upon it.

Their sharp eyes missed no print, no turned stone, no broken branches or trampled brush.

The shadows grew darker, and they began to worry that they would lose the trail in the dark. But it was a light touch on his arm and a silent pointing by Walking Horse that drew Hawk's attention to the pale glow of a fire.

Hawk made silent motions that Walking Horse understood quite well. They would circle the fire and come from both sides so that Thomas would not have a chance to escape or harm Sabrina before they could get to him.

Hawk kept moving silently closer and closer, and when he pushed aside the brush that stood between him and the fire, a scene was unfolding before him that brought a growl of rage from him.

Sabrina, fighting valiantly against a man who was fondling her and pushing her to the ground where his intent was obvious.

It was a scene Hawk could not bear. He leapt from his place and crossed the space between them rapidly. In black rage he gripped Thomas and dragged him from Sabrina. With immense strength he threw Thomas to the ground.

Hawk's rage lit his face and glowed in his eyes as he reached again for Thomas and dragged him to his feet.

Thomas whimpered in fear as he read violent and imminent death.

With a huge fist, Hawk struck a blow that sent Thomas

flying to land near the fire. He lay still . . . and Hawk believed he was unconscious. He fully intended to leave Thomas to Clay's justice.

He turned to reach for Sabrina and drew her gently to her feet. He held her in silence until she regained some control. He wished deeply it was his woman he was holding.

His attention drawn from Thomas, he did not see him stir, or sit up . . . or reach for the rifle that lay in his bundle near the fire. He lifted the rifle stealthily and aimed it at Hawk's broad back, a target he could hardly miss at that range.

He would have killed Hawk if he had had the chance to pull the trigger . . . but he did not have that chance. There was a whispered sound, a soft thud, and the rifle dropped from lifeless fingers. For the moment Thomas gazed in shock at the knife that protruded from his chest . . . then his eyes closed and he fell forward.

Hawk spun about as Walking Horse stepped from the shadows. Their eyes met and Hawk smiled his gratitude and Walking Horse smiled in understanding. Hawk turned back to a still trembling Sabrina.

"Sabrina, are you all right? Did he hurt you?"

"N . . . n . . . no Hawk . . . I'm all right. Clay . . . where is Clay?"

Quickly Hawk explained how they were forced to follow separate trails to be sure they had the right one.

"With the dawn I will send him a signal and he will come. Don't be afraid any longer Sabrina. The evil one is dead."

"I am grateful to you both. I was so afraid, I do not think I could have survived."

"It is all right," Hawk soothed. "You are very tired. Are you hungry?"

"Yes . . . I . . . I refused to eat his food," she admitted angrily.

Hawk's white teeth flashed in a wide grin as did Walking

Horse.

"Come, we will find you something to eat, then you must sleep. Clay will be here very soon."

They prepared the small amount of food they found among Thomas's supplies. While Sabrina ate and Hawk kept her occupied by asking questions about the trial and all that had happened, Walking Horse removed and disposed of Thomas's body. Neither Hawk or Sabrina asked him where or how and he offered no answers.

Sabrina was completely exhausted and at Hawk's urging, she wrapped herself in a blanket Hawk provided and before long she slept.

Hawk and Walking Horse spoke quietly for a while, then they too slept.

It was just before dawn that Hawk rose, quietly built a fire and set the signals of grey smoke that rose in the early morning sky.

Clay had not closed his eyes in sleep the entire night. He stood now in the first touch of dawn, and scanned the sky for a signal.

His heart leapt in his breast as he saw the puffs of grey smoke. Within minutes he was astride his horse and riding at as rapid a pace as the forest would allow.

The sun was rising. Sabrina woke and walked to the fire where Hawk and Walking Horse were seated.

She was about to speak when the thunder of horses' hooves made her spin about. Before she could even speak he was beside her, drawing her into his arms, murmuring her name as he rocked her against him.

She clung to him, feeling the peace and joy of the strength of his arms. Then she lifted her lips to his to seal the deep and overflowing pleasure that coursed through her.

When their breathless reunion could be controlled, they looked into each other's eyes and knew a new peace and future was theirs.

Hawk and Walking Horse walked to them. Clay held Sabrina with one arm, and in silence that was more eloquent than any words he had ever spoken, he held out his hand to Hawk.

Walking Horse smiled at the sight he would tell the entire village about later.

The small, slim golden girl had brought together two brothers that had been split in a tragedy. In her own gentle way she had reunited them. Walking Horse knew within it would be a union that would last a lifetime.

Clay did not question Thomas's whereabouts. He knew he was dead, and he did not care at the moment for anything except the fact that he had Sabrina in his arms and safe.

Hawk and Walking Horse gathered their things, mounted and rode away. Clay turned to a bright, smiling Sabrina.

"It's all over Sabrina," Clay smiled. "Let's go home. I have to tell you about Summer and how we came to be here."

"You're here Clay, that's all that matters."

"And we're together," he said gently, "and it will be that way forever."

"Yes," she whispered, "forever."

Clay took her in his arms and his mouth lowered to blend with hers in a warm and tender promise of all the tomorrows to come.

Then they left the place of anger and pain and death and rode slowly toward peace, joy . . . and eternal love.

Epilog

Summer knelt by the stream examining her changing face in the water. She was pleased with the new and happy face that gazed back at her.

A sound behind her drew her attention and she turned to see a child approaching her. She laughed as he struggled over the rough terrain on his chubby, still unsteady two year old legs.

She loved this child completely. He was her half-brother, and she had loved him from the moment of his birth.

She looked behind him, because if the child was here she knew Sabrina and Clay would not be far behind.

She was rewarded by the sight of them walking together. Her father's arm was about Sabrina's slim waist and Summer was again filled with pleasure at the love they shared both with each other and their children.

Young Clay had now reached her side and promptly plunked himself down in her lap. She laughed and hugged him to her fiercely.

She ruffled his thick mane of black hair and enjoyed the quick laughter and glow in his deep purple eyes.

Summer waved at her father and the step-mother she had grown to love more every day as her father did.

Her eyes would glow with warmth when she saw them together. She could feel it when they smiled at each other. It was as if they had gently reached out to touch each other.

She had the special sight and feeling and now she had begun to understand it. Hadn't she seen the beautiful woman of another tribe who had come for a visit and stayed to become the wife of Hawk? Hadn't she also seen the young white girl who had come to visit Caleb and then Sabrina and Clay? She had captivated Walking Horse and eventually had become his wife. Hadn't she seen the arrival of Ellen and her brother? Ellen had come to stay and make their home even fuller and warmer.

She was quite pleased with herself and her life. It was complete.

She held the child and watched her father and mother stop beneath the shade of a tree and talk together. She saw them laugh and hold each other.

"Oh Sabrina," Clay said, "look at them. Have you ever seen a happier sight?"

"Summer is filled to capacity with love," Sabrina laughed. "She has enough to spread over this entire frontier."

"And you, love?" he said with a warm chuckle as his arms surrounded her.

"Me," she replied, "I am filled with love, Clay . . . for you, only for you. I've never been happier in my life. This miracle world you've given me is more than any money could buy. Little Clay and Summer, oh Clay, my world is complete."

"And mine," he whispered as he bent his head and kissed her thoroughly and warmly with a clear promise that later he would carry the kiss to a much warmer conclusion.

They walked toward their children with their arms about each other and smiles on their faces that made both children smile in return.

Summer felt their love and remembered the strange dream she had been having lately. Was it real? Was it she?

She remembered: a young Indian girl, she stood by a man. He was tall, ruggedly handsome. His eyes the color of jade and his hair thick and gold as the morning sun. He held the Indian girl and kissed her as if he possessed her.

For the first time, Summer was unsure. Was he her future, or were they both someone she would one day meet? The future . . . but that is Summer's story.

MORE TEMPESTUOUS ROMANCES!

GOLDEN TORMENT (1323, $3.75)
by Janelle Taylor
Kathryn had travelled the Alaskan wilderness in search of her father. But after one night of sensual pleasure with the fierce, aggressive lumberjack, Landis Jurrell—she knew she'd never again travel alone!

LOVE ME WITH FURY (1248, $3.75)
by Janelle Taylor
When Alexandria discovered the dark-haired stranger who watched her swim, she was outraged by his intrusion. But when she felt his tingling caresses and tasted his intoxicating kisses, she could no longer resist drowning in the waves of sweet sensuality.

BELOVED SCOUNDREL (1259, $3.75)
by Penelope Neri
Denying what her body admitted, Christianne vowed to take revenge against the arrogant seaman who'd tormented her with his passionate caresses. Even if it meant never again savoring his exquisite kisses, she vowed to get even with her one and only BELOVED SCOUNDREL!

PASSION'S GLORY (1227, $3.50)
by Anne Moore
Each time Nicole looked into Kane's piercing dark eyes, she remembered his cold-hearted reputation and prayed that he wouldn't betray her love. She wanted faithfulness, love and forever—but all he could give her was a moment of PASSION'S GLORY.

Available wherever paperbacks are sold, or order direct from the Publisher. Send cover price plus 50¢ per copy for mailing and handling to Zebra Books, 475 Park Avenue South, New York, N.Y. 10016. DO NOT SEND CASH.